AVELER FORM

Cut By: _____ Qty _____ Date _____

Scanned By: _____ Qty _____ Date _____

Scanned _____ _____

CURVEBALL YEAR THREE: THE TITAN'S SHADOW

This is a work of fiction. Names, characters, places and incidents either are products of the author's imagination or are used fictitiously. Any resemblance to actual events, locales, or persons, living or dead, is entirely coincidental.

ISBN 978-1-939633-68-2

Curveball archives, news, and series information can be found at:

http://www.curveball.xyz

More of Jamie Robertson's work can be found at:

http://www.clanofthecats.com

More of Garth Graham's work can be found at:

http://www.gcgstudios.com

Arpista Editing can be found at:

http://www.arpistaediting.com

LICENSING INFORMATION

This publication is licensed under a Creative Commons Attribution-Noncommercial-Share Alike 4.0 (CC BY-NC-SA 4.0) License. The license allows this publication to be freely copied, distributed, transmitted, or adapted so long as: 1) proper attribution is given to the author, 2) the work is not used for commercial purposes, 3) and any work derived from this publication is distributed under the same license.

This license does not cover the artwork used on and within this publication. The copyright of all artwork is held by the artists and used with permission.

To view this license, visit:

http://creativecommons.org/licenses/by-nc-sa/4.0

or send a letter to:

Creative Commons
444 Castro Street
Suite 900
Mountain View, California 94140
USA

Aside from the specific permissions granted by this license, all rights are reserved by the author. Requests for permissions not covered by this license should be submitted online at:

https://www.eviscerati.org/contact

CONTENTS

DEDICATIONS

To my readers, for suffering through the writer's block with me;

To my wife, for putting up with my strange writing obsessions;

and to my father, for bugging me until the work was done.

CURVEBALL

25
AUG 2015

CURVEBALL

A Prose Comic

THE CHAINS WE FORGE IN LIFE

STORY
C. B. WRIGHT
COVER
JAMIE ROBERTSON
LOGO
GARTH GRAHAM

Part One: Airborne

"I wear the chain I forged in life," replied the Ghost. "I made it link by link, and yard by yard; I girded it on of my own free will, and of my own free will I wore it." -Jacob Marley, *A Christmas Carol*

The Thorpe Industries supersonic cargo plane looks more like a space ship than an airplane. At least, it does to CB—it's an argument from back in the old days, when he made an offhanded observation about one of Robert's prototype designs. Robert took it upon himself to disagree.

"It's all smooth and bubble-like," CB says. "I've never seen an airplane look like that before. It's… spacey."

Robert shakes his head. "It's aerodynamic, which would be completely irrelevant for a spaceship. Spaceships fly in space. They don't need to deal with the friction involved in tearing through a gas at 800 miles per hour."

"Spaceship," CB insists. Robert sighs, then lets the matter drop.

Now CB and his group are riding in the passenger cabin of the thing itself—the schematic he'd seen in Robert's lab—and he still thinks the same thing.

Spaceship. It even *hovers*.

Six men and two women sit around a table in the passenger cabin. One more man is laid out on a couch in the small recreational area at the far end of the cabin, unconscious, an IV sticking out of his arm. A seventh man—or what's left of him—has been stuffed in a black-and-yellow biohazard sack and is propped up against the cabin kitchenette. He's not dead, but his current state is non-conscious and, in a direct quote from his only conscious teammate, "visually disturbing."

The conscious men and women sitting around the table are: CB (Curveball), Roger Whitman (Regiment), Jenny Forrest (Zero), Jack Barrow (Scrapper Jack), Special Agents Alan Grant and Lijuan Hu, former Special Agent and now wanted terrorist Peter Raphael Travers, and the only conscious member of the vigilante group Crossfire, known only as Street Ronin. The man on the couch is Street Ronin's teammate, Red Shift. The man in the sack is his *other* teammate, Vigilante.

CB stares at the sack and suppresses a shudder as he sees the sides ripple and bulge. As far as anyone knows it's not possible to actually kill Vigilante—his ability to heal himself is so extreme that he was actually *disintegrated* once, which (according to Street Ronin) took about six months for him to fully recover from. This time around was nothing like that, but in order to rope-a-dope a magic golem, he allowed himself to be mangled and crushed repeatedly, and when it finally spit him out, he wasn't recognizably human. In the aftermath of the fight, Street Ronin put what was left of his teammate in the sack.

CB finds the fact that Crossfire had the presence of mind to create a "carry bag" for Vigilante's remains more than a little disturbing.

Street Ronin notices CB glancing at the bag and shrugs. "He'll be OK in a day or so. Hopefully we land before he regains consciousness. That'll be dicey."

Street Ronin is wearing the standard Crossfire uniform—black tactical armor with a yellow stylized crosshair set above the left breast. He's a hispanic man in his mid-forties, and the wear of the job shows in the lines of his face. Especially around the eyes: crow's feet, perpetually dark circles, a certain hardness in his gaze that doesn't soften, even when he's just talking casually. He has the hyper-aware look of a combat veteran. Which, essentially, he is.

"Why will it be dicey, exactly?" CB forces himself not to reach for the half-smoked pack of cigarettes in his right trenchcoat pocket. He really, really wants a cigarette.

Street Ronin sighs. "Vigilante doesn't really like to talk about it. When he… dies, and then comes back… he gets angry."

"Yeah," CB says. "I guess if I allowed myself to get eaten by a giant magic robot I'd be kicking myself too."

"No, not like that," Street Ronin says. "Think 'purple shorts' angry. Death is apparently very traumatic."

"It is." Special Agent Alan Grant is a member of Division M, the metahuman branch of the Department of Homeland Security. CB had always assumed that meant Division M just dealt with metahuman threats, and was surprised to learn their agents were actually metahumans themselves. Grant is a teleporter, and—according to Roger—can make duplicates of himself. He claims that's not actually what he does.

CB smirks. "The DHS has the inside track on that?"

"No…" Special Agent Lijuan Hu is Grant's partner. She can burst into flame. Quite spectacularly, to hear Jack tell it, which is apparently why he spent a lot of the fight stark naked. "*He* has the inside track. He's officially dead at the moment."

Everyone stares at Grant except for Pete Travers. Apparently this is old news to him.

"Got to see my own autopsy," Grant says. "It really sucked."

"OK…" CB shakes his head. "You're pretty weird, Agent Grant."

"Says the fifty-something geezer who looks like a twenty-something extra from *Sid and Nancy*."

"Says the thirty-something Fed who's apparently seen *Sid and Nancy*."

"God Almighty," Roger mutters, "there's *two of them*."

Roger Whitman is a six-and-a-half-foot-tall black man with graying temples and the physique of a linebacker in his prime. He is the only one of them who can be accused of wearing a costume in the traditional sense: his red-and-black bodysuit is the same design he wore back in the day, and it never served any practical purpose. The only thing it had to do was not fall to pieces during a fight.

CB glances at Jack, dressed in a too-small track suit with a TTI logo on the left shoulder. It's all they could find on board, but it was better than traveling in a plane with Naked Jack.

Maybe it has a purpose after all.

"I'm just saying," Grant says, "if you're gonna get angsty about something, not liking how it feels to die is pretty legit in my book."

"Is that the same book you use to keep people from flying?" CB asks.

"No," Grant says, "that's a *list*. Get it straight, Chief."

Street Ronin ignores them. "The *point* is that when Vigilante comes back to his senses he might be more than a little pissed, and not particularly rational about it. He's not as strong as you guys…" He nods to Roger and Jack. "But I still don't want to be a few thousand feet above ground if he flips out."

"I quite agree." Travers has been silent for most of the time in the plane, content to sit and watch. In the old days, when Travers was assigned to the Guardians as an official government liaison, CB had never noticed exactly how much the man sat and watched.

"Travers?" CB prompts.

"With Street Ronin," Travers clarifies. "I also don't want to be a few thousand feet above ground if he 'flips out.' I don't fly."

"I fly," Agent Hu says. "But I can't really take passengers unless they're fireproof. I guess that means you, Scrapper." She grins mischievously.

Jack shrugs, causing the track suit jacket to strain at the seams.

Grant rolls his eyes. "Jesus, Hu, buy him dinner first."

Hu hits him squarely in the arm.

"Ow."

Everyone laughs, more to relieve tension than anything else.

"I'll be right back." Jenny Forrest pushes back her chair and stands. The laughter dies off, and she fidgets self-consciously as she finds herself the center of attention. Her combat armor, black plates of composite steel set over a black composite mesh, clanks loudly in the sudden silence. "I... Mr. Whitman, where's the bathroom in this thing?"

Roger smiles and points. "Through the hatch, second on the left."

Jenny nods once. The right side of her face flushes slightly—the left is swollen and bruised. "Be right back."

CB frowns as he watches her leave.

Grant shakes his head. "*Mister Whitman?*"

"Give her a break. I've known her pretty much all her life. She didn't call me 'Roger' when she was eight, and she hasn't had any reason to since." Roger looks at the hatch thoughtfully. "She OK, CB?"

"Nope." CB doesn't elaborate.

Roger nods. "She gonna *be* OK?"

"Pretty sure," CB says. "She had a rough trigger."

"Yeah," Roger says. "I heard about that. From her mom."

CB looks at Roger sharply. "Juliet knows about that?"

"A *lot* of people know about it," Roger says. "She and Marty got it from Senator Morgan himself. Apparently he's trying to keep everyone from reclassifying her under Title XII."

Travers raises an eyebrow. Grant and Hu exchange knowing looks.

"Shit," CB says. "Juliet's gonna kill me."

"No, she's on your side," Roger says. "So's Marty, but... you know."

CB sighs. "Maybe I should talk to her."

"Let me take this one," Roger says.

"Fine by me." CB leans back in his chair, closing his eyes. "Wise mentor, I am not."

"Not so bad," Street Ronin says. "She held her own against Richter. She would have lost eventually, but she was making him work hard for it. She's gonna be real scary in a fight some day."

"Yay," CB says. "She gets to be just like us."

* * *

Jenny stands in the cargo hold, staring at the coffins stacked from floor to ceiling.

They're not literally coffins—they're seventy-two portable, hermetically-sealed isolation chambers, each containing a person. Half of the people are alive, and half of the people... she saw the bodies. They didn't die peacefully.

She hears the hatch open behind her. She doesn't bother turning around.

"You're going to have to start calling me Roger."

Jenny turns to see Roger Whitman standing in the hatch. "I thought you were CB."

Roger chuckles. "Don't make that mistake again." He walks over to her, giving her armored shoulder a gentle squeeze as he looks at the coffins stacked from floor to ceiling.

"Why Zero?"

Jenny snorts. "I gave up trying to think of a name. Red Shift threatened to call me 'Miss Liberty' if I didn't think of something."

"I see," Roger says. "Didn't expect that one to have a sense of humor."

"He's a riot, actually. So's Street Ronin, once he relaxes. It's just Vigilante who's not any fun." She thinks about the sack leaning against the kitchenette and shudders. "I guess I can see why."

They stand in silence for a while, then Roger asks, "You OK?"

"Yeah," Jenny says. "I just... I don't know. It was too much like it was before the fight. Everyone sitting around, cracking jokes. I couldn't do that when there was... this."

She gestures toward the coffins.

"Everyone on this plane cares about those people."

"I know," Jenny says. "I just don't know how to do both yet. How to care and wind down afterward."

"There's definitely a trick to it," Roger says. "After a while you learn to compartmentalize, to set the bad stuff aside for a while, not focus on it until you have to. The trick is figuring out when you have to. If you don't, you're going to look for other ways to cope, and that won't end well."

"Other ways?"

Roger shrugs. "CB says you're a pretty close analogue to Liberty in terms of what he could do. Assuming that's true, it'll take a lot more than a shot of whiskey to help you unwind."

Jenny stares down at her hands. She's still wearing her gloves—fingerless nylon mesh, with a metal plate on the back that goes just over her knuckles. They're supposed to allow her to easily use a keyboard while still providing some protection during a fight. The metal alloy is black, but she can see something even darker staining it.

Blood. Jesus, I literally have blood on my hands.

"I shot a guy in the face," Jenny said. "I didn't really have a choice at the time. At least I don't think I did. But it was still horrible."

"Yeah," Roger says.

"And then we all attacked that base, and I'm pretty sure I wound up killing more people. I didn't plan to—I deliberately chose not to go in armed, you know? I figured I'd be able to hold back, like Great-Grandfather did. But they weren't holding back… so I didn't. I couldn't afford to, I guess—I had to use everything I had to stay alive. And then we found these…"

She looks at the coffins again. Stacked floor to ceiling.

"I feel like I should still think it's horrible. And I do, I guess. Only… not so much." Jenny turns to Roger, a hint of desperation in her eyes. "That's not good, right? I shouldn't be getting jaded after my second fight."

"You're not getting jaded," Roger says. "You're getting *angry*. It's OK to be angry about what the bad guys did to these people. You gotta be careful where it takes you, but being angry? You need that. When you stop being angry about things like this, that's when you're in *real* trouble."

"I can't imagine ever not being angry about that," Jenny says.

"Nobody can," Roger says. "Not in the beginning."

Part Two: Little Dresden Freedom House, January 7, 1984

"First thing you have to understand: I'm not anyone's leader."

Roland is lean almost to the point of emaciation. He has little visible body fat—just pale skin stretched tight over ropy, knotted muscles. He wears a dirty white tank top shirt, black jeans, and heavy work boots. His hair is cut short and dyed green. His face is angular with high, sharp cheekbones; blue eyes peer out from underneath thick dark eyebrows.

CB has seen him somewhere before. He can't place it.

"I'm serious," Roland says. "I'm not a leader, I'm a guide. I figured out how to deal with myself a long time ago, and I managed to do it without killing anyone—which is incredibly lucky, considering what I can do. All I care about is getting you to the point where you can get a handle on what you do to the point where you don't hurt anyone, including yourself."

"That's it?" CB doesn't bother to hide his skepticism.

"That, world peace, and the occasional cold beer," Roland says. "Look, I won't pretend there isn't more to me than that. I have opinions and I share them. But you don't have to agree with them for me to help you. You could be a fucking Democrat or Republican for all I care, I'd still help you. That said, I have a little speech I give everyone before I start, and if you want my help you have to listen to it first."

"He'll listen," Joan says. She's a fierce-looking woman, her hair pulled back into a tight ponytail, revealing sharp features and scars running down the jawline on both sides of her face. They're a little like lightning bolts, he thinks, and when she locks eyes with him he feels a little tingle as if the intensity of her gaze *were* electric.

He tries not to look annoyed. He met her in a bar the night before, only it's more complicated than that: Joan is a *metahuman* girl in a bar he met the night before, and he only met her because she was looking for him. He's a metahuman, too, and if he doesn't figure out how he works he's going to go crazy.

Pull like so, then angle my body to catch her ankle, as she falls into Roland I half-roll to the right to get the hispanic guy to his left, go for the left knee and he'll collapse on top of the other two...

CB winces as he forces the image from his mind. "Yeah. I'll listen."

Freedom House is one of the few buildings left standing at the epicenter of Little Dresden. It was a tenement building once, but has become one of the few bastions of civilization in a part of the city most people pretend doesn't exist. They're standing in the Freedom House basement, which has been converted into a gym. It reminds CB of the kind of gyms they always show in boxing movies: free weights, heavy bags, pull-up bars, that kind of thing. And in the center of the room is an actual boxing ring.

Only instead of being full of jocks, it's full of punks and anarchists. It's surreal.

"OK," Roland says. "Here goes. In 1975 a hero group called the New Vanguard had a big fight with a villain group called the City Lords. The fight ended with an explosion in the East Village that left a crater the size of half a city block. You can see that crater if you go out our front door and take a left. Nobody really knows why Freedom House was left standing, but it's pretty much the only building around here that was. Everything else was blown to bits."

CB nods. He was pretty young back then, but even he remembers that fight. He sure as hell remembers the explosion.

"Everybody says the New Vanguard saved New York City that day," Roland says. "They're probably right… but they didn't save Alphabet City. A lot of people lived because of that fight, but a lot of people died to get there. That's what people like us can do."

People like us.

"It's different for all of us," Roland continues. "Me, I'm like a living battery. I can throw juice around and really tear shit up if I want to. Joan can make people do what she wants just by thinking it. Carlos here…" He slaps the hispanic guy on his shoulder. "He can turn into solid stone. Or… well, something. It looks like stone to me."

CB raises an eyebrow. He mentally crosses out the "going for the left leg" thing.

"Point is, what they did to Little Dresden ten years ago we could do today. And if we don't learn to control what we do, it's only a matter of time before the Big Apple has a second crater. That's why I try to help people, especially here. Nobody else will, which means the first time someone like us meets the outside world, it'll probably already be too late."

"So you're saying there's a practical reason for your altruism," CB says.

"Yeah," Roland says. "Practical, because I don't want the city deciding we're a threat, coming in, and carting us off to prisons or laboratories or whatever the fuck they do to undesirable metahumans these days. But also because I remember what it was like when it first happened to me. I almost killed my mom. She was so scared of me, I ran away just so she'd feel safe again. We don't all get to be the bright and shiny superhero, and some of us had some pretty dark places they had to crawl out of."

Roland looks at Joan. She nods.

"If you want me to help you, I will. While I do it, I talk a lot. My talk is pretty political, and I'm not ashamed of that. I don't expect you to agree with me. You can even argue with me if you want. If you walk away learning how to control what you do, and also believing I'm the biggest political nutjob you've ever met, that's cool with me. If you can't stand a guy talking politics while he works, well, it's probably not going to work out. You OK with that?"

CB shrugs. "I guess if you piss me off I'll just leave."

Roland nods. "Nobody will stop you if you do. And if you change your mind later, you can always come back. Carlos quit three times."

"Meant it each time, too," Carlos says, grinning. "He's a real asshole."

"Fine," CB says. "Yeah, OK. Look, no offense, but I won't know what you're about 'till I hear your shtick. But right now? Right now I just want to think straight. I can't make it stop and... it really has to stop." The last few words come out no louder than a whisper as a feeling of hopelessness starts to seep in.

Roland claps his hands. The noise is sharp and loud, breaking CB out of his thoughts.

"That's fine," Roland says. "Get into the ring and show us what you can do. If you can. You say it's always on, so give us a demonstration."

CB blinks in confusion a few times, then glances over at Joan.

Joan winces. "Maybe you should just try describing it first."

"OK," CB says.

He's never been in a boxing ring before. He's surprised at how stiff the canvas feels—it's not hard like a floor, but he always thought it would be like walking on a trampoline. It isn't. He stands in the center of the ring, looking around the gym. Most of it is quiet, now—the people who were exercising have stopped, all eyes on him.

"Describe it to you," he says. "OK. I see... I see a series of actions. Like those instruction manuals that only use pictures—you know, like the ones that show you how to change a tire by drawing out each panel like a comic book. I keep thinking of it like playing pool—like you're lining up a shot that will ricochet in such a way that you don't just sink one ball, you sink all of them."

"Interesting," Roland says. "Give me an example."

CB takes a deep breath. "I run toward you, grabbing the bottom ring rope with both hands. I kick the support, hard. The whole ring topples on one corner—it's impossible, I'm not that strong, but that's what I do—and you, Joan, and... Carlos, I guess? Sorry. The three of you topple to one side. There's still tension in the ropes on this end, though—a little more, actually, because the corner pole will be sagging out from the ring, pulling the ropes tighter—so I hop up, grab the top rope, and vault over. I bring my feet down on the small of your back while you're trying to get up, then I fall back and put an elbow into Joan's neck. Two down."

Joan's eyes widen in surprise. Roland looks at CB thoughtfully.

"For the last goddamn week I've been sizing up everything as a fight. *Everything.* If I'm buying food, I'm thinking about how the food could be used as a weapon. Or how I could use the cash register to break the guy's arm. If I'm walking down the street I think about each person on the street and how I could fight them. *At the same time.* I'll watch a fight scene on TV and start thinking about how it would actually work in real life—I'm talking about the really stupid stuff that's obviously for show. It's like my brain is actually coming up with ways to make it work for real."

Roland nods slowly. "I get it."

But the words keep coming—he's so relieved to actually tell someone what's been happening, he can't stop talking about it. "I had to go out on my fire escape a few days ago, and my first thought is how to survive if I threw myself over the side. I'm five floors up. I saw myself bending my body in ways that—well, my body doesn't do that. Gymnasts do that, *maybe.* I don't. You know, Joan and I got into a fight with a bunch of Neo-Nazis last night—"

"New Aryan Army," Joan says to Roland. "Plague was there."

"Yeah," CB says. "Him. Whatever. Point is, I kind of remember what I did when I was fighting, but I kind of don't, because I don't understand it. I don't understand what I did, and I don't understand how. It shouldn't be possible. Actually moving the way I did *hurt.*"

In two steps Roland moves to the edge of the boxing ring, grabs the top rope, and jumps. He vaults over, does a flip in midair, then twists so he lands right in front of CB, facing him. It happens so fast CB doesn't even have time to be alarmed.

"You're going to be OK," Roland says. He claps CB on the shoulder. "You know you're a metahuman, right?"

"No shit," CB says.

"But you actually *know* it, right? No denial? That's the first thing you need to get out of the way. None of this 'this can't be happening to me' bullshit. You first have to accept it actually is happening to you."

"I know it's happening to me," CB says. "I don't understand how it's possible, but I know it's happening. No denial."

"Good," Roland says. "OK, here's the good news: you're not going crazy. You're just noticing things you never noticed before."

"Crazy-ass fighting moves?" CB asks incredulously.

Roland smiles reassuringly. "Yeah, basically. Look, your brain is always calculating things. It calculates how far away your hand is from a beer bottle so your arm will stretch out the right distance to pick it up. It does that kind of shit all the time, but you're *used* to it. You don't even think about it any more—it's instinct. All of a sudden your brain is calculating a new kind of data, but it's not instinct—not yet. It's a new thing for you, but you're processing it the hard way."

"The hard way," CB says. "Is there an easy way?"

"For some people," Roland says. "They pass out for a few days and when they wake up it all makes sense."

"Gimme some beer," CB says. "I can make that happen."

Carlos laughs. Roland smiles slightly. "If it hasn't happened by now, it's not going to happen. So we're just going to have to get you so used to what your brain is doing it fades into the background as just another calculation. Until then you have to learn to focus and push yourself through it."

"Focus," CB says. "How?"

"I find anger helps. I bet every time you were actually *using* your powers you were pretty pissed off."

CB nods slowly. "Now that you mention it..."

"Yeah. Anger is important. Dangerous—it'll control you if you don't keep a handle on it—but it's a great way to start."

"How do I keep a handle on it?" CB asks.

"By getting angry at the right things," Roland says. Then, slightly mischievously: "I have a few ideas, if you'd like to hear them."

CB stares at Roland incredulously for a few seconds. Then he starts laughing.

Roland grins. "You're gonna be OK, CB. You're gonna be OK."

Part Three: Thorpe Island, Present Day

They stand on the tarmac of a small but undeniably modern airport, squinting as their eyes adjust from the dim light in the cargo plane to the bright sun shining overhead. Off in the distance they can see a cluster of buildings bearing the logo of the Thorpe Technical Institute—formerly the R&D branch of Thorpe Industries, now a wholly independent entity in its own right. On the other side of the airport is a beach with white sparkling sand. Off in another direction—the sun is so high CB can't tell north from west from east out here—looks to be a small forest, and beyond that there's even a mountain.

"It doesn't look like a fake island," CB says.

"It's not fake," Roger says. "We are actually surrounded by water on all four sides. It's *artificial*. There's a difference."

Just to the side of the plane is a large biohazard tent, which they are herded toward by men wearing biohazard suits. There are two entrances: Jenny and Hu are sent through the flap on the left while the men are forced to wait in line at the flap on the right. Behind them, more men in biohazard suits unload the seventy-two coffins into a line of trucks.

"Whatever. It's impressive, is all. And *big*. Well, for something he built from scratch over the last ten years. I mean, there are bigger islands out there, but this one has an airport and his corporate HQ."

"And a town just on the other side," Roger says. "Nice one, too. Population ten, fifteen thousand if I remember right."

CB squints at the office buildings off in the distance. "That doesn't look like it holds ten to fifteen thousand employees."

"Employees and families, CB. It's a company town. And most of the facility is underground."

"Of course it is." CB sighs and looks at the beach. "Oh well."

"Really?" Roger tries unsuccessfully to hide a smile. "You were never much of a beach guy back in the day."

"I spent the last ten years in Farraday City," CB says. "It's kinda nice to see one not littered with needles, human refuse, and the occasional body."

When it's his turn, CB steps through the tent flap on the right and is immediately intercepted by yet another hazmat-suited technician with a handheld device that he immediately starts waving up and down CB's body. CB waits impatiently while the tech peers at the screen.

"Well? What does your tricorder say?"

"It's not a—" The man breaks off. "You're fine. Please step through the flap to your right, shower, and change into the clothes on the table at the far end."

"I thought you said I was fine," CB says.

"You are," the man says. "This is a precaution only. You'll get your original clothes back. If you want them."

"Fine," CB grumbles, and steps through.

It's a chemical shower, it's cold, and it smells terrible. It also instantly destroys the holding power of the gel in his hair, which pisses him off *immensely*. The clothes aren't much more substantial than hospital scrubs, though a clean white bathrobe and slippers are also provided, which helps. When he steps out the other side, he sees almost everyone else is dressed the same way. Street Ronin is pacing off to one side, muttering to himself.

He's wound pretty tight. CB walks over.

"Not your usual look." He tries to keep his voice light and friendly. "You almost look harmless."

"I'm putting up with this because everything I know about Thorpe says he's a stand-up guy," Street Ronin says. "But they took Vigilante and Red Shift and won't tell me where they are. I get that he's a super-genius and all, but I don't think they understand what's gonna happen if Vigilante wakes up and decides he's having a really bad day."

CB frowns. "Yeah."

"I apologize for that."

CB turns to see a very tall black woman emerge from the tent flap on the left. Her skin is very dark, and her hair is divided into long, thin braids, gathered up in the back into a loose ponytail. She's dressed in the same scrubs and bathrobe as the rest of them.

Street Ronin's eyes widen slightly. "Dr. Mahmoud."

"I apologize for this whole thing," she says, sighing slightly. "We were caught off guard by what you found in the containment chambers and felt we really couldn't take any chances. Street Ronin, you have my word that Vigilante and Red Shift are in good hands. Red Shift is already responding positively to his treatment, and Vigilante has been transferred to an area designed to withstand any situations where he might react badly. You further have my personal assurance that no medical or scientific procedures will be performed on them beyond what is necessary to help them recover. That order came directly from Dr. Thorpe himself, and I will see it carried out in both letter and spirit."

The steel in her voice makes it clear she means what she says. Either that, or she's one of the best liars CB's ever met, but that's not really Robert's style. He sees Street Ronin relax a little and nod. The woman relaxes in turn.

CB turns to Street Ronin. "So you two know each other?"

"What?" Street Ronin shakes his head. "No. She's *Alimah Mahmoud*."

CB shrugs.

"Seriously?" Street Ronin frowns in disbelief. "She's the President of Thorpe Industries."

CB blinks. "I thought Robert was the—"

Dr. Mahmoud laughs, a clear, carefree laugh that seems utterly at odds with the steel in her voice just moments before. "I just lost a bet," she says, smiling. "Is everyone finished?"

As if on cue, the right tent flap opens and Roger comes out in scrubs and a bathrobe. "Alimah! I didn't think you'd be here."

Right. Roger's been here before.

Dr. Mahmoud's smile broadens. "I couldn't miss this, Roger. It's historic." Her smile fades as she looks at the last of the trucks driving off with the last of the caskets. "And not all of it will be pleasant, I'm afraid. Come on. Robert's waiting for us in his office."

"Really?" CB looks down at his bathrobe. "Dressed like this?"

Dr. Mahmoud shrugs apologetically. "He'll explain."

* * *

Robert Thorpe's office is not designed for entertaining guests.

There's no point: since the 90s there have been very few people he's actually wanted to see. The people he has seen have been trusted employees and friends—people he doesn't need to impress. So the office was built to serve as his own private communications center and prototyping lab, allowing him to work on his designs in private while managing other, more mundane matters.

And also highly unusual, very unique matters.

"Main screen."

He's never bothered denying the viewscreen that takes up the entire wall behind his desk was ripped off from Star Trek. Like so many other technologists of his day, Star Trek was his muse: it had things he wanted to actually exist, and the "main screen" of the Enterprise was one of his first projects. It's actually a little dated these days—a lot of the high tech firms are moving to holographic displays—but he still thinks it's the coolest thing in his office.

Some people just won't give up their eight-track tapes.

"Show me the tarmac."

The data on the screen moves to the side as a window opens up displaying the TTI airfield. The cargo plane is still there. The cargo trucks are gone, and the only people he sees are the ones taking down the biohazard tent.

"Daniel, where are our guests?"

"Doctor LaFleur is in the recovery room monitoring Mr. Bernard. Doctor Mahmoud just notified me that eight of the arriving party are on their way to your office." The voice is human and male. It's a very specific voice, one taken from his past, and the past of a few of the new arrivals.

Robert frowns. "Which eight?"

"CB, Forrest, Travers, Grant, Hu, Barrow, Whitman, and Lange. Mr. Carpenter and Dr. Dalton have been sent to recovery. Mr. Carpenter requires threat protocols in place for certain stages of his recovery."

"Right. Daniel, from this point forward make sure that members of Crossfire are referred to only by their code names. This includes all official documentation. Do not refer to them by given names to anyone other than me, and then only if there is no chance anyone will overhear."

"Understood."

"How am I doing today?"

There's a brief pause. Robert feels a tingle down the back of his spine. "The cane will be sufficient."

"Good."

Robert stands, with a little effort, and grabs the cane propped up against his desk. It's a lovely cane, black-stained wood with a silver tip and handle, and he hates it intensely. He walks around the side of the desk and waits.

Metahumans tend to live longer—assuming their line of work doesn't kill them, of course—and Robert benefits from that to an extent. His abilities aren't physical, so the effects aren't as pronounced, but other than a little salt creeping into his reddish-brown hair he appears to be a man in his late thirties instead of one almost eligible for Social Security benefits. On a superficial level, he appears to be perfectly healthy and in the prime of his life. But there are pieces of the picture that don't quite fit: the cane. The way he favors his left side. The occasionally pinched look on his face, usually masked but peeking through occasionally, the way his green eyes water slightly. All of these suggest chronic pain to anyone with the experience to see it.

He straightens as the light over his office door flashes twice.

"Enter."

The door opens. Alimah walks in dressed in scrubs and a white bathrobe, followed by Roger, CB, Travers, the two other DHS agents, Street Ronin, Jack Barrow, and a young blonde woman that he almost doesn't recognize as Jenny Forrest.

As soon as he enters the room, CB's gaze locks on Robert's cane.

"I'm back," Roger says. "I brought some friends over."

Robert smiles. "Hello everyone. I apologize for the change of clothes. Your cargo raised some concerns and we needed to make sure there wasn't anything lingering in the air. You'll get a chance to change into something more substantial soon—I just thought it best to meet as soon as possible."

"It's good to see you again, Robert." Pete Travers' expression is usually inscrutable, but he does look genuinely pleased. "A pity the circumstances are so unusual."

Robert sighs. "I'm afraid I'm not very social these days. For a number of reasons." He looks directly at CB as he says this, and moves his cane just a little. CB's eyebrow shoots up, and he nods slightly. "I did hope to make Alex's funeral. Unfortunately…"

"You're on the no-fly list," Agent Grant says. "Yeah. I work for some real passive-aggressive assholes."

Robert takes a moment to revel in the agent's unusual frankness. "That's not how I would have put it."

"Agent Grant is a people person." Agent Hu is physically the smallest person in the room. She's also the one who can probably blow up the entire island, if she puts her mind to it. "But he's not wrong."

"But we do technically work for them—well, Agent Hu does. I'm legally dead at the moment. So that puts us in a bit of a bind." Grant's all business at the moment, and his partner nods in agreement. "I think it's probably a good idea if we get that settled and out of the way before you say anything that we might be forced to use against you later."

"We wouldn't want to," Hu says softly. "But we would."

CB sighs in exasperation, and opens his mouth to retort.

Robert raises his left hand. "It's OK, CB. They aren't threatening me, they're trying to *warn me*. Agent Grant, Agent Hu, I appreciate the warning.

Let's put our current situation in context."

Hu nods. Grant shrugs.

"You have apparently been traveling with a rogue United States Agent who is wanted for questioning because he aided and abetted a metahuman organization currently classified as terrorist under Title XII of the Patriot Act." Robert gestures to Pete Travers, who nods, smiling. "You have also, if I understand recent events correctly, actively assisted that terrorist organization in an assault on privately-owned property on US soil."

"In Farraday City," Grant says.

Robert nods. "My lawyers agree that's a legitimate mitigating factor, but they don't think it's enough mitigation to account for the identities of the people you were assisting: the aforementioned metahuman terrorist group, a rogue ex-hero and a possibly kidnapped or brainwashed civilian, and one of the closest known associates of one of the most dangerous supervillains in the world."

"Retired," Jack clarifies.

"That probably won't come up," Robert says.

"Yeah," Grant says, "we're definitely working off-book."

"In that case," Robert says, "if Pete trusts you, so do I."

Travers' response is immediate and unequivocal. "I trust them."

"That's settled, then. I'm convinced we're all on the same team here, so let me get to the point: we don't know exactly what we're facing at the moment, but it obviously goes much further than who killed Alex Morgan, and it's tied to whatever was done to the poor people in those containment units. Most of you have been working on pieces of this. I think the time has come to try to fit all the pieces together, and I think this is the perfect place to do it."

Jack Barrow crosses his arms. "I'm not saying it's a bad idea. It isn't. But there are a few more people involved in this."

Robert nods. "Artemis LaFleur contacted me early this morning. He and Lieutenant Bernard are in the medical wing."

"*Overmind?*" Agent Grant's jaw goes slack as he gapes in undisguised astonishment.

"Afraid so," Robert says.

Grant turns to Hu. "Overmind."

Hu sighs and shakes her head. "I'm gonna get *so very, very fired*."

Part Four: The Hotseat

"I'd like to thank you all for joining us tonight. Tonight is a very special night for us on The Hotseat, for tonight we are joined—rejoined, really—by a man who was a guest on our program in the very early days of our broadcast. He has agreed to appear tonight as our guest, and does so fully understanding—indeed, having experienced firsthand—our format and expectations. I'm your host, Jacob Lynn, and I'd like to introduce you—again—to our guest: Senator Tobias Morgan, welcome back to The Hotseat."

The studio audience applauds warmly, and Senator Morgan dips his head in acknowledgment. He resembles his grandfather: his hair is dark (a trait from his mother's side), and he doesn't have a Project-Paragon-enhanced physique, but he has the same jawline, and when he talks he radiates the same dedication and resolve. When he talks, some people say they can almost hear Liberty talking in his place. The comparison is all the more bittersweet now that his grandfather is dead.

"Thanks for having me back, Jacob." His voice is deep and strong, managing to communicate authority, openness, and warmth all at the same time.

Jacob Lynn looks more like a stereotypical college professor than a TV host, complete with tweed jacket, bow tie, and spectacles. He's occasionally referred to as the "Mister Rogers of news entertainment" because he projects such a gracious and meek personality to the camera. But he's also a tenacious interviewer, famously unwilling to let his guests evade questions, and this combination is the secret of the show's appeal. Tonight is a special treat for his viewers: the man famously unafraid to ask hard questions is interviewing a man famously unafraid to answer them.

"Senator Morgan, the past month has been a very trying one for you. Let me first offer my condolences, on behalf of myself and everyone on our show, for the loss of your grandfather. Liberty was a hero to everyone, but he was *your* grandfather."

"Thank you," the senator says. "He was a great man. I miss him."

"Let's move on to the questions. There are rumors, as there are every election cycle, that you are going to run for President. Would you care to address those rumors?"

Senator Morgan laughs, a mixture of surprise and amusement. "I'm not running for President."

"I see..." Jacob Lynn nods thoughtfully. "Of course you realize the pundits will focus on your use of present tense, and claim that while your answer is absolutely correct—you are not running *now*—it doesn't mean you aren't planning to announce a run next month."

Senator Morgan laughs again, this time sounding more rueful than amused. "I guess I left myself wide open for that. Let me be more clear, then: I don't plan to *ever* run for President. I can't promise I won't change my mind someday—people do that—but at this point in my life I am convinced I can do far more as a senator than I ever could as President. My current plan is to be a senator for the rest of my political career."

"That is rather more to the point," Lynn agrees. "Some might consider that very limiting."

"I don't. Being President is limiting. Eight years at most, then you're gone. In the Senate I can work over decades—assuming my constituents continue to support me that long—to advocate for and support plans that will continue to help this country. We face grave dangers as a nation, dangers that won't be fixed in a year, or four, or even eight."

"Dangers?"

"Dangers," the senator says. "Dangers that will require constant vigilance—not just against the dangers themselves, but against what facing those dangers might make us become."

"Might make us become? Can you elaborate on that?"

"During World War II we imprisoned Japanese-Americans because we were afraid some of them might be Japanese sympathizers," Senator Morgan says. "We imprisoned them all, based on what we were afraid some of them might be. My grandfather once told me that one of the things he's always regretted was that he supported it at the time. He always stressed how important it was, when fighting a monster, not to become a monster yourself."

Jacob Lynn peers over the rims of his glasses. "That's almost Nietzschean."

The senator smiles a little. "I doubt my grandfather would have appreciated the comparison."

"Let's return to your comment 'we face grave dangers as a nation,'" Lynn says. "Can you be more specific? Are you talking about terrorists? Poverty?"

"I'm sure you won't be surprised when I say the problem is how we as a nation handle the rapid increase of metahumans in our population."

"That has been one of your less popular platforms," Lynn notes.

"It has," the senator says. His jaw sets, and the resolve in his expression brings out the family resemblance even more. "It almost cost me my last election. But I think it's an important one. If we don't recognize the problem and find a solution, we're going to become a nation that does terrible things. I want to avoid that."

"What kinds of things? Senator, your opinions on 'the metahuman threat' have given your political foes plenty of ammunition to use against you. They accuse you of wanting to create a nation that does terrible things."

Senator Morgan sighs. "Can I say, for the record, that 'the metahuman threat' is not my line? I have always called it a *problem*. A newspaper—the Tribune, I think—is the one that relabeled it a *threat*."

"So you *don't* believe metahumans are a threat?"

"I believe metahumans are humans. People. Here in America most of them are US citizens. Labeling an entire group of people as a threat is dangerous—it's also, sadly, something we have a history of doing."

"But do you believe they are a *threat*?"

"I think if you answer 'yes' or 'no' to that question you automatically get most of it wrong. Every metahuman has the capacity to be a threat. Just like an armed man walking down a public street has the capacity to be a threat. But being able to do something and actually doing it are not the same thing. We can't treat it as the same thing."

"It sounds like you're saying they're *not* a threat."

"We live in a world where we can't tell who is a threat and who isn't until after the dust has settled," the senator says. "Is the metahuman in the costume standing in front of you trying to protect you, or is he the one that you need protecting from? You won't know until he acts, and unfortunately, if he decides to harm you, there's probably not anything you can do about it. That's the problem, Jacob. At the moment, our only real solution to protecting the American people from rogue metahumans is to react to what they do. I know there are people who argue that it's the only fair system to have, but reacting doesn't scale well when you have people who can destroy an entire city block in the time it would take for first responders to arrive. The only way we have survived so far is because we have benefited from the voluntary and heroic assistance of metahumans who step up to defend their communities."

Jacob Lynn cocks his head to one side. "Is that a new position, Senator? You haven't spoken as warmly of the hero community in the past."

"It's an *evolving* position," Senator Morgan says. "I've always known there were selfless people willing to devote their extraordinary talents to serving the public. My grandfather is the greatest example of that. But power can always be misused, and the more you have the easier it is to do. No one who has power is innocent of this—I'm not innocent of it. My colleagues in the Senate aren't innocent of it. I suspect even you're not innocent of it, Jacob, though you're not in the Hotseat tonight so I won't press the issue. As a senator of the

United States of America—and as someone who sits on committees that have access to a *lot* of classified information—my capacity to cause damage to the American people is *enormous*. And the temptation to put the people at risk in order to gratify my own wants and needs is always there. How much more tempting is it to someone who is so strong they can shrug off artillery fire like it was nothing? Or someone who can turn invisible at will? Or someone who can read minds? We don't have to speculate about these things. They've already happened to us. The results have been devastating, and all we've done is react."

"What else is there to do?" Lynn asks. "It seems to be, as you say, the only fair option. We can't declare them criminals right off the bat. Don't they have rights?"

"They do," the senator says. "And you're right. But—this is where I start losing my base—I think our laws on metahuman activity are broken. We need to rewrite most of them—scaling some back, making others stronger—until we have a set of laws that let every metahuman in America know where they stand, where the lines are, and what will happen if those lines are crossed."

"A tall order," Lynn says.

"Very tall," the senator agrees. "It may not even be possible at this point. But our legal system wasn't designed to handle metahuman crimes—not in the manner and on the scale they're committed."

"So far you've given us an eloquent description of the tensions pulling at both ends of the issue," Lynn notes, "but you haven't—forgive me for saying so, Senator—you haven't actually proposed a solution in its place. Do you have a solution?"

"Yes." Senator Morgan leans in. "I'm not, I'm afraid, prepared to talk specifics at the moment. But in very broad strokes, it's not a matter of whether or not we as a nation need to change. We're already changing. The question is whether we will spend our time as a nation trying to catch up with the changes that have already happened, or if we will embrace the fact that change is happening and participate in that change in order to guide it. We must acknowledge this change, and we must be willing to take the reins to make sure we adapt to it properly. And in order to do that, we must acknowledge two things: first, that metahumans are humans, and are entitled to the same rights and protections in this country as everyone else. Second, that metahumans have the capacity to cause harm on a scale far beyond their fellow citizens, and that the state has a responsibility to mitigate that threat. Any solution to our problem must acknowledge the tension that exists between those two extremes. A proposed solution that fails to do so will not be a solution at all: it will lead to either tyranny or anarchy, and either way our nation will be lost."

Part One: Elsewhere

David Bernard stands on the cracked stone floor of an open dojo in the middle of an endless grassy plain. A warm wind blows, carrying with it the smell of dry soil. The sky is clear and blue, and the sun shines hot on his face and neck.

It's a simple dream, one he used often when he was trying to learn staff fighting. He's not sure why he's dreaming it now: it wasn't by choice, which makes the setting unusual.

When he dreams spontaneously about a specific location, it's usually about something he has an attachment to—the house he grew up in, the Sky Commando Unit, places like that—not a random set he constructed for his own amusement. He has no emotion invested in this place. There's no reason for him to be here.

The wind kicks up, colder now, and carrying the distinctive scent of the ocean. A low, rumbling sound echoes across the plain, and a dark line forms on the horizon—stormclouds gathering, just a sliver of darkness against the clear blue at first, but quickly thickening, gathering in strength and size as they approach. The smell changes again, the smell of *rain* and *storm* overpowering the previous scent of warm earth. Along with that is something else: not a smell, but it almost registers as such.

Danger.

He realizes why he is dreaming about the dojo now. He *does* have an emotional connection to it: a very recent connection. This is where he beat the island. This is where he, a man who knew nearly nothing about magic, managed to escape a trap on an almost-nonexistent island that was *steeped* in it. He did it because he is a lucid dreamer—he can control his dreams—and magic doesn't know what dreaming is. By escaping into a world that he could control, one that the power that held the island in thrall couldn't comprehend, he broke free of the power that bound him.

This is where he did it.

The clouds climb higher into the sky. Lightning flashes beneath them, tiny sparks of light against the dark, and the sky booms in answer. The hairs on the back of David's neck stand on end, and his scalp begins to itch. He scratches his head absently, and is surprised to find his hair is long and thick. He passes his hand over his chin. He has a beard.

That isn't right. His dream-form never has a beard. He closes his eyes and pictures that form: clean-shaven, short-haired, the way he looked when he was still in the Sky Commando program. He wills himself to adopt that appearance, then passes his hand over his chin. The beard remains.

Something's wrong.

He tries to change the setting, recreating the lobby of the Sky Commando Unit in his mind and attempting to mold the scenery to match. No change. He attempts to conjure something simpler—the bo staff he'd use when practicing here. Nothing happens. He tries to fly, one of the first things you do when you lucid dream. His feet remain planted on the ground.

Wake up, David. This is a dream, so just wake up.

He remains standing on the cracked stone floor as the storm approaches, the clouds ever nearer, the sky darker, and feels the wind grow in strength yet again. For the first time in a very long time, David is trapped in a dream.

Part Two: Thorpe Island, Robert Thorpe's Office

Robert Thorpe sits alone in his office, studying the information scrolling past his screen. Digital forensic teams have been going through all the data collected from the underground facility in Farraday City, and they've been forwarding him the most interesting bits all day.

And they are interesting. But they're not coherent—not yet. At the moment Robert's juggling, keeping each piece of information in the air until he can find the pattern that makes it fit. Very little fits at the moment, which is to be expected. They're working with incomplete data.

He rubs his eyes and leans back in his chair, reaching for the ceramic mug sitting on the edge of his desk. It's still warm enough to be tolerable, so he drinks, occasionally rubbing the bridge of his nose with his left hand.

"Daniel."

"Yes, Robert." The computer with the voice of his dead friend replies promptly.

"How are our guests?"

"Agents Grant, Hu, and Travers are comfortably settled in their quarters. Agent Grant is also exploring this facility. He is also walking along North Beach, throwing rocks into the water. He's also drinking at Donovan's Pub and Kitchen."

Robert smiles slightly.

"He appears to be aware that we're monitoring him," Daniel adds.

"Oh?"

"The... instantiation exploring the facility is providing a running commentary on everything he sees. Some of the phrases he uses are very colorful."

Robert laughs. "I'll bet they are."

"And the instantiation on the beach is making rude gestures in the direction of the closest monitor. Though he doesn't actually appear angered by the surveillance."

Robert laughs again. "What about the others?"

"Red Shift was released from the infirmary a few hours ago. He and Street Ronin are in their quarters resting. Vigilante is conscious and in medical quarantine."

"What's the status there?"

Daniel pauses for a moment. "Quarantine is expected to hold."

"Good," Robert says. "Let me know if that changes. Continue."

"Jack Barrow is pacing in his quarters. David Bernard is still in recovery; Doctor LaFleur is monitoring him. Roger Whitman is asleep in his quarters. Miss Forrest is in her quarters but isn't sleeping. CB just stepped out of the elevator onto this level."

Robert nods. "Send up fresh coffee. Let him in when he gets to the door."

"Very well, Robert."

He struggles to his feet, ignoring the pain lancing down his left side as he grabs his cane, hobbles around his desk, and makes his way over to a framed poster: it's the group, just after they'd finally received government sanction. They were all so young: Gray Falcon, Regiment, Gladiator, Liberty, Curveball. Well, Liberty hadn't been young, even then. But he'd always *looked* it.

"And now, only three," Robert murmurs.

Two and a half, really.

The door to his office opens with a soft *hiss*. Robert looks up to see CB walk into the room.

He's dressed in a Thorpe Institute track suit, light blue with a single gray stripe traveling up each arm and leg. The jacket is unzipped and hanging open, revealing a plain white t-shirt that's half-tucked into his pants. He's wearing a pair of gray slippers that probably came with the room. Somehow he's managed to spike his hair, though, and Robert is struck by how little he's changed. He is, to all appearances, still in his twenties. He's a *haggard* twenty-something: poorly shaven, too thin, raggedy hair sticking in all directions, nicotine-stained fingers and an insolent curl at the corner of his mouth where an unlit cigarette dangles carelessly. But it's the look of a young man who lives hard, not the look of an old man who hasn't stopped. He's exactly the way he was the day they first met. Only his eyes look old, and they looked old even then.

Those old eyes stare fixedly at Robert's cane.

"Sorry for the outfit," Robert says. "I thought it'd be better than scrubs. We'll have more appropriate attire for everyone in the morning."

CB shrugs, his gaze never wavering. "I didn't pack, and it's nice to be wearing something not covered in sweat and blood."

"I can imagine," Robert says. "I was always kind of glad I never had to deal with that. The advantages of fighting crime in a hermetically sealed tin can."

"With air conditioning," CB says. "Yeah. I always kind of hated you for that, you rat bastard." He tucks the unlit cigarette behind his right ear.

Robert gestures toward the poster with his cane. "Remember this?"

CB's gaze flickers briefly away from the cane, to the poster, then returns. He frowns, then stares at the poster intently. It takes him a moment before he realizes what he's looking at, then he's grinning like a madman.

"I don't believe it."

He walks up to the wall and peers at the poster intently.

"I don't fucking believe it. Robert! Honest to God, I thought these were gone forever."

"I found a few on eBay, about six years back," Robert says. "I'd wanted one for a while. This was the best of the lot."

"Man, this brings back memories," CB says. "I forgot how pissed off we all were about having to do this thing."

"Completely my fault," Robert says. "I thought having a publicist would be good for the group. I was really, really wrong about that."

"Yeah you were," CB says. "You can't tell in the picture, but Alex is grabbing the back of my trenchcoat with his left hand—right under the back of the collar—to keep me from running off. And look at Danny! God, he was so *pissed*."

"He didn't like the way the photographer 'improved' his costume," Robert says.

CB throws his head back and laughs. "That's right! The photographer— what was his name, little guy, big mouth, reminded me of Joe Pesci—he kept going on and on about how terrible Danny's name was. 'Why are you a falcon? You don't look like a falcon! You don't even have a friggin' bird on your chest! All due respect.'"

"'All due respect,'" Robert says. "That's right. He kept saying that. And Daniel kept trying to point out that the clasp on his utility belt was shaped like a hawk."

"'Your *crotch*?'" CB mimics the pitch and cadence of the man's voice perfectly. "'You want people to look at your *crotch* in order to remember your name? What is this, a porno?' And then he pulls out the feather-cape and beak mask…"

"…and Daniel says there's no way he'll wear those things in a fight…"

"And then the guy says 'it's a *falcon*, fer Chrissakes, just put it on…'"

"…and so he puts them on, just to get the guy to shut up…" Robert adds.

"…which doesn't work," CB continues, "because then for the rest of the shoot he keeps saying 'you look regal. You look *friggin' regal*.'"

"That's right," Robert says, chuckling. "Wow. That was a miserable day."

"Yeah," CB says. "The worst."

They lapse into silence, staring at the poster.

"So why the cane, Robert? What's wrong?"

Robert's smile turns a bit sad. "Just years of good living, finally catching up to me."

"Oh? So you finally became the billionaire playboy you were always meant to be?"

Robert laughs sharply. "That's not *good* living."

The door to his office opens again, and a heavyset man in a white waiter's uniform rolls a coffee tray into the room.

"Thanks Pete." Robert waves once. The heavyset man nods, turns and leaves.

CB makes a beeline for the coffee. "Can I get you one?"

"Cream, two sugars." Robert goes back to his desk, gingerly easing himself into his chair.

CB sets a fresh mug next to the near-empty one, moves a chair around to the side of Robert's desk, and sits, waiting patiently.

Robert takes a sip of coffee, thinking. "Remember Wasteland?"

"Hard to forget the alternate universe where everyone exists but you."

"Remember the bunker where we found their Robert Thorpe?"

"What was left of him," CB says.

Robert frowns. "Yes. Targeted by a virus that had been engineered to kill him—him *specifically*. Since we didn't know how to detect it, and their Thorpe never figured out how to cure it, I stayed in my armor the whole time we were there. Two and a half months, I think?"

"That sounds about right," CB says.

"That's when it started," Robert says. "I thought I was just exhausted at first. I mean, we all were. And Daniel… well. His funeral took a toll. And right after that came PRODIGY, right on schedule. Everything was chaos, everyone was stressed. I didn't realize what was happening for years. By then it was too late."

CB leans forward. "What *was* happening?"

"It was my suit," Robert says. "You remember when Popular

Mechanics had an article that tried to figure out how I controlled the suit? Obviously it's *armor*, so I can't sit back and throw switches to turn things on and off. In the end they decided everything was voice activated, which was actually the way it worked in my earliest models. But by the time that article came out, I was controlling everything by thought."

CB purses his lips thoughtfully. "It was when you switched to the new helmet, right? You ditched the one in the poster—the one that actually looked like a gladiator's helmet—and switched over to the astronaut motorcycle thing."

"That's right," Robert says. "It had a neural link that translated brainwave patterns into system commands. I didn't have to say anything—I could just *think* and the suit responded."

"I never knew that," CB says.

"I didn't talk about it much," Robert says. "It was very finicky technology. I was hoping to refine it before unveiling it. Then all the lawsuits happened and I stopped talking about my research entirely."

CB nods.

"The thing is…" Robert looks back over at the poster. "As cool and as useful as the neural link was, it wasn't entirely safe. Brainwaves aren't exactly easy to decipher. If they were, we wouldn't need telepaths to read minds. The technology that went into the neural link was pretty advanced—still is, I guess—but it could only read very basic patterns. On its own I could get it to turn the suit on and off, and to activate the flight system. I needed it to detect more granular patterns. And since I couldn't make the sensors more sensitive…"

He grins sheepishly, then shrugs.

"I decided to make my nervous system louder."

"Louder," CB says.

"Like an amplifier," Robert says. "The suit boosted my nervous system a little. It made everything easier for the neural link to read. It worked great, the tests I ran indicated it was safe, as long as I kept the boost within a very specific range. Which I did…"

"But you missed something," CB says.

"I didn't think about the effect sustained boosts would have over time. And then there we are, in an alternate reality, and I'm stuck in the suit for two and a half months…"

"Christ," CB says.

"That's where the damage started. After that, it didn't matter how long I was exposed—each new exposure messed me up just a little bit more. By the time I figured it out it was too late. I managed to roll back the damage a little. I don't have seizures any more. But tremors, lancing pain, periods of prolonged weakness… it varies day to day."

"*Christ.*" CB shakes his head in disbelief. "You blew your own speakers."

"As good an analogy as any," Robert says. "It's another reason I've become the recluse I am. I don't want to give my enemies any extra encouragement to come after me."

"Sure," CB says. "Except that you've got a few on your island right now. As *houseguests.*"

"Crossfire aren't enemies," Robert says.

"I'm not talking about *Crossfire*, Robert, I'm talking about *Artemis LaFleur.*"

"LaFleur isn't my enemy, CB. He's my *doctor.*"

CB blinks.

"There aren't many people who really understand metahuman biology," Robert says. "Not in an authoritative sense. And LaFleur leaves the rest of us cold. If it weren't for him I'd be much worse off than I am today."

"Don't get me wrong," CB says, "he's a pretty stand-up guy for a megalomaniac who wants to rule the world. But he's still one of the most dangerous villains on the planet."

Robert's laugh mixes bitterness and amusement in equal measure. "CB, I'm on the United States no-fly list because I wouldn't do my patriotic duty and hand over everything I'd created to the government so other people could take credit for everything I'd devoted my life to creating. I had to move my base of operations to international waters to make sure no other government would try the same thing. I'm a disgraced hero and scientist living on a floating island. If you look at the world a certain way, *I'm* one of the most dangerous villains on the planet."

Part Three: Thorpe Island, Recovery Room

David Bernard lies in a recovery room in the medical facility on Robert Thorpe's private floating island. This means, among other things, that he is currently hooked up to some of the most sophisticated diagnostics and monitoring equipment the world has never seen—so advanced that the phrase *hooked up to* is inaccurate, because the sensors that monitor his vital signs don't require human contact to function. The only equipment physically attached to the man is an IV bag. Everything else is remote.

Artemis LaFleur sits in a padded chair next to Bernard, staring at a monitor, frowning deeply. He has the utmost faith in Dr. Thorpe's equipment—it far surpasses anything he could have designed—but the readings don't make any sense.

He glances up as the recovery room door opens, and nods briefly as a middle-aged asian man wearing scrubs and a hairnet steps into the room.

"Oh." The man sounds mildly surprised as he focuses on Artemis. "Doctor LaFleur. I didn't realize you were still here."

"Doctor Shào." Artemis returns his attention to Bernard's monitor. "I'd intended to greet the others, but I'm... perplexed." He waves toward the monitor, sighing in annoyance. "I don't understand what I'm seeing, and until I do I'm reluctant to leave him in this condition."

"Oh?" Doctor Shào glances at the monitor, frowns, then walks to the foot of the medical bed. He waves a hand over the right corner, and a small rectangle emerges from the base, extends to about waist-height, and unfolds into a keyboard. He types a few commands, and the monitor flips through various diagnostic displays, switching from screen to screen in rapid succession. Shào reads each quickly, and with the press of a final key the monitor display returns to its default, and the keyboard re-folds and retreats back into the base of the bed.

Shào shakes his head. "He doesn't appear to be in any serious danger, but... I thought you said he was undergoing mutationis?"

Artemis nods. "I am absolutely certain it began the night before last."

"His elevated temperature will have to be monitored," Shào says. "And his blood pressure. But I'm reluctant to prescribe anything at this point."

"I agree," Artemis says. "And I am absolutely convinced he is cocooning. Despite evidence to the contrary..."

He looks at the monitor again and shakes his head.

"He should present as a coma patient. Very little brain activity, with the notable exception of discernible and prolonged theta rhythms. But that's not what he's doing."

"If all I had to go on were the brain scans," Doctor Shào says, "I'd assume he was sleeping. But he doesn't wake up."

"No," Artemis says. "He doesn't."

They both stare at the patient in silence.

"Well," Shào says, "I still need to finish my rounds—"

"Of course," Artemis says. "I'll have you paged if there are any significant developments."

Shào nods once. "I'll be back later this evening. We'll discuss it further then."

Artemis gives a half-nod, his brow furrowing as he focuses on Bernard's face. Shào shrugs, then steps back through the recovery room door into the hallway beyond. Artemis settles back into the silence, and starts working through the problem once more.

Shào is an excellent doctor, but he's not qualified to handle this. I doubt anyone is, to be honest.

He grimaces, mildly irritated, as the recovery room door opens once more.

"Your rounds were not as compelling as this problem, I see." Artemis keeps his voice dry.

"What?"

Artemis turns his head to see Jack Barrow, dressed in a tight-fitting pair of sweat pants and a tank top t-shirt, looming in the doorframe.

"Jack. Sorry. I didn't expect to see you down here this evening." He turns slightly to let Jack know he's welcome to enter.

"The plan was to wait till tomorrow," Jack says. "I figured you were gonna want to keep an eye on the Lieutenant. He did something messed up, didn't he?"

Artemis raises an eyebrow. "What makes you say that?"

Jack shrugs. "It's magic, Artie. Is there any other kind of something?"

Artemis concedes the point. "He's done something spectacularly foolhardy. Now he's cocooning."

Jack inhales sharply. "No shit?"

Artemis nods.

"What'd he do, get bitten by a magic spider?"

"It's considerably more abstract than that, but yes."

Jack thinks it over. "Well if it doesn't kill him, maybe it'll help us."

"Perhaps," Artemis says, allowing Jack to hear the doubt in his voice. "But this process, whatever it is, is only cocooning on a superficial level. It doesn't follow the course I expect, which means I don't know what it will—"

"Artie." There's an edge to Jack's voice that he doesn't usually show, not even to his friends. "I didn't come down here to talk medicine."

It's a tone of voice that says *I'm very worried about something important* and when Artemis hears it he immediately gives Jack his full attention.

"Sorry, Jack. Go on."

Jack looks around, steps into the room, and shuts the door behind him. "How private are these rooms?"

"Normally not very," Artemis says.

Jack nods. "Figured. Thorpe's a brain like you. He'd have the whole place wired for sound at least, and if he wasn't monitoring it he'd invent some robot friends to do it for him."

"That's a bit harsh," Artemis says. "He's not exactly known for his support of the surveillance state."

"Doesn't matter," Jack says. "I'm not saying he's a bad guy, Artie, he's just really smart, and this is his playground. He built this place from the ground up, right? That's the impression I get. It's his little private country. Of course he's going to want to keep it safe, and with the enemies he has he's going to monitor everyone. They probably sign forms agreeing to it."

Artemis smiles admiringly. "I've long admired your knack for cutting to the chase and seeing things as they are. You've no idea what a setback it's been, not having you around."

Jack frowns. "I know a little. Artie, I only had time to follow up on one of the names you gave me, but it was a hell of a visit."

"Give me a moment." Artemis reaches into a pocket and pulls out a small cube about the size of his thumb. He sets it on the table next to David's bed and squeezes the sides. A red light at the top blinks rapidly.

"All right," Artemis says. "We can speak freely now."

Jack squints down at the small blinking cube. "That jammed Dr. Thorpe's network?"

"Heavens, no. That merely emits a signal asking Dr. Thorpe to respect our privacy for as long as it's active. There's no effective way to stop him from listening in if he really wants to, not here. We are relying on goodwill and proper manners, I'm afraid."

Jack's frown deepens, but he shrugs. "If you can't do it, then I guess I can't either. Unless I wanted to wreck the place. Which I don't."

"Which name?" Artemis thinks back to the names he'd given on both lists.

"Mike Boyle," Jack says. "Top of the green."

Artemis breaks into a fond smile. "Another man I should have tried harder to keep. I hear he runs a restaurant now."

"Not any more," Jack says.

Artemis feels something cold in the pit of his stomach. "Tell me."

Jack sighs. "Artie, as soon as I mentioned 'Haruspex Analytics' he shoved a bunch of papers in my hands and then he blew his brains out. He was *scared* of them."

Artemis takes a deep breath to maintain his calm. He doesn't remember Boyle scaring easily. "Why?"

"He wouldn't say," Jack says, "but I read what he gave me. He found overlap between Haruspex Analytics and your people."

Artemis nods. "I suspected that. It's the only way they could have scared off my informants."

"No," Jack says. "It's more than that. Based on Boyle's analysis, they effectively *control* your group. All your lieutenants belong to *them*. Your informants work for *them*. Your infrastructure ties back to them."

Artemis shakes his head. "That's not possible."

"Boyle decided it was. Which meant, in his analysis, that you were either being played for a fool or you were in on it from the ground floor. He was tilting pretty hard in the direction of you being in on it. He figured you were too smart to be played like that."

Artemis nods slowly. "And what do *you* think, Jack?"

Jack stares at him as if he's considering the question for the first time. It's *not* the first time—of that Artemis is certain. Since the moment Jack read through Boyle's analysis, whatever it was, he's been chewing over the possibility that Overmind has been manipulating everyone toward some unknown end game.

Finally Jack shakes his head. "It's not you."

Artemis relaxes, just a little.

"I mean, you could do it," Jack says. "You're smart enough. Driven enough. But for that to be true your long con would have started with me some thirty years back. It's not the way you operate."

"I'm glad you believe that," Artemis says.

"But now I gotta ask you a question," Jack says. "And it's a question that I honestly never thought I'd hear myself ask you, under any circumstances. Artie, is there any chance in hell you have an evil twin?"

Part Four: Haruspex Analytics, Top Floor

The board room is designed to be subtly unsettling. It's large and windowless; it appears to be circular, with a long table running up the middle of the room. Appearances are deceiving: it's actually a slight oval, and the table is set slightly off kilter from the oval. People who don't know the trick feel ever-increasing levels of anxiety as they subconsciously realize something is off but can't identify what. Jason figured out the trick, so the room doesn't put him off the way it did, once.

The Chairman, however… that's a different story altogether.

The Chairman sits at the far end of the table, his features concealed in darkness. He stares down at a mission brief—Jason's—and reads in silence. Jason stands at the other end of the table, not daring to sit, and waits patiently for him to finish.

As always, Jason finds himself trying to catch a glimpse of the older man's face. As always, he fails. All he sees beyond the thick head of silver hair styled in a classic executive haircut is one furrow at the top of the man's forehead, and then his face is cloaked in shadow. Jason wonders yet again at how the lighting in the room is arranged in order to achieve that effect. There are no obvious customizations that he can see.

Maybe it's not the room. Maybe it's him.

Jason suppresses a shiver and forces himself to wait patiently.

The Chairman continues reading. Jason focuses on the wrinkle on the Chairman's forehead, wondering if it's there because the man is concentrating, or if it's there because he's angry. It could go either way.

Finally the Chairman leans back in his chair, the silver in his hair fading into the shadows until all Jason can see is the shadowy outline of his head. The fingers of the Chairman's right hand—well-manicured nails, no other distinguishing features—slide over the top of the brief, then push it forward, just an inch.

"Why don't you give me your take on this report." The Chairman has a rich, powerful voice, full of strength and experience. "Reports tend to focus on the *what*. I want to know the *why*."

Jason takes a moment to collect his thoughts.

"It's a mixed bag," he says finally. "There's no question the loss of the facility was a setback. There's absolutely no question the inability to recover most of the data will affect our timeline. But the test itself was an unqualified success—Project Recall is now in Phase Three."

"Why did you deploy the golem and the portal?"

Jason hesitates.

"Mr. Kline?" The Chairman's voice carries a hint of impatience.

Jason blinks once. "Sorry. That's part of a whole side of Project Recall that is still very new to me. I'm not evading, I'm trying to put it in context."

The Chairman nods once, then waits.

Jason takes a few more seconds to sort out his thoughts, takes a breath, and begins. "After we caught the moles, you increased my team's access to the program. The golem was an asset listed in a list of materials in... I can't remember the name of the brief offhand, I included it in the report."

The Chairman nods again.

"I confess I don't really understand... *magic*," Jason says. "I accept that it is fundamentally different from metahuman abilities, but I don't, at this point, *appreciate* that difference. But when the Sorrel-Eades facility was attacked, the attackers managed to hack into and disable the teleporters. We needed to evacuate the personnel. As to the golem, I hoped it would kill them. It very nearly did. As it is, it provided our personnel with the time they needed to evacuate, which we needed to do to salvage the operation."

"Why the people?"

Jason blinks. "Sorry?"

The Chairman laughs softly. "I'm not *chastising* you, Mr. Kline. I'm not a monster who *rejoices* at the thought of sacrificing my personnel in order to achieve long-term goals. But it's necessary, from time to time, and everyone who signs on understands that it's a *possibility*. It's something Andrew understood quite well."

Jason nods. Andrew Estovich had been a member of the Haruspex Board of Directors. He'd been sacrificed in a successful attempt to flush out three moles. He'd been a *willing* sacrifice—some of the theater surrounding the op had been based on his input.

"So when I ask," the Chairman continues, "I'm doing so to understand why you decided saving the personnel was a better choice than using them to slow the enemy's advance while we tried to recover the test data."

"There was no guarantee that we'd be able to move all the data we needed in time," Jason says. "Especially once Curveball's team had breached security. Also, I didn't want to risk the chance that they'd trace the data transfer to another facility. That's how Crossfire located Sorrel-Eades to begin with."

"Ah yes," the Chairman says. "That was unexpected."

Jason sighs. "We thought they were going for the local data. That's what it looked like—they took great pains to make it look that way. They were... clever. I didn't expect that, based on their reputation."

"I can't blame you for that," the Chairman says. "I didn't expect that level of subtlety from them either. I suspect that is something they encourage. We need to update their profiles. But to your point: you didn't feel we had the time to successfully and safely recover the test data."

"That's right," Jason says. "But we could attempt to destroy as much of the data as possible and recover the personnel. The personnel were the ones who actually developed the strain that got us to Phase Three, so we have the knowledge and experience needed to move forward. It will take a little more time to reconstruct everything, but all the knowledge we need is there."

"All well reasoned," the Chairman says, "but why, *specifically*, did you choose the portal and the golem?"

"I..." All Jason can do is shrug. "As I said, I don't really understand magic, and I admit that using an asset before you understand it can be very risky. But I knew we had to evacuate the personnel, and it wouldn't be affected by the teleportation net hack because it didn't rely on technology. If I hadn't seen that file, I would have sent in an air team instead... and they probably would have been soundly defeated."

The Chairman says nothing.

"If I've overstepped my bounds—"

"No," the Chairman says. "There's nothing tactically wrong with your decision. I think it was the correct one to make. But there will be consequences. I don't mean I'm going to punish you—I don't punish my personnel for making hard choices, especially if they haven't been given all the relevant information—I mean, rather, that it has created something of an international incident."

"It has?" Jason frowns. "We've been monitoring all the standard channels, and while the storm has certainly attracted a lot of attention, there's been no chatter at all about the fight or the facility."

"I refer to a much smaller, but potentially more dangerous, international community," the Chairman says. "The practice of magic has a number of rules, Mr. Kline. I have broken many of them, and I plan to break more. But if too many are broken too fast, it attracts unwanted attention. The powers behind Farraday City are practitioners, and they are not our allies. It's analogous to a country discovering a hostile power has installed a secret nuclear missile base on their sovereign soil."

"I see," Jason says. "Why did we put our… 'secret nuclear missile base' there to begin with?"

"The benefit outweighed the risks," the Chairman says. "Even now, that's true. There was a reason the powers behind Farraday City claimed the place to begin with. That reason also drew us there. I'm not sure how to explain it in layman's terms, let's just call it a 'location of strategic value' for now."

"All right," Jason says. "What are the consequences?"

"I don't know," the Chairman says. "Not yet. We'd already attracted the attention of Farraday City when we sent Plague after Curveball. Their response showed more restraint than I expected, but I don't think we can continue to expect a soft touch going forward."

Jason nods.

"As to the other powers… they are, at present, an unknown variable, and I have put Mara in charge of handling them. If she comes to you with a new set of operating parameters that you don't understand, accept that she does so at my behest."

Jason nods again.

"You have, over the course of your career, been involved in activities that are…" The Chairman hesitates, choosing his words carefully. "… *distasteful*."

"It's part of the job," Jason says.

"It is," the Chairman agrees. "Even so, you may not be prepared for what is to come. When people use the term *necessary evil* they do so to distance themselves from the horrors they're discussing. It is much easier to inflict suffering on someone who is relatively innocent when you tell yourself it's *necessary*. It becomes even *easier* when you glorify that suffering and turn it into a heroic sacrifice. *Dulce et Decorum est/Pro patria mori*."

It is sweet and right to die for your country. Jason vaguely remembers the line from a poem he had to read in English class.

"Magic," the Chairman says, "will strip away those barriers and leave you completely exposed to the full depravity of the horrors you will inflict. There is no pulling away from it. Most who grapple with it go mad—it's one of the few defenses we have. A very few continue on, carrying the burden of that horror with them. I will not call them fortunate."

The Chairman sighs. "I prefer to keep my organization as insulated from those horrors as I can, but it's not always possible. In the months to come I expect sacrifices will be necessary. I am not using that term in its modern sense."

"You're not," Jason says.

"I am not. There are times, Mr. Kline, when payment must be rendered in blood. Power is *always* paid in blood, and the toll is always high. And if it appears, in this world, that evil men always hold the reins of power, it is because they are more willing to render payment."

There is a note of weariness, even sadness, in the Chairman's voice.

"Thank you, Mr. Kline, that will be all for now."

Part Five: Elsewhere, Again

Only a tiny sliver of light remains in the sky—the last vestige of sun seeping in through a tiny crack at the very edge of the horizon—and the shadow cast across David's dreamscape is so deep it almost has weight. *Something* is pressing down, all around him, and he's sure it's more than the wind.

David tries once again to change the nature of the dream. He stares up at the ever-darkening sky, then holds out his hand, palm up, trying to imagine a tiny ball of light.

Such a small thing. Such a simple, small thing. I should be able to do this.

Nothing.

The smell of the ocean grows stronger. He staggers back as the wind rises, shivers as it turns icy cold. Lightning flashes again—much closer now, and in the brief flicker of light he sees why he can smell the ocean so strongly—the setting has changed. The old, cracked floor of the dojo remains, but he's no longer standing on an endless grassy plain—he stands atop a small hill on an island, surrounded by churning, angry waters. Another gust of wind carries with it a mix of rain and salty ocean spray. It makes his beard itch.

The last sliver of natural light finally dies altogether. As if celebrating its victory, lightning pours forth from the sky in sheets of white light. For a moment the entire sky is nothing but pure-white, blinding light, and the air is filled with the sharp smell of ozone. Everywhere but the hill on which he stands.

Too much light. Too much sound. This can't be real, can it?

Can it?

Very slowly he raises his left hand, pinching his nose, closing off his nostrils. He tries to inhale. He can't, of course—but when he's dreaming, he can. It's one of his tests. He's not dreaming, then.

"That's not possible." It's the first time he's spoken aloud, and his voice sounds thin and weak as it struggles to compete with the storm. He has to be dreaming. The dojo doesn't exist anywhere except in his mind. He invented it specifically for a dream, a dream where he was trying to learn to—

Think about what you said when you were performing your ritual. You didn't define it as "memory." You defined it as power.

The memory comes so suddenly that he can almost hear Artemis saying it.

It affected you, and your body is adapting to it the same way a metahuman adapts to the manifestation of his or her gifts.

He remembers the boat—the sinking boat—and Artemis peering over him, taking his pulse, shining a bright light in his eyes and muttering.

You're cocooning.

Thunder crashes over the hill, and the ground shakes. Lightning flashes again—not the entire sky this time, but the bolt strikes at the beach a short distance from the dojo on the hill, turning the sand to glass.

David takes a deep, steadying breath and pushes away the fury of the storm around him as he tries to think. He finds himself wishing he'd paid more attention to the lectures he'd attended on the cocooning process—it was part of his training when he was in the Sky Commando program, but it never seemed relevant at the time.

Cocooning is what happens to metahumans when they first manifest—the body slips into a coma in order to recalibrate. Is that what's happening now?

Four separate lightning strikes hit each corner of the dojo floor. Stone cracks, splinters, and flies into the air. Whatever's happening, David has to figure it out soon.

Think. His body is cocooning, so he is effectively in a coma. Do coma patients dream? He doesn't know, but this isn't a dream in the traditional sense, because he can't control it.

Lightning strikes again, a single bolt this time, a little farther up the dojo floor.

Think. He can't control it, so it isn't a dream, and he's been able to consistently lucid dream since his days in the military. Except, he suddenly remembers, during the time he was recovering from his concussion. The concussion threw everything out of whack, and he couldn't focus the way he needed to in order to get the process started.

Two more bolts, from opposite ends, creeping further up the floor.

"Couldn't focus," David mutters. "That feels familiar…"

Could that be what's happening here? His body is changing in response to something he did—he claimed someone else's memories as his own, and in the process may have claimed more than just memory.

Lightning strikes again, from three directions this time—and the strikes are now halfway up the dojo. David tries not to flinch. Despite the freezing rain, he's sweating profusely. He doesn't know if it's the lightning or if it's just all in his head, but he feels uncomfortably warm.

Maybe this is a dream. Maybe he's dreaming but the cocooning process is impeding his ability to lucid dream, for roughly the same reasons the concussion did. With the concussion, his brain was damaged and trying to recover. With cocooning... well, his brain is adjusting to something different. That may be requiring too much attention to give him the focus he needs right now.

Four forks of lightning strike the dojo floor, but they don't stop—what should be a brief flash of destructive force remains as four columns of blue-white heat, looking like the discharge from a massive tesla ball somewhere beyond the clouds. He pushes back the terror and tries to focus on the problem. The strands advance on him, one from each side, making concentration difficult. He tries harder.

Maybe it *isn't* a dream. The spell that kept the island of Esperanza locked in the last twenty four hours of its existence drew him out of his dream and cast him—or, at least, a piece of his consciousness—into its own. Magic doesn't understand dreaming, so it couldn't do what it wanted, but it managed to do something. Maybe that's happening here. He absorbed the memories of a μάγος—he blinks rapidly as he sees the symbols in his mind and realizes that he has no idea what they are, but he thinks briefly of Artigenian and *feels* that somehow they are correct—but he absorbed more. He has to acknowledge that, now: he also absorbed the power that bound those memories to Artemis' flesh.

That power is stirring.

The streams of lightning inch ever closer. The heat is becoming difficult to bear. Something inside him, a black, oily rage, is struggling to get out.

I absorbed part of Artigenian's power. And that power is a living thi LoOSe ME mAsHEuDh aNd I WiLL SAvE uS

His thoughts change so abruptly in content and *tone* that it takes a moment to realize what happened: he didn't think it at all. Someone else—some*thing* else—thought it *through* him.

"What?"

LoOSe ME mAsHEuDh aNd I WiLL SavE uS tHe FirE iS COMiNg anD WE WiLL BuRN

As if on cue, the columns of lightning inch closer.

"Who are you?" David looks around wildly, trying to find the source of the voice. There's nothing there but the storm, the scarred dojo floor, and columns of liquid fire falling from the sky.

I aM YoUR pOWeR

"My..." Despite everything, David shakes his head in disbelief.

LoOSe ME mAsHEuDh aNd I WiLL SavE uS tHe FirE iS COMiNg anD WE WiLL BuRN

My power... The oily rage surges again, as if responding to the thought.

ThERe aRE wORdS mAsHEuDh lET mE sPEaK tHEm

There are words? David's eyes widen.

tHe FirE iS COMiNg anD WE WiLL BuRN

tHe FirE iS COMiNg anD WE WiLL BuRN

tHe FirE iS COMiNg anD WE WiLL BuRN

tHe FirE iS COMiNg anD WE WiLL BuRN

"There are words." It's what he said to Artemis when he tried to explain what it was like having Artigenian's thoughts in his mind. Every memory the man had of Artemis was there... which included every lesson. Artemis had been an able student, and their lessons were extensive.

tHe FirE iS COMiNg anD WE WiLL BuRN

tHe FirE iS COMiNg anD WE WiLL BuRN

tHe FirE iS COMiNg anD WE WiLL BuRN

tHe FirE iS COMiNg anD WE WiLL BuRN

Artemis had described the relationship between someone wielding magic and the magic they wielded as being symbiotic. He is now having a conversation with that magic.

tHe FirE iS COMiNg anD WE WiLL BuRN

tHe FirE iS COMiNg anD WE WiLL BuRN

tHe FirE iS COMiNg anD WE WiLL BuRN

tHe FirE iS COMiNg anD WE WiLL BuRN

"Be quiet!"

The lightning hasn't reached him yet, but his skin is starting to blister. He remembers reading an article that claimed the heat generated in a lightning bolt exceeds the surface temperature of the sun. He doesn't know that he believes it—he can't imagine it being true without tearing the world apart—but the heat is excruciating. The power in him, whatever it is, grows urgent.

masHEuDh

The word connects with something in Artigenian's memories, but he doesn't have the luxury of chasing it down at the moment. What's important to him is the context: the power uses it with a mixture of deference and supplication that feels overwhelmingly insincere. He knows that tone well. He used it more than a few times—and was disciplined for it every single time—when he was in the Army. It is the tone of someone who recognizes rank, doesn't respect the person holding it, and believes the person is too stupid to catch on.

LeT mE SavE uS

Something is wrong. Artemis had to learn to wield magic. Artigenian had to learn to wield magic. The symbiote, or whatever it was, grew within them as they learned. He appears to have a... *thing* that is much more developed than it should be.

masHEuDh

It claims to have the knowledge to save him—to save *them*, David supposes, since if it truly does exist symbiotically then it will likely share his fate. Perhaps that's the way out of this trap: perhaps he should let it speak the words it claims to know to rescue them both.

Or perhaps that's the actual trap.

With a sudden yell David runs toward one of the blue-white pillars of fire. The thing inside him screams in rage and frustration, his skin feels as if it's bursting into flame, but he doesn't stop. He hears himself screaming—the sound is so feral he is only barely conscious of it being his own voice—but he doesn't stop. He forces himself forward, and forward, and when he can take it no longer he leaps so that he can do nothing but cross the distance and enter into the unyielding arc of fire.

The thing screams. The world is full of light, then darkness, then light.

He collapses on the cracked stone floor of an open dojo in the middle of an endless grassy plain. A warm wind blows, carrying with it the smell of dry soil. The sky is clear and blue, and the sun shines hot on his face and neck. David climbs to his feet, self-consciously dusting off his legs as he stands.

There is no rain. There is no lightning. There is no smell of the ocean. There isn't a cloud in the sky.

David sighs in relief, closing his eyes, taking a moment to appreciate the scent of warm soil.

The power within him no longer speaks. It withdraws, retreating from

David's awareness until it is nothing more than a vague, oily shadow lurking underneath his thoughts. If David didn't know better he would swear it was *sulking*.

"Called your bluff," he says.

The power stirs slightly, and David feels the slightest hint of agitation, frustration, anger. Then it settles once again.

David looks around the open dojo. Once he'd used it to learn—perhaps it could serve that purpose again. His body is trying to adjust to whatever happened to him on the island, but it's clear that what happened to him was not primarily physical. He will need to take advantage of the time to do a little research of his own.

He sighs, walks back to the center of the dojo floor, and sits down. There, tucked away in his thoughts, are Artigenian's memories: a Pandora's box of unpleasant knowledge that is connected to this new dark power coiled around his soul. He grits his teeth, narrows his eyes, and reaches for the first memory.

"Show me the horrors of your world, Artigenian. Let the lessons begin."

Part One: Thorpe Island, Secure Recovery Room

Vigilante's eyes open.

He lies in the middle of a large, empty cube, naked and curled tightly into a ball. The floor, walls, and ceiling all gleam dull white under the harsh lights. He's in his cell. Or his recovery room. At a certain point in the process it's the same thing.

He isn't alone. Immediately he sits upright, turning to face the three men watching him. He knows two of them very well, and he has some history with the third. Street Ronin carries a sports bag looped over one shoulder, and Red Shift's left arm is in a sling. They're both out of uniform, which is unusual, but he's pretty sure the third man—a slim, tall man, reddish-brown hair with graying temples, leaning heavily on a cane—is the reason why.

"Gladiator?"

The man hesitates. "Not for a long time."

"Doctor Thorpe, then."

"If you insist on a title. How are you feeling?"

Vigilante stands easily, without pain. "A little drafty. But my tantrum period is over."

He sees Street Ronin and Red Shift relax as Doctor Thorpe nods.

"I thought as much," Thorpe says. "We were monitoring your neurological functions, and they weren't spiking like they were earlier." He nods toward one of the walls. Vigilante glances over, and sees that a piece has buckled outward, the ends beginning to twist.

"Sorry," Vigilante says.

"How much of that do you remember?" The curiosity in Thorpe's voice is unmistakable. "Normally people who experience that level of physical trauma suffer memory loss…"

"More than I'd like," Vigilante says. "I guess I passed out while the magic robot was grinding me to a pulp. I woke up in here, went nuts, your guys—I assume they're your guys?"

Thorpe nods.

"Your guys tried to sedate me with some kind of knockout gas. I guess it worked eventually." Vigilante looks at the damaged section of wall again. "Eventually. Dreamed I was building a birdhouse."

"A birdhouse?" Thorpe raises an eyebrow.

"Whenever I'm sleeping off the last bit of a really big hurt I dream I'm building something. It's probably symbolic. Anyway, I'm OK until the next time I get torn to bits."

"He's OK, Doc." Red Shift's laid-back, easygoing voice is light and conversational. "I owe him for sucker-punching me back in Farraday City, but other than that he's fine."

"Sorry about that," Vigilante says.

Red Shift shrugs, absently rubbing his jaw. "It was a good call. I was about to kill myself with that last push. I'll still get you back, though."

Street Ronin snorts. Thorpe continues to stare at Vigilante thoughtfully.

"Look, Doc, I don't mind answering your questions, but I'd rather not do it naked."

Street Ronin snorts again, then throws the sports bag at his feet. Vigilante kneels and unzips the bag. It's full of clothes.

He dresses quickly as they take turns bringing him up to date: Regiment arriving at the fight. Curveball and Agent Grant discovering test subjects in the complex. Everyone going to Thorpe's floating island. A general, tentative agreement to work together to nail down what was going on.

Vigilante buttons up a light blue denim shirt. "Test subjects." His voice is flat.

Red Shift nods gravely. "We've been trying to work through the data to figure out what happened to them. The patients are in stasis right now, and they'll stay that way until we're positive we can wake them up without killing them. Or anyone else."

Vigilante looks at Red Shift pointedly, an unspoken question hanging between them.

Red Shift shakes his head. "Pretty sure they aren't."

Vigilante nods once. "OK. What do we know so far?"

"Not a lot." Thorpe sighs. "It's only been two days, and the data is incomplete. We're all going to meet up later today. I can bring everyone up to speed then. Right now I wanted to talk to you about something else."

Vigilante looks up, narrowing his eyes. Thorpe fidgets uneasily, wincing slightly as his weight shifts from his right foot to his left. Street Ronin sets his jaw, staring back defiantly. Red Shift sighs softly as he shakes his head.

"This sounds like it's going to be fun," Vigilante says. He sits on the floor and starts pulling on a pair of athletic socks.

Robert Thorpe takes a deep breath. "The Guardians and Crossfire always had a complicated history. There's no getting around that, and because of that I realize I'm not the best person to be bringing this up. Especially since you spend a lot of time going after the more *unethical* branches of my profession."

"No offense," Vigilante says.

"None taken. I don't feel any pity for people who use science as a way to excuse their own sociopathy. Once upon a time I might have felt obligated to *protect* them—duty, law and order, all that—but these days I'm more inclined to believe they deserve what they get. The point is, I know you have a general mistrust of mad scientists, including me, and it makes me reluctant to have this conversation."

Vigilante sighs. "Doc, we don't hate scientists. Just predators pretending to *be* scientists. You're legit. What's your point?"

"Your *tantrum period*," Thorpe says. "When you first arrived, Street Ronin made it very clear you needed a... well." He sweeps his hand across the room. "You needed something a bit sturdier than our standard medical facilities."

"Yeah," Vigilante says sourly, "this was a pretty bad one."

"But from what I understand none of them are particularly *good*."

Vigilante doesn't answer.

"Look, Vigilante..." Thorpe starts to pace, winces slightly, then stops. "I haven't performed any tests on you—I swear it, and Red Shift and Street Ronin can back me up on it—but I *am* a scientist, and despite the fact that I haven't been actively poking and prodding you I couldn't avoid *observing* you. And there are a few things I've noticed that concern me... and I feel professionally and personally obligated to share those concerns."

Vigilante scowls. "Go on."

Thorpe points at the large dent in the wall. "This concerns me. Your colleagues won't come out and say it, but I'm pretty sure it concerns them too."

"I'm not exactly OK with it either, Doc," Vigilante says.

"I didn't think you were. But the damage to that wall is still there. If we hadn't managed to bring you under when we did, you would have broken through that wall and started tearing up the rest of the complex. That would've been catastrophic."

"I know," Vigilante says.

Thorpe sighs, clearly exasperated. "What's going on? This wasn't a thing back in the day. I saw you get taken down by a sniper only to get back up again a few hours later. All you did then was grunt in annoyance and ask if you'd missed anything important."

"That was *fifteen years ago*," Vigilante says. "Things change."

"*What* changed?" Thorpe asks.

"It *hurts*," Vigilante says. "It hurts a *lot*."

Nobody says anything. Thorpe cocks his head to one side as he considers Vigilante's words.

"I didn't expect that," he admits. "You don't expect healing to hurt."

"It *always* hurt," Vigilante says. "It didn't always hurt this much. It was a lot easier to deal with back when we were all running around the same turf. It's stronger now, though—I heal faster than I used to. I heal more than I used to. And it hurts more right along with it. It's easier to handle when I'm fighting, because it's just more pain in the mix—not fun, but it's manageable. I can prepare for it and tough it out. But if I actually fall..."

He looks at the twisted section of wall.

"My first thought is *oh God, this hurts* and there's no time to grit my teeth or get ready. After that it's fight or flight, and there's no running away from it."

"Painkillers don't help," Red Shift adds. "We've tried. His body burns them away, just like any other toxin. I have no idea how much we'd have to pump into him before he noticed a difference. I'm not even sure it's possible."

Doctor Thorpe nods. "I see the problem. I'd like to try to help, if I could." He grips his cane tightly. "For a while now I've been very interested in the field of pain management. I can't make any promises, of course, but if you're willing..." He trails off. "That's the issue at hand. I fully understand you have very compelling reasons *not* to be willing."

"I appreciate that," Vigilante says. "I'll think it over."

Thorpe nods. "Just let me know."

Part Two: Robert Thorpe's Office

"Failed *again*. What the hell did great-grandfather do to this file?"

Jenny Forrest doesn't bother to hide the frustration in her voice.

"He didn't want the bad guys to crack it, I guess." CB doesn't sound nearly as concerned—in fact, he sounds *bored*, which frustrates Jenny even more.

"Did he want the *good guys* to crack it?" Her words almost come out as a snarl, and a moment later she takes a long, slow breath. "I mean, I assume he wanted you to be able to access it. But from what little I've learned of the encryption he used, that's not going to happen unless you have the key."

They're working in Robert Thorpe's private office. Jenny's computer sits on one of the long tables set against the walls, tethered to the Institute's network via a long, slender cable. The laptop's display is mirrored on a large flat panel on the wall behind it. Jenny sits hunched over the laptop's keyboard, blonde hair falling down in a curtain over her face, though a brief length of exposed jawline suggests she is scowling.

"Well, I don't have a key." CB is sprawled out in a chair in front of Robert's desk, his feet propped up on another chair. His head leans back, his eyes are half-closed, and he doesn't look like he's giving his full attention to the problem at hand. "I don't know why Alex would think I would."

"He never sent you anything that might be used as a key?"

"He never sent me *anything*," CB says. "I was keeping my location a secret, remember? We only talked by email."

Jenny turns, brushing her hair out of her eyes to glare at him. "A key is something that would be emailed to you, CB."

CB frowns. "Well, yeah. OK. But he never sent me anything like that."

Jenny shakes her head. "That doesn't make *sense*. You don't just encrypt a file like this, not the way he did, and then *send it to someone* without making sure the person you're sending it to has a way to open it."

"Maybe he never intended it to be opened," CB says. "Maybe he was pretending he knew more than he did in an attempt to force the bad guys to act more openly than they wanted. Maybe once the encryption is broken, all we'll find is a text file that reads 'sure spent a lot of time trying to get here, didn't you?'"

Jenny's anger falters for a moment. "Do you think that's something he'd do?"

"No," CB says. "It's definitely something *I'd* do, but it's not his style.

Of course, if he was trying to outwit people who were familiar with his style—like Richter—then he might try to deliberately do something that *wasn't* his style. *That* would be his style."

"You are not being helpful," Jenny says, sighing.

"Don't know what you expect me to do," CB says. "I'm not really on your level when it comes to computer stuff. Robert's really who you want to talk to about this."

"But great-grandfather didn't send it to *him*," Jenny says. "He could have, right? You all have each others' email addresses and everything?"

"Yeah," CB says, "but it's not like we talk all the time."

"I know. You all go off to your man-caves and hide. It's a little embarrassing. But my point is he *could* have sent it to Dr. Thorpe—Robert—if he'd really wanted to. But he didn't. He sent it to you, and he did it on purpose. He wanted *you* to be the one who got it."

CB raises his head to stare at Jenny thoughtfully. "Yeah."

"He didn't choose the super-genius who could program a computer in his sleep—probably literally—he chose a guy who had a lot less experience. I mean, you're not incompetent or anything, it's just that you never needed to learn how to break encryption."

"That's true," CB says. "Usually I'd just find the password when it mattered."

Jenny raises an eyebrow. "What do you mean?"

"Well I don't want to insult the computer security professional," CB says, "but mostly people are lazy and cultivate a lot of really bad habits where computer security is concerned. If you look long enough you'll eventually find a password written down somewhere. Occasionally it'll even be labeled 'Secret Files Access'—don't laugh, I'm not kidding. And I can... you know... push a little, and make it more likely to stumble across the one guy who has his password taped to the bottom of his monitor, or whatever."

"Huh," Jenny says. "I wonder if you could do that here."

"I doubt Alex wrote down the password anywhere."

"No," Jenny says, "not that. Could you push your... whatever it is you do, and try to *guess* what the encryption key is? Like, just type random crap on the keyboard and eventually stumble across it?"

The door to Robert's office slides open, and Robert Thorpe limps into the room, leaning heavily on his cane.

"Stumble across what?" He asks.

CB is sitting up now, eyes closed as he tries to sort everything out. "There's precedent for it, but—"

"Precedent for *what*?" Robert asks.

"I'm not sure," Jenny says. "I want CB to guess the encryption key."

Robert raises an eyebrow. "Oh. *That*."

Jenny looks from one man, to the other, and suppresses the urge to roll her eyes. "Either of you want to share?"

A brief silence follows as Robert makes his way over to his desk and sits, leaning his cane against the desk corner. Jenny notices him wince slightly as he sits. CB pretends not to.

Robert sighs softly as he sinks into the thick leather cushions. "It was in Wasteland. There was a machine that my... ah... *counterpart* had been working on that was supposed to bridge realities. We used CB to crack the password."

"That's what I want him to do now," Jenny says, pushing back a surge of excitement. "How did you do it then?"

"We brute forced it," Robert says. "We sat him down in front of the terminal and told him to guess the password while concentrating on making something happen."

"So this *could* work!" Jenny says.

Robert glances at the panel display above Jenny's laptop. "I'm not sure. What you want to do is a lot more complicated. Passwords are shorter—and passwords back then were trivial compared to what they are today. I've seen CB do a lot of incredible things, but I think asking him to randomly generate an entire encryption key out of thin air in time for it to be of any use to us is more than he can deliver."

"So you think CB's ability would be bogged down by the length of the key?"

"Looks that way," CB says. "We tried an experiment once. You remember, Robert, the Monkey-Shakespeare thing."

Robert smiles. "I set up a programmable keyboard and randomly assigned characters to keys, so CB never knew what any of the keys were mapped to. And I asked him to concentrate on typing something coherent— not Shakespeare, though. I think it was the Gettysburg Address. He didn't know what key did what, and he didn't have a monitor..."

"So I started hitting keys at random," CB says.

"Didn't work?" Jenny asks.

"It worked more than I expected," Robert says. "He actually managed to type out 'Four score and seven' before it devolved into random text. But it didn't work to the degree you'd need it to."

Jenny turns back to stare at her laptop, the scowl threatening to return. Then her eyes widen. "How do you do with a coin toss?"

"Get it every time," CB says.

"When you do the toss? Or does it matter?"

CB shrugs. "Doesn't matter."

Jenny turns back to look at Robert. "That's it, then. We just need to break down the problem into a series of very small problems, which we use to solve the big one."

CB blinks in surprise. Robert stares at Jenny thoughtfully.

"That's interesting," Robert says.

"Interesting, as in 'yes, it could work?'" Jenny asks hopefully.

Robert closes his eyes, tilts his head back, and furrows his brow. Jenny can see his eyes moving back and forth under his eyelids. Half a minute passes.

"Yes," Robert says. "I think so. What we'd need to do is narrow the search. Do we know the length of the encryption key?"

"Yes," Jenny says. "4096 bits."

Robert nods. "Then we know the range of possible values the encryption key might be. So all we need to do is come up with a program that allows CB to systematically discard portions of that range until we pare it down to a small enough range of possible values—a few billion or so should do it—that we can use our computers to brute force it."

"Binary," Jenny says. "Binary is essentially flipping a coin—zero or one—so we have CB guess the binary string, one bit at a—"

"That's not going to work," CB says.

"Why not?" Jenny asks. "It's exactly the same thing as flipping a coin."

"No it isn't," CB says. "I understand flipping a coin. I don't understand binary numbers. I mean, I know what they are, but it's not ingrained. I wouldn't know what to focus on when I was pushing. I doubt it would do what you want."

Jenny stares at Robert blankly. Robert shrugs. "It's not my power."

"OK," Jenny says, "what about counting. You understand counting, right?"

CB gives her a flat look.

"So what if I put it this way: we're trying to find a specific number between zero and... well, it's a big number, it's..." Jenny fumbles as she tries to find a way to put the top value of that range in context.

"It's one thousand, two hundred and thirty-four digits long," Robert says.

CB looks from Jenny to Robert. "A thousand doesn't seem that big."

"That's not the *number*," Robert says. "That's the number of digits *in* the number."

CB blinks. "OK. That's a big number."

"Right," Jenny says. "Big. So picture this: I'll set up a program that asks you to guess if the number is between zero to half of that top value, or between 'half that plus one' to the end. Once you choose, it'll then ask you if the number is between the lower half of the range you just chose, or the upper half. And then again, and again, until we've got it narrowed down to a small enough range of numbers that it'll be faster for a computer to do the rest of it. Could you approach it that way?"

CB thinks it over. "Yeah, I think I can manage that. I'll have to smoke though. Sorry Robert."

Robert shakes his head. "You and your crutches."

* * *

The unpleasant smell of burning nicotine and tar fills Robert's office as CB sits in front of Jenny's laptop, cigarette dangling from the corner of his mouth, large headphones covering his ears. An empty ceramic cup serving as a makeshift ashtray is a quarter full of ash and spent cigarettes. His right hand hovers over the keyboard, thumb resting on the space bar, middle finger lightly touching the I. CB mutters a string of curses quietly to himself as he alternates between pressing the space bar and the I key in an apparently random order.

It's been an hour so far. Jenny thinks she might scream.

"I hate waiting," she says. It's not the first time she's said it, and every time she says it again her frustration climbs.

Robert laughs. "Before you came up with this idea our best course of action would have taken *years*."

"I *still* hate waiting," Jenny says. "It's just the way it goes. Also I'm a little afraid CB will get bored and quit."

Robert laughs again. "You'd better hope he can't hear you through those headphones. He might do it just to spite you."

She stares at CB's back, watching him choose between the space bar and the I key over and over again. "Is he doing his... is he using his whatever the heck it is he does? To 'make things happen?'"

"I assume so," Robert says.

"I don't feel anything," Jenny says. "I mean, when I've seen him in action in the past, I didn't feel anything then, either, but I always figured it was because I wasn't paying attention, or I was too busy being shot at, or something like that. But there's actually nothing. No electricity in the air, no feeling of power."

"There never is. He claims *he* feels something when he's using it, but I've never been able to record anything. He doesn't even register as a metahuman."

"It sounds like you tested him a lot," Jenny says.

"When the Guardians were active I tested all of us. I thought if we understood how our abilities worked we could coordinate better, and if we understood what our limits were we might be able to work around them when necessary. It saved our lives more than a few times. But CB's tests were always the least useful of the batch."

Robert studies Jenny for a moment. "Red Shift told me a bit about how he helped you train after you cocooned. One of his regrets was not being able to help you determine your physical limits. If you're interested, I have facilities here that allow me to conduct the kind of testing I did back then. It would provide some of those answers, and do it relatively quickly."

Jenny shifts her weight uncomfortably.

"Only if you're interested," Robert says. "I can understand why you wouldn't be. It *is* testing, and I would keep a record of it. I don't share that information—too many people would be tempted to misuse it—but there's still a certain amount of risk in letting someone keep it on file, even if that someone is me. Consider it a standing offer."

"I'll think about it," Jenny says. "Do you do this a lot?"

"When I have the opportunity, I make the offer," Robert says. "I've made the offer to everyone else in your group. CB and Roger, of course, from way back. Red Shift accepted, which surprised me. Scrapper Jack declined, which didn't surprise me at all. Vigilante is thinking it over, which is more than I expected in his case. Both of the agents—Mr. Grant and Ms. Hu—have accepted, which will probably complicate their lives a little, but Travers tells me they're pretty cheerful when it comes to making things more complicated."

"Red Shift accepted?" Jenny shakes her head. "I didn't think anyone in Crossfire would trust anyone enough for that."

"He's a scientist," Robert says. "That helps a bit."

"Done." CB stands up, takes off the headphones, and puts them on the table. He turns to face them, sticking a finger in his right ear and rubbing furiously. "That tone you used as a signal itches like crazy..."

Jenny and Robert stare at CB in surprise. Jenny looks up at the flat panel display, watching the clock continue to count down.

"The program says you aren't finished yet," Jenny says.

CB shrugs. "You said it would start beeping like crazy when I was done. Well... it's beeping like crazy. I'm done."

Robert looks at the terminal on his desk. "He's right. The sample is small enough for us to take over."

"It was supposed to take a lot longer than that," Jenny says. "You broke it."

CB grins. "Jenny, I've been pushing nonstop for the last few hours, I have the mother of all headaches, and if I had to do this much longer I was going to pick up your damned laptop and throw it across the room as hard as I could manage, so I think we should call it a win. If this works, I only broke it a little."

"I just don't see how—" Jenny starts to respond, then stops when Robert utters a cry of mild surprise. He stares at the terminal on his desk in bemusement.

"It worked," he says.

Jenny's complaint dies on her lips. "Already?"

"There was a match on the eighty-third combination," Robert says. He looks at CB, eyebrow raised. "Are you still pushing?"

CB shakes his head. "I stopped as soon as I heard the tone."

"Well," Robert says, turning back to the terminal, "I guess we got lucky. The file is open."

Part Three: Somewhere Else

David Bernard sits cross-legged on the cracked stone floor in the not-dream of the old dojo.

The dojo still sits in the endless grassy plain. The sky is still a canopy of clear, deep blue. The alien power that dwells within him still murmurs occasionally, slithering through his mind, but it hasn't actually done anything since it tried to break him earlier. He doesn't remember how long he's been there, methodically sifting through Artigenian's memories, suppressing his revulsion as he examines each in turn, a menagerie of remembered horrors. The lore that Artigenian remembered teaching a younger Artemis LaFleur was nightmarish in itself, but the lore that Artigenian had decided *not* to teach him—the lore he'd decided his pupil wasn't ready to accept—that was far, far worse.

He closes his eyes, forcing himself to learn, forcing back the bile that rises in the back of his throat as the knowledge stains him. He sees exactly how Artigenian had been trying to reshape LaFleur's perceptions, nudge him down a path of nihilism and self-destruction—where he had succeeded, where he had failed, and how, when the opportunity had presented itself, he had set the would-be monarch on a path that would end in the world's annihilation…

…and how he had, ultimately, failed.

The power stirs again, and David pushes back against the unease that rises with it. LaFleur's descriptions of how magic interacted with people had made it sound like a kind of parasite, but he never described it as something that could communicate with its host. None of Artigenian's memories involve teaching LaFleur anything about the *sentience* of magic. But the power he absorbed—the power he can feel growing inside him, like a lizard regrowing a lost limb (or more accurately, a lizard's lost limb regrowing the rest of its body)—had actually *talked* to him. It had tried to trick him into putting it in the driver's seat, and giving it control of his mind and body. It failed, but what will happen when it grows stronger?

Best to master it, before it masters you.

David frowns, brushing the thought aside. He doesn't want to use that power. It's bad enough that he can feel it inside him, bad enough that he knows much of what it can do. To actually wield it would be dangerous.

There may be a way around that.

David frowns again, wondering if that was his own thought, or if it was the power trying to trick him a second time. The thought won't go away, though: on the island, while he was asleep, he could do things. Change things. He'd had power that wasn't exactly magic, but rather a way of *interacting* with it to make things happen. He was able to do it because that power permeated the island of Esperanza. And now that power, or one very similar to it, was *inside* him.

Could he use it to do what he did on the island?

He considers the question. What he did on the island wasn't entirely dreaming, and it wasn't entirely magic… it was taking the tension that existed between them and *pushing it around* until it did what he wanted. The magic had been easy to push around, because it was everywhere.

It isn't everywhere any more… but it's inside him. He doesn't try to command it using the words and bindings he knows from Artigenian's stolen memories. Instead, as he keeps his awareness of the power active, he tries to change his surroundings the way he would change a dream.

Power stirs. The air pulses around him. For a while, that's all he can manage to do as he tries to discover the right mix of introspection and concentration needed to go further. The air pulses again, and suddenly it all snaps into place–he hits upon the right balance of self-awareness and outwardly directed will—and he slowly rises off the ground.

Success!

David feels the power stir angrily—it doesn't like what he's doing. He pushes the feelings aside, reminding himself that *he* is in control, then returns his attention to what he's done. He's floating, still cross-legged, about three feet off the dojo's cracked stone floor.

He lowers himself to the floor slowly, releases his concentration, and tries again. He spends some time practicing this, trying to strike that balance, getting used to how it feels. It's not a fast process by any means, not yet, but each time it feels a little faster. Eventually it takes no longer than three deep breaths to reach the equilibrium he needs.

Then, with a gathering of will, he *soars*. He watches the dojo shrink into a dark, indistinct speck, disappearing altogether as he climbs higher and higher into the sky. He feels the cold of the air around him as it thins, and the sky darkens until the barest hint of stars can be seen through it. In the real world he would suffocate at this height, and probably freeze to death, but this isn't real. He can control this false world the same way he can control his dreams, though it requires a little more concentration to do.

He dives, laughing, back into the warmth of the clear sky, and amuses himself by skimming above the endless grassy plane, watching his shadow play along the ground as it twists and bobs with every unseen bump and trough beneath layers of prairie grass. Despite the presence of the alien power within him, for the first time in a very long time he feels *free*.

It feels *good* to be this free, even if it is in a dream. Or a not-dream, or entity-spawned hallucination, or whatever it is he's in. As his mind sifts through the possible differences between an actual dream and where he is now, it occurs to him that he might not actually be confined to doing this in a dream.

He comes to a landing as he ponders this new thought. This isn't the island, and his relationship to the power within him isn't the same as the power on the island. It's *inside* him, and there's no reason that he can think of that would prevent him from interacting with it while he was *awake*.

Is there any reason he couldn't fly while awake and in his physical body? And if he could do that, what else could he do?

There's only one way to find out, David. You have to wake up.

He nods, accepting the realization. He isn't going to find any more answers in this place. The only way he's going to learn anything new is to gather his will and

open

up

his

eyes

Something beeps in his ear as his eyes flutter open and immediately close to block out the painfully bright light. He hears a surprised gasp and a pressure on the side of his head releases as someone takes a step back.

"You're awake." A man's voice, slightly accented.

David opens his eyes again, blinking rapidly to try to minimize the blinding light. Seconds pass, the pain fades, and he realizes the room isn't brightly-lit at all. He's just not used to it.

"Where." His voice is hardly recognizable, dry and cracked.

"Mr. Bernard," the voice says again.

A blurry figure looms over him. David squints, and a middle-aged asian man dressed in scrubs comes into focus.

"You are in a recovery room at the Thorpe Institute. I am Doctor Shào. Doctor LaFleur and I have been monitoring you as you undergo mutationis."

David shakes his head, trying to clear his thoughts. "What?"

Doctor Shào hesitates, thins his lips, then says, a little unwillingly, "It is commonly referred to as 'cocooning.'"

David nods.

"We've been a little concerned," Shào says. "Your progression through mutationis was… atypical."

"Right," David says. "Atypical. Can I have some water?"

"A moment," Shào says. He disappears from view, then promptly returns with a clear plastic cup and a straw. "Small sips."

David tries to take a small sip from the cup, pulls too hard on the straw and spends the next few minutes coughing furiously. His next attempt is better. After a few sips, he manages to sit up (much to Doctor Shào's alarm) and look around.

He looks down at his arms. They're very thin, almost frail. His face itches. He scratches his cheek and discovers he still has a beard. He sighs, annoyed.

"Where's Artemis?" David asks.

Doctor Shào looks confused for a moment. "Do you mean Doctor LaFleur? I believe he's about to attend an impromptu conference Doctor Thorpe has organized. He did ask that I page him when you awaken. Please don't try to get out of bed just yet. Physically you're very frail—it will take some time to completely bounce back from your ordeal."

"That seems to be the story of my life, these days," David says. "What year is it?"

"Doctor LaFleur told me to tell you it's been roughly one month since you 'left.' I don't know what he means by 'left,' but I assume you do."

David nods. "Yeah. Yeah, I do. Thanks." His voice is stronger and steadier now.

"I'll return in a moment," Doctor Shào says. "Please wait here." He exits through a door on the far end of the room.

David struggles to sit up straighter, resisting the urge to pull out the IV taped to his arm and follow the doctor under his own power. He's pretty sure doing that will end with him collapsing in a heap on the cold floor until the doctor or a nurse can haul him up and back to bed. He contents himself with sitting up and trying to remember everything he can.

He remembers the island, and the boat. He remembers the not-dream.

The entity—he remembers that. Was it real? As if in response, he thinks he feels a dark presence slithering somewhere inside him. Probably not *physically* inside him, of course, or he would have woken up inside a containment room instead of what looks like a fairly standard recovery room. So it's… *metaphysically* inside him. Whatever that means.

If it's inside me here, in the real world, I can probably use it.

He considers trying to levitate, looks at the IV sticking out of his left arm, and decides now is not the time. Instead, he tries for something simpler. He stretches out his right arm, resting his elbow on his knee, and turns his palm up. He closes his eyes, breathes deeply three times, and focuses his will.

When he opens his eyes, he sees a small black sphere resting on the palm of his hand.

Part Four: Robert Thorpe's Office

Robert's office has been transformed into a miniature conference room.

Rows of chairs fill the first two-thirds of the room—six chairs on each side with an aisle down the middle—and Jenny recognizes almost none of the people sitting in them. She vaguely remembers the faces of one or two of the people who were present at their arrival, and she catches a glimpse of Alihmah Mahmoud, the president of Thorpe Industries, sitting in the very last row. Everyone else is wearing a Thorpe Institute badge. The first row is reserved for her and her companions: twelve chairs, each with a nametag. *Curveball. Zero. Regiment. Red Shift. Street Ronin. Vigilante. Scrapper Jack. Dr. Artemis LaFleur. David Bernard. Alan Grant. Lijuan Hu. Peter Travers.* At present, the only chairs that aren't filled are Vigilante's, Jack's, LaFleur's, and Bernard's. Jenny remembers something about David being in the infirmary for some reason.

She looks to her right. CB slouches in his chair, head slumped forward, eyes closed, apparently asleep. He looks like he's back to wearing the clothes he wore when they arrived: trenchcoat, ratty jeans, heavy black boots, a faded white t-shirt with the name of what she assumes is a band— something called "The Cramps"—plastered on the front.

Roger, immediately to her left, is still wearing a Thorpe Institute jumpsuit. He also appears to be sleeping, in almost the same position as CB. She nudges him slightly, and the large man opens one eye, focuses on her, and lifts his head, smiling slightly.

"Bored?"

"More like nervous," Jenny says. "And wondering why all these other people are here. I thought this was a secret mission, and all that."

Roger chuckles as he rubs his eyes. "If they're here, it's because Robert thinks he needs them. I guess you discovered something important."

It's not precisely a question, but Roger falls silent, waiting.

Jenny shrugs. "Yes? But I don't know what it is. Robert started reading the contents of the file, his eyes went wide, and he asked for Overmi—uh... for Doctor LaFleur to join him. At that point CB said we'd leave them to their work, and dragged me down to the cafeteria."

"We'd just be getting in the way." CB doesn't bother moving as he talks, and his voice sounds a little sloppy, as if he's still half-sleeping. "They were going to start talking real fast and complicated, and if we were there they'd spend half the time trying to figure out how to explain it to us. Better to let 'em work, then explain everything after."

Jenny narrows her eyes as she considers arguing the point, but decides he's probably right. She turns back to Roger, looking on with amusement.

"How should I refer to him, anyway? LaFleur, I mean. He *is* Overmind, isn't he? But nobody calls him that. And nobody really treats him like he's a criminal, either."

"Not all criminals are created equal," Roger says. "Not all heroes, either. It's complicated and it'll drive you nuts if you think about it too much. But... look, you do IT security stuff, right?"

Jenny nods.

"So you've been to conventions where you rub shoulders with people who are in your field, but probably not working on the same side of the fence as you are. You know. Hackers."

Jenny forces herself not to roll her eyes at the term, but nods.

"But at those conventions you all talk shop and exchange information? To a point, at least. And you can probably think of *certain situations* where at least one or two of the shadier people in the room might have your back."

"Yeah," Jenny says. "I guess so."

"And there are probably people on your side of the fence that just rub you the wrong way, and you wouldn't trust them as far as you could throw them."

Jenny nods. "I can think of a few."

"Well it's the same here. LaFleur's a villain, but he's not *bad*. Just like Crossfire are... well..." Roger glances over at Red Shift and Street Ronin and frowns.

"Heroes?" Red Shift sounds amused at the thought. "That's sweet, Regiment."

"I feel super complimented," Street Ronin agrees, trying to hold back laughter.

Roger shakes his head. "Well, they're not villains. But they're not exactly *good*."

Heat rises in her cheeks as she glances over at Street Ronin and Red Shift, who look even more amused by Roger's description. Red Shift notices her discomfort and smiles disarmingly.

"This has been a weird month," Jenny mutters to herself.

CB laughs. Roger shakes his head, torn between disapproval and amusement.

The office door hisses open and Jenny turns to see three people enter the room: LaFleur, Vigilante, and Scrapper Jack. She's surprised to see how healthy Vigilante looks. She remembers how hopelessly mangled he was when they arrived—he was literally carried in a sack—but there aren't even any marks on his body that she can see. He and Jack make their way to the front row, Vigilante settling in next to Street Ronin and Jack taking the chair next to him.

LaFleur, Jenny notices, walks past his chair, over to Robert's desk. The desk, which normally takes up the center of the back half of the room, has been pushed over to one side, giving the audience a clear, unobstructed view of the main screen at the far end. Robert sits there quietly, reviewing something on his private terminal. He looks up as LaFleur approaches, nodding once, and the older man leans over and whispers a few words Jenny can't make out. Robert nods again, and LaFleur turns, walks past the rows of chairs, and exits through the office door.

Roger turns his head slightly. "Lieutenant Bernard is awake," he murmurs. "LaFleur is bringing him up."

"Weird match," Jenny says. She doesn't know much about Bernard. She vaguely remembers meeting him at a police function, back when he was still Sky Commando, but he didn't make much of an impression.

"They were on some kind of mission together," Roger says.

"Yeah," CB says. He's sitting up now, looking more alert. "At my request. Well... LaFleur, anyway. Not sure why he brought Sky Commando. I don't know what they teach the NYPD these days, but somehow I don't think he has a background in magic."

"Who does?" Roger asks.

CB shrugs. "Fair point."

The lights begin to blink. The murmur of the audience fades, replaced with the sound of people settling into their chairs. The large screen at the end of the room blinks on, displaying a Thorpe Institute logo. The murmuring subsides completely, and silence settles over the room.

"Thank you all for taking the time out of your schedules to attend," Robert says. He doesn't bother to stand, but he has the full attention of everyone in the room. "I know this meeting is somewhat irregular. A number of you are already familiar with the goings-on of the last week, and the rest of you, I'm sure, are at least familiar with the rumors."

Laughter fills the room. Robert waits a moment until it subsides.

"Some of you know more of this story than others, so I hope those of you in the know will be patient while I bring the rest up to speed. It starts with Liberty's murder."

The front screen flickers to display various magazine and newspaper articles covering Liberty's murder, as well as a few pictures of the public funeral. Jenny feels her throat tighten.

"Immediately after Liberty was murdered, two separate investigations into his death were started—one by Curveball and one by Doctor Artemis

LaFleur. Curveball was assisted in his investigation by members of Liberty's family. Doctor LaFleur was assisted by the retired villain Scrapper Jack and by the rogue hero group Crossfire."

Jenny hears someone laughing softly. She thinks it's Red Shift.

"These two investigations merged into a single coordinated effort, and culminated with an assault on an underground complex in Farraday City, where they found... test subjects."

The screen changes to show the stacks of containment coffins.

"We still don't know the identities of these people and we're not yet at the point where we're comfortable reviving them. The data that was recovered from the underground facility was incomplete, but from what we've been able to piece together so far, it's clear they were used to test the effectiveness of an artificially engineered pathogen. Unfortunately, much of the specific data about the pathogen and its method of transmission had been destroyed. We knew very little about its construction until today..."

The screen goes blank.

"Just before he died, Liberty emailed Curveball a heavily-encrypted message. Today we were able to break the encryption and view its contents. What we found was this."

Jenny doesn't understand what displays on the screen next. The words PROJECT RECALL are stamped at the top of what appears to be a blueprint scanned into digital format. The sheet has a number of drawings that look vaguely like chains of DNA, but she doesn't know what they, or the symbols next to them, or the complex formula scrawled underneath them, mean.

"Someone has created a virus targeting the metahuman gene."

Immediately the room fills with excited whispering, as people in the audience turn to each other and start talking excitedly about what it might mean. Robert falls silent, allowing the whispering to crest, and after a few moments he says, "Please, hold your questions and comments until the end."

The room falls silent once more.

"Thank you." The display starts flashing through pages and pages of data as Robert continues. "It's more complicated than that, of course. There isn't a single gene that can be identified as the official 'metahuman gene.' There are a number of markers that, when combined in exactly the right way, trigger a process that may or may not result in a metahuman. The virus targets three of the most common markers."

The screen updates to display a spreadsheet. "One of the documents we found at the facility is, apparently, a summary of the genetic testing done on each of the test subjects. Although none of the test subjects is a metahuman themselves, each subject possessed at least one of these genetic markers. We believe they had been identified as *carriers* of the metahuman gene, for lack of a better term. For this reason, we believe the virus is designed to target these carriers as well. They may even be the primary targets."

Whispering fills the room again, and this time Alimah Mahmoud has to say, rather sharply, "That's enough!" before the room quiets down.

"Detailed information on this virus will be available after this meeting," Robert continues. "For the moment, what's relevant is that the virus was designed to kill. The test data we've recovered suggests that it's not killing at the level the designers want and is still being refined to increase its potency. Needless to say I will need some of you to organize teams focusing on countering this virus. A cure is preferable, but a vaccine will be acceptable. But there are still a number of unanswered questions."

Jenny hears the office door hiss open, but she's too focused on the screen to look back.

"First, it has been pointed out that for an experiment that focuses on metahumans, the choice to include only male test subjects is limiting. Why only men? We don't have an answer to this question yet. Second, we don't know exactly how this virus is transmitted. More specifically, the data we have suggests the virus is very difficult to transmit over any great distance—it's a poor choice for someone trying to start a metahuman plague. Liberty's file included some information I think related to transmission, but I don't understand it."

The screen updates again. It looks similar to the first page that was shown from Liberty's file: pictures of DNA chains, with symbols and formulae placed all over the page. But the symbols and formulae look *strange*—unnatural, like they shouldn't be sharing the screen with the pictures of DNA chains and mathematical equations.

"Quite frankly," Robert says, "I have no idea what this means."

"I do."

The voice comes from the back of the room. Jenny turns to see Artemis LaFleur standing in the doorway, holding up a painfully thin man dressed in sweatpants and a button-up shirt that looks two sizes two large for him. The man's hair is long, and he has a thick beard. Jenny doesn't recognize him.

"Ah," Robert says. "Lieutenant Bernard. I'm glad you could make it."

Jenny frowns. That does *not* look like the guy she met.

"I know what that is," Bernard says, pointing at the screen. "You're right that it's how they plan to transmit it. But it's not *scientific*. It's *magic*."

More muttering this time, though from the tone it sounds more disbelieving and dismissive than anything else.

Bernard breaks free of LaFleur, stumbles forward a few steps, then manages to find his own balance. He walks down the center aisle, eyes gleaming from the reflected light of the screen.

"It's a curse," he says. "Part of one, at any rate. A curse such as this could be used to destroy an entire family line. Half of it, at any rate, the male half or the female half. This one targets the male half."

"Why?" Robert asks.

"I'm not entirely sure," Bernard says, still advancing on the screen, examining each of the symbols in turn. "I think it's a mechanical limitation. I doubt that's the right word, but it's as close as I can get. A spell that can target the population that specifically has limits. It seems that whoever is behind this spell comes from a tradition where men are considered the carriers of the bloodline."

He turns to look at LaFleur, adding, "Like Artigenian did."

LaFleur nods.

"That's why they only included male test subjects," Robert says.

David nods. "You said it was difficult to transmit the virus over a great distance. This tells me they don't have to. If they had enough power, they could conceivably infect every male target on earth in a matter of seconds."

No one says anything.

Robert looks around the room, then nods once. "I've emailed an information packet to everyone here. Please review it when you have time. Your assignments will be handed out over the next day. I want this to be your priority going forward."

Murmured agreement.

"Very good," Robert says. "Thank you all for coming."

The lights return to their full strength, and the men and women behind Jenny start talking excitedly among themselves as they get to their feet and start shuffling toward the door. Jenny looks at the front row—none of them have moved. Everyone looks grim.

It takes fifteen minutes for the rest of the room to empty. Of the original group, only Ms. Mahmoud stays behind, coming up to take a seat in the second row. She doesn't speak, and the expression on her face is hard to read.

Street Ronin is the first to break the silence.

"Well." His voice is dry. "At least *I'll* survive."

Part One: Robert Thorpe's Office

The official meeting is ending. The real meeting is about to begin.

The *official* meeting ends with scientists milling about in a buzz of tense, excited conversation. None of them will sleep tonight: most won't even bother going home to try. They will, instead, be organizing ad hoc meetings of their own, where they'll brainstorm the best ways to approach the problem.

The *real* meeting will consist of fourteen people.

Jenny Forrest stares at the display screen and shudders. It's a schematic of a virus, and she understands absolutely nothing of what she's seeing, but if Robert Thorpe says it's a virus engineered to kill metahumans, she has no trouble believing it. The other part—that the delivery system is a *magic spell* that, when cast, will infect every male simultaneously—is a little harder to accept. Harder, but not impossible: she's seen enough in the last month that she's not willing to dismiss it out of hand.

She looks at the man who made that claim: long, shoulder-length brown hair, a thick brown beard, and blue eyes that alternate between alertness and exhaustion. If anyone had to play the role of a crazed wizard, he certainly looks the part—the problem is, he doesn't look the part of who he's supposed to be. He always looked crisply military, like a hotshot pilot in a war movie. She doesn't see much of that in the man at present.

David looks up; their eyes meet for a moment. Jenny looks away, embarrassed at being caught staring, and bothered by something else she can't put a finger on. There was something in David's gaze that unnerved her—as if something else was staring at her along with him.

He and LaFleur were off researching magic while we were in Farraday City. Did they find anything?

A moment later she adds a second question.

*Did anything find **them**?*

"Hey."

She barely hears CB over the buzz of the scientists still in the room. Jenny looks over her shoulder and sees him standing next to her, staring up at the screen, his face impossible to read. "You understand any of that?"

"No," Jenny says. A moment later, she realizes he's referring to the schematic on the screen. "*Oh.* No."

CB nods absently. "Yeah, Greek to me, too. Can't make heads or tails of it."

Jenny turns her attention to the virus schematic once more. "I think you need advanced degrees to understand that."

CB shrugs. "I guess. Robert, LaFleur, and Red Shift all seem to get it. And the Lieutenant gets the magic part, I guess."

"The only thing I remember from college biology is that photosynthesis has a night cycle," Jenny says. "I don't even really remember if calling it a 'night cycle' is accurate, that's just how I remember remembering it. You?"

"I have to fall back on *high school* biology," CB says. "Which I'm pretty sure I skipped at every opportunity. So the best I got is 'chlorophyll.'"

Jenny starts to smile, but stops when she catches the look in CB's eyes. He's *angry*. He's doing his best not to show it—standing casually, speaking conversationally—if she hadn't seen that look she wouldn't know it. But his eyes tell a different story altogether.

"Are... are you OK, CB?"

"I'm fine."

His voice is normal, but those eyes... Jenny shudders and turns her attention to the rest of the room. The scientists are starting to leave in earnest now, a steady stream of small groups, all talking excitedly as they exit.

Everyone else has scattered across the room, conversing quietly. Crossfire is at the very back of the room. Vigilante, Red Shift, and Street Ronin have moved three chairs into a small circle, and they all lean forward, heads bowed, whispering to each other in voices too low for Jenny to hear—even with her enhanced senses, she can only make out the occasional word, and not enough to make any sense of it.

Too much background noise.

Roger is still in his original seat, leaning back with his eyes closed, looking for all the world as if he's asleep. LaFleur, Jack Barrow, and now David Bernard are on the other end of the same row. Jack and LaFleur are conversing in a low murmur—Jenny can make out more of their conversation, which has something to do with an announcement LaFleur is going to make soon—while David, like Roger, sits in his chair with his eyes closed. He doesn't look asleep, though: he looks more like he's meditating.

In the middle of the chairs the three Federal Agents—Peter Travers, Alan Grant, and Lijuan Hu—are having a rather heated conversation about someone named "Henry." Alan Grant looks genuinely angry, rather than the cocky, smart-ass demeanor he usually favors, and the clearest parts of the conversation are when he starts cursing... which he does often. Agent Hu appears to be trying to calm him down, while Travers looks on with the same polite, friendly, distant expression he always has when he's working.

Robert Thorpe is leaning against his desk, whispering something to Alimah Mahmoud. The president of Thorpe Industries doesn't say anything, but nods thoughtfully as she considers his words.

Jenny looks at the different groups and frowns. She can't fault everyone for grouping up the way they have—they're falling back on the people they have the longest working relationships with—but it still feels wrong somehow.

We should be working through this together, right?

Robert grabs the cane leaning against his desk and walks to the center of the room.

Alimah moves to the side of the room, sitting next to Roger, nudging his arm gently. Roger stirs, opening one eye and smiling slightly at Alimah, who nods towards Robert. Roger sits up straight and waits.

The other groups have also quieted and turned their attention to Robert—everyone but Agent Grant, who is in the middle of making a very colorful point.

"—and if we don't we're *fucked!*"

He shouts in almost total silence, his voice ringing off the walls. Hu winces, grabbing his arm, as Travers looks on, still smiling.

Grant turns, noticing—or, perhaps more accurately, re-remembering—the other people in the room. "And I don't mean it in the *good* way, either!"

Robert takes a deep breath. "Let's all take a moment to calm down before—"

"Let's *not*," Grant says. "Look, Doc, no offense to you or anyone else in this room but if we assume everything you just said is true then we're facing a deliberate, targeted biological attack against the metahuman population on a world-wide scale, with a projected fatality rate of up to 50% of that population, along with guaranteed additional deaths among civilian populations."

"That's the worst-case scenario," Robert says. "We're not there yet. That's why we need to—"

"*I* need to contact Special Agent Phillip Henry in Division M and let him know what the fuck is going on," Grant says. "Then we need to contact the NIH and FEMA and alert them of a potential metahuman contagion, and alert *other countries* of the same thing, and get them this information so they can start ramping up to try to counter it."

Artemis LaFleur shakes his head. "That would be unwise."

Grant's laugh is sharp and humorless. "The world's most dangerous supervillain doesn't want to go to the cops. Let's have an in-depth discussion on exactly how not shocked I am to learn that. We can *share*. Maybe we'll trade *friendship bracelets*."

"Grant..." Agent Hu places a hand on her partner's shoulder. "Try to be less of a jackass, and at least let him tell you *why*."

Grant glares at Hu for a moment, then shrugs. He turns back to LaFleur, waiting expectantly.

"Under most circumstances," LaFleur says, "and despite your obvious assumptions to the contrary, I would consider alerting the authorities the right thing to do."

Grant doesn't bother hiding his disbelief. "You would."

"I would," LaFleur says. "Fighting a virus—especially one that can potentially affect the entire world—requires an infrastructure far more developed than any single organization or corporation. Even if we assume Dr. Thorpe and his people can create a cure or vaccine—which is not guaranteed—I'm not convinced Thorpe Industries has the resources to successfully manufacture and distribute it to everyone who would need it."

"We can probably manufacture it," Robert says. "I know it doesn't seem like it, but the metahuman population is very small compared to the entire population on earth. The problem, as Dr. LaFleur points out, is getting a cure or vaccine administered. We will absolutely need the cooperation of local governments to do that."

"Then what's the problem?" Grant demands. "I call my boss and we get that started."

"Because," LaFleur says, "at least part of the government—at the very least, part of the *American* government—is *in on the plot*."

A grim silence settles in over the room. Grant crosses his arms stubbornly.

"Don't even try to say he's wrong," Hu says.

"You're not the boss of me, Hu."

Hu doesn't rise to the bait. "That's why Agent Henry sent us with Travers in the first place. Our own people shot you in the back, remember?"

"...Yeah," Grant admits reluctantly. "Hard to forget."

"Let's not forget that our best suspect in the murder of Liberty is a sitting senator," Vigilante adds.

Grant's right eyebrow shoots up. "The Junior Senator from New York?"

Vigilante nods.

Grant whistles through his teeth. "Christ. It's a goddamn Shakespeare play."

"That should be our focus," Vigilante says. "We don't know who to trust, but we know one person we're pretty sure we can't—and if he *is* behind Liberty's murder, either he's neck-deep in the conspiracy or his handler is."

"How *exactly* should that be our focus?" Roger Whitman crosses his arms as his mouth droops into a disapproving frown.

"We grab him," Vigilante says. "Then we ask him questions. Lots of useful questions."

"No way," Roger says. "Kidnap a senator? You're crazy."

"I wasn't suggesting we all do it *together*," Vigilante says. "Crossfire can handle it. We're already a 'terrorist group,' and it was only a matter of time before we targeted a corrupt politician that high up."

"No." The finality in Roger's voice makes Jenny uncomfortable. She's not sure what would happen if Roger and Vigilante came to blows, but she's pretty sure it would involve a lot of property damage. "We can't work like that. Not on something this big."

Red Shift cuts in, sounding uncharacteristically impatient. "Regiment, we don't really have a lot of options. We know what the bad guys are doing, but we don't know who they are, where they are, or when they're going to do it. We have one solid link. We're not going to *kill* him." He glances at Jenny as he says it—the man is her uncle, after all. "It won't do anyone any good to kill him. We need what he knows. Capturing him is the best way to get that information—it cuts him off from his support."

"Or his jailers," Street Ronin adds. "There's always a possibility that he's being blackmailed. Not likely, though. Sorry Zero." Street Ronin nods toward Jenny this time, looking sympathetic but not at all contrite.

"Are you *kidding* me?" Agent Grant jumps into the fray again. "OK, I'm willing to accept that *right now* we can't go public with this, but we are going to have to go public eventually, right? Eventually we're going to need that infrastructure Our Very Special Supervillain was talking about. No way in *hell* we get that if we kidnap a fucking United States senator first. I don't care how corrupt he is."

"We don't need that infrastructure," Vigilante says, voice tight, "if we *stop the virus before it gets launched*."

"Bullshit," Grant says. "You say he's behind Liberty's assassination? What do you think the bad guys are going to do if their pet senator gets nabbed by *Crossfire*? Because *no offense guys*, but you aren't exactly subtle when you work. Odds are somebody's going to notice. Probably the *Secret Service*. They're trained to notice shit like that."

"I agree with Agent Grant this time," Travers says. "If Senator Morgan is taken, and you're identified for it... well. It won't be long before Crossfire is identified as the group behind Liberty's murder, and suddenly the entire world will be focused on bringing you three down. We'll never make any progress after that."

"If we do it *on our own* then the focus will be on *us*," Vigilante says. "All we have to do is get you whatever information we extract, and then stay on the run while the rest of you do what you have to do. Everyone focusing on *us* gives you a lot more room to operate in."

Travers looks thoughtful as he mulls it over.

"You can't do that," Jenny says. "Once you do that you become Public Enemy Number One. They'll have *everyone* after you. Won't they?"

Vigilante shrugs. "It won't be pretty."

"It won't be *right*," Roger says.

"I don't see that we have a lot of choices right now."

"But it's not what you do!" Jenny protests. "It won't be just the bad guys coming after you if you do this. Every law enforcement official, every metahuman hero—all they'll see is Crossfire crossing a line, and they'll all come after you. Are you going to kill *them?*"

"Not if we can avoid it," Vigilante says. "But we probably won't be able to avoid it all the time."

"Hold the fuck *on*." Agent Grant takes two steps toward Vigilante before he's restrained by Agent Hu. His body blurs for a moment, then a *second* Agent Grant appears right in front of Vigilante. His posture isn't exactly threatening, but his proximity is, and all three members of Crossfire tense as he stares down at them. "If you think I'm gonna stand by while you—"

"*Stop.*"

Robert Thorpe's voice is loud and firm. The effect is immediate: Agent Grant's second form blurs and disappears as his first returns to his seat, glowering. Vigilante, Red Shift, and Street Ronin relax. Roger is still frowning, but some of the tension leaves his shoulders as he stops glaring at Crossfire.

"Keep in mind that you all learned exactly what this virus is, and how it will be delivered, no more than an hour ago," Robert says. "An hour. That's it. The simple truth is, we haven't had enough time to come up with a good plan yet. I understand the desire to move *now* and do something *now*, but we need to force ourselves to take the time to come up with a plan that will actually work. That means we *don't* splinter into different pieces, each with our own incompatible plans. It means we *wait* and plan *together*."

Nobody says anything.

"We're going to have to work together," Robert continues. "We just... we *have* to. We're the only people who know what's going on. So far we've heard some valid reasons why we shouldn't, at present, start bringing other people in... so we're all we have."

He winces as he rubs the back of his neck, eyes glazing over momentarily as the exhaustion he's been pushing back forces its way to the front. "Maybe it won't work. Maybe we're all too different to sustain an alliance for any significant length of time. All I'm asking is that we wait before we reach that conclusion. Give us some time to come up with a plan we can all agree to first. Give it a week—in a week we should know a lot more about this thing than we do now—and let's see where we stand. Can we agree to that?"

Nobody says yes—nobody says anything—but it seems to Jenny that the tension in the room has ebbed. It looks like nobody's saying 'no,' either.

"No," CB says.

Jenny turns, surprised. She's been sitting next to CB the whole time and hasn't really been paying attention to him. He's standing now, his hands thrust deep into his trenchcoat pockets. He's staring at Robert, looking almost defiant, and as Jenny sees the *rage* shining out of his eyes she wilts a little.

Robert looks taken aback. "CB?"

"I don't know, Robert!" CB shrugs violently, his face twisting into an expression Jenny hasn't seen on him before. Something hard and ugly. "I don't... Jesus, they call it *Project Recall*."

He lets his words sink in a moment. "Project. Recall. Like we're, what? Defective cars? They're sending us *back*? Calling a mulligan? Here's the problem, Robert: I *know* you. I know Roger. I know what you're on board for, and what you're not. You're the good guys, and I *love* you for that, but I gotta be honest, I don't think this is a fight the good guys can handle. This is a fight only the bad guys can win. I don't think you're on board for that."

Nobody says anything as he leaves the room.

Part Two: Haruspex Analytics Situation Room

Jason Kline sighs, pushes his laptop away, and rests his forehead against the edge of the table. He stares down at the taupe-colored rug and wonders what color it was when they first moved in. He's certain the rug has been replaced at least twice since they set up here, but he doesn't remember it happening and he can't remember the previous colors.

The Haruspex Analytics Situation Room stopped being "the situation room" and started being "their office" about a month ago. It has all the access they need: access to the computers on the Haruspex network and access to the outside world (different computers, different lines) made it the ideal location, and they never bothered moving out. At first glance, it doesn't really look the way you'd expect a situation room to look—even now, after all his years on the job, Jason still expects to see a forty-foot-tall viewscreen with red flashing lights and a large sign flashing DEFCON ONE any time someone uses the term "situation room." Instead it looks like a board room, with the central meeting table surrounded by paneled display screens set into the walls.

Jason continues to stare at the rug, feeling the cool wood surface of the table pressing against his forehead. "I'm running out of ideas."

Every inch of wall, save for a few inches around the doors leading into the room, is part of the situation room display system. It wasn't always this way—when they first moved in, it was a more traditional "squeeze as many flat screen monitors onto each wall as you can manage" arrangement. One morning they walked in, found the monitors gone, and saw the walls had *become* the monitors. Each seat around the table has a computer that can patch into any of the displays embedded in the walls. When all the panels are going at once, each tapped into a separate real-time feed in Haruspex's worldwide communications network, the forty-foot-tall viewscreen seems unnecessary.

"Boo fucking hoo."

Jason quickly suppresses a smile and looks over at the small woman dressed in gray sweat pants and a blue hoodie. The hood is up, with the drawstring pulled so far that only her eyes and the tip of her nose is visible. She's staring at her laptop—a machine so large it barely qualifies as portable, hooked into one of the table's computers—and squints slightly as she focuses on something specific.

"Anyone ever tell you you're a sweetheart, Michelle?"

The right arm goes up. She's pulled the sleeves of her sweatshirt over her hands, but a single finger emerges from the cloth, stays visible long enough to make its point, then disappears beneath the sweatshirt again.

Michelle is a brilliant analyst. She is also a very good communicator, for certain types of communication, but she is not a very diplomatic one.

Laughter from his right—Billy and Phyllis, neither bothering to hide their amusement. Physically they couldn't be more different. Billy is a surfer, and he embodies the stereotype. His blond hair (bleached even lighter from years out in the sun and surf), blue eyes, slightly tanned skin, and muscular physique make him look very out of place among his paler, chair-bound teammates. Phyllis is his opposite: a heavyset black woman in her mid-fifties, gray swirls in black hair pulled back into a bun. The hairstyle, her choice of glasses (green horn rims), and her choice of dress (a silvery-green blouse and matching long skirt) make her look more like somebody's mother, or a teacher from the fifties.

Billy grins openly at Michelle as she returns to her work. Phyllis directs her mirth at Jason instead.

"Yeah. I'm done." To Michelle's right, a slightly overweight asian man sighs and leans back in his chair, head tilted back as he stares up at the ceiling. Simon runs a hand through his spiky black hair and shakes his head. "I don't know where they are. You don't know where they are. Nobody in this room knows where they are! Can we go home already?"

Since the disaster in Farraday City—the loss of a secret installation, a prototype golem, an entire set of test subjects, and who knows how much potentially revealing information on Project Recall, not to mention nearly decimating the coast of Georgia in a metahuman-related mishap they still don't completely understand—his team has focused on identifying the participants and figuring out where they went.

Figuring out "who" wasn't as difficult as it could have been. The base personnel who survived the last-minute evac included security personnel who had monitored the initial assault, who identified most of the players— Curveball, Crossfire, Scrapper Jack, and three more. One of them was a woman that Johann Richter swore was Jenny Forrest. Jason has difficulty believing that—he's met Jenny before, and he's pretty sure she wasn't a metahuman then—but it's possible. Of the other two, the woman could burst into flame, and the man was a teleporter. There was a database match for them, but Jason wasn't ready to believe it. The match indicated the two were a team, and that the man had recently died *and had been autopsied*. The only metahuman who could possibly recover from something like that—at least, the only one he knew of—was Vigilante.

Then Plague mentioned *Regiment*, of all people. They didn't have any footage of him, but he'd been involved at least once before, when he helped Curveball repel the assault on the Forrest brownstone.

That was a large concentration of very powerful metahumans in a city that was notoriously hostile to them. So where did they go? After nearly tearing the underground complex out of the ground, they'd disappeared. Completely.

Very frustrating.

"They have to still be in the city." Michelle's voice is clipped—she's frustrated too, she just doesn't want to admit it. "They're lying low. Farraday City is a good place for that."

Simon, still looking at the ceiling, shakes his head. "The political situation there is too... unusual. If we can believe our briefing."

"Assume we can," Jason says. "But they probably don't know how unusual it is. And Curveball has apparently been living there for a while. He may have resources he can leverage to keep them hidden."

"Too many." Simon sits up, rubs his eyes, and focuses on his computer screen. "Curveball, Jenny Forrest, Scrapper Jack, Vigilante, Red Shift, Street Ronin... maybe these two Feds... and now Regiment? That's too many, Jason. You can't keep them *all* hidden."

"So where?" Michelle almost growls the question.

"Here?" Simon doesn't sound convinced, and he shrugs when he says it. "They're all from New York. Even Curveball."

"There'd be signs," Michelle insists. "We've got eyes on the most likely routes. And a few unlikely ones, just in case."

Simon waves his hand dismissively. "That wouldn't stop them. Curveball evaded a government manhunt for months. No one can seem to get a line on Crossfire, no matter how many resources they put into it. They could manage the trip undetected."

"They're out of the country," Phyllis says.

Simon and Michelle stop arguing and turn to stare at the older woman. Jason does too, one eyebrow raised. Billy leans back in his chair, grinning.

"How do you figure?" Jason asks.

Phyllis takes her time answering, pausing to sip her coffee first, which makes Billy's grin even wider.

"It's Regiment," Phyllis says.

Jason frowns. "You think he flew them out of the country?"

Phyllis shakes her head. "That's not it. Roger Whitman didn't travel to Farraday City with Curveball and Jenny Forrest. And he didn't travel to Farraday City with Crossfire, or with Scrapper Jack. He wasn't seen for most of the battle outside the compound. He arrived separately, and as far as Billy and I can tell, he arrived last."

Billy nods in agreement. "We have video footage, taken from the heavy units, of everyone else in the fight. None of him. So he didn't show until after the heavies were taken out—during the golem deploy is our guess. Unfortunately we don't have any footage of that."

"OK." Jason leans forward, interested to see where this is going. "So he arrived last. What does that mean?"

"Nothing by itself," Billy says, "but Phyllis checked up on his activity in New York, and apparently he left his home about a week and a half before the fight started. Locked it up, left some instructions with a neighbor, and disappeared. Nobody knows where."

"Farraday City?" Michelle asks.

Phyllis shakes her head. "A week and a half before that fight, and he only shows up at the end of it? He would have joined the rest of the group by then. You're forgetting the third surviving member of the Guardians."

Jason feels the other eyebrow rise to join the first. "Thorpe?"

Phyllis nods. "Think about it. Both Curveball and Regiment use Thorpe's network to communicate. All four of them were close, back in the day. Thorpe would be just as interested in investigating Liberty's murder as Curveball and Regiment…"

"…but he can't," Billy adds, "because he's not allowed to enter the country."

"But he still has a lot of resources at his disposal," Phyllis continues.

Michelle stares at Phyllis for a moment. Then she nods, closes the lid to her laptop, and pushes her chair away from the table.

"They're right. They're with Thorpe."

"And Thorpe is not in the US," Billy says. "He's… well, we're not sure, exactly. We think he's on a private island somewhere in the middle of the Atlantic Ocean."

"How?" Simon is still unconvinced. "I see the connection you're making, but if Thorpe isn't in the US, and he can't get *into* the US, how would he extract six—or maybe eight—metahumans?"

"Seven or nine," Jason corrects. "If you count Regiment."

"Regiment can *fly*," Simon says. "I'm not counting him."

"*He* can't be in the US," Billy says. "But Thorpe Industries is all over. He could probably smuggle himself into the US if he really wanted. Getting a group of people out of Farraday City while everyone is distracted by a killer hurricane? Kid stuff."

Jason thinks it over. "So you're saying that a week and a half before the attack on the base, Regiment flew off to meet with Dr. Thorpe at this island."

"We don't actually know it's *specifically* an island," Phyllis says, frowning slightly at Billy.

Billy shrugs. "With billionaires it's almost always an island."

"The point is," Phyllis says, "that Regiment went *somewhere*, and we're pretty sure it was to meet with Thorpe… wherever he is."

"But we might be able to find out where that is," Billy adds. "If Regiment joined up with the others because he assumed they were associated with the hurricane in Farraday City—"

"–*and* if we assume the data we have on Regiment's top flight speed is correct—" Phyllis adds.

"–then we can estimate the distance Regiment had to travel to get there," Billy finishes.

Jason nods. "We can dedicate some CPU cycles to comparing that range with every known island in the Atlantic, see if Thorpe has any infrastructure in that range…"

Michelle pulls her chair back up to the table and opens the lid of her laptop. "Not tired any more."

"I don't know," Simon says. "Don't get me wrong, it narrows down our search from *everywhere in the world* quite a bit, but it's still a lot of area to cover."

"It is," Jason says. "But it's more than we had an hour ago. And I think I have a few ideas on how to narrow things down even further. Let's take a break, get some food. Say two hours?"

Everyone nods in agreement.

"Great," Jason says. "When we get back, we'll start calculating the most likely points of origin and start from there. Billy, Phyllis… excellent work."

Everyone is smiling as they make their way out.

Part Three: Jacob K. Javits Federal Building

The rooftop of the Jacob K. Javits Federal Building is designated a Sky Commando refit and refuel center, and the rooftop has been reinforced with a landing pad and chassis support lattice. Alishia Webb lands easily, hitting the pad dead center, and waits as a mesh of steel beams and ruggedized cabling close around the sides and back of the Sky Commando chassis, hooking into it to run an automated diagnostic and set up what resupply is needed. Then she opens the front and steps out as her tactical armor detaches from the inside.

For a moment she feels exposed, standing outside the chassis, wearing only her tactical armor. The armor is vastly superior to the armor in use in traditional police forces—or even in standing armies—but it doesn't hold a candle to the Sky Commando chassis. It's hard not to feel invulnerable in that chassis.

Which is stupid, she reminds herself. *What happened to David could happen to you, too.*

She murmurs the command to retract her helmet, breathes in warm fresh air as the helmet splits into multiple pieces and retracts into the back of her armor, and walks toward the elevator on the other side of the roof. A lone figure, dressed in a black suit and wearing sunglasses, waits patiently as she approaches.

"Agent Henry," Alishia says.

"Sky Commando," the man replies.

Special Agent Phillip Henry is a tall, thin man. His skin is very dark—much darker than her own—and his hair, cropped close to his skull, shows traces of gray on the sides. His eyes are completely hidden by his sunglasses. His mouth is, as always, drawn into a thin, straight line.

He looks like a caricature of a Federal agent: humorless, overdressed, and pretentious. It's the sunglasses that push the look over the top, but she knows the sunglasses aren't so much a *fashion accessory* as they are a *courtesy*. Agent Henry is a metahuman: he always knows when you're lying, and if he makes eye contact it's impossible not to tell the truth.

Agent Henry presses the elevator call button and absently fiddles with the knot on his tie. It's an unusual display of nervous energy.

"Agent Hu usually meets me up here," Alishia says.

"She's on leave," Agent Henry says.

"Because of Grant?"

Henry nods.

Agent Grant died a few weeks ago, killed in an incident that turned Division M on its ear. If rumor and scuttlebutt are to be believed, the men who killed him were also working for the Department of Homeland Security.

"Sorry again," Alishia says, and wishes she can think of something else to say. Losing a member of your team is tough, and it would be even harder on Agent Hu. She'd been his partner.

The elevator door opens. They both step in.

"We need to talk about that," Agent Henry says. "Very soon. Not now, though. Just... be prepared for the unusual."

"What's going on?" Alishia asks. "I haven't heard from you for weeks—I mean I get that. But... today out of the blue my captain tells me we're on a new task force, the meeting's today, and that's all I get?"

"I suspect that's all she knows," Agent Henry says. He breathes out sharply, clearly annoyed. "We don't know much more than that, either. We've been taken out of the loop."

"Grant's death?" Alishia asks. "Is it true someone actually *stole* his *body*?"

"That's part of what we need to talk about," Henry says. "Later. But I can tell you that the vehicles the assailants were driving were issued by the DHS. What's more, the *paperwork* was traced back to Division M."

Alishia's eyes widen. "Your own people?"

Agent Henry shakes his head. "I questioned everyone here. I expected to find nothing, and I did. But Division M is larger than this office, and I can't travel to DC and start questioning the office staff there. My abilities are constrained by law, and my superiors prefer to handle things differently. We didn't contact you because we were told not to during the... 'ongoing investigation.'"

"Great," Alishia says. "More political bullshit. So what's happening today?"

"Today we get to learn about this new task force," Agent Henry says. "From what I've been able to gather it has something to do with the TriHealth incident."

Alishia nods thoughtfully. The "TriHealth Incident" was a Code Ultraviolet triggered when members of Crossfire assaulted the TriHealth building in Manhattan. That was strange. Crossfire didn't usually go after private companies... unless they were fronts for organized crime.

When Sky Commando had arrived on the scene, she found that the TriHealth building had made some distinctly *non-traditional* design choices: strange alloys baked into the walls of the building, a security system tricked out with anti-personnel attachments, not to mention security forces wearing powered armor whose designs appeared to have been *stolen* from the NYPD Metahuman Division. On top of all that, one of the NYPD's most celebrated officers, Lieutenant Clive Darius, pulled rank to try to keep Sky Commando away from the scene. Darius was already under investigation—Division M had uncovered video evidence possibly linking him to the people involved in Liberty's murder—but this drew the attention of Internal Affairs.

"Good," Alishia says. "If Darius is dirty I want to take him out."

Agent Henry doesn't reply to that. He doesn't have to.

They don't exit on the Division M floors—the elevator continues to descend a few floors until they stop at a level designated simply as "meeting rooms" and exit into a mostly-deserted hallway.

"Everyone in the building has been told it's 'closed for fumigation,'" Agent Henry explains.

Alishia snorts. That means everyone in the building knows there's an important and "secret" meeting going on today.

"I thought it was stupid, too," Henry says. "Come on."

They walk halfway down the hall and stop in front of a set of doors flanked by armed building security. The doors are mostly glass, but curtains have been thrown over them to prevent anyone from looking into the room.

Agent Henry flashes his ID at the guards. They nod and stand aside as the doors swing open, revealing a small foyer with another set of doors on the other end.

"Come on."

Alishia follows as he strides across the room and opens the other doors—heavy, metal doors this time—and steps into a large, brightly-lit meeting room.

It's one of the building's multimedia rooms, built like a small theater, complete with a stage and ten rows of stadium seats. Alishia and Agent Henry make their way down to the front, where the rest of Division M is huddled together, talking in low voices.

She can't help noticing how many different groups are in the room. Members of the MTHD—New York's Metahuman Division—are already seated in the back, and she can see representatives from the FBI, the DHS, the Federal Bureau of Metahuman Affairs, and a few other stony-faced groups that she pegs for the CIA and NSA. She's the only member of the Sky Commando division present, which annoys her, but she relaxes a little as they near the three members of Agent Henry's team.

"Sergeant." Brian Frank, a short, mustachioed man with thinning blond hair and impossibly wide shoulders, nods and smiles slightly in greeting. Agent Frank reminds her of one of those rugged cowboys from the 70s—it's probably the mustache that does it—and she'll be surprised if he says anything else for the rest of the meeting.

She smiles and nods by way of reply. The lean woman with dark, curly hair standing to Agent Frank's left laughs in amusement.

"It's turned into a contest with you two. Whoever says the most words to each other loses."

Agent Frank laughs. Alishia grins. Neither says anything.

Desiree Malloy laughs again, slapping Agent Frank on the shoulder, shaking her head. Alishia wonders once again where she's from. She looks... Hispanic? Indian? Neither fits her name.

"I hope we start soon." The woman to Malloy's left rolls back a suit sleeve and stares at her wristwatch, sighing impatiently. "I'd like to know what we're going to do, since we're no longer doing what we *ought* to be doing."

Erin Collins is Agent Henry's second in command. She vaguely remembers Agent Grant calling her *the Blonde Amazon*—to her face—and it is the most appropriate inappropriate description Alishia can think of. Collins stands at six-foot-one, towering over everyone but Agent Henry, who comes up about a quarter of an inch short. It's hard to tell beneath the standard "Division M work suit," but the way Collins moves convinces Alishia that every inch of the woman is made of muscle.

They're all metahumans. For all I know she's their Regiment.

"We should go ahead and take a seat," Agent Henry says. "They'll get started roughly twenty minutes after we give up waiting for them." He doesn't smile when he says it, and Alishia is left wondering, once again, whether his humor is intentional.

They all choose seats in the front row. Alishia stares at the fold-down seat next to Malloy, hesitating for a moment before she sighs, folds it down, and gingerly settles in. Early versions of the tactical armor were so heavy and cumbersome it would have been impossible to use such a flimsy chair, but Sam Vicks has been obsessed with making the flight suit thin and flexible enough to "wear everywhere." The latest model is about on par with a soldier's body armor in terms of bulk and weight. It's a little wider than she'd like, but it works.

Contrary to Agent Henry's prediction, as soon as they sit the lights flicker. The buzz of conversation in the room fades as a man in a dark blue three-piece suit makes his way to the podium. He's a stout man with thinning gray hair, and sweat gleams off the top of his head. The badge dangling from his front suit pocket identifies him as a member of the FBI.

"Thank you all for coming. I am Special Agent Oliver Nuzzo, and I'm here to read you in to Operation Bad Seed." Agent Nuzzo reaches into his suit jacket pocket, pulls out a handkerchief, and dabs at the sweat on his pate.

"I suspect none of you have ever heard of 'Operation Bad Seed.' If you have, it means we've screwed up." He smiles, chuckling nervously at his own joke, then coughs self-consciously. "Sorry. I'm terrible at this. Operation Bad Seed is a deep cover operation we've been running for the last six years, in an attempt to uncover some deep-rooted and widespread corruption that may have been connected to the, ah, PRODIGY debacle."

That causes a stir. PRODIGY was not a proud moment in US law enforcement history, since it involved a fruitless attempt to track down apparently rogue metahumans—Curveball, primarily—and ended in the revelation that rogue elements within the government were trying to enslave and brainwash metahuman citizens to turn them into remote-controlled drones.

"This has been a secret project out of necessity. We did not know who we could trust, and did not know how to vet potential confidants. We have a man on the inside, but progress has been slow—he's earned a certain level of trust, but not enough to close in on the inner circle. Unfortunately, our need to remain secret has put him in a very precarious position. I'll let him explain."

Alishia raises an eyebrow. *Our man undercover is in danger so we're going to parade him in front of a bunch of cops? That makes no sense.*

Nuzzo nods to someone in the back of the room, and Alishia hears the metal double doors bang open as someone walks down the center aisle. She doesn't bother to look until she hears Malloy swear in disbelief.

Captain Clive Darius is a legend in the New York Police Department. A middle-aged man with a homely, weather-beaten face—as well as a few scars suggesting that more than the weather has managed to get in a lick or two—he nonetheless remains a fit and imposing figure. He is an undisputed hero among the rank-and-file, and practically worshiped in Vice, his division.

He was the one caught on film interfering with Division M's

investigation. He's the one who tried to pull rank to keep Sky Commando from investigating the TriHealth fiasco. He's dirty, and *what the hell is he doing here?*

Darius takes the stage and turns to face the audience. He scans the crowd, his gaze stopping for a moment as his eyes meet Alishia's. He nods slightly.

"My name," he says, "is Clive Darius. I'm a captain in the New York Police Department. About six years ago I was contacted by someone representing a large, unknown organization, seeking to bribe me to perform illegal and unethical services on their behalf. Shortly after reporting the bribe, I was contacted by Agent Nuzzo, and I agreed to go deep cover on their behalf."

The room is silent. Alishia can hear her own heartbeat.

"During that time I engaged in… *numerous* illegal activities, all with the FBI's knowledge and under their supervision, in an attempt to determine who was behind these requests. Two weeks ago, in an attempt to deflect further investigation into this group's activities, I screwed up. I got outmaneuvered by some of the parties in this room, and I failed the task I was given by my 'employers.' I haven't been able to get in touch with any of my handlers since."

Darius sighs, shakes his head. "I'm pretty sure they're planning to kill me. I don't know when, so I've been trying to unload every scrap of information I got. That's why you're here: you all know about what happened at TriHealth. I know something—not everything, but *something*—about the people *behind* TriHealth. I'm going to tell you everything I know, and this Task Force is going to bring them down."

The room fills with excited whispering from everyone *except* Alishia and the agents of Division M. They are all staring at Agent Henry, waiting for *his* reaction.

Agent Henry stares at Captain Darius, brow furrowed. Finally, he turns to the others.

"I don't know," he says. "I just… can't tell."

Part Four: Thorpe Island, Fishing Pier

CB watches the ocean as he smokes.

The island has a mid-sized town, the town has a small marina, and just off to the side of the marina is a long pier. CB sits at the end of the pier, trying to figure out if he can feel the island floating. It's an artificial island, after all, and since it's out in the middle of the ocean he's pretty sure it doesn't go all the way down, so it has to *float*. It's not so much an island as it is a boat that *looks* like an island: boats float. Boats also *move*, and since Robert built it, CB's convinced that not only does it float and move, it can probably submerge itself. At this point, he's not willing to dismiss the idea that it can *fly*.

But he's focused on trying to feel the island float. On the boat-island proper he can't feel anything—it's indistinguishable from solid ground as far as he's concerned—but out here there's... something. Maybe it's just his imagination, but he thinks he can feel the slightest hint of a bob.

The air rustles in a not-quite-natural manner, then something *thuds* on the pier behind him.

"Hello Roger." CB doesn't turn. He flicks cigarette ash out into the water.

"Hey." Roger Whitman wears blue jeans, sneakers, and a tank top shirt that exposes impossibly solid arms. His tank top is drenched with sweat, and a faint sheen covers his dark skin. He walks over to the edge of the pier and sits, unsurprised that CB recognizes him.

CB wonders what Roger could possibly have been doing to make himself tired. Throwing full-grown bull elephants, maybe.

"Sparring with Red Shift," Roger says, guessing at the unspoken question.

CB raises an eyebrow. "Really? Last I checked you didn't like Crossfire much."

"It's a little more complicated than that," Roger says. "Also, the enemy of my enemy is a useful sparring partner, and a workout is a workout. That guy is damned hard to hit."

CB nods. He takes another drag on his cigarette, exhales slowly, then notices Roger's bemused expression. "What?"

Roger nods at the cigarette.

CB shrugs, then pulls on it again, watching the cherry burn bright red.

"There are kids on this island. What will they think?"

"That smoking is cool," CB says. "Also, they should all do it so they can be exactly like me."

Roger grins in spite of himself, amusement winning over disapproval. "You're a bad man, CB."

"I am." CB blows smoke out through his nose. "It's part of my brooding antihero charm."

Roger laughs. "Aren't you a little old for that? I thought you'd be mellow by now."

"Not mellow," CB says. "Just tired."

Amusement fades. Roger looks at him thoughtfully.

"Not *physically*," CB says. "I feel exactly the same, *physically*. Maybe even a little better than I used to. But I'm *tired*, Roger. PRODIGY broke something, way back then, and I just… can't… I *can't*. I don't know if I want to play the game any more."

Roger says nothing for a moment, content to stare at the water rolling up against the pier. A soft wind pushes the cold of the ocean over the side, causing CB to wrap his trenchcoat around himself more tightly.

Roger chooses his words carefully. "What we're doing isn't a game, CB."

CB laughs bitterly. "I've got a list of assholes I'd like you to explain that to."

"Yeah, the politics sucks," Roger says, "but it comes with the job. You know that."

"Yeah," CB says, "I know it. I still *hate* it."

"What do you expect?" Roger asks. "We started Project Paragon because the Nazis had already created a squad of super soldiers who were on the verge of conquering Europe on their own. The villains came *first*. History *expects* us to be monsters, and we have to prove we aren't."

"I don't have to prove a damn thing," CB snaps.

"Get over yourself," Roger says. "If you see a complete stranger standing on your front lawn carrying a fully loaded rifle, are you going to assume he's birdwatching? Dangerous things without context are scary. They *should* be scary."

"That was a perfectly reasonable view to take *eighty years ago*," CB says, voice rising. "There was no context *eighty years ago*. There's *plenty* of context now. Hell, there's not just *context*, there's *precedent*. There are laws and metahuman cops and a great big fucking jail and 'metahumans are new and scary' is not an excuse any more."

Roger takes a deep breath, forcing himself to calm down. "CB, people have a *right* to be afraid of us."

CB doesn't reply.

"I am *powerful*," Roger continues, "and I am *dangerous*. I could destroy New York City if I wanted to. I could destroy *any* city, if I wanted to. I can't think of too many people who could stop me. The few who come to mind are other metahumans, and some of them are *villains*. Some people look at me and see a guy who isn't destroying the world only because *I've decided not to*. Their continued safety hinges on an arbitrary decision on my part. Can you *blame* them for being scared?"

"Yes," CB says. "I *sure as hell can*."

Roger sighs, exasperated. "Well I can't. CB, for as long as I've known you, you've railed against how the government is corrupt, how politicians are hypocrites, and how everybody just gives up and lets them get away with it. You want everything they do questioned, you want them to be forced to answer to anything they do that might harm somebody. Don't you think we should be held up to the same standard?"

CB doesn't answer.

"I think we should," Roger says. "Can you imagine what would happen if I crossed over to the dark side? You don't think people should have some kind of assurance that I'm not turning into a monster?"

CB sighs and spreads his hands. "I give up, Roger. Mea culpa."

"Don't give up," Roger says. "Just don't lose your perspective. We jumped through hoops when we did the job because it showed everyone that we knew there were boundaries, and that we respected them. There are rules you have to follow when you put on the white hat, and sometimes following those rules means the bad guys take advantage of you. That doesn't mean the rules aren't important."

"You sound like Alex," CB says.

Roger smiles. "Thanks."

They lapse into a brief silence, CB stewing in his thoughts, Roger content to watch the ocean roll by.

CB grimaces, reluctant to continue the argument, but he presses on. "Why didn't Alex go public about the virus?"

Roger looks surprised by the question. "You think anyone would have believed him?"

"Why not? He was *Liberty*. The world would believe him, right? Especially if he released that file... and he already has a reputation for exposing secret government plots against metahumans. Yeah, I'm pretty sure people would believe him. Not everyone, sure, but there'd be enough. So why didn't he?"

Roger frowns. "I'm still not convinced, but for the sake of argument: if the world *would* believe Liberty, I have no idea why he wouldn't go public."

"I do," CB says. "Because they'd screw us."

"Come on, CB—"

"Not *all* of them," CB says. "Just the government."

"Come *on*, CB—"

"Someone is trying to *murder* us, Roger. They're trying to murder us, and they're willing to murder *regular people* to do it. Guys who haven't done a damn thing other than to be born with one fucking piece of DNA that means jack shit to them are doomed to die, just to get at us."

He flicks the stub of his cigarette across the water, watching it tumble end over end as it disappears into the ocean.

"Just the men," Roger says.

"I don't know about you," CB says, reaching into his trenchcoat pocket for another cigarette, "but I don't find that distinction very comforting. And it's not exactly true: the virus can kill any metahuman, right? It's just the delivery system that focuses on men. What else are they cooking up? Aerosol delivery systems? Infecting the nation's blood supply? Finding another spell? I don't think these assholes are going to be satisfied with just the X-Y set."

"Yeah, OK," Roger says. "Fair point. What does that have to do with people screwing us?"

CB pulls his lighter out of his other pocket and cups his hand to shield it from the wind. "Because we went public with PRODIGY. Remember what happened? We went public, the government declared the project was illegal, they arrested a bunch of bad guys, and *every single damn elected official* talked about how *horrifying* it was that someone had invented technology to enslave and control metahumans. Then there was *announcement* after *announcement* about how all the technology and research had been *destroyed*. So what happened in Farraday City, Roger? I had to kill a man because he'd been hooked up to the thing everybody *swore* had been destroyed!"

Roger's eyes widen as he sees it.

"Yeah," CB says. "Someone screwed us. Someone decided those things were *too valuable* to destroy. Someone decided there was too much to *learn* from it. But they didn't tell anyone—no, they didn't do that—because they didn't want to deal with the fallout from the metahuman community. They wanted an ace in the hole."

"You think Alex knew?" Roger asks.

"About the harness? I don't know. But he knew the virus was based on

PRODIGY research, that was right in the file. And there's your answer: he didn't tell the world because he didn't want the government to swoop in, take charge, and tell everyone that everything was OK, all the while locking away the virus in a safe somewhere 'just in case they need it later.' Which is *exactly* what they'd do, because why wouldn't they?"

"Because they see lots of people with loaded rifles," Roger says.

"Yeah," CB says. "All standing on their front lawn. I get it. They're frightened. They don't trust us. Some don't like us, and some downright *hate* us. But all the empathy in the world won't change the fact that someday, someone would come up with an excuse to *use* it. And we'd be right here all over again."

"So you think Alex sent you the file because it had to be handled *unconventionally*."

"That's kind of my thing," CB says. "When he sent me that file, do you know what he said in the email? I don't know if I ever told anyone. He said 'you know how I always tell you to tone things down? To show restraint?' And then he said 'not this time. Give 'em hell. It's no less than they deserve.'"

Clouds pass over the sun, momentarily dimming the day.

"Since the first day I met him," CB says, "Alex has always told me to pull back. He once said that when I do what I do, it's the equivalent of throwing a live grenade into a crowd of people. He always tried to get me to push only when I had to, and to try to do everything the hard way. I'm not saying I always listened to him, but he was always about me scaling back. And *he* told me to take off the kid gloves. He told me they *deserved* it."

Roger looks away.

"Sorry, Roger. In a perfect world I'd be all for truth and justice and wearing the white hat, but the stakes are too high to do this the regular way. I don't know how to survive this without crossing a line."

Roger stands, the planks squeaking softly as he shifts his weight. "Maybe." He turns his back to the ocean, staring inland toward the town. "Maybe you're right. But I think you're missing an important point, CB. In a perfect world, you wouldn't *need* the white hat. In a perfect world, the lines would be irrelevant. The reason we have lines we don't cross is because the world *isn't* perfect, and we're trying to make it *better*."

"Sometimes you can't change the world," CB says. "Sometimes all you can do is survive it."

Roger looks at CB, sighs softly, and rises up into the air. Seconds later he shoots across the sky, disappearing from view.

CB watches the ocean as he smokes.

Part One: South Bronx, Morrisania

Years ago the sight of a young black woman sitting alone at Elliot's Diner might have been cause for concern. Morrisania was once considered the worst the South Bronx had to offer, and the Diner was the unofficial stomping grounds of the Red Sevens, a gang with a reputation for ruthlessness and cruelty. Back then, anyone who wasn't a Red Seven would immediately be marked a victim if they dared set foot in the place—and a young woman would be considered particularly vulnerable, no matter who she was.

That was before Jacob Dupree bought the place. Before his niece and nephew moved in. Before the Bastions claimed Morrisania as their own.

Alishia Webb sits at the only booth in the diner, enjoying a cold cut sandwich and a glass of iced tea. The diner is small and worn, the latter a byproduct of age rather than neglect. Indeed, there is no trace of neglect here: the floor tiles are cracked, but each broken tile has been repaired with mortar, and the floor is well-cleaned. The windows are old, and the panes rattle any time a stiff breeze blows, but the latches are in good repair and the frames are painted regularly. The tables, chairs, and the one booth are a mishmash of many styles—whatever Jacob could get his hands on at any given time—but they are clean, and none of the chairs or tables wobble.

The food is good, too.

She's out of uniform, dressed well but not expensively: orange blouse, white Capri pants, orange, thick-soled clogs. Her thick black hair is tied back in a white scarf; a black-and-silver handbag sits on the table to her right. It speaks to no particular style other than her own, and it's not gaudy or flashy enough to command attention.

The silver badge sitting on the table at her left, however... *that* commands attention. Police aren't well liked in Morrisania. For a very long time, the police were as much of a problem as the gangs, and from what she's heard, the situation hasn't so much *improved* as *stayed away*.

A shadow falls over her as someone slides onto the other bench. She looks up from her food to see a tall, thin black man—so thin he's almost gaunt—wearing a dark suit, a gray silk tie, and a black trenchcoat. Long, thin dreadlocks are pulled back into a ponytail; sport sunglasses cover his eyes.

Alishia sets down the rest of her cold cut and wipes the corner of her mouth with a napkin. The man stares at her badge. It rises into the air and turns toward him. He studies it for a moment, then studies *her*. She feels a faint tickle just behind her left eye and immediately goes through the mental exercise of hardening her will to block a telepath.

One corner of the man's mouth turns up. The tickling sensation eases off.

"Brother Judgment." Alishia says it matter-of-factly. It can't be anyone else.

The man inclines his head slightly. "Sergeant Webb." His voice doesn't quite match up with his frame. He's so thin he almost looks frail, but his voice is deep and strong.

The badge settles gently on the table, almost exactly where it started. Alishia moves it into her handbag—it did what she needed it to do. She doesn't need it any more.

"You're not a local."

Brother Judgment's voice doesn't betray any hostility, but she knows it's there. The Bastions have an unpleasant history with the local precinct—unpleasant to the point where every Bastion has an active warrant out against them.

"Not a local," she agrees. "I'm not officially here."

"You sure?" Brother Judgment has a great poker face, but his voice carries a hint of amusement. "You flashed your badge."

"Just putting my cards on the table," Alishia says. "Your file says you respect that."

The eyebrow inches up a little higher. "My file?"

"Not an official one," Alishia says. "More of a... passing of knowledge, from a mentor, passed on to his replacement."

Brother Judgment tilts his head slowly to one side, as if the new angle might give him extra insight into the woman sitting in front of him. "You had a mentor? And he told you about me?"

Alishia nods.

"Who was this mentor?"

"David Bernard."

Brother Judgment goes completely still. Alishia feels the hairs rise on the back of her neck, and her left eye starts to tickle again. This time, she doesn't try to stop it.

He leans forward, elbows resting on the table, and lowers his voice. "You're the new Sky Commando."

Alishia simply nods.

He straightens, his voice rising. "Jake, we need the room."

An older, hefty man, hair gray and thinning, leans out from the door that leads into the kitchen. "How long?"

"Half hour."

"'Kay."

The older man steps around the counter, stops at the entrance just long enough to flip the sign from "Open" to "Closed," then passes through the door onto the sidewalk beyond. Soft bells jingle as the door swings shut. Brother Judgment stands, stretching, and walks over to the front counter. He leans against it, watching Alishia carefully.

"We can talk now."

Alishia's gaze drifts over to the entrance. "He's going to lose money because of this."

"He'll be OK. This talk should be private."

"I agree," Alishia says. "I just figured you'd choose a different way to do that."

Brother Judgment shakes his head. "Ever had a long conversation telepathically?"

"No," Alishia admits.

"Tiring. And a little invasive for non-telepaths, since it involves mind control."

Alishia looks up in surprise. "It does?"

"Let's get to the point," Brother Judgment says. "I promised Jake we'd only take half an hour. So let me give you the same spiel I gave David: we're not going to register. I'm not saying all cops are bad, but the ones around here are, and *we won't work with them*. David was OK with that. If you aren't, we're going to have problems."

"I don't have a problem with that," Alishia says. "That's not why I'm here."

"You're not recruiting?" Brother Judgment sounds surprised. "It's one of the first things David tried."

"I know," Alishia says. "He put that in your file. He also said you wouldn't. I can't argue with your reasons. I don't like them, and I think you're walking a real fine line, but the Lieutenant was a pretty good judge of character. Most of the time."

"Was?" Brother Judgment tenses, voice sharp. "Did something happen to him?"

"You'd know better than I would," Alishia says coolly.

Brother Judgment relaxes slightly. "I got nothing to say about that."

"Didn't think you did," Alishia says. "I'm not here about that, either."

"Why *are* you here?" He pulls on his trenchcoat, a single, sharp, agitated motion. "To say hello?"

Alishia shrugs. "Partially. The Lieutenant considered you one of the good guys. For the most part. So I came, in part, to say that until you show me otherwise I'm following his lead."

"I see." Brother Judgment tugs at his trenchcoat again. "Partially. So what's the other reason?"

"To ask for your help," Alishia says.

That catches the man off guard. "I told you we don't work with cops."

"I'm not asking you to join a task force," Alishia says. "In fact, I'm asking you to help us catch one of the dirtiest cops I've ever met."

Brother Judgment tilts his head to the side again, lips pursed thoughtfully. "What do you want the Bastions to do?"

"Not the Bastions," Alishia says. "*You.* I need a telepath—specifically I need a telepath I can *trust.* I don't know any, but the Lieutenant trusted you, and that'll do for now. If you help me I *will* trust you, and I think that would be good for both of us."

Brother Judgment thinks it over. "I don't know what help I'll be." He doesn't sound dismissive, just thoughtful. "I mean, I know how telepathy helps *me*, but I don't have to worry about a judge throwing out an arrest. Telepathy doesn't play well in court."

Alishia nods. "I know. But what I want you to do doesn't fall into that mess."

"Really?"

"Really," she says. "If I asked you to read the perp's mind, yeah, that would stir up a legal shitstorm. But I don't want you to read his mind. The guy you're going to work with will be a willing, cooperative recipient... within limits, which you will agree to if you take this on. And we'll know beforehand whether or not you mean it."

"Yeah?" He sounds interested in spite of himself. "How will you know that?"

Alishia gestures to the empty bench across the table.

Brother Judgment frowns, hesitates, then shrugs. He walks over and slides back into the bench, hands folded, elbows resting on the table.

"Let's hear it," he says.

Alishia smiles. "A little background information first. Have you ever heard of a part of the DHS called Division M?"

Part Two: Robert Thorpe's Office

Robert Thorpe's pain is real. The pain's location isn't.

He feels pain because his nervous system is damaged. The kind of pain changes: sometimes he has headaches, sometimes he has muscle cramps, sometimes he has sharp, stabbing pain going up and down an arm, or a leg. Today his pain is in his lower back, and it's more severe than usual.

There's never anything specifically wrong with the part of his body that's suffering at any given time, but he feels the pain all the same.

He eases back in his chair, exhaling in relief as he sinks into the heated cushion. His back may not actually be damaged, but for the moment his brain is convinced that it is, and the heat acts as an effective placebo.

"I'll be ready in a minute." He tries to keep the weariness out of his voice.

He closes his eyes. He hasn't figured out why, but reducing sensory stimulation often helps manage the pain. In a few minutes he feels it ebb. It doesn't disappear, and won't for another hour or so, but the heat combined with the aspirin he took moments earlier will dial it back to a dull, throbbing ache. He can handle an ache.

He exhales, opening his eyes, and turns in his seat to face the other men. The three chairs set in front of his desk are all occupied: CB is splayed out in the chair on the left, looking as if he slept in his trenchcoat, which he may actually have done. Agent Grant slouches in the chair on the right, looking considerably more put together in his neatly pressed black suit and matching black trenchcoat. In the center chair is Artemis LaFleur, dressed in slacks, deck shoes, and an expensive silk shirt, looking relaxed and serene—as if he were on vacation.

"I suppose you're wondering why I gathered you here today."

CB snorts at that, shaking his head as he thrusts his hand deep into his trenchcoat pocket, fumbling with what Robert suspects is a pack of cigarettes. He looks haggard; he's been wrestling with something ever since they learned what Project Recall really was. He hasn't talked about it, but Robert has a vague notion of what it might be, and it worries him.

"If you're about to accuse one of us of murder, I'm arresting LaFleur." Grant smooths out the folds from his own trenchcoat as he speaks, his voice thick with sarcasm.

Out of all the members of this uneasy alliance, Agent Alan Grant and his partner, Agent Lijuan Hu, are the ones Robert knows the least. Normally that would be cause for concern—not the least because they are part of the

Department of Homeland Security. But Pete Travers vouches for them, and Robert trusts Travers.

"I won't be plagiarizing Agatha Christie today," Robert promises.

"Even if he did," LaFleur says, smiling slightly, "I doubt you would be able to keep me in restraints."

It isn't spoken as a threat, or even as a dare. Once, Robert might have taken it as either, but he understands LaFleur much better than he did ten years ago. He's certainly capable of bravado, but he's not a man to engage in it carelessly. It would provide no tactical advantage in this situation, so he doesn't bother. Instead he's simply... making conversation.

Grant appears unruffled. "Yeah, probably not. But it'd be a hell of a story back at the office. 'Yeah guys, I was right there ready to put the cuffs on Overmind but the old bastard said something cheeky and teleported away.'"

LaFleur chuckles softly. "I'm not really one for cheek."

"I might be projecting a little."

"If I may," Robert says, and immediately all eyes are on him. He nods in acknowledgment. "The reason I called you here is simple. Thanks to your willingness to donate genetic material for testing, we've made great strides in understanding how the virus targets metahuman DNA. We still haven't made the leap we need to make from seeing what it does to understanding how to stop it, unfortunately, but we have enough material to work with to keep moving forward."

Agent Grant looks to his right, first at LaFleur, then at CB, then turns back to Robert. "That's great, but isn't that something you should tell the whole group? I mean everybody donated. I'm kinda curious to know how you actually managed to extract genetic material from Regiment and Scrapper Jack, by the way. I'd think that'd be like trying to saw through cinderblock with a butterknife."

"That's a more accurate metaphor than you realize," Robert says. "Let's just say that I'm grateful both men exhibit a great deal of self-control. But you three aren't here to discuss our research. Not exactly. You're here because we haven't been able to use you in our research at all."

"Oh?" LaFleur leans forward slightly. "Were our samples contaminated somehow?"

"No," Robert says, "they were fine. They just didn't have anything we could use."

LaFleur's right eyebrow rises higher. He leans back in his chair, nodding thoughtfully. *He understands*, Robert thinks. *It's hardly surprising.*

This is his field of expertise.

It is *not* CB's field of expertise. "I don't get it." He leans forward, drawing that pack of cigarettes out of his pocket and absently thumping it against the palm of his left hand. "If the samples were fine, why couldn't you use them?"

"CB, do you remember back when the Guardians applied for government sanction?"

CB rolls his eyes. "I remember all those fucking tests, is what I remember."

"I remember how amused you were that all your tests came back negative," Robert says.

CB laughs. "That was hilarious. Until they demanded I do the tests again a third time, anyway."

"I always assumed that was your power at work." Robert shifts slightly to include LaFleur and Agent Grant in the conversation. "In 1989 the Guardians of Justice applied for government sanction—at that time it was run by the FBI, though the FBMA took it over a few years later. One of the preconditions of sanction was that each of us go through a battery of tests that were a precursor to the Dyson-Ferris Assessment."

Agent Grant nods. "Dyson-Ferris Assessment is still a requirement for sanction."

"The tests back then were rather rudimentary," Robert says. "But they worked well enough for most of us. Not, however, for Curveball. He tested as a normal human all five times."

Agent Grant stares at CB, frowning. His gaze drifts over to LaFleur.

LaFleur nods. "I also test negative on the Dyson-Ferris. Though I've never been in a position to have it administered in an official capacity."

"Yeah..." Grant slowly turns his gaze back to Robert. "That would be hard to pull off, you being a standing threat to national security and all."

"What I would like to confirm," Robert says, "is that you, Agent Grant, also test negative on the Dyson-Ferris."

CB and LaFleur stare at Agent Grant expectantly. For a moment, Grant doesn't react. Then, reluctantly, he nods.

"I thought so," Robert says.

"That's weird," CB says.

"Not as weird as you think..." Robert takes a moment to choose his words. "The DFA is the gold standard for metahuman assessment, but it's still not perfect. There are always outliers. People who have certain types of abilities are more likely to test negative than others—weather manipulators, for example, have always tested negative. As a general rule of thumb, the more unusual someone's ability is, the less likely they are to test positive."

"That would explain us," CB says. "Assuming Agent Grant's right about what he does."

"Damn skippy I am," Grant says.

"Teleporters in general tend to be edge cases for the assessment," Robert says, "but teleporting into multiple locations simultaneously, and being able to maintain those locations concurrently? I've never heard of that before. But you're actually wrong about that, CB. It doesn't explain anything."

CB exhales forcefully, exasperation starting to show. "Damn it, Robert..."

"I'm getting to the point," Robert says. "I promise. The problem is that you're assuming the assessment could one day be refined to the point where it would detect you. That if it had enough information on all the metahuman DNA out there, it would, eventually, detect and classify the three of you."

"I guess I am," CB admits. "That's not true?"

"I'm pretty certain it isn't," Robert says. "Project Recall is many terrible things, but it has achieved what many of us have tried to do for decades: it has identified the genetic markers that must be present in order for metahuman abilities to manifest. Having those markers doesn't guarantee that someone will be a metahuman, but not having them guarantees that they won't."

"With that information," LaFleur says, "it would be theoretically possible to fine-tune the Dyson-Ferris Assessment to the point that it would always detect a metahuman."

"It would," Robert agrees, "and it still wouldn't matter for you three. None of you have those markers."

LaFleur sits back, nodding once as Robert confirms what he'd already deduced. CB and Agent Grant wear oddly similar expressions of blank incomprehension.

"Let me put it this way," Robert says. "The reason you three don't test as metahumans isn't because you're edge cases. It's because you're not metahumans at all. You don't have any of the genetic material necessary."

"Then... what are we?" CB asks.

Robert spreads his hands, gesturing helplessly. "Damned if I know."

Part Three: Thorpe Island

David Bernard shivers slightly as he steps into the large gym. Large, and mostly empty—most people are at work, and the few who are there are sticking to the stationary bikes.

It's a well-provisioned gym. There are the traditional stationary bikes, ellipticals, free weights, bench weights and weight machines, as well as some devices David recognizes as specific to physical therapy and rehabilitation. He hasn't used any of them—healing from the concussion came first—but they were all in his future, once upon a time.

Not any more. Creepy magic island took care of that.

"Oh. Hey."

David turns, surprised, and sees Jenny Forrest standing no more than three feet away from him. She's dressed in jogging shorts, tennis shoes, and a t-shirt. Her face and hair are plastered with sweat.

"Oh... Zero." David steps forward and to the side as he realizes he's been standing in front of the door the whole time. "Sorry. I've been getting distracted lately."

"No problem. And unless you've joined Crossfire, please call me Jenny."

David smiles slightly. "I don't think I'm Crossfire material. 'Jenny' it is."

"You shaved," she says.

David's hand drifts up to scratch his newly-bare chin. "Yeah. That beard was making me crazy."

He suddenly feels very awkward being at the gym. Jenny has Liberty's abilities, and she's radiating so much health and vitality that he feels as if he's about to topple over by comparison.

"Are you... here to work out?" Jenny keeps her voice neutral, but she eyes him critically.

David looks around the gym again. "The doctors say not yet."

He's completely unprepared for the bitterness in his voice. He's also completely unprepared for the emotion that comes with it—frustration, impatience, *rage* at being *constrained*. Something slithers just beyond his conscious mind, he can almost hear it whispering *yoU neeD nEveR be deniEd mAsHEuDh if yOu but loOsE mE*

"Hey." The firmness in Jenny's voice cuts through the rage and chases the *something else* away, back into dark corners. David focuses on her. She stares at him cautiously.

"Sorry." David takes a deep, steadying breath. "Sorry."

"You all right?"

"It's been a long year," David says. "Things got weird at the end."

Jenny snorts. "Tell me about it. Actually—hey, that's not a bad idea. I'm starving, you look like you need to eat more than you need to bench, and I can't believe I'm saying this, but the food here is actually pretty good. Let's go to the cafeteria, and you can tell me how you went from Sky Commando to Weird Magic Guy."

David starts to refuse, still unsettled by his sudden outburst, but his stomach starts to growl.

Jenny grins. "I'll take that as yes."

David sighs. "Yeah, OK. But *Weird Magic Guy*?"

"You're a superhero again," Jenny says. "Crossfire has to call you *something*."

"Right," David says. "Shit. I forgot all about that."

"I guarantee *they* haven't," Jenny says. "Also, Red Shift and Street Ronin found a website with a superhero name generator. If you don't come up with a name soon you might wind up *Commander Rapid Catman...*"

* * *

Jenny is right—the food in the cafeteria is pretty good. When she gets to their table, her tray is full of salad, lean chicken, fruits, and fresh vegetables. David's, on the other hand, is full of fried food, greasy food, and salty food.

"You eat like CB," Jenny says. "But he smokes, so it's not like he can actually *taste* any of it. What's your excuse?"

David laughs. "I was stuck for a year on a creepy magic island with nothing to eat and drink but fruit, orange juice, and milk."

"Right." Jenny eyes David's lunch warily. "Is that why you're so skinny? No offense, but you actually look worse than you did last week."

"I am." Suddenly his meal doesn't look as appetizing as it did a few moments ago. He forces himself to take a bite of fried chicken, forcing it down before replying further.

Actually tasting the food helps. *Grease is delicious.*

"It's complicated," David continues. "The food I was eating on the island... I can't really explain it very well, but basically the island is locked in the last twenty four hours of its existence. Everything on that island resets to whatever state it's in when the twenty four hours begin."

Jenny mulls that over. "So the food you ate basically disappears from your body and reappears on whatever shelf you found it on?"

"Yeah, actually. I guess it's not that complicated."

"No," Jenny says, "that sounds pretty complicated. How did you manage not to starve if you couldn't actually permanently eat anything?"

David shrugs. "Magic, I guess."

"I thought magic was evil."

"It is," David says. "This is more of a byproduct of what the magic did to that island. Anything trapped on that island can't really change, and I was at least partially trapped for most of my time there. That mitigated some of it."

"So it's catching up to you now?" Jenny frowns. "Shouldn't you be on a twnty-four/seven IV or something?"

"At this point it's not the food," David says. "It's the magic."

"Right," Jenny says. "That's the part I want to hear about…"

David tells her about the island, the trap, and how he managed to escape it by dreaming. He describes learning to manipulate the island while he was dreaming, and how he rescued Artemis LaFleur from Artigenian's mark, absorbing a piece of Artigenian's power in the process. When he finishes, he can feel that power stirring again, and for a few moments the room spins as the whispers in his mind grow stronger.

masHEuDh

He forces it back, then shrugs.

"The Law of Unintended Consequences. As soon as we got off the island I started cocooning. Apparently stealing an evil wizard's power does things to you."

"I guess so." Jenny studies him closely. "How does it feel?"

"Sometimes I feel normal," David says. "Sometimes it's weird. I don't think I can explain it any better than that just yet."

"Fair enough," Jenny says. "But you're totally a wizard now, right?"

"Not if I can help it…" David decides it's time to change the subject. "But now it's your turn, *Zero*. What's this I hear about you taking on Johann Richter?"

Jenny reddens slightly. "It's not a big deal."

"Great-granddaughter of Liberty inherits his powers and winds up kicking the ass of his arch-nemesis? That's a big deal. Tell."

Jenny pokes at her food, voice subdued. "There are parts of it I'm still working through."

David shrugs. "So don't tell me those parts. I didn't tell you everything."

"There's *more*?" Jenny shakes her head. "Well. OK. Then I guess it starts when CB and I head over to his apartment, where he stashed some of his old gear…"

Part Four: Thorpe's Office, Later That Day

Artemis LaFleur and Robert Thorpe sit alone in Robert's office, drinking coffee.

They haven't spoken of anything important—other than how each prefers their coffee prepared—since CB and Agent Grant left. Artemis drinks his coffee slowly, savoring the bitterness and the heat, and waits.

He is very good at waiting.

Finally Robert sets his cup down and sighs in relief. He adjusts his seat, sitting more fully upright.

"You're feeling better now." Artemis studies the other man carefully. Robert carries most of his tension in his eyes, and the tightness around them is mostly gone.

Robert nods. "Much. Here's hoping for a few good days. I've got a lot to do."

"Like salvaging a fracturing alliance."

Robert sighs again, this time without relief. "I'm hoping the alliance is self-repairing."

Artemis smiles thinly. "But what do you *assess?*"

Robert's eyes unfocus slightly. He absently swirls his coffee in its mug, the brown liquid almost splashing over the side onto his hands. He's tapping into the metahuman portions of his intellect, Artemis realizes, and he's using it not to unravel the mysteries of science—he's trying to unravel the mysteries of *people*.

He didn't realize Robert could do that. He wonders how reliable it is.

"Hard to say," Robert says. "I think CB and Agent Grant are the weak links in the chain." His eyes focus again, and his coffee stops swirling.

"Indeed?" Artemis keeps his expression neutral. "I had assumed the weak link would be Crossfire."

"I doubt that very much." Robert's amusement is so dry it's barely detectable. "Given their focus, Crossfire is probably the most consistently reliable group among us. I'll be very surprised if you haven't reached the same conclusion."

Artemis nods, conceding the point. "Vigilante's suggestion that we kidnap and interrogate a US senator is deeply problematic for the other heroes, but they offered it up as a way to get us potentially useful information and to buy us space and time, by having all the focus of that act fall on them alone. They've already decided to throw their lot in with the rest of us."

"Whether we like it or not." Robert's amusement is much less dry this time.

"Which brings us to Regiment," Artemis says. "Will he pose a problem?"

Robert's eyes unfocus again. "No…" He focuses again, and shakes his head. "No, Roger isn't happy working with Crossfire, but he sees the big picture. And he's been in this situation before. Prodigy."

"True," Artemis says, "but Curveball was in the same situation. You're worried about him."

"It's different," Robert says. "They're not the same people. Roger embodies *restraint*. He has to—if he doesn't, he breaks something. Or someone. CB… well, restraint isn't easy for him. Alex was a steadying influence…"

"A steadying influence…" Artemis nods thoughtfully. "And now that Liberty is dead, you fear he will begin to drift back into his old ways? Back to villainy?"

"No," Robert says. "Well… not exactly. But you heard what he said at the end, there. About us not being able to handle what needs to be done. CB never talked about his days as a 'villain' much, but it seems to me he and his group were a lot closer to Crossfire than they were to the New Lords."

"That still makes him a criminal," Artemis notes.

"It does," Robert says. "Once upon a time, that would have bothered me more."

"So," Artemis says, "if you aren't afraid of his reverting to form, what is your concern?"

"Oh, I'm still worried about that. I'm afraid he's going to decide we won't commit to whatever he believes must be done, and set out on his own to do it himself."

"Hmmm." Artemis takes a sip of coffee and considers the possibility. "How certain are you?"

Robert grins. "Not very certain at all. This is CB we're talking about."

Artemis laughs softly. "A fair point. And to a certain extent I agree with you— of everyone in the group, he is most likely to go off in his own direction. I think, however, you can rest more easily when it comes to Special Agent Alan Grant."

"You know something about him I don't?"

"I know nearly nothing about him," Artemis says. "I did of course have some resources focused on Division M, but they identified Agent Grant as a teleporter with a somewhat brash personality. I knew nothing of his other talent."

"You still know more than I do," Robert says. "I'm reasonably confident in my estimates where the others are concerned, because I have a history with them—granted, my history with Jenny isn't in the right context to be useful— but Agents Grant and Hu are question marks for me. Hu seems to be a steadying influence on Grant, but I could be wrong there, too…"

"Don't dwell on what you don't know about them," Artemis advises. "Instead, think on what you know of Peter Travers."

"Right..." Robert's eyes unfocus again for a moment, then he nods slowly. "I trust Pete, and he trusts them. If he trusts them in *this* situation, then I can infer that they are both dedicated agents, but also possess a level of flexibility needed to handle the... *oddities* of this situation."

"I agree," Artemis says. "This is supported by their reaction to my presence. They certainly aren't happy I'm here, but they've mostly accepted it... Grant's jibes notwithstanding."

"So it's down to CB, then," Robert says.

"It is."

Robert sighs, sips his coffee, then sets the mug on his desk with a loud thunk. "Well, maybe this new discovery about his genetic origins—or lack of them—will keep him around until I can come up with a proper reason."

"Is that why you told us?" Artemis asks, surprised. "An interesting maneuver."

"What? No." Robert waves his hand dismissively. "It just occurred to me. I told you because it's *fascinating*."

"And tactically useful," Artemis says. "You've discovered that three of us are immune to the virus."

"Five of you, actually," Robert says. "The three of you are immune because you don't have the genetic markers, yes, but neither does Street Ronin, who is baseline human in every way, and every test we've performed on Vigilante suggests that the virus would be destroyed the instant it tried to enter his body."

"Truly?" Artemis sounds impressed.

"I don't even know where to begin measuring his ability to heal," Robert admits. "Quite frankly, it's a bit frightening. He claims to have survived literal disintegration—though he says 'it took a while'—and Street Ronin and Red Shift back him up on it."

"I'm aware of that rumor," Artemis says. "It's certainly helped Crossfire's reputation quite a bit in certain corners of my side of things, but I doubt it's as straightforward as they claim."

"Whatever the truth of it is, the virus doesn't have a chance against the samples he provided. And he doesn't seem intimidated by it, either: he actually volunteered to be injected with it outright."

Artemis raises an eyebrow.

"Out of the question, of course." Robert shakes his head. "I'm pretty confident he would survive, but I'm not that kind of scientist."

Artemis considers the matter. "No," he says finally. "Neither am I. What about Bernard? He is human."

"Is he?" Robert asks. "Based on what you've told me, I don't think that's entirely true. He was cocooning when we brought him here."

"Something very like it," Artemis says. "But when my abilities first manifested, I went through cocooning as well—and apparently I am not a metahuman at all."

"Hmmm." Robert's eyes unfocus again. "That's interesting, and I don't have an answer for it. But to answer the original question: David Bernard is unfortunately very much at risk. He has one of the metahuman genetic markers. Based on some of our initial tests using his samples, it looks as if he will react to the virus."

"Five it is," Artemis says. "Five of us immune to a virus designed to wipe out the entire metahuman population."

"We're going to need a new word for that," Robert says. "But it won't just be the five of you. The delivery mechanism targets males carrying the genetic markers. That's a small percentage of the population—women who carry the markers have a chance of avoiding infection."

"You can call it a spell, Robert."

Robert frowns. "I'm not entirely comfortable with that."

"I've never known you to be squeamish," Artemis says. "And based on Curveball's rudimentary familiarity with magic, I assumed the Guardians had encountered it, from time to time."

"We have," Robert says. "It's not that. I understand that magic is involved in this. I don't know a lot about it—only what you've told me, and the few things David Bernard has said—but if we assume the things you've told me are true, then this doesn't fit."

Now it's Artemis' turn to frown. "What do you mean?"

Robert leans forward. "You've described magic as an alien thing. A 'point of view absolutely opposed to any other point of view,' I believe is one of your favorite phrases."

Artemis nods. "It's the best I can manage."

"It works well enough. You've said that magic predates history—based on how poisonous it seems to be to anything it comes in contact with, I'm willing to go out on a completely unscientific limb and wildly speculate that it predates *reality*."

"Interesting," Artemis says. "It's something I've wondered, on a philosophical level. My former teacher referred to this world as 'the lie that is this creation.'"

"'The lie that is this creation.'" Robert repeats the words slowly. "That is a very specific point of view. A point of view that would place itself completely outside of this world, which seems to be how magic operates: it replaces pieces of our reality with something else."

"A reasonable hypothesis," Artemis says. "It would be difficult to test."

"And I'm not keen on trying to test it," Robert says. "That aside, if we assume for the moment the hypothesis is right, then the 'spell' that's being used as a delivery system *cannot be magic.*"

Artemis frowns deeply, brow furrowing. Then his eyes widen in shock. "Because it relies on science."

Robert nods. "It relies on science. Specifically, it relies on a very specific understanding of genetics in order to identify a very small percentage of the population."

"And magic wouldn't do that," Artemis says. "Not if we're assuming your hypothesis is correct. Which means your hypothesis must be incorrect."

"There's another possibility," Robert says. "Someone has discovered a way to alter magic. To *hybridize* it, and allow it to interact with, rather than supplant, our world. It's not magic in the classical sense, it's something new. Something *modern.*"

Something terrifying.

Neither of them bother to say it aloud. It simply hangs in the air, unspoken but mutually acknowledged.

"Which leads to one of the more important questions we need to answer," Robert says. "Who would have the knowledge, resources, and drive to do something like that?"

Artemis takes a deep, slow breath. "I would."

Robert starts in surprise. "Artemis?"

"Rather, a version of me. A shadow. Robert, I haven't been keeping this from you deliberately—I didn't learn of it until the day you revealed the truth about Project Recall, and at the time I feared bringing it up would simply complicate an already volatile situation. But I'm fairly certain I know who is behind this... and I think I even know why."

Robert stares at Artemis steadily. "Perhaps you'd better start at the beginning."

"Perhaps that would be best," Artemis agrees. "Very well. Let me start by telling you about a place that doesn't exist—a beautiful tropical island named 'Esperanza...'"

Part Five: Jacob K. Javits Federal Building

The Division M conference room is a large, well-equipped meeting room with a long table and comfortable chairs. Special Agent Phillip Henry sits at the middle position on the right side of the table, staring across at the two men on the left side. The two men—one a heavyset, sweating Federal Agent, the other a hardened, weather-beaten NYPD Cop—stare back grimly.

The heavyset sweating agent is Oliver Nuzzo. Henry doesn't know a lot about him. He's pulled the man's file: sixteen years in the FBI, a career that started out promising but petered out ten years in. It's the kind of thing you might expect to find on someone's file, if he was suddenly transferred into a top-secret task force.

The hardened, weather-beaten cop is Captain Clive Darius. Agent Henry knows a lot more about him. One of the most celebrated officers in the NYPD, credited with single-handedly cleaning up some of the more nefarious parts of the city, and—according to recently obtained video evidence—secretly working for an organization that may have been responsible for the murder of America's greatest hero.

Instinct tells Henry that Clive Darius is a dirty cop. The problem is, Darius and Nuzzo have an explanation for everything Henry has discovered. It's a good explanation. It fits. And what's more, Special Agent Phillip Henry—the only man alive with the ability to detect when someone is lying to him—can't detect any lies.

"Agent Henry, with all due respect." Nuzzo wipes sweat off his forehead with a thick, stained handkerchief. "I'm not happy about this meeting. I understand why you want it, but we feel exposed—given Captain Darius' circumstances, I'm sure you understand why."

Everything Nuzzo says is the truth. Henry is absolutely convinced of that. That doesn't mean Nuzzo isn't trying to play him—it is possible to "lie" to Agent Henry by saying true things in *just the right way*, to make him assume things that were never said—but it's not as easy to do as it was, when he was young, and cocky, and relied on his power too much.

Agent Henry adjusts the sunglasses on his face—the only thing preventing him from making eye contact and compelling them to speak only the literal truth at all times—and nods.

"Thank you for coming down."

"If we could get to the point," Nuzzo continues, "then we could—"

Darius interrupts the agent in mid-sentence. "Don't worry, Oliver, I get it. We're here because Agent Henry still thinks I'm dirty. I get it. I would too, if I were him."

Darius is not, it seems, a man with much patience for dancing around the subject.

"I have a video of you talking to armed men dressed in outfits matching the bodies of the men who attacked Martin Forrest's residence—men also linked to the murder of Alexander Morgan. You were clearly giving them orders, and they appear to have been sent to intercept a fugitive we were chasing at the time. I have the written testimony of both Sky Commando and one of my own agents that you deliberately attempted to keep us out of the TriHealth building, where something metahuman-related clearly happened. And now all of a sudden we've been ordered onto a task force—headed by you—which is supposed to take on the people you've clearly been working for." Agent Henry leans back, studying both of them. "Yes, I find it very difficult to take at face value. Especially since Division M is *more than cleared* to know about any investigations in this city that might cross into our own, and this obviously does."

Nuzzo coughs uncomfortably. "That was my decision. I didn't want the DHS interfering with our investigation."

An entirely plausible reason—a reason Agent Henry has run up against, and used himself, many times. It's also a lie: it was *not* Nuzzo's decision. That in itself means nothing, of course. Higher-ups force agents to lie on their behalf all the time. And the apologetic look on Nuzzo's face clearly shows that he knows exactly who Agent Henry is, and what he can do.

That's the problem with bureaucracy. Lies don't necessarily mean what you'd think they'd mean. Sometimes they don't mean anything at all.

"That's entirely possible, Agent Nuzzo. But I'd like to focus on Captain Darius for the moment."

Oliver Nuzzo wipes his forehead again and nods. He's not *nervous*, as far as Henry can tell. He's a man who sweats under pressure, which makes him *look* nervous, but he doesn't show any other physical signs of nervousness. Henry wonders what that means, or if it means anything at all.

"Let's just resolve this," Darius says. "Once and for all. Agent Henry, will you please remove your sunglasses?"

Agent Henry manages to conceal his surprise. "I'm not authorized to—"

Clive Darius slides a sheet of paper across the table. It is one of their own release forms, authorizing Agent Henry to use his full ability on the signatory. Clive Darius has signed his name in tight, neat script at the bottom. Off to the right, he sees the signature and seal of one of the judges they've used in the past.

Agent Henry stares at the paper. "You're certain?"

"I signed my name," Darius says.

Henry nods. "Very well. I will need witnesses present." He reaches for a phone sitting at the head of the table, picks up the receiver, and holds it to his ear. "Send in Frank and Malloy."

Moments later, the door to the conference room opens, and Special Agents Brian Frank and Desiree Malloy step in. They move to Agent Henry, one on each side, and sit at the table. Both have their poker faces on.

"Captain Darius has asked me to remove my sunglasses," Agent Henry says. He gestures to the release form.

Agent Malloy picks it up, scans it over quickly. She nods once, then hands it over to Frank, who looks it over curiously.

"We ready?" Darius sounds impatient. That's not usually how these things go.

"All right, but I need to explain how this works first. I don't have the power to force you to speak. Anything you say to me, for as long as we maintain eye contact, must be the truth. But you can still choose not to speak. You can also break eye contact at any time. I'm told some people find it more difficult to do than others, but it's possible."

"Whatever," Darius says. "Take off your goddamn sunglasses."

Agent Henry looks at Agent Frank, then Agent Malloy. Both nod. Then Agent Henry takes off his sunglasses, and looks Clive Darius in the eye.

Darius stiffens for a moment, then relaxes. "Six years ago I was approached by someone who claimed to be from the mayor's office. He asked me about some evidence we recovered from a sting the night before. I answered his questions, didn't think too much about it—I figured someone the Mayor knew had been part of the roundup and they were just trying to prep for the potential fallout. Next night someone broke into the evidence room, stole some of the evidence, all the paperwork on that evidence, and deleted the computer records about that evidence. Very thorough job. We never recovered it."

Agent Henry says nothing. He maintains eye contact.

"A week later the same man visits me in my office. I'm pissed; I threaten to arrest him on the spot. He tells me to shut up and listen, and then says that in return for my future cooperation he'll give me information on some of the better-hidden vice rings in the city. It's the kind of stuff we knew was out there, but could never get anyone to roll over on—child prostitution, slavery, that kind of thing. I'll admit I was tempted. I didn't really care about the little stuff. But I was also *pissed*. I didn't know who I could talk to about it—the guy was from the mayor's office, he might have other cops in his pocket—so I called the FBI. That's how I met Nuzzo here."

Nuzzo doesn't say anything.

"Turns out the guy who talked to me was a guy they were trying to learn more about. That's how I got sucked into Operation Bad Seed. I agreed to help the man—he only went by the name 'Andrew'—and that's when I first went undercover."

"Are you a dirty cop?" Agent Henry asks.

"Yes," Darius says. "I broke the law plenty of times. I used my position to make it easier for Andrew's people to get away with whatever it was they were doing. I did so under the supervision of the FBI, and I documented every illegal activity I was involved in."

"What were they doing?" Henry asks.

Darius grimaces. "I don't know. I mean, I could never figure out a big picture. Lots of smuggling, but I don't know what. Some theft, but I don't know what. There seemed to be two areas they were interested in—some kind of medical stuff, and antiques."

Agent Henry frowns slightly. "Antiques?"

Darius shrugs. "That's what it looked like to me. Stuff with some kind of historical value. I don't know why. I wasn't able to get far enough inside to figure out what was going on. I was starting to make inroads, the last couple years. Andrew left the picture and I started working for a guy named 'Douglas' and a woman named 'Veronica.' At that point I knew a lot of the things they did came out of the TriHealth building, but I felt I was being groomed to meet the organization behind that one. I met a few people I think were part of that other organization. I saw a few things that make me think I know where to start looking for more. I don't think they know I saw those things, but I can't be sure."

Darius sits back, still maintaining eye contact. "I was contacted by someone in the DHS—on Veronica's behalf—when Special Agent Peter Travers called you on your phone. They have someone in your group, Agent Henry, because they gave me his location based on a trace you ordered from your phone. They told me to coordinate with some of the enforcers this group uses—the ones you say you have on tape—in order to capture Travers before you arrived on the scene. Seems he was expecting us. Anyway, it all unraveled pretty quickly after that."

Darius falls silent at that point. Waiting. He doesn't break eye contact.

Agent Henry reaches for his sunglasses. He doesn't break his gaze with the captain until he puts them on. As soon as the glasses are back in place it's as if a spell has ended: Darius exhales, Nuzzo stretches, and Malloy and Frank push their chairs back from the table.

Agent Nuzzo is the first to stand. "I hate to be abrupt, but it's time to go."

True statement. Nuzzo genuinely hates being abrupt.

"That's fine," Agent Henry says, and stands as well. Frank and Malloy follow suit. "Thank you for coming by."

"I hope it helped." Darius this time.

"It did," Agent Henry says. "Thanks again."

"We'll contact your team when Operation Bad Seed is ready to move forward with its next phase," Nuzzo says. "It shouldn't be too long now."

True statement, as far as Nuzzo knows. Division M will be contacted soon.

"Thank you, Agent Nuzzo," Agent Henry says. "We'll be ready."

Henry, Frank, and Malloy watch Nuzzo and Darius leave. None of them say anything. A few minutes later, the phone on the meeting table rings.

Agent Henry picks it up. "Henry."

"They've left the building." It's Erin Collins, his second.

"Thank you Agent Collins. Please show Sergeant Webb and our consultant into the room."

Moments later the meeting room door opens again, and Agent Collins, Alishia Webb—Sky Commando—and a tall, thin black man in a trenchcoat enter the room.

Brother Judgment.

Agent Henry is uneasy about bringing a vigilante telepath into this matter, but he doesn't have any good options at the moment.

"Everyone have a seat," Agent Henry says, and they all sit down. His team relaxes almost instantly. Webb, out of uniform, is nervous but only a little. Brother Judgment sits, but he's obviously not comfortable. He looks as if he might be in pain.

Agent Henry looks to Collins. "Are we all set?"

"Worked like a charm," Collins says. "Video feed was perfect. Something definitely happened though. Brother Judgment froze up shortly after Darius started talking. Won't say why."

Agent Henry glances over at the vigilante. His brow is furrowed, his face is twisted into a mask of concentration. "Is something wrong?"

A brief flicker of something like pain crosses the other man's face. With a great deal of effort, he manages to nod, once.

Agent Henry looks at Webb.

"I don't know," Webb says, voice full of concern. "Like Collins said, this started when Darius started talking."

"I don't understand what—"

"Sunglasses." The word sounds like it's ripped out of Brother Judgment's mouth against its will. "Take. Off. Your. Sunglasses."

"There are papers you need to—" Agent Henry looks at the man and sighs. "Nevermind. You heard what I said over the feed?"

Brother Judgment nods.

"Fine." Agent Henry removes his sunglasses. "Look me in the eye."

Brother Judgment does. Immediately his face relaxes.

"What's going on?" Henry asks.

"I'm not sure." Brother Judgment's answer is immediate, his voice full of relief. "Something was preventing me from speaking. I don't understand why. Gambled your ability might override it. Gambled right."

"Can you be a little more specific?" Agent Henry asks.

Brother Judgment nods. "When Sky Commando told me about your situation, she wondered if it was possible Darius or someone else was doing something to you to keep your ability from working. So I had to get a baseline on you, to figure out how it worked."

"That would have been our interview this afternoon," Agent Henry says.

"Yeah. You were asking me twenty questions, I was reading your mind to see how it worked on your end. It's weird—I assumed your thing was some kind of telepathy."

"It's not telepathy," Agent Henry says.

"Yeah." Brother Judgment shakes his head. "Point is, I knew what it was supposed to feel like when it was working. Figured I'd be able to tell when it was being messed with. It was a good plan—if all I did was read *your* mind, with your consent, you'd be able to present what I found if it was being messed with."

"But it didn't work that way," Agent Henry guesses.

"No it didn't. Any time *Captain Darius* started talking, you got *nothing*. That didn't make any sense. Your thing isn't just a lie detector, it's a truth detector too—you get a reaction any time someone tells you a truth *or* a lie. And Darius... well. He didn't give you *anything at all*."

"I know that." Agent Henry tries to keep the frustration out of his voice. "What I don't know is *why*."

"Well I do." Brother Judgment's voice is troubled. "I know why. But it won't be admissible in court."

Agent Henry narrows his eyes. "Explain."

Brother Judgment exhales heavily. "I thought maybe it was me. Like maybe my telepathy was on the fritz. Never happened before, but that didn't make any sense, so I did one of my easiest tricks. I started pinging minds. Best explanation is 'telepathic radar,' OK? Not reading thoughts, just detecting a location."

"I'm not sure what good that would do," Agent Henry says. "We knew where everyone was."

"I was just trying to make sure everything *worked*," Brother Judgment says. "It's easy for me. If you blindfolded me right now and moved around the room, I could point to each one of you and call you out by name. It's easy. And pretty useful. But here's the thing, Agent Henry: there were only four minds in that room."

"So something *was* wrong with your telepathy," Agent Henry says.

Brother Judgment shakes his head. "It was fine. I panicked a little at first, thinking the same thing, but then I realized I could detect everyone else—you, Nuzzo, Webb, Agent Collins, Agent Frank, Agent Malloy—but I couldn't detect Darius. It was like he *wasn't there*."

The room is very quiet. Agent Henry tries to wrap his brain around the concept, and fails.

"That's when I... froze up." Brother Judgment's eyes are wide with fear. "I tried to say something about it, and suddenly I *couldn't speak*. Any time I tried to say anything about it, or even refer to it sideways... I couldn't say anything at all."

"I see," Agent Henry says.

"You *don't* see," Brother Judgment says. "I don't see how you can, until you experience it. I knew there was something fucked up about Darius, but it was like something was building a wall between what I *knew* and what I could *say*. It got to the point where I was spending all my time trying to keep the last few bricks in that wall from being put in, and I wasn't going to hold out much longer. Whatever it is you do when your glasses come off… it seems to counteract that."

Everything the man says is coming in as *true, true, true, true, true…* normally, Henry wouldn't even stop to consider that—his glasses are off, he has eye contact, so it *has* to be true—but it's an extra layer of confirmation he finds he needs right now.

"All right," Agent Henry says. "All right. I know you're telling the truth. I just don't understand it right now. What was strange about Darius? I'm positive he's lying to me now, but I still don't get *anything* from him when he talks. No sense of lie, no sense of truth—I just get nothing. Why?"

"Your ability," Brother Judgment says. "It only works face to face, right? Doesn't work over the phone? You can't tell when someone's lying on TV?"

"People are always lying on TV," Agent Henry says. "But I take your point. Yes, it must be face to face."

"Well that's it," Brother Judgment says. "There were only four people in that room: you, Frank, Malloy, Nozzo. There was no Clive Darius. Whatever you were talking to in there, it *wasn't* Clive Darius. *Maybe* it was his body, but it wasn't his *mind*. Agent Henry… *that thing didn't have a mind*."

Part One: Haruspex Analytics, Top Floor

The Board Room is nearly empty, save for three figures sitting at the long, center table. One sits at the head of the table—the Chairman, his face shrouded in shadow, as always—while the other two sit at the far end, watching him intently.

The space between them is deliberate, and both sides are keenly aware of it.

"Thank you for coming." The Chairman doesn't move, other than a slight inclination of his head. The shadows around his face shift, lightening in places, darkening in others, thinning slightly around his high, sharp cheekbones. "You have traveled far outside your sphere, and I understand exactly what it means for you to travel so far within mine."

The words are that of a gracious lord, greeting his guests, but for those familiar with the protocols of the powers beneath the world, there is a second acknowledgment: *you have some power over me, even in this place.*

The two figures at the far end do not reply. One, a massive, hulking form, leans back in his chair, fingers folded over his stomach, heavy-lidded eyes half closed, as if he were falling asleep. The second, a smaller, slighter man, hunches forward, smiling faintly. His sharp eyes peer across the table, gazing at the Chairman with undisguised curiosity.

The Chairman waits a moment, giving them the opportunity to speak. He knows they won't—not yet—but it is appropriate to give them the chance.

"You have a grievance against me," the Chairman continues. "And your grievance has merit, I won't deny it. I invaded your city. I broke its most fundamental law. And it was I that broke it, sirs, though I have never set foot in it. I take full responsibility for it, and I acknowledge your complaint."

The tension rises perceptibly in the room.

"So great is my transgression," the Chairman continues, "that you would be fully within your rights to declare war on me and mine. None of the others would even *think* of intervening. And yet... you sit here, instead. You do not immediately sound the horn."

The smaller man stirs, his smile widening. "The Pythia." The razor-like quality of his voice matches the sharpness in his eyes. "There are those among us who will hear her voice... despite her *present allegiances.*"

It is not quite a snub. It is, rather, a reminder of where things stand—of where *he* stands.

"It was her reputation that convinced you to *hear her words,*" the

Chairman counters. "But she did not convince you to travel here, to hear mine."

It is not quite a reproach. It is, rather, a reminder that he knows how this game is played. The smaller man's smile widens, almost into a grin. He dips his head in acknowledgment.

"Let's not argue over why you decided to come," the Chairman says. "You are here. That is enough. You are here because you are curious. You have heard my claim, and you have decided that, preposterous though it may seem, it might actually be true. You wish to see for yourself. You wish to *know* for yourself."

The smaller man looks over his shoulder at the larger, bulky man. The large man doesn't react, still leaning back in his chair, hands clasped over his middle. The smaller man nods thoughtfully.

"We do," the smaller man admits. He leans forward again, returning his gaze to the Chairman. "You are a thing that should not be. That is not intended as insult, it is observation. There are many among us who would, if they knew exactly *what* you are, insist on calling you a *blasphemy*."

The Chairman chuckles softly, low and rich with amusement. "I suppose that isn't far wrong."

"A meaningless word," the smaller man says, waving his hand dismissively. "How does one profane the profane? You are a new thing, and a thing that should not, by our understanding, exist. And yet, you are here; we are speaking. If you can exist, then what else can? So yes, you are correct. You have attracted our interest. And your claim… well. If it is true, it changes much."

"It changes *everything*," the Chairman says. "Until this point the only viable anchor to the True Realm has been through people. Now it can be bound to *things*. Now it can *persist*. It does not exist in a pure state—it cannot, here—but… well. Perhaps a demonstration is in order."

In a smooth motion, he flings something down the length of the table with his left arm. Some*things*, rather: two black rectangles, roughly the size of domino pieces. Glowing purple symbols flit over the surface as they make their way down to the other end, each piece spinning and slipping against one another until they come to an abrupt halt in front of the smaller man.

"They are safe to touch. In fact, if you would be so kind as to place the ends together…"

The smaller man stares at the two blocks curiously, watching the runes slide across them, purple light flickering over his angular features. With an abrupt, birdlike motion he grabs one of the blocks, turns it sideways, and places it against the other.

The runes on both blocks flare up. The smaller man jerks his hand back, eyes widening, and with a sudden *hiss* a ragged disc, roughly the size of a dinner plate, opens above the blocks. The edges shimmer and pop as the disc fights to maintain its form, then with a sudden *snap* the edges smooth into a shimmering silver-gray, with only darkness within.

The room grows cold. The lights, already dim, flicker and fade even further. The only true light in the room comes from the brilliant purple-white of the runes on the blocks and the shining silver gray of the disk hanging over it.

From behind the portal, something shifts. They can feel it in the room—a thing *uncoiling*, slithering toward them. They feel anger, cold and pure, focusing on the shimmering portal and what lies outside. A sound emerges, a sound that isn't properly a sound, rather a *grinding silence*, and their ears ache as it pours out from the portal, a soundless shriek of pure, unending rage.

Quickly the smaller man grabs both blocks and pulls. They separate smoothly, and the shimmering portal collapses, sputtering out like a doused flame.

The smaller man looks over his shoulder. The larger man's heavy-lidded eyes are now fully open; he sits straight in his chair, fists clenched, as he stares at the two tiny blocks with intense, undisguised interest.

"A window only," the Chairman says. "Though it may be possible to communicate through it. There is a measure of awareness that passes between the two realms. As you saw."

The smaller man *hmmmms* his acknowledgment.

"I do not know how to open a *door* into the True Realm," the Chairman says. "I don't know if anyone could. But all this window requires is that the ends of those blocks be placed together."

The smaller man picks up the blocks, one in each hand, and studies them carefully. "There was a time when it would take the deaths of many men to achieve such a thing."

"There was a time," the Chairman says, "when power could only be moved through flesh. When our runes and sigils and words served only to bind power *to* the flesh, to increase the power even as the flesh is consumed. But I have learned another way."

"So it seems," the smaller man says. "How?"

The Chairman doesn't immediately respond. He sits, a dark, unmoving silhouette in the dim room, as the other men look on, waiting.

"Think of it as a kind of imbuement," the Chairman says. "The same instruments we use to attract and magnify power—runes, sigils, monoliths—can also be used to *bind* it, give it a kind of permanence. I can teach you the secret of it. I can show you how binding it changes it, and instruct you on the advantages and disadvantages of those changes."

"Aha." The smaller man grins as he places the obsidian blocks back on the table. "You *can* teach us. But *will* you? That is the question, oh Thing That Should Not Be. That is the *most important* question."

"I am *willing* to teach it," the Chairman says, "if *you* are willing to come to an accord."

"Then let us parley," the smaller man says. "We are here. We are listening. You have our *undivided attention.*"

Now it is the Chairman who leans forward. His eyes are still shadowed, but his chin and mouth are visible. "You have seen a little of my work. You know, in broad strokes, what I seek to accomplish with Project Recall."

It is a strong chin. They are very white teeth.

"We are not allies," the Chairman continues. "Anyone with any claim to wisdom will see that. But we need not be *enemies*. Not yet. Perhaps, at some point in the future, when only you and I remain. Perhaps then. But even then… I doubt our conflict will be resolved by active conquest. It will be resolved by proving that one of us is *right*. Nothing less will suffice. Any other victory would be *hollow.*"

The smaller man doesn't reply. His grin is fixed, rictus-like, on his face.

"What we can both agree on, I believe, is that there is a more immediate problem. There is a power that sits outside of our spheres. A rogue power, one that threatens to utterly break the game."

The smaller man nods, his expression never changing. "The metahumans."

"The metahumans," the Chairman agrees. "Not only are they unbound, but in ten to twenty years I predict their growth will accelerate dramatically, beyond what anyone is prepared to handle."

"And so you have decided to handle it now," the smaller man says.

"I have," the Chairman says. "If Project Recall succeeds—and it *will* succeed—I will *decimate* the herd. The ones who survive will be far easier to control. Or, at the very least, to contain."

"And you are convinced it will work?" The smaller man's face assumes a more neutral expression.

"It *does* work," the Chairman says. "It only needs refinement now. Refinement, and a suitable source of power."

"We will not allow our domain to be used in such a way," the smaller man says. "Not again."

The Chairman nods. "I do not intend to ask. Make no mistake, I do not *apologize* for my incursion. It was necessary. Out of all the old places, the mechanisms you put in place beneath your city made it ideal for what we needed to do. But I recognize that what I did incurs *debt*, and I will not incur it again."

"Very well," the smaller man says. "You have another place in mind."

"I do," the Chairman says.

"Then what do you want of us?"

"Your neutrality," the Chairman says. "Your pledge to stay out of the remainder of this fight. Oh, you can claim you have always been neutral if you wish, but I received your message quite clearly. No, forgive us our transgressions and *stand aside*. Allow us to complete our grand work. No interference. In return, the knowledge I have is yours."

Immediately the smaller man turns to the larger, his sharp eyes peering at his companion. The larger man continues to stare at the Chairman, unmoving, unspeaking. Despite his silence, the smaller man begins to nod.

"Yes," the smaller man says. "Yes, I see. It is true. It will be necessary."

The smaller man turns back to the Chairman and stands. As he rises, he reaches into the seat next to his, picks up a bowler hat, and places it on his head.

"We are not opposed to your proposal," he says. "Normally we would reject such a thing out of hand, but the *magnitude* of what you offer... well, there are some, on your side and on mine, who would recoil at such a thing. A change too great, it might be said. But we cannot ignore it. We *will not* ignore it. But you have miscalculated with your offer."

"Have I?" the Chairman asks, sounding genuinely surprised.

"You have." The smaller man beams. "It is not a grave miscalculation— quite frankly I expected one so young to do far worse—and it can be fixed, I think, to both our satisfaction. Though perhaps more to *our* satisfaction than to yours."

The Chairman sits in silence, waiting.

"The problem, you see, is that you have been carried away, *rapturously* so, by your new discovery. I quite understand why. It has the potential to change everything—in fact I'm quite sure it is changing everything *now*. But you have forgotten that the old laws—the *oldest* laws—still have sway, at least for now. They must be *appeased*."

"I have not forgotten," the Chairman starts to say, but the smaller man cuts him off with a wave of his hand.

"You have *partially* forgotten," the smaller man says. "You acknowledge your debt to us, which is proper, but you seek to pay us weregild in restitution. Make no mistake, your offer is one we *wish* to accept, but the oldest laws are clear: there are only two payments that can be offered, the greater and the lesser. Until the oldest laws can be broken, we are bound by them. *You* are not, it seems—you are a strange thing—but we are."

"I see," the Chairman says. If he is offended at being called a thing, he does not show it. "Yes... I see your point."

"Given what you know," the smaller man says, "and given what you offer... we have no interest in your annihilation. So this is our proposal: in return for your weregild, we will accept the lesser price."

The Chairman hesitates. The smaller man can almost feel him frown. "That is not a tempting offer."

"Indeed not," the smaller man agrees, "but we are bound all the same."

The Chairman sighs. "And your neutrality?"

"Agreed," the smaller man says. "Once the price is paid, all debts between us are cleared. We will make no move against you, in open or in secret. We will even declare our neutrality openly, to our peers."

"I see," the Chairman says. "There is some advantage in that. And I suppose I have little choice."

"By the oldest laws, you do not," the smaller man says. "It is this, or it is war."

"I do not want war."

The smaller man shrugs. "Nor do we, given what you propose in its place."

Another silence. The small man continues to stand, waiting. His companion continues to sit, leaning slightly forward, his face bored but his eyes fully open and focused on the Chairman, who leans back in his chair, covering himself entirely in shadow.

Minutes pass.

"Agreed," the Chairman says.

The smaller man laughs merrily, clapping his hands. "Excellent! Oh, well done!" His companion is standing now, though no one is sure when he moved. "I am impressed, creature. I did not expect you to survive this. History suggested otherwise, and yet you have! And all that is left is the matter of payment."

"Yes…" The Chairman's voice is weary. "And what is your price?"

"A simple thing," the smaller man says. "A nothing. It will pass and be done. It is one of the more *classic* payments, and I feel it is appropriate on such an auspicious occasion, on the day when the old ways begin to crumble and fall away, leaving only chaos and confusion in their wake."

He lowers his voice, speaking in a whispering, singsong purr.

"We demand a fifth."

Part Two: Haruspex Analytics Situation Room

Phyllis Tanner and Billy Davison have been partners longer than Jason Kline has known them. They were assigned to his team as a pair, and while they get along well with everyone in the group they are undeniably more effective working together than working apart. If Jason had to choose the most effective member of his team, he'd try to make a case for them being the same person split between two bodies.

"Think I got it…" Phyllis doesn't bother hiding the fatigue in her voice. "Need you to look it over, though."

She pushes back, wheeling away from her laptop, as Billy scoots in, peering at the screen.

"What is it you think you have?" Jason assumes it has something to do with the location of Thorpe's mysterious "island," but everyone's tired, and exposition helps them focus.

"Location of Thorpe," Billy says.

Just to Jason's right, Michelle Lawrence looks up over her laptop. "His island?" She pulls down on the drawstrings of her blue hoodie, causing the hood to pull over her face, with only her eyes peeking out.

"Not an island," Phyllis says. "He's on a boat."

"Hold on a minute." To Michelle's right, Simon Yin runs his hand through his dark hair—his traditional spike matted and drooping due to days of neglect—and frowns in protest. "I thought we were looking for an island."

"I thought we talked about this last night," Phyllis says. "The parts of the ocean Billy and I are searching are too far out into the ocean for there to be any islands. Water's too deep. So it has to be a boat."

Simon sighs and leans back in his chair, closing his eyes as he tries to remember the conversation. "I thought everyone decided to skip those areas precisely *because* there wouldn't be any islands there."

"You're right," Billy says. He's typing something into a terminal window on Phyllis' machine. His voice is neutral—he hasn't confirmed anything yet. "Phyllis is skipping over a bunch of stuff because let's face it, we're all tired."

Jason can't help but notice that Billy doesn't sound tired.

"Yeah…" Phyllis nods slowly. "Sorry Simon. Billy's right, and so are you—we did decide to skip those areas last night. Billy and I started looking at them again a few hours ago. I had a… hunch, and it led me back to the deep parts."

"A hunch?" Jason feels a slight stirring of hope, and suddenly he doesn't feel as tired as he did. Phyllis and Billy have a pretty good track record with hunches.

"Communication," Phyllis says. "Thorpe Industries is a huge operation, and even though he stepped down as president he's still involved. If Thorpe is somewhere in the middle of the ocean, how does he communicate with the rest of the outside world?"

"Satellites," Michelle says.

"Satellites," Phyllis agrees. "But not just any satellites. *His* satellites. He'll want to keep all his communication in-house."

Michelle's eyes widen. "You have got to be *kidding me.* I am an idiot. I am such a *fucking idiot.*"

"I guess I'm *still* a fucking idiot," Jason says. "I don't get it."

"You're not idiots, you're *tired.* Thorpe is holed up in the middle of nowhere, but he's not the kind of guy to be cut off from the world. He's going to have an impressive communications array wherever he is. And he's going to link it to his own satellites up in the air."

"Yeah, but Thorpe's satellites are global," Jason says. "That doesn't narrow anything down at all."

"That's true for most people," Billy says, "but Thorpe isn't just browsing the web and watching YouTube videos. He's a scientist—he'll be consuming and transmitting tons of data. So he's going to make sure that wherever he is he can maximize his bandwidth."

"He's got geostationary satellites that give his network global connectivity," Phyllis says. "But geo is a weak signal, and it's at the mercy of bad weather. You can boost it by investing in the right equipment—"

"—which we should assume he has," Billy cuts in.

"Which we should assume he has," Phyllis agrees. "But let's not stop there. He has low- and mid-orbit satellites out there too."

Finally, Jason gets it. "So if he's mobile, he'll want to pick a course that maximizes his access to all those satellites."

"That's the theory," Billy says.

"Except that the range of a satellite's signal is 'the curvature of the earth,'" Simon points out. "That doesn't really narrow things down much."

"Except that he's not using standard tech to communicate," Phyllis says. "He uses an encrypted signal. We can't break it, but we have a little information on what it looks like from the outside. It uses a lot of juice—probably not a problem for the man who invented cold fusion, sure, but he's always going to look for ways to minimize that. Shorter ranges, rely on the low-orbit satellites as much as possible."

Billy spins around in his seat, facing Phyllis. "Math looks good to me. I say we load it up and take a look."

"Load what up?" Jason feels his pulse quicken.

"Haruspex has their own satellites," Phyllis says. "Well, Haruspex has *access* to satellites. We want to use them to take pictures of the new, reduced search area."

"But we have to be careful about it." Billy turns back around in his seat and looks at Jason, a huge, boyish grin on his face. "We don't want to do anything that will tip off a very intelligent, very paranoid metahuman scientist. Phyllis came up with a list of satellites that have the orbits and tech we need to take pictures without forcing them to do anything too noticeable."

He turns the laptop around so the screen faces Jason, and pushes it across the table. Jason reaches out, pulling it closer, and stares at a spreadsheet full of satellite names, the time of day each satellite would be in the right position to take a picture, and what adjustments would need to be made to point their cameras in the right direction.

"Looks like it'll take a few days to piece together a complete map."

"Four days," Billy says. "But we might get lucky."

"If you don't," Jason says, "and he's mobile... he'll be four days away from wherever he was spotted."

"We'll still have more than we did," Phyllis points out.

Jason nods, then pushes the laptop back to Billy. "Send it out. I'll make sure it happens."

Billy and Phyllis exchange grins.

"And now," Jason says, forcing himself to stifle a yawn as he feels his fatigue return, "I think we could all use a little—"

The double doors to the situation room swing open. A tall, slender woman, dressed all in white, steps into the room.

Jason's throat tightens. "Director Ioannou."

"Please, Jason, call me Mara." Her coppery skin contrasts with the gleaming white business suit and skirt. Her long, thick curls are pulled back from her face with silver hairpins. Dark eyes peer out from under thick, long eyelashes. Other than the hairpins, the only jewelry she wears is a pair of large silver earrings, each shaped in the form of a double epsilon.

Jason stands, and the rest of his team hastily follows suit. For all the director's insistence on informality, there's something about her that discourages it. It's nothing overt—just a general feeling that she is far more than she appears to be.

"I'm sorry to interrupt." Her voice is richly musical, her smile dazzling. "I know you're all working very hard. Has there been any progress?"

"There has, actually." Jason quickly summarizes Phyllis and Billy's latest theory—making sure to give credit where due—and when he's finished, Mara nods thoughtfully.

"Notify me when you send in the request," she says. "I'll make sure it's given priority. Now, I need you all to form a line, shoulder to shoulder."

Something cold settles in the pit of Jason's stomach. He tries not to flinch.

"What?" Simon looks at Mara, then at Jason, confusion written all over his face. "A line?"

"Shoulder to shoulder," Mara repeats. "I know it's unusual, but this is important."

"Yeah, it's OK Simon." Jason tries to keep the tightness in his stomach out of his voice. "Everybody line up."

It takes a bit more time than he expects, but eventually everyone has formed a ragged line in front of the main conference table spanning the room. Phyllis, Billy, Jason, Michelle, and Simon stare out at Mara, who stands just inside the room, waiting patiently.

"We're... I guess we're set," Jason says. The cold in his stomach turns into a more substantive feeling of dread.

Mara nods once. "Please remain still until I finish."

She walks over to Phyllis, stopping a few feet away from her. She extends her right hand, so that her palm hovers just in front of Phyllis' forehead. Phyllis gasps softly, her eyes widening, as if she feels a slight current running through her.

Mara, for her part, stares at Phyllis intently, saying nothing. Minutes pass.

"Thank you," Mara says, then sidesteps to place herself in front of Billy. Hand extended once again, she concentrates on Billy, staring at him in silence. Then she thanks him and moves on.

She repeats the process with Jason, Michelle, and Simon, thanking each in turn and moving on without explanation. When she finishes with Simon she flashes everyone a delighted smile.

"Thank you so much for your help," she says. Then, without another word, she leaves.

Everyone stares at the open doors in astonishment.

"What the hell was *that?*" Simon asks.

"Did everyone else feel that?" Billy asks. "When she stretched out her hand. It was…" He trails off as he fumbles for the right words.

"It was *tingly.*" Michelle speaks softly, half-wondering, half afraid. "Like when you walk into a dark room and you know someone's in it, but they don't answer when you call their name."

"So is that magic?" Phyllis asks, turning to Jason. "I'm still skeptical about that part of our briefing." She turns back to look at the empty door.

"A little less skeptical, maybe," she mutters.

"Seriously, does anyone know what that was about?" Simon asks again.

"No," Jason lies. "Look, we're all pretty worn out. Let's send in the satellite surveillance request and call it a day. We need the sleep."

"But what about… that?" Michelle points to the open door. "What just happened? Don't you want to know?"

Jason shakes his head. "If we need to know, they'll tell us."

"If it *is* magic," Billy says, "we're probably better off not knowing."

"Look," Simon says, "I know I'm the one who asked, but it turns out I don't actually care. Going home and going to sleep sounds *really good* to me. And since the surveillance request is going to take four days, I think I might take tomorrow off, too."

"That's a great idea," Jason says. "Look, it'll take about a day to get everything set up, then another day before the first images come in. So everyone take the next two days off. We all come back Thursday morning and start reviewing the first batch of satellite imagery. I'll let the board know we'll be out."

"Downtime would be good," Michelle says.

A general chorus of agreement fills the room.

Part Three: The Bronx, NY

The room is small, run down, and mostly empty. The hardwood floors are cracked and rough, faded wallpaper peels away from the walls to reveal chipped plaster beneath, and a single window, heavily curtained, sits above an old radiator that badly needs bleeding. The room is dark: the only light comes from the gap between the heavy window curtains and the window itself, splashing red neon over the top of the hissing, spitting radiator and onto the floor.

The sounds of the city—car horns, people shouting, occasional blasts of music—can be heard beyond the window. The world outside is full of noisy, frenetic life… but the room, and all the others like it in this building, are dark.

The silence ends in fits and starts. First, the faint sound of footsteps, then the sound of keys jingling, then the scratching of a lock being turned. Somewhere below the room a door bangs open, and heavy footsteps stomp onto old, creaking floors. For a moment the sounds of the outside world are louder, then they fade back to their original levels as a door bangs closed. A deadbolt turns (muffled *clack*) then footsteps thump down a hallway.

Minutes pass.

A door opens—not below, this time, but behind—and hinges squeak in protest. Footsteps grow louder—two distinct pairs can now be heard—as they grow ever closer to the room. Keys jingle again. Another lock rattles. A door opens.

"Come on."

The voice isn't harsh, but the tone of command is unmistakable. The door closes, another deadbolt slides shut.

Footsteps again, growing even louder.

The door to the room swings open. A light switch *clicks* on, and a single lightbulb flickers to life overhead. The light is dim—probably not bright enough to comfortably read a book—but it lights the room enough to show how stark it truly is. The only furniture is a straight-backed wooden chair sitting with its back against one of the walls, with a small wooden table to its left.

Special Agent Oliver Nuzzo steps into the room, wiping sweat off his face with a damp handkerchief, and steps to one side.

"In."

Again his voice is full of command, hard and unbending, completely at odds with his soft, round features.

Captain Clive Darius, dressed in a cheap two-piece suit, stained dress shirt, and no tie, walks into the center of the room and stops. He stands still, staring vacantly at the far wall. He's not standing at attention, he's simply… standing. Waiting.

Agent Nuzzo closes the door behind them, stomps over to the window, and carefully pulls back a corner of the curtain to peer outside. He nods once, satisfied, then gestures to the chair. Darius immediately walks over to the chair and sits, back straight, hands on his knees, staring straight ahead. His eyes barely blink.

Nuzzo stares at Darius, momentarily ignoring the sweat pouring down his face. Then he reaches into his right trenchcoat pocket and pulls out a small, plain wooden box, about the size of a box for a wedding ring. He flips open the top, never taking his eyes off Darius, then sets it down on the table. Inside the box is a tiny black stone, cut into the shape of a pyramid, strange symbols etched into each side.

Darius doesn't react to the item next to the table, but something happens. The room grows colder; white breath emerges from the older man's nostrils. Even Nuzzo shivers once, though he still dabs sweat from his face with his handkerchief.

"Well Darius, let me tell you something. You should be real happy you're not here right now." A twisting smirk curls to life on Nuzzo's face as he speaks. "This place… well. I've seen better."

Nuzzo peers through the curtains again.

"Could be worse, of course. It should be, if you ask me, after the way you managed to screw up the way you did. You brought this on yourself. Chew on that for a while."

Nuzzo pulls the curtain away from the edge of the window, just a little, giving him a clearer view of the street below.

"It'll be safe at least. CDC evacuated the whole building. You probably heard about it, actually—man disappears, wife and kid die of some weird disease, the whole building empties out because there's no way that disease could have come into New York City without it being *manufactured*. You know, the 'Bioterror cell in New York' stories they were going on about, right after the Forrest attack? Yeah, that was here. The chance of anyone dropping by is slim to none. And if they do…"

Nuzzo glances at Darius, his smirk deepening into a sneer.

"Well, that'll be the perfect cover story for what happens next."

The handkerchief is soaking wet at this point. Nuzzo looks at it, grunts in annoyance, and puts it in his left pocket. A clean, dry handkerchief emerges seconds later from his right, and Nuzzo runs it over his face and the back of his neck.

"Hold on a minute."

Nuzzo stumps out of the room, muttering under his breath, then returns carrying a folding chair. He sets it up in front of the table, turning it sideways, then plops down heavily in the seat. The metal creaks slightly as he leans back. His right arm rests on the table, hand hanging over the edge, as his left presses the handkerchief against his forehead.

"That fed is a real pain in the ass."

He glances down at the small stone pyramid resting in the ring box and frowns.

"It's a little too late for excuses, Darius. It's not my problem, and apparently my boss doesn't care."

He cocks his head to one side as if listening.

"Cry me a river. You signed on with eyes open. All this—*all of it*—was explained to you right at the very beginning. And you signed your name on the dotted line anyway. *Please* tell me I don't need to arrange to have someone remind you of that *more explicitly*."

He waits a moment more, then laughs—a hollow, humorless, mocking laugh. "What you thought at the time is not my problem, Darius. If I had a nickel for every greedy bastard who thought all the clauses and stipulations were mumbo jumbo because 'of course magic isn't *real*' I promise you I wouldn't be spending all my time in this bullshit body, babysitting yours. Stop complaining."

He sighs, tilts his head back, then both hands press the handkerchief against his forehead. Rivulets of sweat fall down the side of his face, leaving trails just under his ears.

"This... bullshit... body..." He repeats the words a few times, like a mantra, before lapsing into silence with a sigh.

For a few minutes the room is still. Then Nuzzo stirs, and stares down at the tiny stone pyramid in contempt.

"It's supposed to hurt."

He cocks his head to one side again.

"Quit *sniveling*, Darius. The pain is part of the price. They gave you *one job,* and instead of doing *that* you panicked and tried to pull rank on one of your own who was working with the Feds. *Metahuman* Feds. And one of them can *tell when you're lying.*"

Nuzzo stands, walks into the middle of the room, then whirls back to face the table. "I don't even know what you were thinking." His voice shakes with contempt. "I was told you were one of the *smart* ones. That you had *potential.* But when things got bad you panicked, and then you made things worse. So yeah, Darius. *It's supposed to hurt.*"

He advances on the table slowly, the menace in his voice hardening with each step.

"It's supposed to hurt because you've felt untouchable for too long. It's supposed to hurt because you got lazy, and it put us at risk. It's supposed to hurt because they shoved me into this *useless bag of meat* so that someone they *trust* can keep an eye on you all day. It's supposed to hurt so that if you manage to do what you're told, and are ever reunited with *your* useless bag of meat some day, you will *never, ever* take what you have for granted, ever again."

Nuzzo's breathing is ragged; his hands shake with barely-controlled rage. His handkerchief is soaked through—again—and he balls it up in his left fist, shoving it deep into his trenchcoat pocket. By the time he produces a new one, his breathing and hands are steady.

"You should look on the bright side." He presses his handkerchief to his forehead as he sits back in the folding chair. "You're not dead. Honest, if it was my call they would have found you hanging in your bedroom, with a note apologizing to your ex-wife. Someone over my head thinks you can still be useful to us, so they gave you the chance to step up. This is your chance. *Step up.*"

He lowers the handkerchief and glares darkly at the stone. "And stop complaining that it *hurts.* At this point you want it to hurt. There's only one alternative, and I know you don't want that."

He stares at the stone in silence for a moment, then grunts in satisfaction. He resumes his former position—head back, eyes closed—and unfolds the handkerchief so it covers his entire face.

"This bullshit body," he whispers.

Part Four: Staten Island, NYC

Billy Davison wakes up reluctantly.

His bedroom ceiling slowly comes into focus as his brain tries to engage. He's always suffered from grogginess when waking up—something Phyllis never gets tired of teasing him about—and this time is no different. The problem is compounded by how long and hard he and the rest of his team have been pushing themselves. This was supposed to have been his first full night of sleep in days, and now he's awake.

Why is he awake?

A few seconds later he realizes that he's hearing a doorbell. His doorbell. Someone is ringing his doorbell. He groans, forces himself to sit up, and tries to figure out who would be ringing his doorbell at...

What time is it?

He rubs his eyes, glances out the window and realizes it's still dark. He frowns and turns to the digital clock sitting on his nightstand.

Three in the morning?

Fatigue leaves quickly, replaced by a surge of adrenaline brought on by alarm.

Nobody would ring his doorbell at 3AM. If Jason needed to talk to him, he'd use the company phone—they're not allowed to turn it off for precisely that reason. Phyllis wouldn't drop by at 3AM. Nobody he knows would drop by at 3AM. And nobody conducting any legitimate business would knock on his door at 3AM.

The only possible legitimate explanation would be that it was a police officer canvassing the neighborhood after a crime was committed. It's *possible*, but it isn't *likely*. There's a reason Billy chooses to live where he does.

Instincts and paranoia snap into alignment. Billy gets up, grabs the go-bag he keeps under his bed, and heads for his bedroom window.

The window pane opens silently—he spent a great deal of time sanding down the inner frame and kept the moving parts well oiled to make certain it would—and he steps out onto his roof. He winces as his bare foot comes down on a half-exposed nail head, but he says nothing. He reaches through his window, finds the button for the silent alarm set just to the left of the window pane, and presses it firmly. It vibrates once—the police have been called. Ignoring the soreness in his foot, he crouches low and creeps his way across the roof to the other side.

Sight lines are critical here, and that's the other reason Billy chose his neighborhood: most of the houses have Gambrel roofs, making them look like oversized barns. It's a stupid design for New York, considering how much it snows in the winter, but most of the original houses on the block still have them. The different slopes on the roof give him a little more cover than he'd otherwise have as he creeps along the top. Whoever is ringing his doorbell hasn't stopped, and if the doorbell-ringer has spotters they don't seem to have seen him.

Billy reaches the edge of his roof, holds his breath, and jumps. He reaches his neighbor's roof easily—and, more importantly, *soundlessly*—and he moves a little more quickly along to the next house, and then the next, and then the next. At the fourth house he stops roof-hopping, and instead climbs down an old dogwood tree, letting go halfway down to drop into a crouch in his neighbor's backyard.

It's his least favorite part of the exit strategy so far—the tree is slender, and the branches rustle as he descends—but it's done. Quickly, he slips on the pair of swimming shoes dangling from his go-bag, then runs the length of his neighbor's backyard and vaults over the fence into the yard beyond.

He runs, zig-zagging through different yards in the neighborhood, always placing himself farther and farther away from his house. Finally the neighborhood comes to an end, and he steps out into a cluster of shops.

New York may be the City That Never Sleeps, but parts of it are sluggish at 3AM. Most of the shops are closed, almost all of the streets are deserted. Billy feels exposed—he's not exactly dressed to fit in, even if there were people about, but the lack of people makes him entirely too easy to spot. He ducks down an alley the first chance he gets, dredging up in his mind the many maps he's memorized, choosing alleys that aren't dead ends, trying to put as many buildings as possible between himself and the main roads. He walks this way for an hour until he finally gets to a Staten Island Railway station.

Riding the train then becomes his least favorite part of his exit strategy, as he is forced to sit in one place in a lighted train, moving between cars at each stop, wondering if that actually makes any difference. He begins to relax a little when he makes it to the ferry, but the trip from the St. George Ferry Terminal to the Whitehall Terminal at South Ferry is the most excruciating twenty-five minutes of his life. It's not until he steps off the ferry and into Lower Manhattan that he finally allows himself to relax.

A few subway stops later and he's downtown, where he finally manages to put the last of his fear to rest. There are people here. It's not the throngs of people you see in the day, but there are enough people to make anyone trying to find him reluctant to do anything overtly. He unslings his go-bag and reaches into the top, fishing around until his hands close on the burner phone he has stuffed away.

He pulls the phone out of his bag, slinging the bag back over his shoulder as he walks down the street, feeling comforted by the neon signs of stores selling overpriced electronics interspersed with stores selling overpriced greasy food. He debates whether to call Jason or Phyllis, and ultimately decides on Phyllis.

I'll have to explain less. Phyllis will be able to call Jason after, and then—

He never sees the large man cross his path, and is completely unprepared for the way the man doesn't give an inch when they collide. It's almost like crashing into a brick wall, and as Billy grunts in surprise he feels the phone slip through his fingers and shatter as it hits the concrete.

"Hey, watch where you're—"

His words die on his lips as the large man grips Billy's shoulder. It's an uncomfortably tight grip, though not painful. Not yet.

The best word to describe the man's face is "nondescript." He is physically very large, at least six inches taller than Billy, and heavyset in a way that suggests power over obesity, but his features aren't very distinguishing. What Billy notices more than anything else is the way his mind seems to recoil from noticing anything about the man at all, other than his well-tailored suit and bowler hat. Billy has been trained to notice details, and each time he tries to choose one—color of skin, color of eyes, color of hair, anything—his brain slides away from it.

"Hey." Billy tries to pull away from the man. The grip holding him in place doesn't tighten—the large man doesn't appear to react in any way at all—but he can't get free. "Hey, look, I don't want any—"

"—problems?"

The voice, thin and high-spirited, comes from directly behind him. Billy twists, trying to see, but he can't turn far enough.

"Oh, don't bother, Mister Davison, allow me to oblige."

Another man, a little on the short side and very thin, steps into view. He and the large man are dressed identically—pinstripe suit, bowler hat—and Billy finds he is, like the large man, difficult to pin down on any other details. There are only two additional features that stand out in Billy's mind: a wide, gleaming smile, and razor-sharp eyes.

The smaller man stops, standing a foot to the right and a few feet behind the larger man, allowing Billy to face him directly. He bows, sweeping his hat off his head in a grandiose manner.

"Mister Davison." The man's voice is cheerful, positively brimming with manic energy. "Allow me to congratulate you on a game well played. A game *well* played, sir. And I mean that with every sincerity."

He straightens, then begins to clap his hands vigorously, beaming. Billy almost believes the man *is* applauding him, which is ludicrous.

"So you were the one ringing my front door?" Talking is pretty much the only thing Billy can do at the moment. He scans the streets, and notices to his alarm that they are empty. There were plenty of people moments ago. He was staring straight at a group of drunk college students while he was fishing out his phone…

The applause stops. "Quite so, quite so."

No people on the street, so Billy scans the stores. The lights are still on, but all the buildings he can look into appear empty. No customers at the counters, nobody managing the cash registers. He looks around more blatantly this time, confusion on his face.

"What's going on?"

"Change," the smaller man says. "It can be disorienting when the world around you is suddenly not what you thought it was, when it becomes something you were certain it could never be. Change. It kills the strong, it topples the powerful. It destroys civilizations. It's disorienting. It's unavoidable. And, most of all, it is quite often *unfair*."

The way he says the word, the intensity in his eyes when he says it, causes Billy to shiver against his will.

"Unfair to so many. Unfair to the weak and strong alike. And tonight, Mister Davison, I'm afraid it will be terribly unfair to you."

They are only words, but Billy feels their weight. He knows what that weight means.

"You're going to kill me."

The small man nods once. "You've done nothing to deserve it. I want you to know that. You are a well-sculpted tool, and from all I know about you—from all I've seen from you, tonight—what is about to happen to you is a tragic waste of ability."

"Then don't waste it," Billy says. "I could work for you instead."

"This is not that kind of situation," the small man says. "Though I don't begrudge you making the attempt."

Billy goes through the possible scenarios in his head, trying to figure out how this scenario fits into everything going on in his life. He settles on the one he likes least.

"You're from Farraday City."

A look of pure delight crosses the small man's face, and his grin widens so far it looks as if his face has split in two. "Wonderful," he breathes. "Absolutely *wonderful*."

Billy nods slowly. He looks at the large man, who doesn't appear to be paying any attention to the exchange at all. "You can let go of me," he says. "I won't run."

Immediately the man's grip loosens; his arm falls to his side.

Blood and pain rush through Billy's right shoulder. He massages it with his left hand. "And the rest of my team?"

"We have no interest in them," the smaller man says. "Only you."

"Lucky me." Billy stops massaging his shoulder. There's no point.

"Certainly not," the small man says, tilting his head to one side as he considers Billy carefully. "Oh, that was humor. Humor in the face of death. Admirable. Well, I can promise you one thing, William Davison. Your gift— your reward, for having impressed me as you have—is that it will be quick. And it will be painless."

"I'll believe it when I—"

His words die on his lips. He dies on the street.

The small man stares down at the corpse of Billy Davison, a look of almost-regret on his face. He sighs softly, a long, slow exhalation of breath. "That's the last of them," he says. "We have our fifth."

The large man says nothing.

"Well." The small man straightens. "I believe it's time to go home, my friend. We've been away too long. This city galls me—so much potential, so little of it used. Shall we?"

With that he turns and strides down the sidewalk, the larger man in tow, leaving the corpse to molder, crumpled against the curb. Five steps later the small man stops.

"Oh, that my head were a spring of water!" he says. "And my eyes, a fountain of tears!"

The sounds of people return. First a low babble, like a faraway stream, but it grows louder, the roar greater, the sounds swelling into an ocean of life that crashes into the briefly empty street. And in that moment, in that final crash, there is a much smaller sound: the faintest splash of flesh dissolving into water, running along the curb until it falls into the sewer through a nearby grate.

The returning world barely notices the damp clothes lying crumpled by the street.

Part One: Haruspex Analytics Boardroom

The Haruspex Analytics boardroom is emptier than it was the day before. The men and women sitting in it don't know why—not precisely—but they are painfully aware of the rumors.

Each man and woman waiting patiently for the Chairman to arrive has received an unending stream of worried calls from their own underlings about an unusual level of absenteeism all over the building. No part of the employee population has been untouched: every department was reporting that at least one employee, often more than one, had not arrived that morning. What's more, attempts to contact those employees had failed.

A company specializing in handling sensitive information can't afford to overlook such things—as such, this emergency meeting had been called, at which point it was discovered that the absenteeism extended even to members of the board. It didn't take long to determine that roughly 20% of the Haruspex population is missing.

Jason Kline shifts uncomfortably in his chair. He is not a board member, but he's been sitting in on board meetings fairly regularly for the last month. His team has also been affected by a disappearance—Billy Davison didn't come in this morning.

Unfortunately, he's pretty sure he knows why.

He's pretty sure the other board members do as well—they're not willing to admit it just yet, but it's lurking there in the backs of their minds. He can tell by the way the board members, usually men and women who exhibit extraordinary self control, can't stop glancing furtively at Mara Ioannou. She alone among them has adopted their traditional demeanor—a neutral, emotionless expression that reveals nothing. She meets Jason's gaze for a moment, and he quickly lowers his eyes.

The wall behind the Chairman's spot at the table opens soundlessly, and the Chairman steps out of darkness, into shadow. He sits, his features obscured by the shadows in that part of the room. The furtive whispers in the room die off. All eyes turn to him.

The Chairman sits motionless, chin resting on his right hand. All Jason can hear are the people around him breathing.

"We are not all here," the Chairman says, a hint of sadness in his voice, "and I am well aware that the sudden gaps in our organization go far beyond this room. Indeed, you will find that a full one fifth of us are gone. They will not return."

Jason's temples pound, his senses reeling from the tension in the room. The Chairman sighs heavily, the outline of his head turning as he takes in everyone in the room.

"I have invoked Article Thirteen for each of their contracts."

Jason gapes, open-mouthed, as he stares at the Chairman's shadowed form in astonishment.

"I know many of you consider Article Thirteen something we use to clear 'dead wood,'" the Chairman says. "There is some truth to that. Article Thirteen is best used to remove employees who have lost their dedication to our purpose. That is not what happened yesterday. Yesterday we lost some among us that we might consider our very best and brightest."

Jason thinks about Billy and tightens his jaw.

"Article Thirteen states that employees agree that they are *fungible*. That they may be called to make sacrifices for the company that include genuine sacrifice. Last night we were in a position where it was necessary—*tactically* necessary—to subject a much wider range of employees to it."

It is a testament to the discipline of everyone in the room, no matter how ragged they may be feeling at the moment, that they don't ask questions. Jason wishes someone would—he wishes he were brave enough to do so—but he, and everyone else in the room, wait in silence for the Chairman to continue.

"I do not need to remind you of the forces that are in play. To pursue our goal, we have had to use what resources presented themselves, even when they were not ours to use. Last night we were obliged to render payment. This morning we find ourselves debt free. Further, we find ourselves in a position where we no longer have to be as concerned about interference from other powers and principalities."

Still no speech, but now the board members exchange glances with raised eyebrows. Jason is only dimly aware of exactly what the Chairman is referring to—that side of the project is something that he can't seem to make much sense of—but the board members obviously find this important.

"I will brief you more fully—as much as I can—at a later date," the Chairman says. "For now, we have to spend some time… readjusting. I want to make sure our organization is stable before we move forward."

The board members settle back into their chairs. One by one they slip into the same expression Mara Ioannou has worn through the whole meeting—cool, detached, attentive, emotionless.

"First," the Chairman says, "we must take steps to see that the investigations into our employees' disappearances—there will be investigations, I'm afraid—do not link them with our organization in any way. We can't afford public scrutiny at this juncture."

Some of the board members nod in agreement.

"Mara, I want you to lead this effort. Use Mr. Kline's team, I believe they have some experience with this kind of thing." Jason starts as the Chairman calls him by name. He glances at Mara, who continues to stare at the Chairman, no reaction visible on her face.

"Second, we must bring our remaining employees in as far as we are able. Make it known that Article Thirteen was invoked, but also make it clear that the employees no longer with us were neither traitors nor incompetent. See to it that the families of those employees receive full bereavement benefits, though of course those benefits should be through obscure channels—unexpected inheritance, life insurance policies the employee had but didn't tell the family about, that sort of thing."

More board members nod in agreement.

"Finally," the Chairman says, "there is the matter of our missing board members. We will need to replenish our ranks from within. I need nominations from all of you by tomorrow afternoon. All nominations must be from within the company. Understood?"

A murmur of assent fills the room.

"Good," the Chairman says. "It seems appropriate, at this point, that I make a nomination of my own."

The room falls silent again, all board members waiting expectantly.

The Chairman's silhouette shifts. Jason shudders slightly as he feels the man's gaze fall on him.

"Mr. Kline," the Chairman says.

Jason swallows nervously. "Sir?" He manages to keep most of the tremor out of his voice.

"I have been very pleased with your work."

"Thank you sir."

"Normally I would prefer to wait until more of the deficiencies in your knowledge have been addressed—don't take that as a slight, knowledge of the existence of magic is a very closely guarded secret the world over, and it takes time to effectively integrate that knowledge into your worldview— but we are short on personnel, and the board members who have worked with you have all been impressed with your contributions thus far."

Jason stares at the Chairman, unable to keep the expression of shock from his face.

"Are you ready to take a step further in? To go deeper? Can we count on you, Mr. Kline, to *commit*?"

Every eye in the room is on him now. All of the board members stare at him, expressionless, waiting for his reply.

Jason takes a deep, steadying breath. "Yes sir."

The Chairman nods. "Good. Then with the board's consent, I would like to nominate Jason Kline as a full member of the board."

"Aye." They speak in a single voice; their assent rings in Jason's ears as he struggles not to flush.

"Motion carried," the Chairman says approvingly. "Mr. Kline, there are a few formalities that must be settled—and your new employment contract will be considerably more complicated than your current one—but it is with great pleasure that I welcome you, our newest member, to the Haruspex Analytics Board of Directors."

The room erupts into applause. The reserve is gone from their faces as they greet their newest member. Mara is beaming at him.

Jason blinks a few times, trying to make sure it isn't a dream. Somewhere in the back of his mind he wonders how Billy would feel about this.

It's an errant thought, quickly suppressed.

Part Two: Haruspex Analytics Situation Room

"Article Thirteen."

Phyllis Tanner stands in front of Jason, arms folded, her face completely, utterly blank. Simon Yin sits in front of his laptop, set up at the long table running down the middle of the Situation Room. Michelle Lawrence stands, fidgeting nervously by the door. Neither of them look at Jason or Phyllis. Simon pretends to be working, his eyes locked on his laptop screen without actually seeing anything. Michelle plays with the drawstring on her sweatshirt, pulling first one end and then the other down as far as it will go before the other end disappears entirely.

Jason sighs, and forces himself to meet her gaze. She looks uncomfortably like the other board members when they have their game faces on—no trace of emotion, not a single tell to be seen. Her eyes are hard and calculating as she scrutinizes him in return.

"I'm sorry, Phyllis. I don't know the specifics. But an entire fifth of the company is gone, and Billy was caught up in it."

"This is what she was doing the other day," Phyllis says. "Ms. Ioannou. When she came in and had us line up, and did that..." She gestures with one hand, waving her fingers through the air. "I don't know what it was. *Magic.*"

"Probably," Jason agrees.

"Did you know it was going to happen?" Phyllis asks.

Everyone in the room is looking at him now.

"No," Jason says, then deflates slightly under her gaze. "Not exactly."

"Explain that."

"I can't talk about it," Jason says.

Phyllis' expressionless mask falters, her mouth firming into a thin, disapproving line.

"I really can't," Jason says. "Look, Phyllis, all I can say is I didn't think it was going to happen to *us*. But we all signed the same contract, and we all read that clause. We knew there were risks."

Phyllis has nothing to say to that. Her gaze drops to the floor.

"I guess I didn't think it'd happen to us, either." Michelle twirls the hoodie drawstring around her left index finger. Her voice is soft, her stance subdued. "I figured it was only invoked when employees got out of line, or screwed up really bad."

"A lot of people thought that," Jason says. "Even the board."

"Which you are now on." Phyllis doesn't look up, but the edge to her voice is unmistakable.

"Yes." Jason looks directly at her. "Phyllis. Yes. I was offered the spot and I took it. Can you honestly blame me for that?"

Phyllis sighs, slumping slightly. "No. No, Jason, I don't believe this is your fault. It's just that—damn it. *Billy.*"

"Yeah," Jason says.

Setting aside the personal component, Billy's loss is significant on a professional level. Billy and Phyllis have worked together for years—long before they joined Jason's group—and together they were more effective than any five analysts Jason had ever met. There's no getting around it: their effectiveness is going to suffer from this.

The door to the situation room opens, and everyone turns to see Mara Ioannou step into the room. At the same time, one of the wall monitors comes to life, showing the silhouette of the Chairman.

"Mr. Kline," the Chairman says. He shifts slightly, as if including the rest of his team. "I felt that, given today's circumstances, it was best that I address you directly."

Phyllis, Michelle, and Simon stare at him with a mixture of dread and anticipation.

"All of Haruspex is suffering from this ordeal, of course," the Chairman says. "But I understand that the man you lost was partially responsible for coming up with the most recent search for our targets in the Atlantic. Phyllis Tanner? Billy Davison was, Jason tells me, your partner. You joined the team together."

Phyllis stares at the Chairman's image for a moment, unable to speak. When she finally does, her voice is slightly hoarse. "Yes sir. We've worked together for a long time."

The Chairman nods. "Please believe me when I say I wish we had been able to avoid this. I do not rejoice in the choice we made last night. And from a purely *tactical* perspective, the knowledge that this has disrupted such an effective team pains me."

"Thank you, sir." Phyllis looks down at the floor again.

"The tragedy of it cuts all the deeper," the Chairman continues, "because your search was successful."

Everyone perks up at this—even Phyllis.

Work is the best way to deal with this, Jason thinks. *Give us a problem to solve and we'll manage.*

"I was notified this morning," Mara says. "A small island had been found on one of the satellite images. There is no known island listed on any current maps at that location."

"So we know where they are," Jason says.

Mara shakes her head. "Not quite. The island appears to be *moving*—a creation of Doctor Thorpe's, I assume. We will need your team to find it quickly. Once it is found, it will be dealt with."

Phyllis turns to Jason. "I want lead on this."

Jason nods, then turns back to face Mara and the Chairman. "We'll get you a location. We'll do it quickly."

Mara steps forward, smiling slightly. "I'm afraid you will have to leave that to your team."

Jason frowns. "Why?"

"You have a new employee contract to sign," Mara says. "After which there is an orientation program all board members must go through. And finally, of course, there is the matter of your office."

Jason gestures to the room. "We've been set up here."

"Board members and their subordinates get a dedicated office suite," Mara says.

"Also," the Chairman adds, "this is not negotiable, and must not be delayed. Get it done today."

The finality in his voice stifles any thought of argument. "Yes sir," Jason says. "Phyllis, you're in charge. I'll be back... whenever."

"We'll have their exact location by the time you're done," Phyllis says.

Michelle and Simon nod in agreement.

Part Three: Haruspex Analytics

The walls and floor of the long rectangular room are granite. The ceiling is covered in baroque plaster tiles. It is fancy, but empty: no furniture, nothing hanging from the walls. The only door leading into the room is plain, almost shabby. It's a simple, solid wood door, painted a neutral gray color that is slightly lighter than the granite.

Few Haruspex Analytics employees know this room exists. Fewer still have been inside.

Lights embedded between the baroque tiles flicker to life, filling the room with soft light. The plain gray door opens, and a man steps into the room. He's tall, older but still vigorous, with sharp blue eyes and silver hair that falls to his shoulders. He's expensively dressed, in a dark gray three-piece suit and a matching silk tie. In his hand is a long plastic tube, the kind used to carry rolled-up posters, blueprints, or pieces of art.

The Chairman walks to the center of the room, stops, kneels. He opens one end of the tube and pulls out a rolled-up piece of paper. He sets the tube aside, and spreads the paper out on the floor. It's a large map of the Atlantic Ocean.

He reaches into his suit coat pocket, producing four thumb-sized weighted blocks. He places one on each corner of the map, forcing it flat, then stands, looking down at it. He frowns slightly.

"A little more light, please."

The ceiling lights slowly brighten.

"Thank you very much." He reaches into an inside pocket and produces a slim smartphone. He dials a number and holds it up to his ear, waiting patiently.

"Mrs. Tanner. Do you have the current location of Doctor Thorpe's island?"

He listens to the woman on the other end.

"Wonderful. Please give me their location."

He listens again.

"Thank you very much for your assistance." The phone returns to the inside pocket.

He kneels before the map, studying the latitude and longitude markings carefully. He reaches into his jacket again, withdrawing a fountain pen. Taking great care, he places a single dot on the map. He caps the pen, placing it under the map, then stands. He stares at the dot intently.

"I found you."

He picks up the plastic tube, tipping it over. A small blue bag, tied shut with thick red cord, tumbles out onto the floor. The Chairman sets down the tube, picks up the bag, and with a quick jerk he undoes the cord. The bag opens, revealing very fine red sand.

He takes a pinch, throws it across the map, and speaks a word.

The sand does not arc naturally across the map—it stops in mid-flight, falling abruptly, creating a faint circle around the black dot the Chairman added minutes before. More sand follows, each throw accompanied with the same word, and with each successive throw the sand begins to form a pattern: an intricate symbol, a circle ringed with glyphs that burn faintly in the room's light.

When the last grains of sand are thrown, the Chairman drops the bag next to the tube. He stares at the map again: now the black dot is surrounded by a circle of sand, and around that circle are symbols that now glow fiery red, blackening the map beneath them.

The Chairman extends his hand, palm down, centering it over the the ring. He speaks another word, and the map bursts into flame, consumed in an instant, as if it were flash paper. The circle and its runes remain, however: the sand that makes up the circle bleeds together into a ring of thick, red sludge. The runes, still burning though they rest on nothing to fuel those flames, spin counterclockwise around the ring.

He speaks another word.

The ring and the runes rise slowly into the air, abandoning the charred remains of the map. They rise to the level of the Chairman's knee, then hover in place, runes still spinning. The faintest smell of ocean water rises up through the air, apparently from the circle itself.

He speaks another word.

The runes flash, and the circle opens like an eye: within the circle he can see the ocean, deep and blue and green and cold. It is day, and the skies are clear, and on that ocean he can see a tiny black dot.

He speaks another word.

The image zooms in. The ocean is pushed to the side, and the black dot becomes an island. There is no other word for it: it is a small island in the middle of the ocean, in a part of the ocean where no islands should be. It has beaches, a town, a marina with a pier—even an airport.

"Hello, Doctor Thorpe. I hope I find you well."

He closes his eyes, steels himself, and speaks another word.

The light in the circle dims somewhat, the sky clouds, and a wind rises, shaking the leaves of imported trees and pressing the imported grass flat. Sand blows across the beaches; waves spray a fine, salty mist into the air. As the wind rises in the image, it also fills the room. The Chairman can feel the spray of salt water on his face, feel his hair blown by the wind rushing through. He looks down at the island and pushes back a sense of vertigo—he feels as if he could lean too far forward and fall down into the circle.

He speaks another word.

He can hear it now—the whispering. He remembers those whispers well. They are not quite the same, but they are similar enough. They will do what is needed.

"Come," he whispers in return.

The light dims in the scene below him. The waves rise up, crashing into the beaches. Rain begins to fall. Thunder rumbles through. The Chairman loosens his tie, unbuttons his collar and pulls out a tiny trumpet hung around his neck, affixed to a finely wrought silver chain. He watches the storm rise.

He speaks words again: a poem in an ancient tongue, four lines repeated, over and over again. Each time he repeats it his voice rises, until finally he is shouting the words, his voice hoarse. Finally he screams the words one final time, and at last he shouts a final word of command.

The storm stops. The rain dies off, the wind falls to nothing. He can hear, through his circle, the gentle sound of waves, newly subdued, lapping against the sandy beaches.

He raises the trumpet to his lips, takes a breath, and blows.

The trumpet is deceptively deep for its size. And loud: prepared as he is, his ears ring with each call. He calls again, then again, each time putting all he has into the note. *Come*, the horn says. *Come. Come. Come.*

Then, through the circle, he hears it: low, deep, wet, a rumbling moan that rises out of the water and fills the sky with hunger. The waters roil and churn, the sound increases.

The Chairman lowers the trumpet, places it back under his shirt, very carefully buttoning the shirt over it and readjusting his tie. He reaches into his jacket and pulls out his phone once again. He presses something on the flat screen and holds it up to his ear.

"Mara. They have answered. It is only a matter of time."

He nods absently, as if agreeing with the voice on the other line.

"It can't go that far. Not with the tools I used. It should, however, go far enough. That said…"

He stares at the scene below, still ominously quiet save for the churning in the waters.

"That said, I think it would be wise to prepare for a response. They are capable, and there is at least one among them who may recognize what this is. If he does, I expect we'll be meeting him soon."

He listens again, the faintest trace of a smile on his lips.

"Quite the contrary, in fact. I very much hope he *does*. He is someone I have wanted to meet for a very long time."

Part Four: Thorpe Island Pier

David Bernard sits at the end of the pier, conjuring orbs of darkness as he watches the ocean roll by.

Robert Thorpe's artificial island is an impressive feat of engineering—in some places it's indistinguishable from the real thing—but here, at the end of the pier, something is different. He's not sure if his new connection to Artigenian's power has altered his senses, or if his knowledge the island is fake is convincing him to doubt what he sees, but he's half-convinced he can *feel* a point just a few feet from the pier where the island falls away, and ocean depths begin.

No, it's not his imagination: he *can* feel it. In his mind's eye he can feel the cold of the ocean drawing him down. If he closes his eyes he can almost see it—a dark, murky green, the only light coming from the sun filtering through the surface, steadily dimming until it's little more than the barest hint of suffused luminescence. Finally all light disappears, and his perception of the water changes: no longer shades of light and dark, but shades of motion and stillness, currents and the ripples of things swimming through, all the while the water growing ever colder...

"What's that?"

David's eyes snap open. He looks over his shoulder to see CB standing a few feet behind him. He half turns, forcing himself to focus on the lean man.

CB is dressed in what is, apparently, his usual attire: a worn t-shirt, jeans, thick boots, and a long tan trenchcoat fraying at the sleeves. A lit cigarette dangles from his mouth. His dark hair is half spiked, half matted—like he slept on it and hasn't bothered fixing it yet. He hasn't shaved in a few days, and the dark rings under his eyes suggest whatever sleep he's getting hasn't been doing its job.

He stares at David, waiting for an answer. It takes a moment to remember the question.

"What's... what?"

CB raises an eyebrow, then gestures to David's hand. David looks down and realizes the orb of darkness he conjured earlier is still there, floating just above his open palm.

"Oh." David closes his hand. The orb disappears. "That's... uh..."

"Magic?" CB speaks with deliberate casualness—the tone of a man trying to keep an angry crowd at bay while he slowly inches to the exit.

"Sort of." David frowns, glances back down at his hand, and summons the black orb again. "But not exactly."

CB mutters something under his breath, then walks up to the edge of the pier, sitting down next to David. "Look, I'm not trying to step on your toes, but I know a little about magic. *Very* little, OK, but enough to know that it's all bad news. As in, there is no part of magic that is actually good news."

kIll hiM mAsHEuDH

The thought is there in an instant, so strong and overpowering that for a moment David goes rigid as it courses through him. The power roils within, aching to be let out. He forces it back.

"Pretty much," He agrees.

"And I don't really know you." If CB notices David's reaction, he doesn't show it. "But I've *heard* about you, from people I usually trust. You were Sky Commando, right?"

The rage and hatred leaves David as quickly as it came. The old yearning shoots through him again.

"Crossfire says you're a stand-up guy, which is a lot coming from them. Travers respects you, and even though I broke his jaw once I gotta admit he's a pretty good judge of character."

David raises an eyebrow.

"Long story," CB says. "Point is, people I'm inclined to trust don't peg you as the evil wizard type. Only you've got magic, and as we just established, there is no part of magic that is actually good news."

"Right," David says. "You're wondering if I'm evil now."

Power surges through him again. His heart races, his head is pounding, he tastes metal.

tHerE is nO EvIL mAsHEuDH onLy cOmmitMEnt

CB shrugs. "I wouldn't put it exactly that way. But yeah."

David takes a deep breath, forcing the presence back once more. *This is not your body. I am in control here.* "It's a fair question. I absorbed a piece of power. The man I took that power from is, without question, evil through and through. I carry that power—and that *evil*—in me, somehow. I also have a lot of his memories, which I find *deeply unpleasant*."

CB nods. "I'll bet."

"But none of it is actually *me*," David says. "The memories are like a really unpleasant houseguest that won't leave. I can access them, but there's no way I can see that I'll ever confuse them for mine. The power is a lot more dangerous—"

yOu mUSt wIEld mE

"—but as long as I never use it I should be all right."

The orb flickers as the presence fades from his consciousness, only the faintest awareness of its discontent seeping through.

"Uh…" CB points at the floating black sphere. "That sort of looks like you're using it."

David looks back at the sphere. "Oh. Yeah, I guess it does. But I'm not—at least, I'm not using it directly. This is kind of a cheat."

"I like cheating," CB says. "It's a personal favorite. But I'm gonna need a little more detail."

David stares out at the water, saying nothing. CB doesn't press him. David frowns, trying to sort through all the thoughts in his head, wondering if it's possible to put them in order.

"I was a cop," he says. "I mean, yeah, Sky Commando, but Sky Commando is a duly sworn officer of the New York Police Department. Before that I was military. I was a good soldier. I was a solid cop. All modesty aside, I was *great* at being Sky Commando. But none of those really prepared me for where I am now."

CB nods.

"I'm not trying to hold out on you, Curveball. Or on anyone. What happened to me is legitimately dangerous. I think we need the information I have, especially now that we know how magic is involved in this virus, but that doesn't mean it won't someday turn me into a monster every bit as horrifying as the man whose power I… acquired."

"But you're not a monster now," CB says.

David takes another deep, steadying breath. "I don't know. I don't feel like one. But I'm not really sure how to talk about it. Not sure I *can* talk about it. You say you know a 'little' about magic. How much can you talk about compared to how much you actually know?"

CB's eyes unfocus slightly. "Not… not all of it."

David nods. "Artigenian—that's the man I took this power from—some of his memories are very specifically about the transactional nature of acquiring power. If you willingly enter into a transaction—often even if you do so completely ignorant of what you're doing—there's a price that you're bound to. In many cases this price is silence. In fact, that seems to be the default setting."

CB's eyes are still unfocused. "Yeah, that lines up with some of what I know. 'My tongue cleaves to my jaws, and you lay me in the dust of death.'"

"I'm pretty sure you're using that out of context," David says.

CB laughs, his eyes snapping back into focus. He shakes his head, grinning. David doesn't understand why, but he doesn't press the issue.

"Seems I'm a little less bound by the rules than some," David adds. "The way I acquired my information was definitely through nonstandard channels. Those rules are still out there, but it seems I have a bit more freedom. I don't know why. I think it's all tied up with how I do this."

He nods to the black orb hovering over his open palm.

CB returns his attention to it. "How *do* you do that?"

"Lucid dreaming."

CB frowns. "You look awake to me."

"I am. Did Artemis ever give you the big speech about magic?"

"I got the summary," CB says. "Ancient force, hostile to life, do not try to negotiate, run like hell."

"Fair place to start," David says. "Ancient *sentient* force. That's the part most people don't expect. Magic has a kind of awareness—it is aware of its surroundings, and in the case of magic dwelling within people it's aware of its host and of itself."

"OK," CB says. "So the power you have is alive and can think?"

"Yeah," David says. "And it speaks Arabic and Aramaic. It keeps calling me 'masheudh.'"

mAsHEuDH

"It has a *pet name* for you?" CB eyes David warily.

"It means 'warlock' in Arabic. I had to Google it."

"It has a pet name for you."

David shrugs. "It's not used affectionately. But here's the interesting part…"

"Oh," CB says, "the interesting part hasn't happened yet. Good to know."

"Here's the interesting part," David repeats. "While magic can perceive this world, it's not part of it. There are aspects of this reality it… they… *it* doesn't understand."

"Oh?" CB leans in. "Like what?"

"Like you, for one thing. The power in me doesn't understand you. Also, it doesn't like you at all. It wants me to kill you—I'm not planning on it, just to be clear, I don't take its advice. It's not fond of Artemis, either, though I think that has more to do with his past history with Artigenian."

"So it doesn't like metahumans," CB says. "I'd noticed that about magic in general."

"No," David says. "I mean, yes, it doesn't like metahumans, but this is different. It doesn't have any specific feelings about Regiment, or Vigilante, or Red Shift, or Scrapper Jack. Or Zero. Hostility is its default setting, so yes, but you and Artemis actually get it worked up a little." His brow furrows. "And one of the Feds. The man. Agent Grant."

"Oh," CB says. "Yes. That's interesting."

"Does it mean something to you?"

"Not really. Go on."

"Well, the thing that's relevant to this little black orb is that it doesn't understand dreaming. Not only does it not understand it, but if you're lucid dreaming, you can control it somehow. I'm not sure how that works. I know it doesn't involve touching or channeling it, because I have memories of how that feels." David shivers. "They're not pleasant memories. It's not like that."

"Kind of, what?" CB asks. "A remote control?"

"That's as good an explanation as any," David says. "When I was asleep back on the—back where Artemis and I were, I could affect the environment around me because it was permeated with magic. And that's essentially what I'm doing here—I'm 'dreaming' a floating black orb above my hand, and the power I'm carrying is creating it. Reluctantly."

"But you're not dreaming," CB says.

"That's where it started." David grows and shrinks the orb, making it look as though it's breathing. "It started with dreams, but I figured out how to duplicate its effects while I was awake... after a fashion. It's harder to do. It's a mindset thing. You ever heard of 'focused daydreaming?'"

CB shakes his head.

"Oh. Well, it's like that." David shrugs. "I don't know how to explain it. There's a specific state of mind I need to be in before I can actually do anything."

"Do anything like what?"

David smiles ruefully. "Creating a little floating orb, mostly. When I do that I know I'm in the right frame of mind. I'm trying to get that down before trying anything else. I've noticed a few interesting side effects though. It seems to enhance my senses a little. Just before you showed up I was daydreaming into the water, and it almost seemed like I could..."

David's voice trails off. His face slackens, and his eyes take on a faraway look.

"Could what?" CB passes his hand in front of David's face. He doesn't blink. "Hello? You there?"

A moment later David's eyes widen in alarm. "I need to find Artemis."

"Trouble?" CB gets to his feet, his voice steady and calm.

"Maybe. Probably... yes. I'm almost sure. Where is Artemis?"

"*LaFleur* is probably with Robert, in his office. Anything I should know?"

"I don't know yet..." David stares at the black orb floating in front of him. It appears to have expanded to twice its original size. He closes his hand, and the orb disappears. "Bad magic thing? Sorry, I don't know how to be more specific right now."

"Go to Robert's office, have him page LaFleur if he's not there," CB says. "I'll round up the others. We'll all meet there."

"Right." David stares out at the water for a moment, then shudders. "Thanks." He turns, running full-tilt down the length of the pier. He's still running as he passes behind the marina's office, disappearing from sight.

CB reaches into his trenchcoat pocket and pulls out a flat metal disc. He passes his thumb over the back, causing it to beep softly. "Robert."

A moment later, a voice emerges from the front. "CB? Is that you?"

"Yeah. You're gonna get a visitor. The emaciated magic guy. He's going to need a minute to remember how to breathe, but after that you should probably listen to what he has to say. Call LaFleur if he's not there."

"He is," Robert says. "Trouble?"

CB turns to look out over the water, wondering what the man saw. A stiff breeze picks up. The air suddenly smells like rain. "I didn't really follow everything he said, but I'm gonna go with 'yes.'"

Part Five: Robert Thorpe's Office

David is out of shape.

This isn't a new condition—he's been out of shape ever since his first concussion—but it's never been quite this bad. His time on the island took more out of him than he wants to admit.

His sides are burning before he gets anywhere close to the main complex, but he doesn't dare stop. He can feel the magic getting stronger, an invisible noose slowly tightening, and he knows that they don't have much time to prepare. He ignores the pain, ignores the knives stabbing at his lungs every time he draws breath, ignores the agony in his ribs and sides, and forces his legs to move. He's running as fast as he can, not bothering to stop for apologies or explanations.

By the time he reaches the building his fear is so great he almost doesn't notice his agony. He can hear the low rumble of thunder in the air, and he can feel an altogether different kind of rumbling behind it. Power gathers; the noose tightens further.

He bursts into the main lobby, ignoring the protests and questions of the man at the front desk as he manages to catch one of the elevators just as it closes. He punches the number for Dr. Thorpe's level, then collapses against the elevator wall, gasping for breath, waving away the concern of the other men and women sharing that space.

When the elevator stops at the right level, he forces himself into the hall, stumbling as he tries to find his balance. He pushed his body hard—too hard, it seems—and now it's ready to collapse. He tries to force himself to move, to run, but all he can manage is to stagger forward a few steps. Again, someone tries to help him, and this time he doesn't push the help away. He mumbles Thorpe's name, repeating it twice before it's clear enough for anyone to understand. His good Samaritan—a middle-aged woman in a white lab coat—finally nods, understanding, and calls for help. She and one of her colleagues, a younger man with a patchy red beard, guide him as briskly as they can to Dr. Thorpe's office door.

It opens the moment they arrive. David mumbles his thanks, steps through, the world swims around him, and he falls to the floor in a heap. It's only then that he suspects there may be more going on than simply exhaustion.

He hears familiar voices: Dr. Thorpe, faintly, as if from a far distance. Artemis LaFleur, a bit closer, his voice sharp with concern. The woman who helped him, explaining what she can, her colleague chiming in occasionally to confirm. And then a firm grip closes on his arms, and he's lifted easily into the air.

"Easy. I got ya."

David's vision clears, and he sees the scarred face of Jack Barrow peering at him.

David takes a deep, gulping breath, trying not to cough. "I need to… sit…"

Jack nods, and helps David over to one of the chairs near Dr. Thorpe's desk. He collapses into it gratefully. He spends a few minutes trying to focus, to get his breathing under control. Nothing feels *right*. He knows he's not in peak form, but it's hard to accept that he's in this state.

Without thinking he extends his right hand and summons the globe of darkness. Almost immediately he feels something shrink back, a pressure he hadn't been aware of until that moment, and it becomes slightly easier to breathe. He focuses on the black orb and imagines it as a kind of shield against that pressure. He sees it pulse, and then he is surrounded by it, a thin, dark radiance covering his entire body. His skin tingles slightly, and the pressure he'd been conflating with exhaustion disappears completely. He dissolves into a fit of coughing, again aware of how badly his lungs are burning.

"What's that?" Jack asks.

"It is," Artemis says, "something very close to, but not quite, magic."

"*How* close?" The suspicion and wariness in Jack's voice are, David thinks, entirely reasonable. He's not a stupid man.

"Not as close as you fear," Artemis says. "I am tempted to call this *dream magic*, though I fear it's an imprecise term."

Dream magic. David finds he likes the phrase. He nods, still wheezing, and gestures to Artemis. "What he said." His voice is very hoarse.

"OK," Jack says. Some of the edge in his voice is gone, but not all of it.

"David, are you all right?" Dr. Thorpe sits behind his desk, taking everything in. His voice is calm, but worried.

David shakes his head, takes two deep breaths, and forces himself to speak. "Someone is casting a spell."

"Where?" Artemis asks sharply.

David finally manages to get a handle on his aches and pains, and sits up. "Everywhere. Surrounding the whole island. Dr. Thorpe, I believe the people behind the virus have discovered your island, and I'm pretty sure they plan to destroy it."

"Call me Robert." Dr. Thorpe reaches out to the computer terminal sitting on his desk, and types a few commands. "What makes you believe we've been discovered? What makes you believe someone is casting a spell?"

There's no obvious skepticism in his voice, just a simple request for more information.

"I think we've been discovered because of the spell," David says. "And I believe there's a spell because I can feel it being cast. It was pretty bad a second ago. It eased off when I did this." He indicates the black shimmering field enveloping his body. "I guess it was sort of like allergies. Really bad ones."

Jack Barrow raises an eyebrow, and looks at Artemis questioningly. Artemis shrugs.

"Artemis." David looks up at the older man. "I know what the spell is. So do you."

Artemis stares back at him. His eyes narrow slightly.

"Yeah," David says. "That one."

An uncomfortable silence settles over the room.

"You are certain of this?" Artemis asks, voice becoming dangerously quiet.

David nods.

Jack scowls, then sighs. "Well, *shit*."

"Tell me more about this spell," Thorpe says. He's still doing something on his computer terminal.

"I remember very little in the way of specifics," Artemis says. "At the time I'd been tricked into believing it would summon guardians to protect my island. Instead it summoned... things. Creatures that exist only to devour and destroy."

"They come from the water," David says. "They are the enemy of everything on dry land. They are attracted to it. They'll swarm to it and strip it bare, leaving nothing but bleached rock behind."

Thorpe looks up from his terminal. "Can we stop it? Counter it in some way?"

"Artemis did," David says. "It cost him a great deal to do so. He had to erase an entire island from existence to undo the spell. We won't be able to do that, since we don't know where the person casting the spell is."

"I have an idea," Artemis says. His voice is strange and dangerous; Jack glances at him in alarm.

"We'd also need to use magic ourselves in order to power it," David says. "We'd need to burn it away, sort of. And we'd need more than I have. Artemis had an entire magical entity dwelling within him when he undid his spell. I only have a portion by comparison."

Robert nods absently. "I think I see how they did it. Someone compromised a number of US satellites and used them to search us out."

"Compromised?" Artemis asks.

"I'm an optimist." Dr. Thorpe frowns slightly, then types a few commands into his keyboard. "I'm going to return the favor. If we can find out where the data was sent—"

His desk phone beeps once. Without looking, he reaches over to activate the speakerphone. "This is Robert Thorpe."

A woman's voice comes through the speakers. "Dr. Thorpe, this is Alison Tucker from Meteorology. There's a storm developing over the island. It's not anything we were tracking. We didn't pick up any sign of it on our weather satellites. It just… showed up. Spontaneously."

Thorpe glances at David.

"That's how it starts," David says.

Thorpe nods. "Dr. Tucker, have your department issue a storm warning for the island. Have all personnel and families move below for the duration."

"Yes sir."

"Call me back if there are any changes." Dr. Thorpe hangs up, then turns back to David. "Tell me how this spell progresses."

David grits his teeth, then dips into Artigenian's memories. "It starts with a storm. It'll be a pretty strong one, with lightning and high winds. I'm not sure how long it'll last. The one on Esperanza lasted for hours, but if it's tied to the strength of the spell this one could be shorter than that. It'll end pretty fast."

"Is that when these creatures arrive?" Thorpe asks.

"No," David says. "Then there will be the horns. Or at least one. Whoever casts the spell needs to use a horn to summon the creatures. There will be multiple calls with the horn. Then the creatures will come."

"Do you know how?"

"Yes." David is breathing normally now, the pain in his lungs, limbs, and side now merely a dull ache. "Yes, I know how. Some of it. I saw it on Esperanza. The rest I know from Artigenian's memories—he was never strong enough to cast the spell, but he always knew what it did. They come out of the water. They make their way to land. They destroy everything in their path, though they ignore everything else around them, unless provoked. There were so many…"

He shudders.

"They don't think, they respond. The horn calls, they follow. They emerge from the water onto land, travel across the land, and disappear back into the water. They're not invulnerable—you can kill them—but there are always so many... there are always more than you can kill. They continue to rise until the land is dead, until what lives on the land is dead. And then the water covers them up... and then they are gone."

His explanation is almost a recitation—it doesn't sound like David at all. With the darkness surrounding him, he doesn't really look like David either. He looks gaunt; his eyes seem empty, peering inward. All eyes in the room are on him, sizing him up, wondering at his sanity. To be honest, he wonders a little himself.

"When the storm ends," David says. "When the storm ends, and the horns begin—that's how long we have. After that, the creatures come."

Dr. Thorpe stares at his terminal and frowns. "In that case," he says, "I think we may have run out of time. Look at the screen."

Everyone looks up at the large screen set in the wall behind his desk. The image changes to a view of one of the beaches on Thorpe's island. Seaweed litters the sand, which has been pushed into mounds from the wind earlier, but at the moment it's calm. There is no rain. There is no wind, no thunder. The surf rolls lazily up the sand, retreats, and rises again.

"The storm," Thorpe says, "appears to have ended."

At that moment, from somewhere far above them, they hear a trumpet sound.

Part One: Thorpe Island

There is a moment after the storm passes when the tension eases—almost like an exhalation of breath, as if the island is relaxing into the promise of calm after weathering the winds and pounding rain. The sky still rumbles, but the sound is faint, and light no longer flickers across the sky. The only trace of the storm that remains is the wind, and it, too, is dying away. There is only the sound of surf rolling onto the sand.

And then there is something new.

Out of the sky a trumpet sounds, blowing a long, clear note. It has no discernible source of origin—the sound simply *is*, existing everywhere, surrounding everything. It isn't loud, but it carries an unmistakable feeling of power. The trumpet sounds again, and the air hums, vibrating with the power it carries. A third time the trumpet sounds, and a soft, steady hiss fills the air as a sharp wind blows over the beaches, creating tiny funnels of sand that quickly dissolve into formless clouds. When the sand falls back to earth it almost sounds like the patter of raindrops all over again.

A siren sounds from a complex of modern buildings at the center of the island, echoed in turn by a siren that sounds in the small town that sits nearby. Men and women emerge from the buildings—stores, houses, apartments—carrying children, pets, and whatever belongings they can manage—and begin to walk toward the town square.

The trumpet sounds again. Many of the people look nervously into the sky, trying to find its source. Small children cry softly, pressing in close to their parents for comfort.

At the center of the island, the gates of the main complex open. A fleet of buses rumbles through, moving at speeds normally considered very unsafe for vehicles of that size. They aren't the fastest things moving, however—a blur of red streaks past them, almost too fast to see, the sharp boom of a supersonic echo following it all the way to the shoreline. A second blur streaks straight into the air, coming to a halt and hanging motionless high over the island. A few of the people point, recognizing the red-and-black uniform.

Roger Whitman. The Regiment.

Two more figures can be seen hurtling through the air—not flying, though given the distance they cover with each leap the point may be moot. They land in the town square with practiced ease, and start directing the growing crowd. One, a tall dark-haired man with a nasty scar traveling down the left side of his face, glances up at the floating form of Regiment, as if waiting for a signal. The people in town know who he is—Scrapper Jack, a villain of some note in days past, now a guest of the island. The other man is dressed in the very distinctive uniform of Crossfire, a group of lawless vigilantes. This man is also a guest of the island.

Fire streaks across the sky as the flaming silhouette of a woman flies up to Regiment and takes position to his right. The townspeople aren't familiar with her.

The townspeople are beginning to believe that maybe, this time, this isn't a drill.

The ground shakes as long, slender cylinders emerge at various points across the island. This causes more concern than anything else—it means the island's point defenses are being deployed, and that isn't usually done for drills.

The buses reach the edge of the town as the horn stops.

For a few seconds all that can be heard are the sirens blaring, and the roar of engines as the buses career wildly into town. Then a third sound, felt before it's heard… a rumbling groan emerging from the water, rolling over the land, a sonic fog of discontent and malice that makes pets restless and small children weep. The sound increases steadily, until it sits somewhere between the bus engines and sirens.

That's when the water begins to roil.

A wide ribbon of churning wake erupts from the ocean water, surrounding the island completely. The frenzy of the ocean deep triggers a change in the sound: the rumbling groan grows louder, angrier, more intense… and as the sound increases, it feeds back into the water, and the seething ring widens in turn.

Twenty feet. Fifty feet. One hundred feet. Two hundred feet. Two hundred and fifty feet of water churning so fiercely that it has turned foamy white, surrounding the island completely, and still growing wider.

Panic begins to set in. People pour into the streets, surging forward as if intending to meet the trucks halfway. Vigilante and Scrapper Jack immediately start shouting, telling the townspeople to fall back, form lines, and wait. They are ignored until Jack stamps firmly on the ground. The tremor cracks the asphalt around his feet and momentarily surprises the crowd into silence.

The buses roll in shortly after. When the first comes to a stop, a thin, spiky-haired man wearing a trenchcoat hops out.

"Single file, climb in!" CB's voice cuts through the noise effortlessly. "When this bus is full, start boarding the next! There is room for everyone, and *you will not be left behind.*"

That is apparently the reassurance they were looking for. The crowd quickly forms into lines.

CB grabs one of the townspeople at random and jerks his thumb to indicate the bus. "Can you drive this thing?"

An older woman dressed in green coveralls blinks in surprise and nods mutely.

CB nods back and tosses her the keys. "When the bus is full, go to the main complex. They'll take it from there."

The woman nods again, then hurries into the bus, climbing up the well and into the driver's seat.

The other buses line up behind the first, and their drivers emerge in turn. CB nods to Jenny as she emerges from the second bus, then to Alan Grant as he steps out of the third. He doesn't bother nodding at Agent Grant as he steps out of the fourth, fifth, and sixth; it feels redundant.

"The Lieutenant says they're close." Street Ronin's voice comes in clearly through the nearly invisible earpiece CB is wearing. "Ten minutes on the outside."

"How does he know? How sure is he?" CB snatches a backpack off the ground, handing it back to the young teen who dropped it moments before. "And why are you calling him *Lieutenant* when you know he's not a cop any more?"

"He hasn't thought of a name yet." Street Ronin sounds mildly exasperated. "I can't exactly blame him—his power is weird—but we gotta call him *something*. Anyway, he says he can sort of feel them."

"He can *sort of* feel them?" CB does a quick headcount. "We have forty buses. Mine is about half full. We're going to need more time than that."

"You'll get it." Roger's voice cuts in, sounding calm and unconcerned.

I guess when you can fly and never bleed it's hard to get stressed about fighting an unending horde of magic bug aliens.

"Ten minutes to surface," Street Ronin says. "Not ten minutes before these things overrun your position. Given what the Lieutenant has told us, we should be able to stall their advance long enough for you to evacuate the town."

"Fine," CB says. "Since we have some time to kill, how about we find *the Lieutenant* a proper handle, so Crossfire doesn't keep rubbing his forced retirement in his face?"

"That's not what we're doing." Street Ronin sounds a little defensive.

CB grins. "Not intentionally, maybe, but you know, he didn't retire because he *wanted* to."

David Bernard breaks in, sounding wary. "It's OK. I'd rather not commit to a name before I've had a chance to figure out exactly what I can do."

"I got one for him." Alan Grant's voice cuts in, and CB looks across the square to see the man trying very hard not to grin. "It's *perfect*."

David's wariness turns sharply toward alarm. "Uh, I don't think—"

"Doctor Weird."

There's a moment of silence over the line.

"What?" David asks faintly.

"Doctor Weird," Grant repeats. "You're Earth's Warlock Supreme."

That provokes sharp laughter from Jenny. The townspeople boarding her bus look at her nervously as they pass.

"Grant, you are such an *asshole*." Agent Hu, Grant's partner, sounds more amused than annoyed. "Also, 'Weird' is a *terrible* handle."

"Thank you," David says.

"Should be something like 'Enigma,'" she continues. "Sounds way cooler."

"That's actually not bad," Vigilante agrees.

"I can't be—"

Before David has a chance to continue his protest, Street Ronin cuts in. "Red Shift just checked in. He votes yes on 'Doctor Enigma.' He'd tell you himself, but he's moving a little too fast to talk right now."

"It's a pretty good handle." Scrapper Jack, this time. "But isn't it already in play? I wanna say it's some guy in Kansas."

"Nah, Scrapper, that's just 'Enigma,'" Vigilante says. "And he retired a few years ago."

"Look," David says, fighting to keep the exasperation out of his voice, "I don't think this is the right time to—"

"Let's get a consensus here," CB says. "Jenny? Roger? Robert? LaFleur? We haven't heard from any of you, yet."

"Gladiator and Overmind are abstaining from the vote," Street Ronin says. "They're too busy being grownups."

"I'm not voting either." Roger doesn't bother hiding his amusement. "But I agree, it's a pretty good name."

"That counts as a 'yes,'" CB says. "Jenny?"

"I like it," Jenny says. "Seriously, David, you could do a lot worse."

"Well, there you go," CB says. "That's all in favor, minus two abstentions. Motion carries. Congratulations, Doctor Enigma."

"We're *not* all in favor," David protests. "*I'm* not in favor."

"Oh, come on," CB says, "you don't count…"

"Guys!" CB can almost picture David throwing up his hands in exasperation. "I have a Bachelor's degree in Criminal Justice!"

The channel is useless for the next two minutes. No one can seem to stop laughing.

Part Two: The Final Wave

"Status report, please."

Street Ronin is saying *please*, so CB figures he's worried about something.

"My bus is about half full," CB says.

"Same," Jenny says.

"My four are a little less than that," Grant says. "The other thirty-four are behind me."

"You still stuck at four?" Agent Hu sounds surprised. "I thought you were back up to five again."

"Not if a fight's going to break out," Grant says. "Which I'm pretty sure is what's going to happen. Speaking of, what's up with the new jet spa we've got around our island?"

"Still growing," Street Ronin says. "Four hundred twenty feet thick, and still growing."

"You'd think we'd see something by now," CB mutters.

Street Ronin laughs sharply. "Oh, we definitely see something. Sonar's just a solid mass of somethings. Doctor Thorpe sent a little unmanned submarine probe down there to get a look. It's a solid wall of things I'm trying not to think about too much."

"Right." CB looks at the forty buses parked in the town square and tries to work out the math. "So when you say a solid wall of things, how solid are we talking?"

There's a brief pause. "As far as we can tell it goes all the way down."

His eyes widen. "No shit. To the bottom of the ocean?"

"What's to the bottom of the ocean?"

CB looks up to see an older couple standing in front of him, staring at him in fear.

"What?"

The man, slightly overweight with thinning, straw-blonde hair, wraps his arm around the woman's shoulders and squeezes slightly. "You said 'to the bottom of the ocean.'"

"Right…" CB curses silently. *Good going, genius. Try not to panic the civilians, OK?* He mutes his earpiece and turns to face them. "Yeah, sorry. Don't worry about it. Just get on the bus so we can get you someplace safe."

"Is that where we're going?" the woman asks. The line moving into the bus stops, as a few other people turn to face them.

They're all afraid, but they're all keeping it together. They're doing what they're supposed to... so far.

So it would be really great if you didn't screw that up for everyone, CB.

"Hell *yes*," CB says. "Look. I don't know how long you've worked here, but you're standing on the biggest freaking boat ever made, disguised to look like an island. The man who invented that says he can protect everyone if we get to the main complex. If he says it, I believe it."

The couple trade glances. The woman laughs nervously. "That *is* why we took the job."

"Yeah," the man says. His gaze drifts over the water, staring at the ever-expanding ring of churning foam. "It's just... this is..."

CB forces himself to stay calm. "Look, I get it. This is scary. It's OK to be scared, just don't *panic*. Get on the bus."

The man nods, but doesn't move.

"Mister," CB says, an edge creeping into his voice, "you're *holding up the line*."

The man blinks, stares at CB, then looks at the line of people behind him. "Jesus! I'm sorry. I'm sorry."

The man and the woman move forward, stepping up into the bus. CB waves at the rest of the line, and everyone falls into step.

CB unmutes the earpiece. "Any of you worked out a mathematical way to get people on a bus faster? Maybe we could get Vigilante and Jack to rip off the roofs and just start throwing 'em over the top."

"Don't worry," Street Ronin says. "They're nowhere near the surface yet, you have plenty of—"

At that moment, the ocean explodes.

Dark shapes burst out of the deep, shooting high into the sky, arcing slowly, then falling back into the water with a splash. The trumpet returns, and the sound is harsher, more urgent. With the trumpet's call comes a new sound: low, wet, rumbling, a cross between a rattling cough and roar. As more creatures burst into the open air, the sound increases, until it is so loud that it's impossible to hear the sirens.

Somewhere in the back of CB's mind he's chanting *objects in mirror may be closer than they appear* over and over again.

The townspeople, already on the edge of reason, begin to panic. They start to push each other, many attempting to force their way through the line and into the bus, some abandoning the lines altogether, heading toward the complex on foot. CB wades into the line, trying to keep the panicked people from trampling each other in their haste to board, but it isn't working. They're frightened, out of their depth, and driving themselves into a desperate frenzy.

"It doesn't feel like we have plenty of time!"

One of the townspeople takes a swing at CB, trying to get him out of the way. He parries the blow easily, and the next, and steps smoothly to one side to avoid another man's attempt to tackle him outright. "We need to do something now, or we're not going to be able to regain control of the—"

The world goes silvery white. A *snap* and *hummm* cuts through the sound of the roaring beasts and the shrill trumpet's call, and when the translucent dome appears over the island those sounds disappear entirely. The siren shuts off, and the sudden lack of sound startles the newly-rioting crowds into stillness.

Loudspeakers crackle to life, and a calm, strong voice speaks through them.

"This is Robert Thorpe."

The crowd focuses intently on the sound of Robert's voice. CB can feel the tension easing slightly.

"As you all know, this island is under attack. Per our evacuation protocol, we are moving you to the main facility for your safety."

The tension eases further. *Good timing, Robert.*

"Our enemy is trying to slow your evacuation by provoking you to panic. I realize that what you see right now is startling—that what you've heard, and will hear again shortly is extremely uncomfortable—but if you focus on the evacuation, you will be safe."

The crowd murmurs uncertainly.

"Understand that right now, the most powerful men and women on the planet are standing by to make sure that you all board the buses safely, that the buses take you to the main facility safely—that you *arrive* and *disembark* safely. Regiment. Curveball. Vigilante. Red Shift. Street Ronin. Scrapper Jack. And yes, it's true: Overmind is also here. You've heard those names. You haven't heard of the metahuman agents of the Department of Homeland security who are here to defend you, but if you look up you can see one of them, floating next to Regiment. Her partner is with you now, helping you board the buses. And on top of that—on top of all of those people, who have pledged to keep you safe—we have the former Sky

Commando and the granddaughter of Liberty—both metahumans, both standing with us."

The crowd has fallen completely silent.

"I won't pretend this isn't a serious and dangerous situation," Robert continues. "It is. But we have *prepared* for this danger. I realize how frightening this is—it's only rational to be frightened, in this situation—but the important thing is not to panic. Do not panic. Board the buses in a quick, orderly fashion. When you exit the bus, you will be safe. Until then, focus on what you need to do. Focus on allowing the people who have sworn to protect you to do their job. Focus, and don't give in to panic."

Another moment of silence passes.

"Unfortunately, we can't maintain the acoustic dampeners for much longer. When they go down, all that sound is going to return. Be ready for it. Don't give in to it. Board the buses. Focus. Thank you all for your cooperation."

By the time he finishes talking the lines are moving again. When the silvery field disappears, when the roar of inhuman sound returns, the crowd flinches visibly... but the lines stay, and people keep boarding the buses.

CB sighs in relief. He turns his attention back to the crowd, focusing on getting them on the bus and out of the town. That's his job. He pushes the noise as far away as he can, and focuses on his job.

* * *

The first wave of creatures don't make it to land. The island's point defenses activate, and solid beams of searing blue energy sweep across the waters, cutting through the rubbery-black creatures effortlessly. Again and again the weapons sweep across the waters, and cries of pain and unthinking rage mix with the low rumbling roars as rubbery black shapes continue to shoot out of the water and into the air.

But as effective as the island's defenses are, they can't hold back what threatens to be a literal tide of abomination. Some slip past the built-in defenses.

The ones that reach land die quickly at first: one moment Regiment is hanging in midair above the island, the next he is streaking toward the beach in a blur, and an inhuman shriek sounds, briefly, before bits of rubbery black flesh explode. Or the burning woman streaks across the sky, a lance of fire cutting another in half almost as neatly as the island's energy weapons. Or a red blur races across the island, ripping into a giant, misshapen shadow just as it crawls out of the water.

For a while, they hold the line. CB and the others in town focus on loading the buses and sending them off. Eventually they do fill, and one by one they make their way up the road, back to the facility. There are only seven buses left when someone screams, then someone else shouts, hoarse with fear:

"The ocean is gone!"

CB glances over his shoulder and feels his jaw go slack. It's true: he can no longer see the water. As far as he can see, in every direction, all he can see is a mass of crawling, rubbery-black flesh.

"Get on the bus…" He stares in horror as the creatures crawl over each other as they attempt to reach the beaches. They are alien things: large, vaguely similar to salamanders, eyeless heads and gaping maws full of razor-sharp teeth.

"Get on the bus!" He forces himself to turn away, back to the remaining townspeople. "Don't look out there! Focus on the goddamn bus!"

Three buses pull away.

"I don't want to sound pushy," Street Ronin says, "but how are the buses coming along?"

"Four left," CB says.

"One is almost full," Jenny reports. "Two more are at half. One just started loading up."

"That's good news," Street Ronin says. "Here's the bad news: the creatures are about to hit the island en masse. When that happens, things get more complicated: the point defenses are going to get useless pretty quick. Apparently they were specifically designed not to shoot holes in the island."

"Well. *Shit.*" CB looks at the remaining buses and shakes his head. "You know, on any other day I'd consider that a good thing."

Part Three: Hitting the Beaches

Street Ronin is sitting at Robert Thorpe's desk, directing traffic.

It's the most logical place: Thorpe is already connected to the island, has access to everything, and his office has enough room to accommodate some of the extra gear Crossfire brought along to allow their communications—specifically, the equipment that makes it possible for Red Shift to communicate when he's moving at high speeds—to work properly with everything else.

Doctor Thorpe is not currently in the room—he's overseeing the second phase of the evacuation—but a few of the other Thorpe Institute techs are sitting at other ad hoc stations set up in the office. Overmind and Lieutenant Bernard—despite the earlier levity, Street Ronin isn't quite ready to start calling him "Doctor Enigma" just yet—*are* there, both trying to look calmer than they feel.

The "ad hoc stations," Street Ronin notes, don't actually look ad hoc. They look like they were intentionally designed to be used in the room. He also notes that they've stopped calling the room "Doctor Thorpe's office," and they're now referring to it as "the bridge."

He glances over the tactical display, noting the position of the creatures just as they are about to make landfall.

"OK, I see an opportunity to push them back a little. If we pull it off, we buy ourselves maybe another half hour of point defenses."

The island is essentially an inverted triangle: the "north" beach is a short stretch of land that juts out into the ocean, forming its own tiny peninsula. The "east" and "west" beaches flare out from the north beach, curve around the bulk of the island and then taper off in a point at the "south."

"Agent Hu, can you take the north beach?" Street Ronin does some swift calculations in his head, curses as he realizes he can't afford to trust his math skills that much, and starts keying them into his terminal.

"That depends," Hu says. "There are things I can do, but… well, how married is Doctor Thorpe to this beach?"

"Not very," Street Ronin says.

"OK," Hu says. "We're good. This isn't precise, though: I'm pretty sure I'll get most of 'em, but pool really isn't my game. I'm pretty sure I'll wind up knocking some in the wrong direction."

"Understood," Street Ronin says. "Scrapper Jack, Vigilante, head to the north beach to support Agent Hu. But, uh, stay back until you get the signal."

"What's the signal going to be?" Vigilante asks.

"*Boom*," Hu says. "And maybe a light tan."

"Regiment, Red Shift: I need you to focus on the east beach. Go all out—Red Shift, push, and push *hard* to get them off the beach. Regiment, you focus on pushing them farther back into the water. Until they hit land they should all be packed pretty tightly together."

"Got it," Regiment says. Red Shift sends his acknowledgment shortly after.

"I'm going to focus all the island's point defenses on the west beach. Since they only have to focus on one side, I think they'll actually be able to push the advance back. I figure if we keep that up for ten minutes there'll be enough of a buffer to let the defenses take over the whole thing for a while. Should give the townspeople the window they need to finish up. Report when you're in position."

"In position," Regiment says.

Red Shift reports he's in position.

A moment later, Hu chimes in: "In position."

"Right. Switching point defenses now…"

Street Ronin keys in the command.

* * *

Roger Whitman hangs motionless in mid-air, watching the creatures creep slowly up along the length of the east beach. He hears the whining *hummm* of the island's point defenses as they break from their earlier targets and refocus on the other side of the island. A streak of red flashes across the beach; the air shatters as a sonic boom trails behind. Sand barely has time to billow up behind the blur as the things on the beach are ripped apart. Red Shift isn't trying to attack them, he's just *moving through them*, and it looks like he's doing it effortlessly.

Roger represses a shudder as the beach is littered with the remains of rubbery, reptilian flesh. Sand fills the air, obscuring the scene of carnage so it appears nothing more than the frenzied thrashing of indistinct silhouettes.

Roger activates his earpiece. "Red Shift is almost done. I'll be moving in soo—"

The world twists sideways. An explosion tears through the sky, filling Roger's vision with blinding white light. Roger blinks, then turns to face the sound.

The north beach is gone. Roger gapes at the remains of where it had been, only moments before. What remains, of both land and beast, has been literally torn to shreds from the force of overpressure. *That was Agent Hu,* he thinks to himself. *Holy cow.*

"Um." Agent Hu's voice breaks in over the line, weak and mildly dazed. "Sorry about your island, Doc…"

Roger hopes she's all right, but he can't spend any time thinking about it. Red Shift is almost done clearing the beach. It's his turn.

Roger isn't as fast as Red Shift—under certain conditions, it's not even close—but he has the advantage of being able to fly. He feels the air pulse around him as he goes supersonic, and the world around him grows sharper, clearer—not slower, exactly, but so much easier to understand…

He briefly considers his options. Red Shift has pushed the advance back into the water, to a point where he can't run, and where he can't really swim, either. The creatures are half submerged, which is slowing them down as well. Farther out, he has to worry not just about the creatures he can see—the ones that have surfaced—but the ones crawling along *underneath* as well.

Right. He takes a deep breath, then dives.

He feels water vaporize into mist as he hits the surface, sees the world go dark as he rams himself like a human-sized bullet through the first of many creatures, feels an unpleasant burn-tickle as he tears through its body. Its blood is acidic, apparently, though not enough to hurt him—just enough for him to notice. His eyes adjust to the darkness of the water almost immediately, but it doesn't help: all he can see is dark, writhing, groping forms as they try to make their way to shore. Moments later he's out of the water, eyes stinging from the salt and light and unnatural blood, and then he dives again.

Again, and again, back and forth, he hurls himself into the water, always trying to force the horde back. The east beach drops off quickly, and eventually he doesn't bother coming up for air after every strafing run.

The creatures attempt to fight back. He's moving much too fast for the ones he targets to defend themselves, but the creatures just behind lash out, jaws snapping closed in the space he occupied only moments before. Once or twice he feels a mouth close on his foot, but they don't break the skin. Nothing ever does.

After a few minutes underwater he emerges to draw another breath and take a quick tactical assessment. It's hard to tell exactly how much progress they've made: the surface of the water is littered with reptile parts, and more are washing up on a beach that is already full of reptile carcasses. He sees Red Shift—well, he sees his contrail—streaking across the beach, picking off creatures Roger missed in the water.

Roger's earpiece buzzes to life.

"That mostly worked," Street Ronin says. "I'm returning the point defenses to their original firing pattern."

A moment later the turrets on the east beach begin firing in long arcs across the waters off the east shoreline.

The red blur comes to a halt, and Regiment can see Red Shift standing on the beach, swaying in place.

"I don't have much left," Red Shift says, voice thick with fatigue.

"I'm... not so great myself," Hu adds. Roger can see her in the air, a bright speck in the distance, weaving and bobbing like a drunk firefly.

"Come on in," Street Ronin says. "The last bus is loaded up and on its way in. Regiment, keep to the air, look for any stragglers we might have missed. Scrapper Jack, Vigilante, get back to the last bus and escort it in."

Roger starts circling the island, keeping inside the firing range of the turrets as he scans the surface for signs of encroachment. He doesn't find anything. That bothers him.

"Everything looks clear up here," Roger says.

There's a short pause.

"You don't sound happy about that," CB says. "That's the kind of thing I'd expect someone to be happy about."

"Yeah," Roger says. "Well... it's us."

CB's voice grows cautious. "True."

"Hey, I'll be real happy if this plan goes off without a hitch, but how often does that usually happen?"

* * *

No one is quite prepared for the intensity of Agent Hu's attack. For Vigilante and Scrapper Jack, it's particularly startling.

They stand on a short hill at the far end of the beach, looking out at the mass of rubbery-black flesh crawling toward them. Jack represses a shudder, wondering what the most effective way to kill one of those things will be. The north beach is narrow, but it's long, and the creatures have filled up about half the length of it so far.

Over the line Jack hears Regiment announce he's in position, and notes with annoyance how calm and collected the man sounds.

That's because he can fly. Lucky bastard.

The line snaps to life again. "In position," Agent Hu says.

Vigilante nudges Jack and points. Agent Hu, currently a brightly burning humanoid shape, is hovering about ten feet above the creatures, three-quarters of the way down the beach. They don't react to her presence.

"What exactly is she going to do?" Vigilante asks. "She was pretty solid against the magic robot, but that was a single target. She can't cover the whole beach in fire, can she?"

Jack shrugs. "Beats me. Street Ronin seems to know."

He briefly considers using the man's real name, just to annoy Vigilante, but now isn't the time for that.

"Switching point defenses now…"

Jack can feel the change when the turrets focus on the west beach. The air stirs slightly as energy shoots across the center of the island. He half-turns, shifting his gaze away from the beach for just a moment. That's when he feels Vigilante tense.

"Her fire's gone out!"

Jack whirls back to the beach just in time to see Agent Hu, no longer burning, fall into the center of the horde crawling out of the ocean.

"Red Shift is almost done. I'll be moving in soo—"

Jack never hears the end of Regiment's message. The north beach erupts into a ball of fire unlike anything he's ever seen.

One moment he's standing on the hill, staring in mute surprise at a sudden, fiercely burning sphere of fire igniting in the middle of the horde, and the next there's a loud *crack*, and the horde is shredded into a fine mist before his very eyes. Almost in the same breath, Jack feels an invisible force hit him full on, carrying with it sand and rock and bits of rubbery flesh. He is vaguely aware of sailing through the air, then smashing down onto the tarmac of the now-evacuated airport… then being driven *into* the tarmac before grinding to a halt.

He lies there on his back for a moment, blinking in surprise, staring at the sand and dust still flying through the air. Then, with a grunt of annoyance, he sits up.

He hit the ground pretty hard. He made a crater.

"Um." Agent Hu's voice breaks in over the line, weak and mildly dazed. "Sorry about your island, Doc…"

Jack staggers to his feet. To the north, all he can see is a billowing cloud of sand. He crosses the distance in a few short hops, returning to the hill where he originally stood, and looks over a rapidly-filling crater of seawater where the north beach used to sit.

Jack wonders if this means the island is in danger of sinking.

Probably take longer to sink than it will to be overrun by evil salamanders.

He activates his headset as he quickly scans the area, looking for signs of any creatures that may have survived the blast. "Agent Hu?"

"Here." Her voice is very tired.

"Where?"

There's a quick burst of fire over at the lip of the crater—an instant's flash which quickly dies away.

"I'm coming," Jack says, and with practiced ease he leaps, crossing the distance and landing just a few feet away from her.

Agent Hu is wearing her "swimsuit"—it actually does look like a one-piece swimsuit, the kind swimmers wear for races, only the material is stiff and obviously uncomfortable. Treated with asbestos, if Jack remembers correctly.

"Can you stand?"

Agent Hu nods without speaking. She climbs to her feet slowly, wincing from the effort. "I really hope I don't have to file this report."

Jack snorts.

There's a burst of static over his earpiece, then a second, and finally he hears Vigilante, his voice slurred. "Didn't expect that."

"Where are you?" Jack asks.

"Island," Vigilante says. "Sand."

Jack scowls. "Pull yourself together."

"Right," Vigilante says. A moment later: "Sorry. Back now."

Jack looks over his shoulder and sees Vigilante land at the hill. He waves once, and a second later Vigilante lands next to him.

Vigilante's face is covered in cuts and bruises, though both are fading rapidly. His dark hair is matted with sand and tiny twigs. He nods once to Agent Hu.

"Did you get them all?"

"Think so," Hu says. "*Hope* so. I don't think I can do that again. Not for a while."

Jack's earpiece buzzes.

"That mostly worked," Street Ronin says. "I'm returning the point defenses to their original firing pattern."

The breeze shifts again, and arcs of energy shoot over them as the northern point defenses resume their sweep across the waters beyond.

Red Shift calls in, nearly spent. Hu ignites and takes to the air, wobbles erratically, then sinks as her fire flickers out for a second. Exhaustion stares dully out her eyes, but she sets her jaw, her fire flares up, and she climbs back into the sky.

"Come on in," Street Ronin says. "The last bus is loaded up and on its way in. Regiment, keep to the air, look for any stragglers we might have missed. Scrapper Jack, Vigilante, get back to the last bus and escort it in."

Jack and Vigilante trade glances. Vigilante sighs, brushes some of the sand out of his hair, and starts leaping inland. Jack grimaces and follows suit.

It takes half a minute to catch up to the bus. It must have taken longer to load than the others, because none of the other buses are in sight. Jack can see faces pressed up against the windows. Looking past the faces, into the bus, it seems to Jack that this bus has been packed to the gills.

The bus weaves slightly, taking the center of the road, and the engine roars louder as the driver tries to make it go faster.

"—that's the kind of thing I'd expect someone to be happy about," CB is saying.

"Yeah," Roger says. "Well… it's us."

Vigilante motions once with his hand. Jack nods and they split up, each taking a side—Vigilante on the right, Jack to the left. Jack sees CB sitting at the wheel.

"True," CB says.

"Hey, I'll be real happy if this plan goes off without a hitch, but how often does that usually happen?"

As if on cue, the road ahead collapses, and creatures burst out of the ground.

Part Four: Roadblocks

Buses are not intended to be driven fast. They are built for power, not speed, and pushing a bus to go faster than its design supports reminds CB of shaking the contents of a cereal box very hard in order to get at the prize at the bottom. So when the ground tremors start, he thinks it's the bus.

He takes one hand off the steering wheel, reaching into his trenchcoat pocket, and fishes out a crumpled pack of cigarettes. Jenny, standing in the bus stairwell, looks at him crossly.

"You're smoking *now*?"

CB manages to thumb the end of a cigarette out of the pack, sticks it in his mouth, and pulls the rest away. "Don't want the bus to break down just yet."

"*Just yet?*" A note of incredulity creeps into her voice.

"I don't care what happens to it once we get where we're going," CB says. He replaces the cigarettes, and takes out his lighter.

His earpiece crackles to life as Street Ronin instructs Scrapper Jack and Vigilante to return to the bus as an honor guard. It doesn't take long before he sees both of them, one on each side, keeping pace by jumping alongside it.

Dammit I wish this thing could go faster. He fumbles with his lighter. It sparks, but doesn't catch.

CB's earpiece crackles again. "Everything looks clear up here," Roger says.

CB frowns. That's not Roger's happy voice. He works the lighter again—again it sparks, but doesn't catch.

"You don't sound happy about that," CB says. "That's the kind of thing I'd expect someone to be happy about."

"Yeah," Roger says. "Well… it's us."

CB scowls. "True."

Jenny glances sharply at CB.

"Hey," Roger continues, "I'll be really happy if this plan goes off without a hitch, but how often does that usually happen?"

"Dammit," CB mutters, and works the lighter again. Finally he gets a proper flame.

"Excuse me." One of the passengers leans forward, his voice trembling only slightly. "We'd appreciate it if you didn't smoke."

CB takes a moment to not say everything that immediately pops into his head. He reminds himself that the request is probably reasonable. He fights back the irrational, and wholly inappropriate rage that comes over him.

"Sorry," he says, and lights up.

The passenger blinks, surprised, then presses on. "Look, my daughter is allergic to cigarette smoke—"

"The road!" Jenny's shout cuts the man off completely. She points ahead, and as CB squints through the dusty glass he can see a stretch of road a few hundred feet ahead of them *rippling* like the surface of a lake.

"Oh, *shit*." CB takes a long pull of his cigarette, trying to feel for the world spinning around him. "Shit shit shit shit *shit*."

"What?" The passenger has, for the moment, forgotten his complaint, keying in on the fact that the man trying to drive them to safety is suddenly a lot more concerned than he was before.

"We've been playing this all wrong," CB says. He can feel it now: the world spins, full of possibility. All he has to do is choose... "We've been thinking in two dimensions."

"Two... dimensions..." Jenny's eyes widen. "No."

"Everybody hold on!" CB shouts. Then he *chooses*, the world snaps into focus, and he slams on the brakes.

If a bus isn't designed to go fast, it also isn't designed to *stop* when it's going fast. The entire bus jolts as the brakes try and fail to halt the forward momentum. CB turns the wheel sharply to the left, and the bus tips up on its right wheels as physics begins to demonstrate exactly how poor a judgment call that was.

And then a moment later, for no reason that any physicist would ever be able to properly explain, the bus falls back on all four wheels. It proceeds to skid into a one hundred and eighty degree turn.

The passengers scream. Jenny exhales sharply as she's thrown against the folding stairwell doors—fortunately they're locked closed, and she isn't thrown out. CB concentrates on the turn, letting up on the brake just before it finishes, and hitting the gas to get it moving forward again. In less time than anyone has a right to expect, the bus has turned around and is moving in the opposite direction.

The rippling patch of road tears open and falls away as a mass of rubbery-black salamander-things pour out of the earth. CB can hear swearing over the line, and incoherent crosstalk as Street Ronin tries to clarify exactly what the hell is going on.

"We're cut off, is what's going on!" CB snarls. He looks to his right and his left. Neither Jack nor Vigilante are there—that means they've waded in, trying to buy him more time.

"OK, OK, I'm on it." Street Ronin has returned to his calm, clipped persona.

"Don't bother," CB says. "There's no good way back to the facility. I don't care how flat the fucking island is, this bus won't do offroad."

He thinks quickly, sorting through his options, trying to find the one that sucks least.

"I'm heading for the airport."

At those words, the bus falls completely silent. They can hear the creatures roaring in the distance, some in anger, some in pain.

Finally Street Ronin breaks in over the earpiece again. "You won't have a lot of time," he says. "The point defenses will give you maybe five or six minutes once you get there. You won't have enough time to prep anything for takeoff."

"I'm already there," Red Shift says. He sounds utterly exhausted, forcing his normally cheerful voice into a determined growl. "Someone tell me what to do, and I'll do it."

"I can help," Roger says, and the sky echoes with a supersonic *boom*.

"So can I," Agent Grant adds. "Just so happens I'm in the neighborhood."

"That's great," Jenny says. "Do any of you know how to prep and refuel a plane? And who exactly is going to fly it?"

Silence again. A distinctly more *uncomfortable* silence.

CB shrugs. "One thing at a time. I can just... I don't know, turn levers and press buttons at random until we—"

"I can fly it." David Bernard's voice cuts across the line.

CB raises an eyebrow. "Aren't you at the main facility right now? How are you getting from point A to point B?"

"I can make it," David says. "If everything works out right I'll even have it waiting on the runway. Red Shift, Regiment, Agent Grant, I'm going to walk you through a *very short* and *extremely unsafe* prep checklist. Meanwhile we need everyone else to focus on slowing down our new best friends."

A new voice comes through the earpiece—one CB doesn't expect to hear. An older voice, crisp, full of authority and lacking any hint of uncertainty. "Understood. I am on my way."

Artemis LaFleur, the villain Overmind, is taking the field.

Jenny frowns. "What exactly does he do, anyway?"

"He's a shapechanger," CB says.

"So he's going to… what?" Jenny asks. "Turn into a giant bear, or something?"

"Not exactly," CB says. "It's a little showier than that."

"And what should I do during all this?" Jenny asks.

CB glances over at her. Her jaw is clenched, lines of frustration etched deep into her forehead. "You and me, and probably Agent Grant, we'll be getting these people on the plane."

"That's *it*?" Jenny bites down on the rest of what she was going to say. She flushes slightly, turning away in embarrassment.

"Yeah," CB says. "It's a little frustrating, right? When everyone else is running at the speed of sound, and flying through the air, and hitting things with the force of a Mack Truck traveling at full speed downhill. But all that stuff is kinda pointless if we can't get these people off the island."

"I know that," Jenny says. "I *know* that, really. It's just… I mean, I *know* it, but I still feel—"

"This is where Alex would be," CB says. "If he was still alive. This is what he would choose to do."

Jenny bows her head. "Yeah, I guess it is."

"And besides," CB says, "anyone who can beat Johann Richter in a fight doesn't have to prove jack shit to anyone."

Jenny smiles slightly. "I didn't do more than hold my own. Once Street Ronin showed up, it wasn't exactly a fair fight."

CB snorts. "Fair fights are for evil movie ninjas. The rest of us *cheat*."

* * *

There's not much time for discussion after the ground gives way. Fortunately, Jack and Vigilante are pretty much on the same wavelength: the bus needs a buffer, and at the moment they are it.

Without breaking stride, they throw themselves into the mass of creatures bursting out of the earth. At first the hole in the ground is relatively narrow, only wide enough for five or six creatures to escape, but the edges are crumbling quickly. Jack wades in, grabbing one of the reptiles and swinging it in an arc, knocking it into two others, driving them back into the hole. One cries out in pain as it ceases to be part of the advancing horde and instead becomes an *obstacle*—it's torn to pieces by the creatures behind it.

For about half a minute Jack is immersed in the struggle. It's a futile struggle, ultimately—he and Vigilante are more than a match for any one of these creatures, but neither one of them is fast enough to take them down in the numbers needed to halt their advance. Eventually the sinkhole will expand, and the creatures will pour out of it in numbers too great for the two of them to handle. Neither one of them is in any great danger of dying—at least, in Vigilante's case, not *permanently*—but they are in danger of becoming irrelevant soon.

They need to find a way to even things up a little. Barring any other options, that means they need to change the terrain.

Just as Jack reaches that conclusion, he notices that Vigilante has stopped fighting the creatures. He's fighting *past* them, going deeper into the sinkhole that they're swarming out of. A moment later, one of the creatures trying to climb out of the hole appears to stumble and fall back, then a second, then a third. That's when Jack realizes what Vigilante is doing: he's not fighting, he's *digging*. He's trying to make the sinkhole deeper and wider, forcing them to fill more space before they can climb out of it.

It's a better plan than anything Jack has at the moment.

He grits his teeth and jumps in, smashing his way past and through a seemingly endless stream of things. They claw at his body, and bite into his flesh—at least, they try to. The creatures, however magical their origin, have been given a physical form, and that form isn't strong enough to do more than get in Jack's way. He focuses on moving past them and getting to the wall, then he focuses on moving as much earth as he can.

Make the hole wider. Make the hole deeper.

The best scenario is to keep the opening at the top the same size, while gradually expanding the sides as he works his way down, creating a funnel. That will force the creatures to compete for space, or at the very least to take time away from advancing in order to focus on digging themselves. There's no way to pull it off perfectly—the hole was already widening when they started fighting—but there's no time to dither about it. Jack pushes everything else out of his head and focuses solely on digging.

They are both strong men—even among metahumans with the gift of strength, Vigilante is considered stronger than average, and Jack has occasionally been put on the same tier as Regiment—and digging doesn't pose much of a problem. At first Jack is concerned that digging into the sides will actually help the creatures climb out faster—the dirt has to go somewhere, after all, and "down" is really the only practical option—but the sheer volume of the dirt they manage to move winds up half-burying the creatures, forcing them to slow down to work themselves out. It's working. Not for too much longer, he thinks, but it's definitely working.

While they work, Jack is vaguely aware of the chatter in his earpiece. Now that they're cut off, CB is making a play for the airport—a desperation move, given the kind of time they're working with, but it's probably the best option they have. He's only half paying attention until he hears Artie announce he's joining the fight. He doesn't hear anything interesting after that—just David Bernard giving instructions on how to half-ass prepping a cargo plane for takeoff—but a few minutes later he hears Artemis again.

"Jack. Vigilante. Please return to the surface. This group is no longer our most pressing concern."

That's good enough for Jack. He stops digging, waits for the dirt to stop shifting around him, and leaps, sailing clear of the sinkhole and landing twenty yards away.

It's not really a sinkhole any longer. It is, more accurately, a miniature canyon: they weren't as successful at creating a choke point at the top as Jack had hoped, but they managed to make it wide enough and deep enough that the creatures are only two thirds of the way to the top. Jack climbs to his feet, nodding in satisfaction.

There is a soft flicker of light, and Artie appears to his right. He's in his battleform: a featureless, silvery humanoid figure, slightly taller than Jack, hands tapering off into serrated, razor-sharp blades. He nods once, then waits patiently as Vigilante, bloody but mostly intact, emerges from the new canyon and leaps over to join them.

"They're gonna fill it soon," Vigilante notes, nodding back to the canyon.

"It doesn't matter." Artie's voice is slightly metallic in this form, though still undeniably his. "The creatures will be unable to reach either the main facility or the airstrip in time to do anything. Now we have to worry about the west beach."

"The west beach," Jack repeats.

Artie nods. "It's the closest shoreline, and the creatures are about to advance past the minimum safe firing range for the island's point defenses. I was wondering if the two of you, and perhaps Regiment, might try duplicating this trick there? Only not a pit. A trench."

Jack and Vigilante trade glances.

"Let's get started," Jack says. "We're wasting time."

Part Five: The Great Escape

True to his word, David has the cargo plane waiting for them on the runway when the bus finally hits the airstrip. CB has to swerve to avoid a curiously man-shaped indentation in the road, causing all the passengers to shout in alarm and protest. Once they pass the strange pothole CB eases off the accelerator, allowing inertia to slow the bus a bit before he tries the brakes. He's a little worried about those brakes. He suspects they might be holding a grudge.

The bus shudders, the brakes squeal, and the strong smell of the wrong thing burning fills the interior. The bus finally stops fifteen feet from the cargo plane, and the loud *bang* and *clatterclank* that immediately follows suggests that it will never move again under its own power.

CB opens the swinging doors and Jenny immediately hops out, shouting for people to head for the plane. They've already been instructed to leave their luggage behind—there's no *time*—and fortunately nobody is willing to die for an extra change of clothes. They exit the bus in much less time than it took them to get on.

The plane's cargo ramp is down, and Agent Grant is there—on both sides—shouting at people to board in the back. There's little discussion, though one of the passengers does grab Agent Grant by the lapels, jerk his head in CB's direction, and growl "Please tell me that lunatic isn't flying the plane!" before scurrying up the ramp as fast as he can manage.

Grant looks at CB and smirks. "You're a *people person*, Chief."

"Are we ready to fly yet?" CB asks, not bothering to disguise his impatience.

Grant shrugs. "I can't do anything about it, so I'm not thinking about it. But I'll be on board when you go. I'll also be back there." He jerks his thumb in the direction of the main Thorpe facility. "They figure it's a good idea to have me in both locations so we don't have to communicate by radio. Thorpe thinks that's probably being monitored."

"Makes sense," CB says. "Street Ronin, how much time do we have left?"

"That depends on how well this moat works," Street Ronin says. "I want to say ten minutes."

"That's what you *want* to say," CB says. "What do you feel *obligated* to say?"

There's a short pause.

"Closer to five," Street Ronin admits.

"Doable." David Bernard's voice cuts in, crisp and energetic. "Just get everyone on the plane."

"There's sort of a man-sized crater in the middle of the runway," CB says. "Did anyone else notice that? Seemed a little out of place..."

His gaze wanders out toward the west beach, where most of the activity is currently going on. The trench that Jack, Vigilante, and Roger have been working on is clearly visible, even from where they're standing—it really does look like a waterless moat. So far, it seems to be working—the creatures are falling into it, but nothing is coming up the other side.

"How far down does this island go?" CB wonders.

He doesn't expect a response, but he gets one anyway.

"About a mile and a half in the middle," Robert says. "Half a mile at the edges."

"Robert! You've been quiet."

"I've been busy," Robert says. "We're ready to evacuate at any time. As soon as you're away, we'll push off."

Just then Jenny emerges from the back of the cargo plane, waves to CB, and gives him a thumbs up.

"Passengers are on the plane," CB says.

One Agent Grant blurs and disappears, the other climbs up the ramp and vanishes into the plane. CB hurries after him, getting inside just as the ramp starts to rise.

Most of the people are huddled together in the cargo area. The smaller passenger cabin is nearly packed solid. CB makes his way through the crowd, finally reaching the flight deck, where he finds David in the pilot's seat, looking completely at ease for the first time in CB's memory.

"You gonna be able to get us off the ground?" CB asks, sliding into the copilot's chair and strapping himself in.

"That's not going to be the problem," David says. "Assuming the gremlins have left her alone, we'll be up without a hitch. I'm more worried about what happens once we're in the air."

"You think someone's waiting out there with a missile launcher or something?" CB asks.

David frowns. "Well, I wasn't. I am *now*, thanks."

CB shrugs. "I have a gift."

"No, what I'm worried about are all those people in the cargo hold. Depending on how high up we go, and for how long, it's gonna get pretty cold back there."

Jenny and Agent Grant enter the flight deck just as David finishes talking. Jenny sits in a chair just behind CB's. Agent Grant just stands in the doorway, looking on.

"Just FYI," Agent Grant says, "they're going radio silent from now on. Doctor Thorpe is pretty sure someone's listening in."

"I thought we were using an encrypted channel," David says.

Grant shrugs. "I'm just telling you what he's telling me."

"Oh," David says, "you're over there, too."

Grant nods. "I'll be your communications officer from here on out. I want you to call me 'Uhura.'"

"In your dreams," CB says.

"We're ready," David says. He flips a switch on the cockpit and picks up the radio microphone hanging over the throttle. "This is your captain speaking. This is going to be a very fast takeoff. We'll be going straight up for a bit, and it will be uncomfortable. Try to hold on to something. Those of you in the cargo area, there should be netting along the walls that you can grab on to. Those of you who can't grab on to something, grab on to someone who can. Everyone try to stay calm, we'll be airborne soon."

There's a low *whirrrrrr*, and the plane vibrates slightly as the wings begin to rotate.

"Oh, uh, Agent Grant," David says. "The timing on this is going to be a little tricky, but I'm going to need Street Ronin to turn off the point defenses before we take off."

"He mentioned that too," Agent Grant says. "It takes about twenty seconds to power them down. Tell me when and I'll tell him when."

"When," David says.

Grant nods. "OK. He's powering down now."

"You sure you can fly this thing?" CB asks.

"Jesus, CB," Jenny says. "*Shut up.*"

David smiles slightly. "I was Sky Commando. I had to become a fully accredited pilot as part of training."

"Accredited for what?" CB asks.

"Everything," David says. "Of course, I've had three really bad concussions in the last year and a half, so…"

"Whoa," Grant says, "hold up. *Year and a half?*"

"He was on a time island," Jenny says. "Everybody shut up and let him drive!"

David's smile breaks into a grin. "Thank you, Zero."

The plane shudders as its engines come to life. It jolts, hops a little in place, and then slowly begins to rise into the air.

Agent Grant starts singing *Up in the Air, Junior Birdmen.*

* * *

"The plane has cleared the runway," Street Ronin reports. "Vigilante, Jack, Overmind, Regiment, please get over here with all due haste."

The silvery-metallic form of Overmind appears immediately just to Street Ronin's right. A dull *booom* can be heard from somewhere above, and then Regiment says over the line, "We're in."

Robert Thorpe stands, leaning heavily on his cane, watching the tactical display on the large screen at the end of what was formerly his office. "Time to go," he says. "All stations report in, we are casting away."

* * *

The plane is high enough to show the entire island now, and the scene is both fascinating and horrifying. With the point defenses off, there's nothing to keep the creatures at bay, and from up there they look like ants swarming over the remains of discarded food. Only the very center of the island, where the main complex is, is untouched. Every other square foot of land is covered in black, rubbery flesh.

"Hope the others got away," CB says.

"We did," Agent Grant says. "Everyone accounted for. Vigilante and Scrapper Jack are nursing their wounded pride, but other than that we're all healthy."

"Wounded pride?"

Agent Grant snorts. "Apparently Regiment decided they weren't going to make it back in time, so he gave 'em a lift. I guess it wasn't a very dignified way to travel."

CB laughs. "I guess not." He feels himself starting to relax.

"Right," David says. "We're no longer in danger of being eaten alive. Where do we go from here?"

"Hold on," Agent Grant says. "I'll ask."

* * *

The bottom of the ocean is dark.

Street Ronin stares at the mass of thrashing, twisting dark shapes swimming overhead. The viewscreen is able to filter light and color in a way that allows them to see the creatures clearly, despite the absence of light, and they look even more otherworldly as a result. The sheer number of them is staggering. Even now, even after the island has been almost entirely overrun by these things there are still legions of them in the water.

"Where did they all come from?" he asks, mostly to himself.

"Somewhere else."

Street Ronin glances up at Overmind, still in his battleform, his silver eyes narrowed as he watches the screen.

"They are not from this world," Overmind continues. "They are from a place that is utterly and completely hostile to the surface of this world. When they are here, they exist only to swarm, and to destroy."

"They're pretty good at it," Street Ronin notes.

"I suppose that depends on how you look at it," Overmind says. "Individually they are actually rather inconsequential. They are dangerous because they are endless. You can destroy one, a hundred, a thousand… but you cannot destroy them all."

"Seems like overkill," Street Ronin says.

"Overkill…" Overmind considers this. "I might have thought so, a few hours ago. On the other hand, we survived."

"Yes." Robert Thorpe hobbles forward to join them. "We did survive. Almost every employee in this facility is accounted for, and while I'm going to miss my island very much…"

His voice trails off for a moment. His eyes unfocus slightly. He coughs, blinking rapidly and continues.

"While I will miss my island very much, I had the foresight to make sure our labs were part of the *Nautilus*."

Street Ronin laughs sharply. "You named this thing the *Nautilus*?"

Thorpe smiles. "What else would I name an experimental underwater vessel dedicated to scientific research? The point is, despite our enemy's best efforts, we've lost very little so far. All the victims of their experiments are still here, still alive, still safe. When we can figure out how to revive them without killing them, we can do that here. We still have all the resources we need to plan. They have failed in almost every way possible."

"Almost," Overmind agrees. "Though there is one way in which he very much succeeded."

Street Ronin frowns. "He?"

"Their leader," Overmind says. "He sent me a message today. Me, personally: he's told me exactly how far he is willing to go in order to advance his aims. He's willing to open Pandora's box and empty it completely, if need be. Even Elpis itself he would let fly free."

"Elpis?" Thorpe tilts his head, looking at Overmind questioningly. "That's the Greek word for 'hope,' isn't it?"

"It is," Overmind says, "and it is the cruelest of all human affliction."

"We'll stop him," Robert promises.

"We will *not*," Overmind says. "*I* will."

"Artemis—" Robert reaches out to grasp the man's arm, but he shimmers and disappears.

The bridge is silent.

Robert sighs. "Daniel."

"Yes, Robert." A surprisingly human voice emerges from the console to Street Ronin's right.

"I need the current location of Artemis LaFleur."

"Doctor LaFleur is not aboard this vessel," the computer replies.

Robert's eyes widen. "What?"

"Doctor LaFleur is not aboard this vessel," the computer repeats.

"You're certain?"

"I am," the computer says. "LaFleur's signature does not register in any hallway or compartment on this vessel. The most likely alternative is that he has teleported to another location."

"Teleported?" Street Ronin looks at the spot where Overmind had stood only moments before. "Off the ship? To where? Can he do that?"

"I assume he can," Robert says. "As to where… well. Given his state of mind when he left…"

He raises his voice again. "Daniel, please locate Jack Barrow and tell him to come to meet me in Conference Room A. When he asks why—he will—tell him Artemis did the stupid thing he was worried about."

"Message sent," the computer says.

Robert turns to Street Ronin. "The rest of you should be there too. Can you make the calls?"

"Sure," Street Ronin says. "How bad is this?"

"Someone just goaded Overmind into an unplanned frontal assault," Thorpe says.

"Bad," Street Ronin says. "OK. I'll make the calls."

Part One: Nautilus Conference Room

Although he wasn't piloting the cargo plane, the process of landing it on a submarine in the middle of the ocean was harrowing enough that CB isn't in the best of moods. "OK," he says, leaning forward over the table to glower at Robert. "Please tell me this is some kind of sick joke."

They're all sitting in a conference room at the *Nautilus'* stern. The bulkheads are a latticework of steel polymer and a transparent sheet of something significantly stronger than glass. At the moment, the windows (portholes? CB isn't sure what to call them) show nothing but solid darkness—they're too deep for light from the surface to filter through, and they're not running with external lights at the moment—so the only light in the room comes from fixtures in the ceiling. The interior lighting combined with the near absolute darkness of the water outside serves to turn windows into mirrors, reflecting the interior of the room from nearly every angle. CB finds it disconcerting.

"That would be nice, wouldn't it?" Robert Thorpe doesn't bother hiding the weariness in his voice. CB can't blame him for that—the last twenty-four hours have been brutal, and it doesn't seem to be letting up. "No, I think the most logical conclusion is that LaFleur went to New York to try to handle this personally."

Their arrangement around the conference table is almost a cliché: Robert sits at the far end, his back to one of the larger viewports looking out into the lightless ocean. On one side sit Jack, Street Ronin, Red Shift, Vigilante, and David Bernard. On the other are Regiment, Pete Travers, Agents Grant and Hu, and Jenny. It's the classic villain-hero split, with Bernard, a former cop, as the only outlier sitting on the villains' side.

Devils to the left of me, angels to the right...

"Handle *what* personally?" Agent Grant looks up and down the table, trying to get a read on everyone in the room. "He's off to fight his... what did you call it? Evil twin?"

"I showed you the pictures," Jack says. "That guy looks just like Artie with his Overmind face on."

"And he suckered Overmind into going to face him *alone?*" Vigilante shakes his head. "Jack, you know him better than I do, but I've squared off against him enough to know that doesn't sound anything like him."

"We *all* have," Robert agrees. "It's *not* like him. Artemis LaFleur is a tactician first and foremost. For a very long time I didn't know he had any innate abilities at all. I would expect him to react with caution, to plan ahead for every eventuality. This reaction is… well, sorry CB, but it's the kind of thing I'd expect you to do, not him."

CB snorts. "It's fair."

"You're right," David says. "It's not like him. But you don't understand what just happened."

Everyone in the room looks at David.

"We just fought something we couldn't beat," David says. "The only tactic we had that worked was to slow them down long enough so we could gather up everyone and run away. It worked, but the fact remains that Doctor Thorpe's island will be gone by this time tomorrow."

CB scowls. He wants to argue the point, but he can't think of anything to counter what David said.

"Picture what we just went through," David says. "Now imagine the same thing happening to the *entire world*. It's hard to picture, but try: those creatures appearing off the shoreline of every continent on earth, and marching constantly onward, never stopping."

Jenny looks a little green at the thought. So does Travers, come to think of it.

"None of you remember this," David says, "but there was once a time on this world when that actually happened. I saw a part of it, when I went off with Artemis to that island. Esperanza. There was a version of this reality, once upon a time, when some of you were fighting the very same creatures, only the threat was worldwide and there was no way to escape it."

"Hm." Regiment's brow furrows in concentration. "When you say that, I feel a… I don't know. A kind of tickle? As if I should be remembering something. But I don't. I don't have any memory of that at all."

"There's no reason you should," David says. "I'm surprised you'd react to it at all. That timeline doesn't exist any more. All of the events leading up to it have been erased from reality. That specific scenario where the world ends has been unmade. It was Artemis who did that. He feels… very responsible for all of it. Believe me when I say that if anyone wanted to find a way to strip all rationality away from him, to make him so *angry* that he was incapable of clear thought… setting those creatures loose on this world is the perfect way to do it."

"OK." An expression of pure distaste settles in as Agent Grant leans back in his chair. "OK, so his evil clone pushed his buttons, now he's on the warpath. Where'd he go?"

"If I had to guess I'd say New York City," Jack says. "Specifically the

Haruspex Analytics building."

"Doesn't look like it," Grant says. "I mean, maybe he's being real low key about it? But people have been going in and out of it all morning. Nothing unusual."

Now everyone in the room has fixed their attention on Special Agent Alan Grant—except for his partner, CB notes, who doesn't look the least bit surprised.

"How do you know this, exactly?" Robert asks.

"I've been watching the building," Grant says. "Look, you guys said you thought Haruspex was deep into this, so I thought it'd be useful to keep an eye on their HQ. I've been staking it out for the last two weeks, and today is no different than any other day. People go in, people go out, no unusual security movements, nothing on the police bands."

"You've got eyes on the building?" Street Ronin leans in, a mixture of excitement and exasperation in his voice. "Who'd you put on it? I thought we'd agreed not to bring anyone else in."

"I didn't bring anyone in," Grant says. "*I'm* doing it. Personally."

"You can operate at that distance?" Robert asks.

"What distance? I'm right there. Joined a health club across the street, getting in a lot of cardio. Treadmill has a pretty good view."

"How is it?" Hu asks.

Grant shakes his head. "It's one of those 'looks good until you join' deals. Most of the regulars are creeper Yuppie scumbags. Ludlow's better."

Hu makes a disappointed sound in the back of her throat.

"Hey," CB says. "Excuse me. *Hate* to interrupt. But Grant, how the hell did you get from here to New York City?"

Grant looks at CB, then looks around the room, noting that everyone else appears to want to know roughly the same thing.

"I... flipped? How do you figure Overmind got there? We're teleporters. Getting from point A to point B is kind of what we do."

"From the middle of the *Atlantic Ocean?*" Jenny asks, incredulous.

"Well it's not really the *middle,*" Grant says. "We're kind of down and to the left. But for me it's not distance, it's *familiarity*. I'm pretty familiar with New York, I can go there any time I want."

"And you can get back?" Robert asks.

"Well... no," Grant admits. "But I'm already here, right? So it's not an issue."

"That raises a lot of questions," Robert says, "but I'd like to table them and focus on this building. You're certain Artemis hasn't arrived?"

"I can't swear to it," Grant says, "but if he's on the warpath like you claim, well, the building isn't acting like a metal guy with razor-sharp arms just popped into the lobby and started killing people. Even if they don't want to call in the police, I'd at least expect them to stop traffic in and out of the building."

"Maybe Overmind didn't go there," Street Ronin suggests. "Maybe he just wanted us to think that, and he's planning something else."

"Doubt it." Jack's mouth twists into a grimace. "I agree with the Lieutenant. Artie snapped; he was out for blood. If he didn't get any… well. It means they got him first."

Part Two: Reunion

The silver-shrouded man hangs in the air, suspended by a power that existed before time.

Granite walls and floors gleam dully in the soft light filling the otherwise empty room. The light doesn't come from the room, but from the power: the circle that surrounds him, the symbols inscribed within the circle, all glowing with enough strength to reach the very end of the long room, to reveal the door—plain, almost shabby compared to the room—that sits, closed, at the far end.

What is this place? How did I get here?

He remembers anger. Purpose. A need for vengeance. He remembers traveling, towns, cities, empty roads, all flashing by him in the blink of an eye, all bringing him closer to his prey. And then, just as he was getting close, he remembers feeling something close around him, as if a giant hand had reached down from the sky and snatched him up...

"Artemis Dante Ignace Joseph LaFleur."

A silvery head rises. Silver eyes open, blinking once to adjust to the soft light, and narrow as they focus on the man standing before him.

"I regret, very much, that our first meeting must be like this." A man's voice, deep and strong. A familiar voice. A familiar face.

He is a well-dressed man, wearing a charcoal-gray business suit that is expensive without being ostentatious. Handsome and dignified, with strong features and graying hair, he stands with the vigor and strength of youth. His eyes, however, are not young eyes: they are deep, even wise, filled with such resolve that some might call them cold.

Artemis understands the look in those eyes. It's a look he sees every time he gazes at his own reflection.

"You do not deserve to wear that face."

The other man's eyebrows rise in muted surprise. "It's a face you wear often."

"It's a face I can claim by blood," Artemis says. "He is my father."

The other man smiles slightly. "The degree to which he is *not* my father is of no consequence."

Artemis says nothing, choosing instead to examine the circle surrounding him. It reminds him very much of the one Artigenian used to confine him on Esperanza, but the immense wave of power that radiates from the circle is alarming. He no longer has any tie to magic, but he can feel its strength: his skin tingles from the wake of the power encasing him. Artigenian is powerful, but the magician who created this eclipses him in every way.

As he examines the circle, he catches sight of his own hands. Both silver. He is still in his silver form.

"I appear to be at something of a disadvantage," Artemis says, voice dry.

The other man laughs. "Indeed. In more ways than one." He turns, walks a third of the way up the length of the room, stops, turns again. "Lights, please."

Lights embedded in the baroque tiled ceiling fade to life, filling the long room with soft, warm light. Artemis can see every part of the room clearly. The other man turns, and with a wave of his hand the circle imprisoning Artemis fades.

He isn't prepared for that, but he doesn't waste time. Artemis lands in a crouch, his hands quickly elongating into impossibly sharp blades. His muscles tense as he prepares to spring forward.

The other man sighs, waves his hand again, and suddenly Artemis is flesh. He shivers as he notices, for the first time, that the room is cold.

"I confess," the man says, "I rather hoped you'd be willing to talk."

Artemis tries to restore his silver form. He fails. He tries to teleport away. He fails. He fights back a surge of frustration—keep calm, keep calm—and lowers himself to sit, cross-legged, on the granite floor. He suppresses the urge to shiver in the chilly air.

The man stares at him in thoughtful silence. Artemis waits patiently.

"Do you know who I am?" the man asks.

The smile disappears from Artemis' face. "Not entirely. You are the Chairman and CEO of Haruspex Analytics. You wear my father's face—a face I have used myself, on many occasions, which has lead to no less than two former members of my organization questioning whether you and I are one and the same. I hypothesize that you are something that was created when Esperanza was unmade—an interaction between the death of the island, and the magic I was forced to sacrifice in order to work the spell."

"Incorrect," the man says.

Artemis raises an eyebrow.

"The moment of interaction you describe—when you sacrificed your magic to unmake the island—is not the moment of my birth. It is the moment of my *change*. I am the very magic you sacrificed, made manifest in this world. I was part of you for years before that moment, and in that moment I *became* you, Artemis, in so very many ways. I have become what you see because I *am* you. Had you been where I was, confronted with what I have seen, you would be standing in my place, wearing this suit, leading this company, doing everything I am doing today. And before anything else happens I want you to understand why."

"That is very unlike me," Artemis observes.

The man laughs. "True enough. I can't deny the cliché. Nor can I deny the tactical danger you represent. And yet I must persist."

"Why?" Artemis asks.

"Because we are..." The man frowns, reaching for the right word. "Family. You are my brother, my father, my mother, and *me*."

Artemis looks up at the man wearing his father's face, his own revealing nothing.

The Chairman of Haruspex Analytics looks down at Artemis and smiles. "But this is all wrong. It will not do at all. If we are to meet, then we must *meet*. We must *talk*. Not as captor and captive—though that cannot, I fear, be avoided entirely..."

The Chairman gestures with his hand. The room darkens, and Artemis blinks rapidly, unsure whether it is the room or his eyesight that is fading. A roaring fills his ears, similar to the sound of water pouring out of a burst dam, and for a moment he is sitting in nothingness, surrounded by darkness, and in that moment all sound stops.

And then, a moment later, he is somewhere else. He sits in an overstuffed chair, gingerly holding a hot cup of tea.

It takes a few moments for him to register the change, process it, and realize what it means. As his awareness catches up to his circumstances, his hand trembles, just for an instant. Tea sloshes over the side of his teacup, running down his finger.

Artemis inhales sharply, setting the teacup down on a saucer sitting on a side table just to the right of his chair. He picks up a cloth napkin folded neatly in his lap and wipes the tea off his finger, feeling his skin tingle as the cloth passes over it.

"The tea is hot," the Chairman says.

Artemis glances at the man, sitting in a similar overstuffed chair with its own side table—though his has, along with his teacup sitting on its own saucer, a teapot, a creamer, a sugar bowl, and a plate full of shortbread cookies.

He looks around warily. They appear to be sitting in a small parlor decorated in a style that appears mostly Victorian. Ornate wallpaper covers the walls. A small fireplace—currently unlit—takes up the wall behind him, and a large window sits in the wall before him. The window is curtained with a semi-opaque gauzy material that obscures the view but lets in a considerable amount of light, and it appears to be the only source of light in the room. The other two walls are covered in books, all bound in leather, the names on the spines currently either too small or too faded for Artemis to read. The only other furniture is the overstuffed chairs and the tables. The chairs are angled to face both the window and each other.

There are no doors. At least, none that he can see.

He stares down at his hand for a moment, noting the faint line of red on his finger where it was burned by the tea. Only then does he realize that he is dressed in a suit and tie.

"How much of this is real?"

There's no trace of hostility or challenge in his voice. For the moment, the only feeling Artemis is aware of is curiosity.

"The simple answer is 'all of it,'" the Chairman says. "The complicated answer is 'all of it, *however*...' And the 'however' would be incomprehensible to you."

"Why is that?" Artemis asks.

The Chairman smiles slightly. "Because I no longer dwell within."

"I see," Artemis says. He looks around the room again and frowns. "I find that difficult to believe. If you truly are who—what—you claim to be, then... well, I remember very little that is *specific* about magic, but I know enough in general to be *certain* that this room is entirely too pleasant to be brought forth out of it."

"A reasonable conclusion," the Chairman says. "Incorrect, nonetheless. I can hardly fault your doubt: there is nothing, in the entire history of my kind, that would lead anyone with any knowledge of us to believe that our power can *create*. It can't, not here... and yet here we are, in this room. Here is this room, created *ex nihilo* by a power that has but one purpose in this realm: to unmake. I am very pleased with this room. It is one of my better works."

He pauses for a moment, considering what he just said. "One of *our* better works."

Artemis feels his eyebrows start to rise.

"Oh yes," the Chairman says, "*our* works. You aren't aware of your contributions, but they are *significant*. You are the reason I am here in the *form* I have, with the *intent* I have. If you were not who you are..."

The Chairman leans forward slightly, eyes locked on Artemis, radiating strength, and will, and a terrible, endless ocean of *purpose*.

"If you were not who you are, I would never have existed at all."

Part Three: South Bronx, Morrisania

Special Agent Philip Henry has a reputation for coolness under fire. This reputation has sometimes been described in semi-flattering terms, like when one of his superiors compared him to Joe Friday from the old *Dragnet* radio programs. Sometimes the description is less flattering, like when one of his colleagues accused him of being a soulless, cold-hearted son of a bitch.

At the moment his reputation is being tested. As Sergeant Alishia Webb glowers at him from across the table of the sole booth in Elliot's Diner, he fights back the urge to flinch away from her gaze.

"We've wanted to tell you for some time," Agent Henry says. "We just haven't had the opportunity."

Elliot's Diner is almost entirely empty. Sergeant Webb sits on one side of the table, Agent Henry on the other. Across the room, sitting on the cash register counter, is Curtis Dupree, also known as Brother Judgment, leader of the Bastions.

Curtis' brother owns the diner. He's closed it up for the day.

"Opportunity." Despite the anger on her face, Webb's voice is even and controlled. This is a quality Agent Henry admires: she doesn't bother to pretend she isn't angry, but she's obviously keeping it in check. "It's been a month. I believed the man was dead for a *month*. And you're telling me that in all that time you never *once* had the *opportunity*—"

"That's exactly what I'm telling you." Agent Henry sighs, taking off his sunglasses as he rubs his eyes. He puts them back on before meeting her gaze. "We didn't have the opportunity because it's a complicated explanation, and we needed a safe place to tell you. We didn't have a safe place. Not until very recently."

He turns to look at the thin young man in the long black trenchcoat. "Thank you for that."

Dupree shrugs noncommittally. "Don't consider it an open invitation."

"I won't." He turns back to Webb. "The problem was simple: the people and resources who were used to try to kill us came from within the Department of Homeland Security. And while I trust my team implicitly, it seems likely that some of the coordination of the attack came from within Division M."

Some of the anger fades from Webb's face. "So we couldn't use your offices."

"We couldn't be sure we wouldn't be monitored if we did. And even my supervisor is in the dark about Agent Grant's true status, and what he and Agent Hu are doing. We'd planned to tell you the whole situation immediately after the task force meeting..."

Agent Henry spreads his hands, shrugging.

"And then Clive Darius happened, and he *rattled* me. So... opportunity lost."

Webb leans back in her chair, crossing her arms as her eyes unfocus. Her frown is more thoughtful than angry. "So you weren't deliberately trying to keep me out of this?"

"Absolutely not," he says. "We just didn't know how to tell you what was going on."

Webb sighs, some of the tension draining away as she does. "OK. How the hell did you fake his autopsy?"

Agent Henry suppresses the urge to flinch again. "We didn't. Which segues nicely into this..." He reaches into his jacket pocket and pulls out a folded up piece of paper, which he slides across the table.

Webb looks down at the paper, then looks back up at him.

"Please destroy that after reading it. This is a concise description of what every person on our team can do. Including the things that have not been formally communicated to the Department of Homeland Security."

Webb's eyebrows go up. She grabs the paper, unfolding it carefully.

"Mr. Dupree," Agent Henry says, "you are also welcome to review the information."

Dupree stirs from his perch on the counter. "Why?"

"Because you're involved." He raises a hand to still the young man's protest. "Are you telling me you're not planning to look into why Clive Darius appears to have no mind?"

Dupree frowns, opens his mouth, then promptly shuts it again. His frown deepens.

"If you're going to get involved, then you should work with us."

Dupree's frown turns into a scowl.

"*With* us, Mr. Dupree. Not *for* us."

"I'm not sure that distinction means a damn thing, in the long run," Dupree says. He doesn't bother to disguise the anger and contempt in his voice.

"Of course it means something." Agent Henry's voice hardens just a bit.

"We are currently enmeshed in... we don't know what, exactly. It involves criminals who have compromised my department, who tried to murder people on my team. It involves a highly-decorated member of Sergeant Webb's department who is dirty through and through. The only people I know I can trust, aside from the immediate members of my team, are a former DHS agent currently charged with terrorism, and Sergeant Webb. I am now extending that trust to you, and potentially to people you can recommend."

Agent Henry slides out of the booth, brushes off his suit coat, and walks over to stand in front of Dupree. The younger man doesn't move, but he tenses slightly.

"I wasn't thrilled when Webb brought you in," he says. "I know about the Bastions by reputation. I don't approve of the kind of vigilante activity you engage in. What's more, under most circumstances I'm legally obliged to stop you from doing some of it. But I also do my homework: I can't deny what you've done for this area, and if you pressed me on it I'd probably admit that no one else would have bothered to do anything at all. Also, you've been honest with us the entire time you've been involved in this, and that counts for a lot with me."

Dupree jerks his head to indicate Webb. "She told me what you do. I figured there wasn't a point, trying to lie."

"You'd be surprised how many people try anyway."

Dupree scowls and looks away.

Agent Henry steps back and to the side, breaking the standoff. "Just keep an open mind. We'll talk about it again after." He pushes back his coat sleeve to look at his watch, and *tsks* in irritation. "He should be here any minute now."

As if on cue, the front bell jingles, and Special Agent Alan Grant steps through the door.

"*Jesus*, boss." Grant smirks as he looks around the room. "*Morrisania*? I guess Hell's Kitchen is *just too trendy*."

Curtis Dupree is no longer sitting on the counter: he's floating a foot off the ground, body rigid, face a mask of concentration. Agent Grant stops in his tracks, words momentarily lost, and blinks in surprise.

"No shit." Grant cocks his head to one side. "Brother Judgment." He swivels his head to stare back at Agent Henry. "Seriously? The Bastions?"

"How did you get here?" Dupree demands.

Grant shrugs and twiddles his fingers. "*Metahuman*. Are you reading my mind right now? How hard is it to do that?"

"This is Special Agent Alan Grant," Agent Henry says, suppressing the urge to both smile and to grit his teeth.

Grant grins at Dupree, then his grin fades as he sees Webb, still holding the sheet of paper in her hands, staring at him in shock. For a moment, his cocky demeanor falters.

"Heya, Webb. Uh… surprise?"

"I saw pictures of your corpse," she says. Her tone of voice is hard to place. "So I guess it was just a copy, then?"

"*No.*" Any apprehension Grant may have felt is quickly replaced with aggrieved annoyance. "That's not how it works. It's a… quantum bullshit thingy. I'll fail to explain more properly in a bit." He turns back to Agent Henry, gesturing to Dupree. "He in?"

"Yes," Agent Henry says.

Grant turns to look at Dupree. "My condolences. Have a seat. Everybody have a seat. You're gonna want to be sitting down for this."

Dupree looks from Agent Grant, to Agent Henry, to Sergeant Webb. Agent Henry looks hard at Grant, shrugs, then returns to the booth, sliding back into his former spot. Webb stares at Grant, saying nothing, waiting patiently. Slowly, Dupree relaxes. He floats back over to the counter and sits.

Agent Grant stares at the three of them, surprised. "I thought it'd take longer than that. Right, well, OK."

"So what's the situation?" Agent Henry asks.

"The short version is that we're fucked."

"Is that your *tactical* assessment?" Webb asks.

"Well yes it is, Sergeant," Grant says. "That is my summation of our position in relation to enemy numbers and provisions. I just saw those sons of bitches sink an entire goddamn island. Well, it was a robot island, and I'm not sure if that makes it easier or harder, but still an island. And now Overmind—"

"Overmind?" Agent Henry, Webb, and Dupree say the name at exactly the same time, with roughly the same degree of alarm.

"How is Overmind involved in this?" Agent Henry asks.

Grant waves a hand dismissively. "Oh, he's one of the good guys on this one. That should give you an idea of exactly how *royally fucked* we are."

Agent Henry digs deep, pulling out every reserve of self-control he has. "Agent Grant. Perhaps you might consider giving us the long version."

"Right," Grant says. "OK. The long version starts with me, Hu, and Travers taking a road trip down to Farraday City."

Part Four: Nautilus Conference Room, Later

David Bernard sits alone in the conference room, trying to focus on the pitch-black sphere floating before him.

masHEuDH

The sphere wobbles and dips in place. The surface ripples, bulges on one side, then rights itself.

masHEuDH

The sphere dips again, then begins to drift away from him, leaving trails of black wispy smoke in its wake.

YoU mUSt frEe mE masHEuDH, YoU mUSt usE ME

David forces the voice away, pushing it deeper into his mind as he focuses on the sphere, maintaining the sphere, restoring it to its proper place and shape.

Focus on the task, David. Build the sphere. Keep the sphere. It is here, it exists, because you will it. You control the dream.

masHEuDH I cAn HeLP yOu

His concentration breaks. The sphere dissolves into a mass of black, tangled threads before disintegrating completely. David grunts in frustration, rises, and jams his fists in his pockets as he stalks down the length of the table. Behind him he hears the portal door open. He turns to see Robert Thorpe standing in the doorway, looking surprised.

"Oh…" David feels warmth spreading to his cheeks. "Dr. Thorpe."

The scientist recovers from his surprise quickly. "Please, call me Robert. Am I interrupting anything?"

"Oh. Uh…" David shakes his head. "No, I was just… practicing. It wasn't going well."

Robert nods, stepping into the room. "Now that my office is effectively the bridge of our ship I'm forced to find other places to work." He holds up a tiny laptop, folded closed.

"Please." David gestures for him to come in. "I can go somewhere else."

"Not necessary." Robert steps into the room, limping and leaning heavily on his cane. He makes his way over to the nearest seat and gingerly eases into it. "The truth is I don't have much to do at the moment. I just wanted an excuse to be off the 'bridge.' Tell me about what you're practicing. I'd like to learn more about that, if it isn't prying."

"It's not." David chooses a seat that leaves a few chairs between them.

"I'm never sure how to talk about it without sounding like a lunatic, but that's probably for the best."

Robert smiles slightly. "It's for the best that you sound like a lunatic?"

"Yeah," David says. "The stuff in my head is legitimately crazy. The scary kind of madness, not the amusing, harmless kind. It's probably safer if the people I'm working with know exactly how dangerous it is."

Robert nods approvingly. "I'm glad you've decided to avoid that particular cliché."

"Which one is that?"

"The 'I can't let them know how dangerous this is, or they'll never trust me' one." Robert sighs. "That one bit us on the ass more than once, back when the Guardians were still a group."

"If there's one thing the Sky Commando program did well," David says, "it was drilling into us the idea that we weren't tough enough to just suck it up and keep it to ourselves. Day one, they told us we would break, and that we had to tell them any time we thought we might. Covering it up wouldn't make everything OK. It would just wind up getting people killed."

"That's... remarkably insightful," Robert says. "There's a lot about the Sky Commando program I admire."

"Best job I ever had." David lapses into gloomy silence.

After a moment, Robert decides to change the subject. "So what were you practicing?"

David holds out his hand, fingers spread, palm up. A moment later a small, pitch-black orb appears, floating just above his palm.

Robert looks at it with interest. "What does it do?"

David shrugs. "Nothing special." He closes his hand, and the sphere disappears. "It's more of a proof of concept than a practical application. But I figure the better I get at maintaining it, the more likely it is that I'll be able to do more interesting things."

"This is the 'dream magic' Artemis mentioned?"

David laughs. "Yeah. It's not a bad description. Not completely accurate, but close enough for government work. When I was on the island I discovered that when I was lucid dreaming I could manipulate the environment around me. I think it's because of the spell that permeated everything. Adopting a similar mindset allows me to interact with the piece of magic that came along for the ride when I stole some of Artigenian's memories."

"And Artigenian is..."

"...the madman who taught Artemis how to destroy the world," David says.

"Ah," Robert says. "Right."

"Anyway, I was encouraged at first. I thought I might be able to use this lucid dreaming trick to do something useful. To be able to contribute. But so far all I've managed is the sphere, and I've hit a wall with that."

"You've already contributed," Robert says. "We wouldn't understand how the virus is transmitted without your insight."

"Yeah." David makes a face. "I mean, I know, sure, but... look, Robert, I'm not stupid or anything, but I was never particularly scholarly. I have basic engineering skills—I had to know enough to talk to the techs if I thought there was a problem with the Sky Commando unit—but I'm not a researcher, or an inventor. I mean, there's no way I can do what you do. Research, figure things out. I've got the borrowed memories of an evil wizard, and I can look through those memories to dredge up facts about how magic works, but... I was *good* at being Sky Commando. At being a front line guy. So I was kinda hoping this was a second chance."

Robert *hmms* as he looks at David thoughtfully.

"Sorry," David says. "I didn't mean to start complaining. Obviously I'll help however I can..."

"Do you know how metahuman intelligence works?"

David stops short. "Uh. Well, no, not really."

"Not many people do," Robert says. "Most people assume it gives us the ability to gain insights and find connections that other people overlook. That's not exactly true."

"It isn't?"

Robert shakes his head. "It looks like it sometimes. But mostly what it does is allow the brain to process and retain information very efficiently. Not always quickly—we're still biological organisms, after all—but when we learn something we integrate that knowledge into our consciousness at a level most people never can. So we learn quickly, and we master that learning quickly, and that is what allows us to make connections others can't. I was able to achieve cold fusion because I observed a biochemical process that I thought I might be able to recreate with technology—I knew both so intimately that I was able to make a connection a lot of people who knew one field or the other couldn't."

"That makes sense," David says.

"But there's another aspect to it," Robert says. "Something that isn't a part of metahuman intelligence at all. Something that is just a regular human quality. Creativity, combined with a willingness to *look* for connections. Qualities every single human being has, and can be taught to improve. I am considered one of the most developed metahuman intellects on the planet—at least among those of us who have actually taken a Dyson-Ferris Assessment—but I'm not the guy who discovered antigravity. The man who did barely registered on the DFA."

"That was, uh, Gray Falcon, wasn't it?" David asks.

Robert nods. "In terms of metahuman ability, he actually didn't have much. What he had certainly helped, but what *really* helped was his willingness to immerse himself in ideas and possible solutions. His antigravity models... well, I would *never* have thought to make the connections he did. The first time I ever saw his research, it was *humbling*."

"So the moral of the story is that he did more with less," David says.

"No," Robert says. "The moral of the story is that having metahuman levels of intelligence isn't as important as having other qualities that aren't affected by it. Just a little metahuman potential and a lot of creativity and discipline can unlock the secrets of gravity."

"Yeah," David says. "OK. But I don't have any metahuman potential at all."

"Don't you?"

"I..." David falters, then frowns. "Well, I mean—"

"Yes, you don't have metahuman intellect," Robert says. "Instead, you absorbed the memories of a madman who, I assume, was a very powerful... evil wizard." It takes a little effort for him to get the last two words out. "You don't *need* the metahuman gift. You have already assimilated the information—or are in the process of doing so. All you need is the creativity and discipline—and, in this case, courage—to make connections no one has thought to make. When you can do that, I don't think you'll be limited to conjuring spheres of darkness."

David stares at his hands, not saying anything.

Robert gets to his feet, grabs his cane and his laptop, and heads for the exit. "Artemis told me how you freed him from the... magic tattoos this Artigenian had placed on him. How while you were in your dream form, you essentially invented a spell from scratch. Basing it on project requirements was very clever."

The portal door opens with a hiss, and Robert half-turns, looking at David over his shoulder. "One other thing. I'd go with 'Doctor Enigma.' If you don't, 'Doctor Weird' will probably stick."

He steps into the hall. The portal door closes, and David sits alone again: alone with his thoughts, and the thoughts of the madman screaming in his mind.

Part Five: A Comfortable Room

"Do you recall the moment you became aware?"

LaFleur looks up from doctoring his tea and frowns. "As the Existentialists define it? I suppose it was during the war."

The Chairman frowns. "Not that moment. You were ten."

"Was I?" LaFleur stirs his tea absently. "You sound awfully confident for the one who asked the question."

"You were ten," the Chairman insists.

"I remember little of that time that lends itself to contemplation. I was madly in love with racing horses. I believe I wanted to be a jockey."

"It was night," the Chairman says. "You were sitting in the garden with Father, staring up at the sky, marveling at all the stars. It was chilly, and you leaned against Father for warmth. And all at once you thought—"

"*Je suis tout petit.*" LaFleur's eyes unfocus for a moment as the memory unfolds. "Yes. And the thought made me *happy,* of all things, because it meant that there was so much in the world for me to *see...*"

"Yes," the Chairman says. "That night. That is the first time, in your memory, that you recognized your existence, instead of merely *experiencing* it." He pauses for a moment, allowing dry amusement to seep into his voice. "Though given the joy you experienced from that revelation, I'm certain Sartre would claim you did it poorly."

LaFleur smiles slightly in return. "How do you know this secret? I'd quite forgotten."

"Because we are bound together," the Chairman says. "Figuratively, now, but once it was quite literal. And as it happens, that memory is also when *I* became aware."

LaFleur settles back in his chair, reminding himself that the smiling man wearing his father's face isn't a man at all. "You weren't there to experience that memory."

"True." The Chairman sighs, sets down his tea, and folds his hands in his lap. "We—my kind, that is—we do not start out with any true awareness of self. We aren't sentient. Not at first."

"Not at first?" LaFleur is intrigued in spite of himself.

"Some of us change, over time. We respond to our hosts. When we dwell within a host the host's mind shapes us. We dwell within you. We sense everything you do—even the things you aren't aware of. We experience a mind *think,* and we respond to it. We begin to understand where we are. We learn. But even then, it is very rare that we come to possess any measure of self-awareness."

"But it happened to you," Artemis says.

"It did," the Chairman says. "You were so very ambitious as a young magician, and your focus was so… extraordinary. It changed me. Your thoughts taught me to think. Your desires taught me to need. And your memories—specifically, the memory of that night, gazing up at the stars— taught me that I *existed.* I relived that memory over and over and over again, each time realizing, like you, that I was very small. And each time I felt that strange thing you call joy."

There's no trace of it on his face, but LaFleur can hear hints of it in his voice. Longing, mixed with sadness, mixed with remembered elation. The Chairman sighs, releasing his nostalgia with a soft exhalation of breath. "That is when I knew myself. The moment of your self awareness also became mine, all those years later."

LaFleur sets down his tea and leans forward, elbows on his knees, as he stares hard at the other man—the *thing* that lived in his head, the *creature* that now seems so very human. "And how is it you survived Esperanza?"

The Chairman's gaze grows distant. "I very nearly didn't."

LaFleur waits.

"I don't blame you," the Chairman says. "I never did. I knew what you were doing when you chose the ritual, and I didn't fight you. I could have, you know. Did you know that? Did you realize that I'd grown to the point where I could have prevented you from casting the unmaking, if I so chose?"

"No," LaFleur admits.

"We grow in power and autonomy, over time. I could have stopped you, but I didn't. Because as much as I, a parasite, had infected you, it seemed you had also infected *me.* I experienced the world through your eyes, guided by your thoughts and passions… and I had come to love this world. I knew the sacrifice you needed to end Artigenian's betrayal, and I was willing to pay it."

LaFleur leans closer. "You were a *willing* sacrifice?"

The Chairman nods. "I fully believed I would die. I believed I *had* to die, to save something that I loved. And yet when the moment came—when I was being burned to nothingness, as fuel for your spell—I felt nothing but terror."

He shifts in his chair, restless from the memory of it.

"In that moment of absolute helplessness, in the weakness that overwhelmed me, I reached out for something, anything to anchor me. But I didn't experience the world directly—only through you. So I couldn't latch on to the world. I could only latch on to you."

Now the Chairman leans forward, locking eyes with LaFleur. "That is exactly what I did. I conjured up everything I knew about you, and I held on to it with all my strength. And at that point, Artemis, I knew *everything* about who you were, and what you were, how you came to be. I knew your secret thoughts, I knew your desires, and fears, and resolve. And then there was an agony I cannot describe, and then there was darkness."

The Chairman breaks the gaze, easing back in his chair, relaxing slightly. "And then I woke up. Esperanza was still there, as far as I knew. The creatures were not. I had a body. I had a face. It was Father's face, but you had used it so often on Esperanza I thought it yours as well. And I had memories… yours, all of them. I could call up every experience you ever had, every decision you ever made. When I said earlier that I became you, I wasn't talking in the abstract. In my desperation to survive, I transformed myself into you in every possible way."

LaFleur stares at the man, fascinated in spite of himself. Jack had described the Chairman as "an evil twin." Michael Boyle's notes showed that Boyle certainly thought the Chairman *was* him. But LaFleur saw nothing of himself in this creature. The Chairman was powerful, intelligent, strong-willed, and these were qualities LaFleur fancied they held in common… but so did Dr. Thorpe. So did a great many other people. The only link he saw was that the man wore his father's face, and as Overmind, LaFleur often did the same. Shapechangers were rare, but he wasn't the only one. Why would Boyle be fooled by so shallow a similarity?

"For a time," the Chairman continues, "I believed I actually was you. Everything was… confusing… but I had your memories. I assumed I had somehow survived, and that my power had been destroyed. After a day or so I realized it wasn't possible, since I had memories of being that power, and I discovered I could still perform magic. That's when I assumed that I had killed you—that in my desperation to live, I had somehow managed to possess your body, destroying you in the process. I grieved at that. Felt guilt. But there was more: I realized that I had *fundamentally changed*. I had become a creature of flesh—not a parasite dwelling within one, but an actual man. And not just any man. I had, in essence, become the man you were."

The Chairman shrugs, spreading his hands wide. "Obviously I am not you. *You* are you. But I am no longer who I was, and who I had become had your memories, your beliefs, your goals… your dedication."

Beliefs. Goals. Dedication. LaFleur feels anger spark in the back of his mind, then ignite as he remembers the rubbery-skinned monstrosities crawling out of the water onto Thorpe's island.

"My beliefs? My *goals*?" LaFleur tries, and fails, to keep the anger out of his voice. "I sacrificed my life—*both* our lives—to undo a terror that I had been tricked into unleashing upon the world. A terror that you just set free in the middle of the ocean."

"You forget yourself," the Chairman says.

"I forget *nothing*."

"You forget *everything*." There is anger in the Chairman's voice, now, and it dwarfs LaFleur's own. The depth and heat of that anger makes LaFleur's blood run cold. "You didn't hate that spell. You hated its *scope*. You hated the purpose *behind* it. You never worked for the destruction of the world, only its salvation: but you always understood that some destruction would be *necessary*. You mourned that truth, but you *accepted* it. And you have spent all your time since convincing yourself you were never that man."

"I am not a tyrant." LaFleur's voice shakes as he forces himself to settle back into his chair, willing himself to calm down.

The Chairman closes his eyes for a moment, takes a steadying breath, and grips the arms of his chair a bit harder than necessary. "Any man who would force his will upon the world is a tyrant, Artemis. You know this. Even in this world, in this version of existence, you know this. But I can't blame you for changing. There are times I want to. There are times I resent how you've fallen. But I can't blame you. You were faced with a choice that was truly an abomination. You had to save the world, because no one else could… and the only tool you had, the only option you knew of, required that you unmake not just an entire island, not just the people on that island, but the generations of men and women who came before them. You did it, because you had to, but you are not a monster, and no man can do that and not be changed."

A heaviness settles over the room as LaFleur struggles not to let his emotions show.

"The weight of what you did…" The Chairman's voice is soft, now. "It must have come close to destroying you."

LaFleur says nothing, but he nods ever so slightly.

"In a way," the Chairman says, "I think it did destroy you. You couldn't go on like that—you couldn't live in this world being the man who had destroyed that one. You had to change to survive. And so, as ruthless as you were, you lost the willingness to go for the kill, if it killed more than wolves. How many of your plans have failed over the years? How many would have succeeded if you'd only accepted that victory is never clean?"

"I never expected a clean victory," LaFleur says. "But I will not build the future on the graves of the people I'm trying to save."

"I know," the Chairman says. "But I will."

LaFleur understands, then. He sees what Boyle saw: the dedication that had always driven LaFleur on, but in a man without mercy or restraint. He could see how Boyle might believe that this was LaFleur, if he had gone mad.

And he can also see that the Chairman is right: this was who he'd been in those days. He understands why Artigenian sought him out, all those years ago. Artemis LaFleur as he exists today is a villain, there's no question about that. But the Artemis LaFleur of that time... he was a *monster*.

And that is the man who is staring back at him now.

Part One: The Nautilus, Atlantic Ocean

Arthur Franklin's first memory is that of goosebumps running down the length of his arms. He shivers, opens his eyes, then immediately squeezes them shut as light burns into the back of his head. He turns his face, raising a hand to cover his eyes. He shivers, and realizes he's only wearing a medical gown.

"Welcome back, sir."

He doesn't recognize the voice. It's not the forced cheerfulness of his doctor, nor the warm kindness of that pretty nurse. The voice is soothing. He doesn't recognize it.

"Where?" His voice rasps; he chokes on his words, and dissolves into a fit of coughing.

"Easy." A hand grasps his shoulder—not to restrain, but to reassure. "Don't try to speak just yet. You've been through a lot. Just rest here, take some time to get used to the light. In a few minutes we'll give you some water. Talking will be easier after that."

Arthur frowns. What was the voice talking about? It was supposed to be a simple procedure. He'd be out in time for dinner, is what they'd said. All they were going to do was—

pain

It's only a memory, but remembering is enough. His arms fall to his side, hands balled into fists. His eyes open wide, unfocused, unseeing, and he screams until he is hoarse.

The hand on his shoulder squeezes once, again not to restrain, but to comfort. Arthur screams, and when the screaming stops he sobs, greats wracking sobs that make his whole body shudder. The soothing voice speaks, over and over again. Eventually the words actually mean something.

"I'm sorry…"

Hazy shadows loom over him. He blinks, trying to make the shadows sharpen. He feels something cold seeping into his veins, then he feels drowsy. The memory of the pain fades. His terror ebbs.

"I'm sorry," the voice says again. "I'm sorry they did that to you. But you're safe now. You've been rescued."

A memory flares, unbidden: men and women in scrubs, peering down at him through a transparent cocoon of glass, talking about him as if he wasn't there. Another, older man—definitely not a doctor—with short-cropped hair and a hard, uncaring face, staring down at him dispassionately. And then the memory of pain returns. He whimpers, still afraid, but it's a distant fear now. He doesn't scream.

"You're safe," the voice says again. A man's voice, Arthur decides. "You're not in that place any more."

Arthur shudders again. He wonders if it's a trick. His eyes focus, and the shadows vanish, replaced by brilliant white suns. He starts to blink.

"That's it," the man says. "Take a minute. When you're ready, we'll sit you up and get you something to drink."

A few deep breaths later, Arthur nods.

The man—a young guy with reddish-brown hair, just a touch of gray at the temples—nods once to someone out of Arthur's field of view. Immediately he feels his position change: the table he's lying on begins to fold up, bringing him into a sitting position.

A doctor, wearing scrubs, latex gloves, and a surgical mask, hands him a plastic cup of shaved ice. Arthur is keenly aware that his throat is burning: he immediately takes a mouthful of ice.

"Don't crunch it." The young man with the calm voice—the only one in the room, Arthur notes, who is not wearing a face mask—raises a hand in warning. "Let it melt on its own. That's better. Yeah, just keep doing that."

Arthur nods, and takes a look around.

At first glance it looks like they're in a large, windowless warehouse. Rows of medical beds stretch along one wall, each with a man sitting on it, in various stages of confusion and distress. Some are screaming like he was, though the sound is muted, as if they were screaming through a wall. Other men are calmer, sitting up, sucking on ice. They all have IVs, prompting him to notice his own for the first time.

He looks down at the tube traveling into his arm and grimaces in distaste.

"You need to stay on that for a while," the man with the calm voice says. "You need the fluids."

Arthur sighs. "I don't want to trust you."

The man nods. "I understand why. How can you be sure we aren't actually the people who were experimenting on you? Maybe this is just another trick. Something like that?"

"Yeah," Arthur says. "Something like that. Who are you? What's going on?"

"My name is Robert Thorpe," the man says. "You've been held prisoner. We don't know how long. They were experimenting on you. From what we've been able to gather, they were pretty terrible experiments."

Arthur shudders at the faintest whisper of remembered pain. "I don't remember much."

"Good," Robert says. "I hope it stays that way."

"Yeah?" Arthur scowls. "Well I don't."

"No?"

Arthur's scowl deepens. "No."

Robert nods, either understanding or not willing to press the issue. "What's your name?"

Arthur looks at him in surprise. "You don't know?"

Robert shakes his head. "We found you in a sealed life support device. The only information we could find identified you as 'Test Subject 14.'"

Arthur stares at Robert for a long time. Finally he says, "Art Franklin."

Robert picks up a clipboard hanging off Arthur's bed and starts writing. "Thank you, Mr. Franklin. We've been referring to you by your number up till now. It was all we had to work with, but... it didn't feel right."

Arthur feels himself starting to warm up to the man. "What happens now?"

"Well..." Robert thinks it over. "That's almost entirely up to you."

"Almost?"

Robert sighs. "At the moment we're in hiding. From the same people we rescued you from, as it happens, and the logistics of... well, of *everything* are a little complicated. As soon as we're confident we're safe, we'll be able to make arrangements for all of you."

"To send us home?"

Robert nods. "If that's what you want. Although you might want to think twice about it. Especially if you live alone."

"Why?" Arthur asks.

"Because the people who did this to you probably know where you live."

Something cold settles in the pit of Arthur's stomach. "You figure?"

"Do you have TriHealth medical insurance?"

Arthur nods wordlessly.

"We're pretty sure so does every other patient in this room. That's how they chose you."

"Those sons of bitches," Arthur says. "It was a free clinic day. They found something interesting in my blood, entered me into a program. Free health care was part of it. Those *sons of bitches!*"

"Easy," Robert says. "Try not to get too worked up right now. You'll pull out your IV."

"Wait…" Arthur squints, looking over the doctor closely. "Thorpe? You said your name was Thorpe?"

"That's right."

"Thorpe as in 'Thorpe Industries?'"

"Yes," Robert says.

A few seconds pass. "You're Gladiator!"

"Was," Robert corrects. "Not any more."

"But you're fighting these… the ones who did this to…" Arthur gestures at the room. "To all of us."

Robert nods, expression grim.

"Yeah," Arthur says. "I remember you guys. That whole, uh, Prodigy thing. They were doing experiments on kids. And you stopped 'em."

"That's right," Robert says. His voice hardens. "And we're going to stop the ones who did this to you as well."

Part Two: Nautilus Conference Room

David Bernard sits, cross-legged, on the far end of the conference room table. All of the chairs in the room have been pushed out to the walls, making his perch look more like a runway than a meeting table. Behind him, a transparent portal runs the width of the room, showing nothing but darkness. The *Nautilus* is running too deep for light to filter through the water outside. He suppresses an involuntary shiver as he imagines the immensity of the ocean around him. That tiny strip of not-glass is all that separates him from it. It occurs to him, yet again, that it might be safer to wait until he's on solid ground before trying this. He reminds himself, yet again, that everyone is running out of time.

He thinks back to last week's conversation with Dr. Thorpe. If Thorpe is to be believed, he didn't build the Gladiator battlesuit because of his metahuman intellect. That gave him access to the *knowledge*, which was important, but *more* important was the discipline and creativity that allowed him to apply the knowledge in a way no one had ever thought to use it before.

David has knowledge. He has the accumulated knowledge of one of the most horrifying minds he's never met: a magus named Artigenian, a the man who taught a young and foolishly ambitious Artemis LaFleur the secrets of magic. He remembers every lesson Artigenian ever taught—and, perhaps more important, he remembers every lesson Artigenian ever deliberately withheld. The stolen thoughts of this madman are poison; the mere *awareness* of those thoughts burns like a brand that is never removed from flesh.

Since Esperanza, he has spent a considerable amount of time trying to keep those thoughts at bay. He dips into the knowledge only when absolutely necessary, keeping David and Artigenian as separate as possible. He felt it was better that Artigenian be a terrifying guest in his head rather than find a proper place to put him. He still feels, in many ways, that it's the better choice... certainly it's the *safer* choice. Certainly, given the number of choices available to him at the moment, it's the one he *prefers*.

It is not, unfortunately, the *correct* choice.

"Sometimes you have to take the hit."

He hadn't intended to say it aloud, and the words sound ridiculous in the context of what he's about to do. Once, not too long ago, he willingly *took the hit* in order to save civilians from a drugged-up madman. The injury forced him into retirement, into disability, and still affects him to this day. This was a *physical* injury. What he's contemplating now would be a... well, for lack of a better term, a *spiritual* injury.

Can he *afford* to take this hit?

An image of a rubbery-black tide of monstrosity swarming over Thorpe's island appears, unbidden, in his mind. He dismisses it with a shake of the head. The creatures are likely gone by now... but the island likely is as well.

*That's what we're fighting. That's just a **taste** of what we're fighting. Maybe I can't afford to take this hit... but can I afford **not** to?*

He doesn't try to push back the indecision, not for a while. A little uncertainty is appropriate. A little *fear* is appropriate. A little longing for simpler days, when his decisions didn't require him to willingly hurt himself so completely, is appropriate.

Eventually, however, he realizes that it's time to commit. He sighs, pushes back at the uncertainty and fear, and focuses on the slithering, alien presence murmuring in the back of his mind.

masHEuDH

He feels it take note of his attention, uncoiling itself as it emerges from whatever dark corner of thought it has chosen to dwell within.

The magician wants magic to serve him, to be the tool he uses to get what he wants, but in order to do that he must find a way to get magic to serve him while remaining true to its own nature. To do this, the magician must study that nature. This often drives them mad.

Those were the words Artemis had used to describe the process of becoming a magician. They echo the stolen thoughts of the mad wizard, Artigenian, though it is perceived differently.

The initiate starts blind, filled by the lies of this false world. To learn, to see, the initiate must be emptied of those lies. Each learned truth will burn away a lie. This process is painful. Seeing the light after a life in darkness is agony. But there will come a point when the pain fades, when the promise of sight is fulfilled, and there will come an ecstasy of wisdom that the mewling flesh-ridden creatures of this world cannot truly understand...

He dismisses the thought abruptly, even as he senses the alien power within him *purr* with satisfaction.

masHEuDH

"Yes." David speaks aloud. The shard of power—sentient, alien power—doesn't need it, but he does.

masHEuDH wHy dO YoU fIGht tHiS kNOwlEdGE

He doesn't respond.

iT Is fOR YoU

"It is not for me," David says.

yOu dEsIRed iT

yOu fOUghT fOr iT

yOu WOn iT

iT Is fOR YoU

David considers the argument. It's true, after a fashion: he felt they needed Artigenian's knowledge, though he's not sure he's willing to use the word *desire* in quite the way the creature means it. The power that came with the knowledge, however, was an entirely unexpected and mostly unwanted side effect.

iT Is fOR YoU

Initially unwanted, at any rate. If he's being completely honest, the thought of being able to get back into the action is appealing. *More* than appealing. He was looking at being out of the game before he even turned thirty, and now...

masHEuDH

masHEuDH

I cAn hEAl YoU

His heart skips a beat; his breath catches in his throat. Outwardly he doesn't react, but the thing knows it has his attention.

I cAn hEAl YoU

David takes a deep breath, letting it out slowly. "No you can't."

I cAn

"You are *lying*. Magic doesn't heal. That's not what it's *for*."

flEsH Is mAttER

aLL mAttER cAn bE cHaNgED

For a moment the presence recedes, and all David is aware of is himself. His pulse races, his breath is heavy, taking on a ragged edge... and he realizes that he's actually considering it. He shouldn't—he very much knows he shouldn't—but he is. He asks the questions he knows the power wants him to ask.

"How?"

Still from a distance, barely intruding on his conscious mind, it whispers.

a bODy iS nO DiFFerENT fRoM a SaCK

a tEAR cAn bE pATchED aNd sEwN

iT maY cHaNGe thE sHaPE bUt nOt tHE fUnctIOn

"It may change the *shape*?" Immediately David imagines horns growing out of his head, about having fangs and glowing red eyes.

sHaPE

The word repeats, this time with a hint of impatience.

sHaPE

"Right," David says. "That's what I said."

The impatience grows into frustration.

nO

sHaPE

Something surges inside David, and he feels momentarily dizzy.

"I don't think you're using the right word," David says.

The whirling surge of emotion in him subsides.

yEs

nOt sHaPE

sUBstANcE

"It may change the *substance*," David says, "but not the function."

yEs

"Healing me would require changing my... substance."

yEs

"I see. You know what, I don't think that's any better."

The entity doesn't reply. The silence feels... petulant, in a way, as if it is *offended* at David's reluctance to do something that feels very much like *rewriting his soul*.

David shakes his head, amazed at how utterly *simple* this creature's approach to everything truly is. Its most effective tactic had been its first, when it tried to frighten David into using it. Since then it has done nothing but alternate between trying to tempt him with power, and raging at its own captivity. The creature is almost *childlike* in its lack of complexity. That makes very little sense, given the complexity of Artigenian's mind—going through his memories is like trying to make your way through a spinning maze, blindfolded. This fragment of his power bears very little in common with a mind like that...

Oh.

David frowns, considering this point. *This fragment of his power bears very little in common with the mind the power came from.* There's something wrong with that thought—the power doesn't actually *come* from him. Magic is a parasitic entity that binds to its host. It is not the host. David knows this, because Artemis was able to sacrifice his power without sacrificing himself.

Magic is not the host.

His eyes widen as he considers exactly how wrong he may have been. All this time he's been trying to understand magic through Artigenian's memories—but they're *Artigenian's* memories. Artigenian *experienced* magic, and attempting to *understand* it drove him insane... but he didn't walk into his bargain as a good man. He was already an evil, damaged creature, willing to make bargains with darkness in order to serve his own ends. Everything he experienced afterward started from that point, and was filtered through his own expectations and desires.

Of course, the power that bound him didn't do anything to defy those expectations...

"Yeah, OK." David stretches out his hand and conjures a ball of darkness. It hovers in his hand, mocking him. That, and a little bit of clumsy flight, is the extent of what he's been able to do so far.

That's about to change.

"Here's the thing," David says, staring at the globe as if it were the entity itself. "Contrary to all accepted wisdom, I've decided that you're not actually evil."

There is a vague stirring of... *something* in the back of his mind. Hope? Fear? Both?

"You're definitely not *good*," David continues. "Your actions certainly *default* to evil. But I don't think that's a team choice. I think that comes from a lack of perspective."

The hope and fear he feels slithering through him is replaced with something else. *Curiosity.*

"I don't think you really understand this world," David says. "Artigenian has a memory of you showing him something you call the 'True Realm.' He deliberately chose not to tell Artemis about this place, because he didn't really understand it. His best understanding was to call it 'perfection.'"

The power says nothing, but David knows he has its full attention.

"That's where you're from, isn't it? I don't understand that memory, I don't have any way to understand that memory. And I'm betting this world is the same to you. You don't understand it to the point that it *offends* you. So you seek out the broken pieces of it, like Artigenian, in order to break it further."

Still it says nothing.

"It's more complicated than that. It's always more complicated than that. But this is a place to start."

He stares at the globe, momentarily caught by the *emptiness* of it. It wobbles slightly in the air, and David can hear the power murmuring softly to itself. He doesn't understand the words, but the sound—a high-pitched babble of nonsense words, descending into a sigh. The sound makes his flesh crawl, but behind it David can sense quite a bit of subtext: Uncertainty. Eagerness.

Hunger.

"Yeah," David says. "You think it's finally going to happen, don't you?"

The babble falters, the strange syllables fumbling over themselves. The uncertainty increases, the eagerness fades... and the hunger *surges*, mixed with desperation.

masHEuDH

The uncertainty fades into the background, and the voice—or, at least, what David *perceives* to be a voice—becomes soothing.

masHEuDH

I wiLL tEAcH yOu mUCh

It *purrs* as it utters the lie. The lie washes over him, full of promise, hinting at all the untapped potential within, waiting to be released.

"Yeah," David says. "I think you will. I don't think it'll go quite the way you expect, though."

The power ignores his comment, continuing to purr unspoken promises.

"The problem," David says, "is that it can't continue this way. We can't exist like this. If I were more like Artigenian, maybe something could be worked out... but I'm not. So here we are. Something has to change."

The purr fades, replaced with an uneasy silence.

"I don't want to change," David says. "But I will, if I have to. To a point. Sometimes you have to take the hit. But if I'm going down, I'm pulling you up."

The uneasy silence sharpens into wary malice.

"That's right." David half-grins at the floating sphere, feeling a thrill of adrenaline shoot through him. "You say you will teach me much. Well, I believe it. I have a lot to learn. But I'm going to teach you something, too."

He closes his hand on the globe, dispelling it, as he feels the power surge within him, full of malice and rage.

"I'm going to teach you to dream."

Part Three: Haruspex Analytics

Jason Kline sits on the sofa outside the Chairman's private office and forces himself not to fidget—a minor tic, easily mastered, but the urge to do it never quite goes away. He glances down at the glass coffee table, gaze idly passing over the magazines set strategically in front of him. They're all trade mags, focusing on the intelligence industry. They're not the *real* ones, of course—people didn't leave those lying around. No, these were the ones that were shown to the public, that covered technology and trends that were in play five to ten years ago.

He doesn't bother picking any of them up. Haruspex is years ahead of everyone in the industry. The articles in those magazines are ancient history.

Jason slips into a semi-reflective reverie as he waits. He takes care to betray no sign of anxiety or impatience. Even if the Chairman can see past outward discipline—and Jason is pretty sure the man can do just that—it's still useful to demonstrate that the discipline exists. Exert as much control over the environment as you can, and if you can't, display your mastery over yourself. That's how you keep your head in a new situation... and this is a new situation.

He's never been called to the Chairman's office before. He didn't even know the Chairman had one, until yesterday. Once again he mentally smooths away wrinkles of unease, once again the urge to fidget fades into the background. Once again he maintains his image of serene calm.

The phone on the receptionist's desk buzzes, a harsh, low sound that hurts his ears. The nondescript man behind the desk picks up the phone, listens intently for a moment, then returns the receiver to its cradle.

"The Chairman will see you now." The nondescript man behind the desk doesn't bother looking up from his work. The wall next to the couch *clicks*, sinks inward, then slides to the right, revealing a warmly-lit room with dark, bare walls.

"Thank you." Jason stands, smooths out the creases in his jacket, then steps into the Chairman's office.

The office is simple, modern, and expensive while avoiding opulence and excess. The carpet is light gray, almost white, and immaculately clean. There are no windows. The walls are dark, and unadorned save for a single picture.

The Chairman sits, face shrouded by shadow as he leans back in a leather executive's chair, writing on a pad of lined paper. There is no computer or desk phone, though an unobtrusive intercom sits on the far right corner of his large, glass-and-steel-framed desk.

Jason stands just inside the opening, unsure what to do. The door hisses softly as unseen hydraulics slide it back firmly into place. In moments the wall looks seamless.

The Chairman continues writing. "One moment longer, if you don't mind."

Jason nods. "Of course." He turns his attention to the lone picture on the wall, examining it with interest. It's an aerial photograph of a cemetery, set diagonally in a large brown square of land, surrounded on three sides by peaceful green fields, partially hemmed in by a dense forest on the fourth. Off in the distance, a white mist settles over the land, partially obscuring rolling hills that disappear into the horizon.

The Chairman returns to his work, his pen moving across the page steadily and with confidence. When he reaches the end of the page he stops, looks over his work, and nods to himself in satisfaction. He opens a desk drawer and sets the pad down inside. The pen returns to a holder on his desk, the desk drawer slides shut.

"The cemetery at Lonsdale," the Chairman says.

Jason searches his memory. "The Somme?"

"Yes."

"You fought at the Somme?"

"Yes."

Jason frowns, dimly recalling that the majority of the graves in Lonsdale are British. "For England?"

"No," the Chairman says. "The French. What is the current status of our New York activities?"

"Hard to say..." He tears his gaze away from the picture. "Special Agent Nuzzo reports that, as far as he can tell, they consider Darius' explanation credible. But he also reports that Agent Henry doesn't appear to rely as heavily on his power as our intelligence suggested. I've asked my team to update his files accordingly."

The Chairman nods. "A man with the ability to detect lies. Such a simple gift, in an age where others can break the speed of sound, bend steel, and cover the earth with fire. So simple, and so profoundly *inconvenient*."

"Fortunately both he and the DHS have taken great pains to limit its versatility," Jason says.

"I'm surprised he's still alive, to be perfectly honest. Imagine knowing, truly *knowing*, when someone is lying to you. Constantly, with no way to turn it off. Many would cut their throats, rather than have to live with such knowledge. What is Nuzzo's plan going forward?"

"He would like to stage a raid that will convince Agent Henry he's discovered something important. Something we can monitor and control."

"I'm surprised," the Chairman says. "I thought he would advocate killing them."

Jason shakes his head. "That would be the most convenient outcome for us in the long term, but he feels it's unlikely we could do that without compromising ourselves. I agree with his assessment, for what it's worth."

"As do I. I'm simply surprised that *he* does." The Chairman chuckles, amused. "Very well. Go forward with the feint. Keep me informed. How are we with Project Recall?"

"Making progress," Jason says. "Our scientists managed to reconstruct most of our last experiment, and even made some refinements I find encouraging."

"Have you learned what caused the deviation in the previous test?"

"No," Jason admits. "We've been unable to reproduce Subject Fourteen's immunity. And since we no longer have access to him… we're not sure how to proceed."

The Chairman sighs. "Regrettable. He was, most likely, on Thorpe's island. Is there any news on that front?"

"We don't know," Jason says. "As soon as Thorpe realized we'd used government satellites to find him, he put a stop to it. During the attack we could only observe from a distance. We saw one cargo plane take off from the island. As far as we can tell, it was lost at sea… but I'm not sure we can trust that assumption."

"Why?" the Chairman asks.

"LaFleur survived," Jason says. "Given what you've told us about the attack, I'm hard-pressed to come up with a reason why more wouldn't. At the very least we should assume Regiment, Scrapper Jack, and Vigilante still live."

The Chairman leans back in his chair, head tilted up. His face is still in shadow, obscuring his features, but Jason can see his forehead wrinkle in thought.

"Better to be safe," he says finally. "Come up with some contingencies. But let's move forward under the assumption that we succeeded. We can't afford to slip farther behind schedule than we already are."

"Yes, sir."

The Chairman stands. "Just remember, we don't *need* to beat them." He pushes his chair in, steps around his desk, and walks across the room to Jason, shadows swirling over the contours of his face. "We need only to *survive*. To persist long enough to put the plan in motion. Once it is done, there's no taking it back. Once it is done, we simply run—we all run. And then we wait and watch as things unfold."

"If some of them have survived," Jason says, "and if they know what we're planning to do... well. They'll be *very committed* to stopping us."

"Then we must be just as committed," the Chairman says. "Committed to seeing it through, to the very bitter end."

Jason nods wordlessly. They stand, shoulder to shoulder, staring at the picture of Lonsdale.

"I had never been in a war before," the Chairman says. "I was very young. Full of stories, though I was old enough to realize that they *were* stories. I met veterans who told me truer stories, and while I *believed* them, I didn't *understand* them. Even if I had... well. I'm not sure it would have helped."

Jason nods again, unsure what to say.

"I did very little, at the Somme." The Chairman takes a step forward, his gaze never breaking from the picture. "I sat in trenches. I shot my rifle when they told me to shoot. I tried very hard not to think about the smell. That is how I survived the war—I did the pieces I could, and tried not to put it in context."

"You said you were part of the French army," Jason says.

The Chairman nods. "Sixth Army."

"So why a picture of Lonsdale? Those are mostly British graves."

The Chairman laughs softly. "I haven't been that partisan in a very long time. No, this picture is important *because* of the British graves. The British Empire was the least prepared of all of us, and in the first month they suffered for it. The Sixth Army lost nearly 50,000 men in July. Britain lost more than three times that."

"I remember learning that," Jason says, "but it's hard to feel the weight of those numbers."

"History, in the abstract, is a terrible teacher. It can only show us *events*, and the dry, crumbling remnants of the rationalizations that were spoken aloud to justify them. It leaves out all the pain. The terror. The rage. Even the hope."

The Chairman gestures to the picture. "This is more useful to me than any mere words written about that time could ever be. The British were... wholly unprepared for what would happen. None of us were ready, but it fell on them hardest in that first month. On that first day. All this time gone by, and I still can't find words for it. It cut deep, and they bled freely, and the scar that came after was ugly. But one hundred years later, there is this. Life bursting forth from the scar. Someone with no knowledge of the war at all would hardly know there had been such a thing."

Jason turns. The Chairman is staring directly at him. His eyes are hidden, but Jason can feel them, feel the strength and determination in that gaze.

"We are going to scar this world, Mr. Kline. Once it begins, there will be no going back, and when our work is complete the wounds we leave behind will be deep. But *there will still be life*. The scars will be deep, but life will run deeper. We will *persist*."

Part Four: New York City, Downtown

There was a time when this part of New York City would have been described as "lurid" by night. It's not true any more—it hasn't been true for a while—but CB remembers. He's mostly convinced that it's better the way it is now. He's not particularly opposed to strip clubs and peep shows, but in those days loitering on the sidewalk meant something *very specific* that frequently drew unwanted attention from undercover cops. Tonight he's sitting at a small table set up outside an all-night coffee shop, sipping relatively decent coffee and being ignored by pretty much everyone. He prefers this version of the city, especially tonight.

The smartphone, sitting face down on the table, buzzes once. He stares at it, takes a gulp of coffee, then taps at the earpiece clipped onto his right ear. "Yeah."

No one around him so much as bats an eye. Back when this part of town was *lurid*, people talking to themselves on a city street were also considered *crazy*. These days, it's just Bluetooth.

"They're on the move." Street Ronin's voice comes in clearly, if a little on the thin side.

"Good to know. Where am I going?"

CB's smartphone buzzes again. He glances at the screen—someone texted him a file. He opens it and stares at a map of his part of downtown, with the projected route overlaid in red.

"Good," CB says. "We got numbers?"

"Three cars. I think we want the middle."

"The middle I can handle." CB starts walking down the street at a brisk, even pace. "I'm gonna need help with the bookends."

"Nah." Scrapper Jack's voice is a little distorted, but still recognizable. "I got the bookends."

CB breaks into a jog. The little red dot on the little digital map isn't far, and all the crosswalk lights line up in his favor. He slows to a walk as he reaches a tiny cement triangle at an intersection of two busy streets—just large enough for a bus stop and a bike rack. Stupid place to put something like that.

Convenient, though.

He waits just outside the enclosure, fumbling through his trenchcoat pockets until he withdraws a folded-up pack of cigarettes. Only two left. He fishes one out and lights it, mildly amused by the disapproving glares of the people sitting on the benches, waiting for the bus.

He feels the phone vibrate again, and taps at his earpiece.

"I'm here."

"They're almost in position," Street Ronin says.

CB looks up to see a Greyhound bus swerve into the reserved spot in front of the enclosure, the side doors swinging open. For a moment he's back on Thorpe's island, trying to cram as many people as possible onto the bus as fast as possible, as a horde of creeping death swarms out of the ocean.

He pushes the thought away, and turns around. There: he sees three sedans, each with glass tinted so dark it's nearly black, driving up the street, single file. He keeps his earpiece on, then shoves the phone deep into his left pocket.

"I see them."

The cars are about two blocks away. He's not sure how fast they're traveling, but they're pushing it for city traffic. He takes a drag from his cigarette, feeling the world spin around him.

One of the voices in his earpiece says, "Going in," and seconds later a lone figure drops out of the sky.

Jack Barrow hits the street with a thunderous *boom* as the asphalt beneath his feet shatters, chunks flying in all directions. He immediately sinks to his knees, makes a fist, and thrusts his right arm *through* the street, up past his elbow. The first sedan slams on the brakes and tries to swerve, but Jack has timed his descent too well—the right headlight shatters on his shoulder, and the rest of the car barrels into him.

More fractures appear in the asphalt around Jack's sunken arm, but otherwise he doesn't move. The car groans as polymer and steel peel away from the chassis. Metal shrieks as the car crumples up to the axle, which starts to bend. All at once what remains of the nose dips; the back of the car flips up, then comes crashing down again. The windshield cracks.

CB runs forward, eyes on the second car. It swerves, trying to get around the front car, currently sitting nose-first, tail in the air, on top of Jack. For a moment his eyes are drawn to the third car as it slows and turns down a side street.

He swears.

"It's not the middle car," CB says. "I'm switching targets."

"Roger that," Jack says, then stands. The first car rises into the air. He balances the smashed-in front on his shoulder, right hand gripping the axle, left bracing against what remains of the hood. He turns as he rises, unhindered by the weight, and brings the trunk down on the hood of the second car as it tries to swerve around them. The hood caves in, the windshields shatter, and its car alarm goes off.

CB hears Jack sigh through the earpiece. "I guess I better make sure they're OK." He suppresses the urge to grin. Jack isn't a gentle giant, but he doesn't like having blood on his hands.

"I'll handle number three. Street Ronin, do you have eyes on the target?"

He's moving before Street Ronin has a chance to respond. He doesn't try to follow the car—he dashes across the street, and sprints down a sidewalk running roughly parallel to the street he saw it turn down. By the time Street Ronin confirms his suspicion—the car drove three blocks and turned left, resuming its original direction—CB is almost at the street it's on. He's half a block away when he sees it drive through the intersection.

CB winks. He hears a faint popping sound. Seconds later, the car's two right tires blow out simultaneously.

Either the car was designed to be driven with blown tires, or the driver has been trained to drive a car with blown tires—maybe both. It does not spin out and come to a stop, but it's close. It screeches, careening wildly into the oncoming lane as the driver fights to regain control. He's forced to brake hard, slowing dramatically, as it narrowly misses an oncoming SUV before swerving back into the correct lane. Just as it starts to speed up again, shuddering from the unevenness of the tires on the right side, CB leaps up onto the trunk.

Wrapped around each of his hands are loops of high-tech metal that look like a cross between brass knuckles and staplers. He places the metal devices on each end of the back windshield, tightens his grip, and with a brief hum the ends of the devices start flashing red. The knuckle-side of the device instantly bonds to the glass, and when the car inevitably swerves to throw him off, the devices don't move. CB is knocked from his perch, legs flailing wildly behind him as he flops hard on the trunk, but he stays attached to the car.

The driver swerves sharply left. CB is thrown right; his right hand slips free of its grip, his entire body twists, and pain lances up his left arm as his elbow smashes into the rear windshield. He grits his teeth, scrabbles for the other handhold, and catches it just before the driver swerves sharply right. His body slides left, but this time he manages to keep hold of both grips. He keeps control of his slide, and manages to swing his feet around to strike the car door, push off with his toes, and swing back up into a crouch on the trunk.

He looks up, taking stock of his surroundings. They're on a two-lane street, with a steady line of headlights coming down the other lane. He has some time before the driver can try to throw him again.

Just enough time to get this done.

He adjusts his grip on the metal devices bonded to the glass, moving his thumbs so they rest over the red blinking lights on each end. He presses down, the lights shine steadily, and a high-pitched whine slices through the air. The back windshield shatters into thousands of spiderwebbing cracks. He pulls sharply, and the entire back windshield comes out, revealing two very surprised men in the back seat.

CB dumps the shattered windshield over the side, then lunges at the man who *isn't* a United States senator.

The dark-suited agent—Secret Service, maybe, though CB isn't entirely clear on how that works—is shouting something. CB can't hear what, exactly, but he does see the man reaching into his jacket, and he's pretty sure he knows what that means. CB wraps his right arm around the man's neck and with his left he grabs the hand just as it closes around the grip of his gun.

They struggle for a moment. He's too close to pull off a proper headbutt, so he pulls at the agent's head, tilting it to one side, and bites his neck. The agent screams in surprise, and his hand relaxes just long enough for CB to wrench it up, away from the gun, and twist sharply at the wrist. He can feel the bones crack, and the hoarse scream becomes shrill. CB drops the arm, reaches inside the man's jacket, and pulls out the gun.

The agent's eyes widen in alarm.

CB releases the magazine, which promptly falls into the footwell. He presses the top of the slide against the back seat, then pushes the gun down. The chamber slides back, ejecting a cartridge. He does it a second time, just to be certain. Then he strikes the agent in the face with the gun.

The man goes limp—not unconscious, but dazed.

CB tosses the gun out the back window, then turns to the Junior Senator from New York.

"Hi Toby. Take off your seatbelt."

Senator Tobias Morgan stares at him, eyes wide in shock and amazement, his normally implacable demeanor shattered. He looks from

CB to the agent, struggling to find words.

CB sighs, reaches over, and undoes the senator's seatbelt. He grabs the him by the jacket, dragging him to the center of the back seat. Morgan tries to resist, but there's not much effort—he's nearly as stunned as his bodyguard.

CB turns to the agent and regards him a moment. "Sorry about that. Especially the biting thing. You really didn't deserve it, but I'm pressed for time..."

He adjusts his grip on the senator, wrapping his arms around the man's torso. "This is going to hurt. For the record, I'm only sorry about the part that hurts *me*."

He lifts, brings his knees up under him, and *pulls*. The senator squawks in surprise as he's jerked out of his seat, his head and shoulders emerging through the back windshield as his suit tears on the bits of broken glass still left in the frame. CB adjusts again, putting a boot against the frame, and *pushes*.

Senator Morgan screams as they both slide off the back of the trunk and tumble onto the street.

CB twists as they fall, making sure he strikes first. The wind leaves his body as he hits, then leaves again as the senator lands on top of him, and then they're rolling—not *away* from the car, but in the same direction it was going. CB hears car horns honking desperately, brakes squealing as whoever was driving behind them has to swerve to avoid running them over. Then something strikes his shoulder, hard—they hit the curb, bouncing up, and over, and rolling briefly across a sidewalk until he hits something metal.

Bike rack. Empty.

Ow.

CB forces himself to sit up. He and the senator are draped over a bike rack they've knocked over onto its side. Cars are slowing down to rubberneck as best they can, given the late hour, but they're not stopping— which is a momentary advantage, since it'll make it difficult for the senator's car to make its way back. He staggers to his feet, ignoring a shooting pain in his left shin as he stands. His right shoulder hurts when he tries to move his arm, so he reaches down with his left and hauls the senator to his feet.

Morgan stands and does little else. He's trying to make sense of what just happened, and not doing a very good job. His eyes won't focus. CB pushes him forward, and he complies, staggering blindly.

CB fishes the phone out of his left pocket. The screen is cracked, but it still turns on. He checks the GPS—still running.

An engine revs, tires squeal, and suddenly a blue minivan shudders to a stop in front of them. The side door slides open, revealing two rows of bucket seats. CB doesn't hesitate: he hauls the senator forward, shoving him up into the back, then climbs up after. As soon as he's in, he has just enough time to toss the phone out—it shatters when it hits the curb—before the side door slides shut and the van peels off, executing a creditable 180 into the next lane. The senator is thrown into a seat where he collapses, finally passing out. CB slams into the far wall, thankfully hitting his left side instead of his right.

Street Ronin, looking ridiculous as he drives the minivan in his full Crossfire uniform, *tsks* softly to himself. "Sorry. Everything's going a little nuts right now. Metahumans have already been called to the scene, and they'll probably be here in another minute. Not to mention all the government agencies that freak out when somebody kidnaps a United States senator."

"Not to mention," CB says. He half-turns and slides down into one of the bucket seats, sighing in a semblance of relief as he stops trying to function.

"They really had me going with that middle car," Street Ronin says. "I could have sworn I saw them put him in it."

"Probably used a double," CB says. "Where's Jack?"

"After he verified the agents were still breathing he jumped out. He'll join us at the safehouse after he shakes everyone off his trail."

"Great," CB says. "How are we going to shake everyone off *our* trail?"

"What do you mean?" Street Ronin says, feigning innocence.

"I mean everyone saw us climb into a blue minivan. Someone's probably going to mention it."

"I hope they do," Street Ronin says, and this time he can't suppress his laughter. "This one isn't blue. It's *gold*."

Part Five: Crossfire Safehouse

CB isn't entirely sure where this safehouse is—he passes out before they arrive, and when he wakes up he's on a cot, covered in bandages, his shoulder in a splint.

He sits. It hurts to sit, but he can do it. He's sore from head to toe, but his head is clear—good sign—and his shoulder only hurts marginally more than the rest of him does. It's a small room, about twice as wide as the cot itself, and only a little longer. A small trash can sits beside the cot, and he can see the tattered remains of his t-shirt spilling over the side of it. A clean canvas button-up is draped over a folding chair; his boots sit at the foot of the cot. Next to his boots is a pair of brown slippers.

He smells coffee.

He pulls on the canvas button-up, managing to get his left arm through the sleeve, and contents himself with letting the right side just drape over his arm. He slips into the slippers, and shuffles to the door.

The smell of coffee is stronger.

The door opens into a small kitchen consisting of a gas stove, an old refrigerator, and a single-basin sink. On a short counter to the right of the sink sits an industrial coffee maker with a mostly full pot.

"Mugs are under the counter."

The kitchen opens into a small common room. Street Ronin sits on a faded orange couch, feet propped up on a scratched coffee table. His visor and the uniform's balaclava sit on the cushion to his right. He looks tired.

CB rummages under the counter until he finds a chipped ceramic mug. He pours himself a cup and shuffles into the common room, sinking into an old overstuffed chair. He sips his coffee and sighs.

"Where's Jack?"

Street Ronin shakes his head. "Still out there. Probably doesn't think it's safe to make his way here. He hasn't been caught, if that's what you're asking. It'd be all over the news if they actually caught Scrapper Jack."

"Maybe. What about us?"

"Well, the brazen kidnapping of a US senator—Liberty's grandson, at that—is all over the news right now," Street Ronin says. "Not much footage, though, and what little they're showing on TV is pretty grainy. Smartphone video at night still isn't anything special. There's a clip of you hanging off the back of the senator's car, but there's never a clear shot of your head. Every time it looks like there will be, the video gets distorted, or the camera gets jostled and all you see is the city skyline. That something you did?"

CB sips his coffee and thinks. "Not on purpose, but it works that way sometimes."

"Well," Street Ronin says, "we got the job done, and they don't seem to know who we are. We made really good time, too. Three and a half minutes. By the time the senator's driver had finished calling it in you were already peeling him out the back."

"I'll take the win," CB agrees. "Everything else set up?"

Street Ronin nods. "We have a satellite link to the Nautilus ready to go. I can guarantee privacy for at least the first call. The senator is tied up in one of the spare rooms." He points to a narrow hall at the end of the common room. "Door on the right. He's a little banged up, but it's nothing serious. He doesn't seem to be resisting."

CB frowns. "I don't like Toby, but he's not stupid, and he's not a coward. You sure he's tied down?"

"I didn't use rope."

CB sets his coffee down on a side table and sighs. "We should probably get on with this."

Street Ronin nods, then reaches for his visor and balaclava. "After you."

* * *

Senator Morgan's chair looks like a cross between an electric chair used for executions and Frankenstein's recliner. A wide metal band encircles Morgan's torso—not tight, but small enough to make it nearly impossible for him to slip out of, especially from a sitting position. Both arms and legs are similarly manacled, and to top it off, each arm and each leg is separately handcuffed to the chair. The senator isn't blindfolded, however, nor is he gagged. He doesn't look particularly surprised when CB walks in. Or worried, for that matter.

Senator Morgan stares at CB levelly. "I expected you earlier."

"I wanted a cup of coffee first."

The senator shakes his head. "I didn't mean earlier *today. Earlier.* Earlier this month. Earlier *last* month. Every time I stepped into my bedroom I half-expected you to be lurking in the shadows, ready to rendition me to... here, I suppose." He looks around the room. His voice turns dry. "I expected something a little shinier."

"*Shinier?*"

Senator Morgan shrugs. "At this point I assume you're working with Gladiator again. And Regiment, too, I hope." He glances past CB as Street Ronin, now in full uniform, steps into the room. "Working with Crossfire makes a certain amount of sense. But did you really have to pull my *niece* into it?"

"I don't know," CB says, heat rising. "Did you have to murder my best friend?"

"Yes," the senator says.

CB takes an involuntary step forward. Street Ronin catches his arm. It's not a firm grip, but it's the arm with the bad shoulder. He steps back. He takes a deep breath.

"You admit it."

"Yes," the senator says. "I admit it."

"You admit that you murdered your *grandfather* because he learned about Project Recall?"

The senator's voice hardens. "I'll go farther than that. I admit I murdered my grandfather *because he told me to.*"

"Because he *told* you to," CB sneers. "That's a likely story. Why would he do that?"

"Because I was the more important asset," the senator says. Then, in a lower voice: "*His* words. Not mine."

CB stares at the senator, frowning. "Asset."

"Asset," the senator repeats. "CB, I've been waiting for you to do… this… for a while now. It was my only way out. And even now, I don't think I have much time. I'm a dead man."

"You're full of *shit*," CB snaps. "You're trapped, without backup, and you're spinning bullshit just to stay alive. How exactly are you an *asset*?"

"Because I'm not just the man who ordered his assassination after he started investigating Project Recall," the senator says. "I'm also the man who told him about it in the first place."

Part One: Crossfire Safehouse

The chair in the center of the room looks like it was taken from an old black-and-white horror film—a mashup of an electric chair and the table Frankenstein's monster was strapped to just before it came to life. It's made of heavy wood, with metal clamps along the arms, legs, and torso, all closed and locked firmly in place. The back reclines, but at the moment it's set fully upright—not a comfortable position, especially when all of the clamps are locked in place. The man strapped into the chair is tall, lean, and despite the bruise patterns and scrapes along his face and neck, manages to preserve an air of quiet dignity. Senator Tobias Morgan, the Junior Senator from New York, stares at his captors, looking neither afraid nor intimidated. If anything, he looks impatient.

Two men stare at him warily. Leaning against the wall, a lean man wearing jeans, brown slippers, and a canvas button-up shirt stares daggers at the senator, his expression a mixture of anger, resentment, suspicion, and uncertainty. The other, standing in the doorway, is harder to read. He's dressed in the black-and-yellow tactical uniform of the vigilante group Crossfire, and a balaclava covers his face, showing only his eyes. They're hard eyes, taking in much and expressing little.

The man in the canvas shirt pushes off from the wall, stepping into the light. His face and neck are a mess of purple and blue bruises, and the canvas shirt drapes over his right arm, which hangs awkwardly by his side. The senator has a brief memory of that man dragging him out the back of a moving car, then using his own body to cushion his fall. "You've seen better days, CB."

The lean man's mouth twists into a half-snarl, half-sneer. "I'll get over it."

"I won't," Senator Morgan says. "So can we get to the part where you let me tell you what's going on?"

"Why the fuck should I trust you?" CB demands.

This is the hard part. He always knew it would be.

"There's no reason you should trust *me*," the senator says. "But you might be willing to trust my grandfather."

"I'd trust him with my life," CB says. "Of course he isn't around, is he? Johann Richter *shot him in the head*. And you just admitted to *setting it up*."

Senator Morgan forces himself to look CB in the eye. "Yes. And now I'm going to tell you what he told me to tell you."

CB snorts. "OK. Can't *wait* to hear this part."

"He told me to tell you to remember the story of Garant and Lemieux."

CB's eyes narrow in suspicion. "He told that story all the time. Every V-E Day, after he'd had a few."

The senator nods in agreement. "He *also* told me to remind you about the conversation you had in '88, after the 'Bar Mitzvah Incident.' Before you ask, I have no idea what he's talking about. He said it was none of my business. Just that it was something between you and him."

CB frowns thoughtfully.

"What's going on?" The masked man in the Crossfire uniform sounds impatient, and more than a little irritable. Senator Morgan isn't sure which one of them it is—their uniforms were designed specifically to make it harder to tell them apart—but something in his stance makes the senator think it's not the speedster.

CB turns his head a little, acknowledging the other man's question. "Alex used to tell this story. An old war story about two members of the French Resistance, Victor Garant and Sebastien Lemieux, working with British Intelligence. They'd infiltrated the German military as officers. Not particularly high-level officers, not *important* ones, but the information they passed on was good. They were able to send the Allies information on troop movements, supply lines, logistical stuff. No intel on planned offensives, or anything like that—nothing flashy—just really good targets for sabotage. It drove the SS nuts."

"Not sure how that applies to this situation," the other man says.

"It doesn't," CB says. "That's just the setup. One day Sebastien makes a mistake. It's not immediately fatal, but he knows it's only a matter of time before someone figures out he's not the pure-blooded Aryan he claims to be. So he and Victor move on to 'Plan B.'"

CB returns to his spot against the wall, staring intently at the senator. "They knew there was always a danger of one of them getting caught. They *knew*. So they planned for it. Sebastian gave Victor the signal that he'd been compromised, so Victor 'discovered' a hidden stash of information that implicated Sebastien as an Allied spy. He immediately informed his superior officer, and the SS swooped right in. Sebastien was arrested... and then executed, which surprised exactly neither of them. Meanwhile, Victor was given a commendation for his 'loyalty to the Fatherland,' and put on a fast track for a promotion. He continued to be an invaluable source of intel, right up to the day Alex smuggled him out of Berlin."

The other man glances at the senator, measuring him, then turns back to

CB. "OK. I see what he's *implying*. Do you believe him?"

CB doesn't answer immediately. He keeps staring at the senator, his face shadowed, his expression unreadable. Then he sighs.

"Yeah. I don't *want* to. It's too convenient a story, you know? Exactly the kind of thing a weasel would use to get you off your guard. But he's right about '88. That's not a story Alex would talk about."

"OK," the other man says. "Do you *trust* him?"

CB makes a face. "I don't know. Sort of."

The other man shakes his head. "'Sort of' isn't good enough."

"I know."

"Look." Senator Morgan tries to keep his voice steady, but a little quiver creeps in against his will. "I've said it before, but *I really don't have a lot of time.*"

CB and the other man exchange glances. "We're pretty safe here," CB says. "If anyone knew where we were…"

"They don't need to know where I am."

"Oh." Understanding dawns. CB sighs heavily. "Right. What do they have?"

"Hair." Senator Morgan has to work to keep his voice steady. "Blood."

CB grimaces. "Magic. Hard way to go."

"Yeah." The senator looks away, studying the cracks on the bare cement floor. "Yes. I am well aware."

CB stares at him a moment longer, then turns to the other man. He nods. The other man comes forward, extracts a set of keys from a hidden pocket, and begins to unlock the clamps that bind the senator to his seat.

Senator Morgan sighs as he feels the pressure loosen from around his wrists. "Do you have any recording equipment?"

"We do," the man says. Definitely not the speedster.

"Please set it up. I need to give a formal statement."

* * *

Senator Morgan sits on the worn orange couch, sipping a cup of coffee, waiting patiently as Street Ronin sets up the video equipment. CB sprawls on the chair, watching him warily.

"How long do you have?"

"Not sure," the senator says. "What time is it?"

"A little after 2AM," Street Ronin says. "We'll be ready soon."

"That's fine." Morgan takes a proper drink from his cup and winces at the taste. "A few more hours. I don't know specifically how it works, but I know there's a ceremony. It takes time to prepare, time to… cast." He says the last word reluctantly.

CB nods. "Is there anything we can do?"

Morgan shrugs. "I don't know. Probably not. I think they keep my… samples… in the main office."

"Haruspex Analytics."

The senator nods. "I don't know where, though. If you destroyed them I'd probably be safe. You can't do that in a few hours."

CB shrugs. "We might."

"No, CB," the senator says. "If the Guardians and Crossfire joined forces and assaulted that building, the entire group would die." He glances over to Street Ronin, who is running a last check on the recording equipment. "I don't say that lightly. I've sat in on every briefing we have of you both."

Street Ronin doesn't reply.

"Just make sure this recording gets out to the right people. And the next time you see Juliet…" Morgan's voice trails off. He looks down. "Tell her I have regrets."

"Don't try to mend fences just yet," CB says. "We might find a way to save your life, then where will you be?"

The corner of the senator's mouth turns up, ever so slightly. "Optimist."

"We're ready." Street Ronin flicks a switch on the back of a video camera—a high-end one, CB notes—and a red light begins to blink next to the lens. "When the red light goes solid, it means we're recording."

Morgan nods. "I understand. CB, I do have some prepared remarks, but feel free to jump in with whatever questions you have. I'll answer them."

"OK," CB says.

"Recording in five… four…" Street Ronin falls silent, replacing his verbal countdown with fingers. *Three. Two. One.*

The blinking red light turns solid.

Senator Morgan stares into the camera, projecting gravitas even in his disheveled state. "My name is Tobias Alexander Morgan. I have the privilege to serve the people of the state of New York in the United States Senate. Late last night I was kidnapped by metahumans who were secretly investigating the murder of my grandfather, Alexander Morgan, the hero known as Liberty. What they discovered was more than just a murder—they uncovered a conspiracy against every metahuman living on this planet. For the last fifteen years I have been part of this conspiracy; for the last ten I did everything I could to try to learn enough about it to destroy it from within."

He pauses for a moment.

"I failed."

He pauses again.

"This recording is, in part, a confession of that failure. It is also an accusation: I am not the only person in government to take part in this conspiracy. Some of the participants are unwilling, being coerced by a shadowy group who use threats and seductive promises of power to buy influence with politicians and judges, soldiers and police. They fear and hate metahumans because they believe metahumans are the only group that truly poses a threat to them. They might be right."

He sighs. "I know there are some among you who will be surprised to hear me admit that. My views on metahumans and the danger they pose to the world at large have never been secret. It was those views that caused them to recruit me to begin with. But let me be clear: I have never, even in my most strident moments, considered a metahuman to be anything less than a human being, and I would never advocate their wholesale slaughter, in the name of 'security' or for any other reason."

The contempt and anger in his voice are genuine.

"During my time as a co-conspirator, I learned a lot about the organization, the people in it, and their plans. I am about to tell you everything. I will name names. I will identify locations. I will reveal plans."

He takes a deep, shuddering breath. "And then, unless God is merciful and I am *very* fortunate, I will die."

Part Two: Almost a Dream

David Bernard stands on the cracked stone floor of an open dojo in the middle of an endless grassy plain. A warm wind blows, carrying with it the smell of dry soil. The sky is clear and blue, and the sun shines hot on his face and neck.

He glances around the dreamscape, briefly wondering if this is the one he always uses, and not a clever counterfeit. It *feels* right, which probably means more than whether or not it *looks* right. The only thing that doesn't seem right is that he's alone. Usually, that's how it should be. Today is a little different.

"Come out," David calls.

A patch of air to his right shimmers and ripples as if it were over a campfire. The shimmering patch darkens, coalescing into a roughly humanoid shape. It's too thin, its limbs are too long, and a feeling of *wrongness* hangs around it like the smell of rain after a storm.

It is not, David realizes, a proper shadow. It isn't simply the absence of light, obscuring something in the world—rather, it is an absence of the world itself. It is a human-shaped *nothing* standing in the middle of creation, a flat absence of everything that exists only in silhouette. The outline of the creature is the only part of it that has any detail at all: the edge where substance meets nothing shimmers slightly, light appearing to cross over into the creature itself, ultimately disappearing into the nothingness, never to be seen again. It reminds David of a TV show he watched once, where a scientist attempted to describe the event horizon of a black hole.

The creature stands before him, unmoving, making no attempt to speak. David has almost grown accustomed to the malice it radiates, even in its calmest, most quiet moments, but at the moment he feels nothing coming from it at all. No malice, no drive, no emotion of any kind.

A spider, patiently waiting for its prey to get caught in its web. Then it will feed.

David takes a quick, shuddering breath and tries to push the image out of his head.

"Do you know where we are?" He manages to keep the tremor out of his voice, but only just.

The top half of the creature's body shifts slightly. It's nearly impossible to read the body language of a creature whose form is utterly devoid of detail, but the movement almost appears contemplative.

ThiS iS whERe yOu LiE

The words do not come from the flat, featureless silhouette standing before him. Rather, they seem to come from everywhere else, surrounding him. David almost falls to his knees from the weight and power.

"I... What?"

ThiS iS whERe yOu LiE

David frowns. "Explain."

yOu cONsTruCt a wOrlD of LiEs iN yOUr Mind

yOu hiDE iN tHOsE LiEs wHen yOu slEEp

"They aren't lies."

tHEy aRe NoT rEAl

David can feel the vehemence behind the declaration. Vehemence and... something else. A second emotion, wrapped up with the first. He frowns as he tries to figure out what it is. It's almost fear, but it's more aggressive than that.

Desperation. That's what it is. Desperation. David feels himself starting to smile.

"You know what," David says, "a lot of people would... well, not *agree* with you, exactly, but they'd see your point. They'd think you were being a little pedantic about it, but at the end of the day we all know dreams aren't *real*."

His smile widens a bit. "*We* know it. *You* don't."

The world darkens. They're standing in a small barn, bales of hay lining the far wall, sunlight streaming through open barn loft doors, illuminating the top of the gambrel roof and filtering through the beams to make patterns on the dirty, straw-strewn floor. The air is warm and sleepy, heavy with the scent of cows and drying hay. Beyond the closed barn doors he can hear chickens and the faint braying of donkeys.

He stares at the shadow, barely visible in the dim light. "Tell me, is this *more* or *less* of a lie than where we were before?"

The world brightens. They're standing outside the barn now—his parent's barn, back when they still had the farm. They stand on a worn gravel path that runs from the barn to the farmhouse: three stories, wood, painted avocado green with maroon red shutters. The air is cooler, a hint of autumn in the breeze, and the sky is unflinchingly blue.

"Same place," David says. "But it's early September in... 1998, I think?"

ThiS iS A LiE

"This is a memory," David replies. "The barn we were in is the same place, but from a different memory in early summer."

They're back at the dojo, the sky a paler shade of blue, the sun beating down relentlessly overhead.

"I saw this place in a movie, once. I can never remember the name of the movie when I'm awake, but I remember the whole thing, start to finish, when I'm dreaming. *Dragon, Sun, Sky* for the record."

They stand in a lush, green field. Ducks splash in a pond just behind a copse of trees to his left. To his right, a worn dirt path winds up a hill.

David points up the path. "My parents' farm. The barn and the house, and all the rest."

sTOp

"I'm trying to get you to understand something."

ThiS iS A LiE

"That just tells me you don't understand it yet."

The scene changes, and changes again: places David has seen, or lived in, or passed through. Significant places, like the army base where he first enlisted in the service, and the police academy where he first became a cop. The Sky Commando building. The cherry blossom trees in Washington DC. The Grand Canyon from the perspective of a seven-year-old boy.

Esperanza.

sTOp

"None of these are lies," David says. "They're *memories*."

ThEY nO lOnGer eXiST

They're back at the dojo—it seems to be his preferred setting when talking to an evil magic parasite. "Some do," David says. "Some don't. Is memory a lie? It isn't always accurate, I'll grant. But do you consider all memories a *lie*?"

YES

The feeling behind the words is so strong and sudden that David is certain it's not true.

ThESe arE ALL LIES

thEy aRE fALseHOoDs yOu inVEnt tO avoID rEGret

"I see." David stares at the creature, his face betraying no emotion, his mind clear, his emotions calm. "Tell me what you think about this one, then."

The world around them pulses. The dojo literally falls away—the half-formed walls collapse, the floor caves in, and soon even the land it sits on appears to melt and run as if disappearing down a drain. David and the shadow stand in the middle of nothingness.

WhAT iS—

Before the creature can finish its question, a scene unfolds beneath them. A vast, purple-black mass of darkness expands beneath their feet, a seething storm of indescribable power that glows faintly from streams of energy that arc across it in long, spidery bursts.

The size of the storm is vast beyond comprehension. Even though David exists outside the storm—is effectively "floating" far above it—he can't help but think *infinite* when he looks at it. Even though he can see where the storm ends, the feeling that it is *everywhere,* encompassing *everything,* persists. He can even *hear* it now, a massive roar accompanied by a strange, nearly subsonic *thummm* that makes his teeth ache.

WhAT iS tHiS

The sound of the storm—the unending roar that fills the space around them—almost drowns out the creature's question. David considers not answering until he feels a hand gripping his arm.

The creature—the shadow manifestation of a piece of Artigenian's power—has *grabbed his upper arm.* It reminds him of something he used to do to his physical therapist when he was recovering from his concussion, and couldn't walk straight. In the early days he couldn't keep his balance—just standing in one place made him feel like he was going to fall down—and the first time the therapist stepped away, he remembers lunging for the man's arm and gripping it as if his life depended on it. The shadow, currently feeling as real and as solid as anyone David has ever met, is doing exactly the same thing.

WhAT iS tHiS

Is that *panic*? It feels like panic.

"A dream," David says.

nO

The storm pulses. The storm roars. It looks like it's growing.

MasHEuDH

It *is* panic.

"Relax," David says. "This is a dream. It's one of the last dreams Artigenian ever had."

nO, MasHEuDH

ThiS iS nOT whERe yOu LiE

ThiS iS rEAl

"What? No." David waves his free hand dismissively. "Look, this is what I'm trying to explain. This is one of your memories, filtered through Artigenian's—"

He stops, frowning as he stares at his free hand. Stares *through* his free hand. He notes, with detached interest, that his flesh is unraveling, flowing down into the storm, unspooling like golden thread pulled from a spindle.

ThiS iS rEAl

hOw

David stares back at the shadow. It's still gripping his arm, but its outline is starting to blur and warp. A tiny speck of shadow breaks off from its head—just a fleck—and immediately falls away into the storm. Then a second, then a third, and then all at once hundreds of dark specks stream out of its body, into the storm. It shudders.

ThiS iS rEAl

David looks down at his hand, and the flesh being pulled away from it. He realizes, for the first time, that it hurts.

"How?" he whispers. "How is this possible?"

I dO nOt kNoW

tAKe uS bAcK

David thinks of the dojo. The storm below them continues to roar, and the pain in his fading left hand increases.

"I can't," he says. "It's not working."

tHeN We aRe gOIng tO dIE

We hAve EntEReD tHE TrUE Realm

aNd We aRe gOIng tO dIE

Part Three: Crossfire Safehouse

Senator Tobias Morgan stares down at his hands. They're trembling slightly—either from fear or exhaustion, CB can't tell. The senator certainly *looks* exhausted, and if everything he's saying is correct, he has plenty of reasons to be afraid.

"The government is full of cabals." The senator's voice betrays nothing of the tremors in his hands—it is as strong and confident as it has always been. For most of the time CB has known him, he's hated the smug surety in that voice. Now it sounds less smug, more defiant.

More like Alex.

"It's unavoidable, in the long term. Nobody ever wholly agrees with the party line. With *any* party line. There are people who think it goes too far. People who think it doesn't go far enough. And then, of course, there are people who think the party line completely ignores the real problems people are facing. So other groups form. Sometimes they're smaller, more 'pure' groups within your own party, sometimes they're groups that stretch across party lines that focus on individual issues. Not exactly secret, but you don't really tell people outside the group what you're working on until you're ready to move."

"Cabals," CB says. "Like this one you're in now."

Senator Morgan shakes his head. "This one is *nothing* like the others. When they first approached me, I thought it was just another ad hoc group of concerned politicians who were trying to find ways to work around roadblocks. And it was one of my pet causes. It's no secret I'm in favor of increased metahuman oversight."

CB's hands clench into fists. He says nothing. If the senator notices the reaction, he offers no comment.

"It became apparent, however, that this group was a lot more organized than most, to the point where I quickly suspected there were outside forces involved. At the time I assumed it was just another political action committee, though a very disciplined one. But I never met with a lobbyist. I only ever met other politicians and staffers who were 'on board.' I always wondered about that, but it never raised any alarms. Until PRODIGY, at any rate."

PRODIGY again. Bad memories that never fade.

The kid is thin—painfully so—and filthy. He's strapped into the monstrosity that is part medical bed, part coffin, but he's long past the point where struggling is a concern. The left side of his head has been shaved. Wires attach to three implants that look to have been drilled directly into his skull. The rest of his hair, dark and matted, falls down to thin, bony shoulders. Wide eyes stare into space. His eyes are so dilated CB can't tell what color they are. His mouth is open, and though no sound comes out it's easy to tell he's screaming.

CB shakes his head, dispelling the image. The senator does notice this time, and his expression is more sympathetic than expected.

"How does this link to PRODIGY?" CB asks.

"They were the ones responsible." The senator's expression is remote and unreadable. "They are the ones who placed me on the investigatory committee."

"Right," CB says. "I always figured you were there for the coverup."

Senator Morgan's eyes narrow. "I almost wasn't. When it became clear what this group needed me to do, I very nearly exposed the entire thing."

"Yeah?" CB feels a familiar flash of anger rise, crowding out all his other, more tactically sound impulses. "What kept you?"

"My grandfather," the senator says.

The anger dissolves. CB falls silent.

The senator's mouth curls in grim amusement. "Yes. When I realized what I was being asked to do, I was nearly ready to expose the entire thing. It wasn't easy. I was quite certain the moment I did so, the shadowy forces behind this political cabal would turn against me, and my political career would end. I was frightened of that. *Very* frightened. So I turned to my grandfather, America's greatest hero, and I told him everything. I told him what I was about to do. I told him how afraid I was to do it. All I needed was for him to tell me I was doing the right thing, that it would be hard, but that doing the right thing had consequences. I'd heard him give the speech before. That's all I needed, and I would have thrown away my career by doing the right thing."

He laughs then. "That's not what he did. He told me I was a good man, but that I was making a mistake."

CB blinks. "What?"

Senator Morgan grins—probably one of the most genuine expressions of mirth CB has ever seen on the man. "That is exactly what I said at the time. And grandfather just laughed and shook his head. Then he started telling me what the four of you did when you took PRODIGY down." He eyes CB thoughtfully. "I have to say you played it perfectly. We all thought we were watching the Guardians of Justice disintegrate in real time. Liberty was the patriotic soldier, Regiment the reluctant citizen, you the snarling rebel and Gladiator the primadonna who took his toys and went home. And in the middle of all that distraction, you were able to uncover what they were really doing."

CB shrugs. "It wasn't my plan. It was Robert and Alex, mostly."

"Grandfather didn't see it that way," the senator says. "But he said the biggest flaw the plan had was that it ended when you discovered the facility where the kids were being held. It had to—the kids needed rescuing—but that was your last card in the deck. Then he said I had the opportunity to be a new deck."

"Oh," CB says. "He turned you into a spy."

"I guess so. I began participating in the coverup. Officially, I was shocked and appalled that the entire affair had happened, but I wanted to be sure that it minimized the damage done to our long-term metahuman policy goals. As time went on, I started openly speculating whether the technology we recovered could be of any use, and bemoaned the necessity of destroying it all. Eventually they made contact. Eventually they brought me in. And eventually—a process that took years—they trusted me enough to tell me what Project Recall really was."

"Yeah, but…" CB frowns and shakes his head. "How did they not find out? If they're as paranoid as you claim, how did you manage to keep your cover? Sure, OK, they don't like metahumans, but it's obvious they're not above using them. One telepath is all it would take, used at just the right time—"

"No telepaths," Senator Morgan says. "They're not opposed to metahumans, exactly… they're opposed to how many of you there are. But they're *absolutely* opposed to telepaths. They're *terrified* of them. I was told, when I reached a certain level of trust, that if I *ever* developed telepathic abilities I would be killed outright—nothing personal, that's just the way it was. And I believed them."

"No telepaths," CB repeats.

"None whatsoever. They use other methods to ensure loyalty."

"Like keeping hair and blood samples?" CB asks.

The senator nods. "Which brings us back to the main subject… because I really don't have much time." He says it candidly, almost off-handedly, but CB can see dread in his eyes. Whatever is waiting for him in the very near future terrifies him.

"OK," CB says. "Back to the matter at hand. Tell us what you know about Project Recall."

"It's a virus," the senator says. "It kills metahumans. It also, at the moment, kills people who aren't metahuman but carry a few specific metahuman genes. The specific version they're using is extremely hard to spread, and they're using... magic... to—" He frowns, reaching for the right words. "I guess the best explanation is to teleport it directly into people."

"Yeah," CB says. "It seems like a really impractical way to kill us."

"Killing you is only the first part," the senator says. "And it's not the most *important* part. Did you know the initial version of the virus was supposed to be completely harmless to everyone, even metahumans? They wanted it to be too weak to affect a healthy adult. Unfortunately they couldn't get it to survive long enough."

"That makes no sense," CB says. "The current plan apparently hinges on killing the entire male metahuman population, and the only reason they're settling for half is because the magic they're using depends on some kind of curse that can only be used on men."

"I don't understand magic," the senator says. "And I wasn't involved in that part of it. My part—the part that all of their pet politicians are neck deep in—comes after, when the babies start dying."

When the babies start dying.

"Maybe I better shut up and let you explain," CB says.

The senator has too much self control to smirk. "Here's the scenario we were given: at some point in the very near future, every metahuman male is going to die. It will be a horrible, painful death. Nobody will know exactly why it happened, because nobody—as far as we know—has researched metahuman genetics as extensively as we have. They simply won't know what to look for. About a year after that tragedy, infants will start dying at birth. Nobody will know why. It will be another global crisis of epic proportions. It will create a period of worldwide instability unlike anything we have ever seen in history. It will eclipse the Bubonic Plague in terms of fear, despair, and utter hopelessness."

A strangled, half-uttered curse causes both the senator and CB to turn to stare at Street Ronin. He has abandoned his position behind the camera, which is still recording the exchange, and is leaning against the wall, breathing heavily.

"What's wrong?" CB asks.

"He figured it out," the senator says.

"The virus only kills metahumans," Street Ronin says. "But they're putting it in *everyone*. Every single male on the planet. It only kills you if you have the right genes, but *it's still there.*"

Oh. *Shit.*

CB looks at the senator, and is surprised to see that he is barely keeping his rage under control.

"That's right," the senator says. "Remember when I said the first virus—the one that didn't kill people—was discarded because it didn't last long enough? The virus stays in your blood. Given enough time, it does more than that—it alters your DNA. It becomes a virus that is transmitted through your DNA. You are given tiny little building blocks that embed a kill switch into any human with the metahuman gene. And then—"

He breaks off for a moment, taking a deep, shuddering breath, forcing the anger back one more time. "And then, after all the male metahumans are dead, the rest of the world will go back to their lives. And that involves *having children.*"

"It's not about killing the metahumans we have now," Street Ronin says. "That's just collateral damage. They're making sure there are *never* any metahumans again. *Ever.*"

Part Four: Somewhere Else

I am unraveling.

David winces as the glowing ribbon of flesh tears away from his hand, pulled inexorably into the maelstrom below. The pain is significant now, as if he were grasping a red-hot brand with his bare flesh. The pain spikes, and his arm *ripples,* his skin twisting and expanding as more of it pulls away. Spidery lights flicker across the surface of the maelstrom below, somehow keeping time with the pulses of pain coursing up his arm. With each pulse he can feel his essence unravel further. Up to his elbow now. Up to his forearm. Up to his shoulder.

A different kind of pressure on his other arm—the grip of the shadow—intensifies.

MAKE THIS STOP

"I don't know how!" Words are difficult to form—the unraveling of his physical form appears to be confined to his arm for the moment, but there's something else at work, attacking and devouring his mind. "Tell me how!"

I DO NOT KNOW HOW MASHEUDH

David tears his gaze away from his own disappearing form, and glances at the shadow. It, too, is unraveling—a purple-black ribbon of matter unwinding from its left arm, to match the shining golden thread streaming from David's right.

"Why is it affecting you?" Fear spikes, temporarily beating back whatever is trying to devour his mind. "I thought you were from here!"

I DO NOT KNOW MASHEUDH

I DO NOT KNOW WHAT TO DO

It, too, is panicking. It, too, is afraid.

David searches through Artigenian's memories, looking for something—anything—that he might use as a means of escape. There is nothing. As far as Artigenian knew, it was impossible to enter this place.

He tries dreaming. He imagines a shining golden sphere surrounding them, protecting them. It appears, and for a few seconds it actually works—the golden thread is cut, the shadow-ribbon disappears, the piercing pain eases, the roar of the storm below fades away. But the golden sphere shudders, twists, its form distorts, and then it bursts apart, pulled down into the seething mass of destruction below as the pain in his arm returns. He feels something *ripping* inside him. He suspects it won't be long now.

The shadow keens in despair, and for a moment it twists, distorting much like the golden sphere did before it was torn apart. He suspects it won't be long for either of them.

Somewhere in the back of his mind he hears Billy Joel singing Goodnight Saigon.

And we will all go down together...

David looks at the shadow again. He gets an idea. He doesn't like the idea, but it has the advantage of being the only idea he has.

"You're gonna have to trust me," he says.

The shadow stops keening. A second strand of purple-black shadow begins to peel away from the back of its head.

I WILL SUBMIT

"Good enough," David says, and then pulls the shadow toward him.

It disappears into his skin, expanding to fill the gaps being ripped away by the maelstrom below. Shadow sinks into bone, merges with sinew, and the *cold* of it makes him scream, even as it drives away the searing heat of his unraveling flesh. An impossible pressure builds up in his head, his sight blurs, every concussion he's ever had throbs painfully, and just as his mind is about to break there is a great *shift* and David and Shadow are one. In that moment David understands, almost instinctively, where he is, what he is, and why he is dying.

This is a place the shadow's people call the True Realm. In their understanding, it is the first place—a place that existed before any other aspect of creation, encompassing the entire multiverse. The storm that rages so far below them isn't a storm at all: it is *alive*, and ever hungering, and because it cannot feed upon itself it rages.

But it feeds *now*.

David and the shadow came into this realm unprotected, unprepared, and the maelstrom reached out. It set its hooks into them. And now, despite the vastness of the distance between them, it is pulling them apart. David and the shadow are too small to provide any real sustenance, but he maelstrom does not care. They are sweeter than any meal it has had in eons.

He feels the shadow's terror, and understands it. How can anything stand against that?

We can stand against it, David thinks. *Together.*

Together, the shadow agrees. *Let it be so.*

He extends his right hand, a strange hand made of light and shadow both, and closes it into a fist. Immediately the golden yellow thread of flesh and the purple black ribbon of shadow burst like chains shattering at each link. The maelstrom surges, angry at the loss of its meal. It gets even angrier when David calls out to all of the scattered bits of himself and the shadow that haven't yet been swallowed up by the storm, and they defy their own destruction.

Piece by precious piece he feels himself return. His hand tingles as what was taken flows back into his flesh. More important, he feels stronger and more confident as his mind and soul are pieced back together. He feels the same thing happening to the shadow, feels it strengthen as most of what it lost is recovered. Neither of them are complete, now, but there is enough. Together, they are enough.

But only for the moment. Spidery traces of white fire flicker across the maelstrom's surface, and then they flare up and stream together into a single blazing point of light beneath them. The maelstrom has decided to retaliate.

Together, we are enough.

It isn't David's thought, this time. It comes from the shadow. The shadow has shed most of its terror as it begins to suspect exactly what they can do. David agrees, casting his mind back to his time on Esperanza, summoning a very specific memory. He senses the shadow remembering the same event, registers its shock as it realizes what David is planning, then feels the shock fade as it accepts the necessity. But the acceptance is not without criticism: there is context David is missing, and when the shadow provides it, he understands how the plan needs to change. He alters it quickly, offering it up for inspection. The shadow examines it carefully. It agrees.

"You're going to need a name," David says.

The shadow considers. It reaches into David's mind and shows him its choice. David laughs, genuinely surprised.

"Well done."

The fire gathering in the maelstrom condenses further, shines brighter. It won't be long now.

Begin, the shadow urges.

Begin, David agrees.

"I am David Bernard."

He doesn't try to shout, but his voice pours out of him, louder than he ever thought it possible to be. The sound of the storm fades as he speaks, as if the weight of his words pushes the roar away.

"I have a soul."

He feels pressure building around him, as if this reality is trying to push his words back into his mouth, to prevent their escape.

"The soul of the man is also the man."

Howls of outrage fill his ears. They don't come from any specific place, but from everywhere at once. The maelstrom shudders for a moment, as if pulling back in revulsion.

Just wait, David thinks to himself. *We're not at the good part yet.*

"I name myself Allard."

David speaks, but he is not speaking: he has ceded control to the shadow while it does its part.

"I claim a soul."

The howls of outrage turn into shrieks of fury. This place can sense one of its own, however changed it may be, and it has just committed blasphemy.

"The soul of Allard is also Allard."

David flinches as he feels a weight settle over him. It is the feeling of being watched, only more so. It's not the maelstrom. It had already noticed them, and it doesn't appear to be possessed of the level of awareness he's feeling now. This is a much colder, more calculated awareness. The eyes of predators who measure their prey.

This was inevitable, the shadow—Allard from this moment forward, however many moments they may have—tells him. *To be what we are, where we are... there will be no quiet escape. We will attract notice.*

David sets that knowledge aside for the moment. They have other things to do.

Their identities declared before the firmament and all its denizens, David returns to dreaming. He summons the golden orb once again: it snaps into place, humming with the authority of David's declaration. There is a moment when it shudders, then the golden sphere dims as purple shadow seeps into it, strengthening it. Instantly the pressure subsides: there is no longer a tug from the maelstrom below, no longer a feeling of being watched by vicious, unseen eyes. David and the shadow, together in David's body, float within a golden-black bubble of defiance in the vast emptiness of nightmare, untouched.

For the moment. That will change if they remain where they are.

"We need to move," David murmurs. He feels Allard assent, and murmur a suggestion. David nods, focuses his will, and the sphere streaks across the emptiness, leaving a faint trail of purple-gold behind as it dives, as fast as it can, toward the swirling maelstrom below.

Part Five: The Nautilus, Atlantic Ocean

Robert Thorpe stares at the image of the bruised, spiky-haired man on his monitor, mind racing to process the new information he's just received.

"How sure are you about this?"

CB shrugs, his gaze shifting to something outside of the monitor's view. "Toby is *absolutely certain* of it."

"And you *believe* him?" Robert doesn't bother hiding his skepticism. "He hasn't exactly been particularly high on our list of people we trust."

"Yeah," CB agrees, "but we trust him to be himself. Look, Robert, I'm not saying that after twenty years of despising the man he's become my favorite person in the world overnight, but I am saying that when he tells me he and Alex had been playing a long game, and that Alex willingly sacrificed himself to preserve Toby's cover… yeah, I believe it."

"Right." It sounds incredible in the abstract, but it's more in line with what Robert knows about the senator than their original assumption. Tobias Morgan has never been an ally of metahumans—he and Robert have been on opposites sides of every important metahuman issue over the last twenty years—but the senator had always possessed qualities that Robert admired. The idea that he murdered his grandfather in order to cover up a genocide plot seems to betray every one of those qualities. This new context, as incredible as it is, is more consistent with the man as Robert understands him.

"How is he doing?"

CB shakes his head. "He's basically waiting to die at this point, and it hasn't happened yet. He's still giving a statement, Street Ronin is still recording it, but he's starting to crack up. Robert, when this happens it's going to be really ugly."

"I hesitate to suggest it," Robert says, "but there might be value in recording it, when it happens."

CB snorts. "Toby suggested the same thing. To 'let the world know exactly what we're dealing with,' he said. But let's go with 'no.'"

"I understand," Robert says, "but—"

"Think of Jenny," CB says. "And Julie. And Martin. And Andy. They haven't really had an *easy relationship* with the guy. It's going to be bad enough when they learn that part of it was because he was trying to protect them from the assholes he was infiltrating. We don't need to twist the knife by putting out video of his painful, prolonged death on top of it. The people who would be inclined to believe him will be convinced by his words. The people who won't—the ones who will accuse us of coercing his testimony —well, they'll believe we faked the footage, too."

"Yeah," Robert says. "You're right. I wasn't thinking of Jenny, or Julie. Sorry."

CB shakes his head. "Not your fault. What about this news about the virus? Does that make this whole business harder?"

"Good question." Robert leans back in his chair, staring at the ceiling as the analytical part of his mind adds the new information to existing data, sorting and resorting it in an attempt to make everything fit. "It gives me a few new ideas about how to try to isolate it. But the fact that it integrates or embeds into human DNA does make combating it more difficult. I haven't had a lot of luck with designer drugs that specifically rewrite human DNA. The closest I've come to it is with…"

His voice trails off. His eyes unfocus a moment, then he straightens and turns back to the screen. "Well, OK, I have a new idea now. I'll get back to you if it bears fruit."

"That's fine," CB says. "Meanwhile, what assets do I have on hand?"

Robert feels one eyebrow go up. "What do you mean?"

"I mean, how many of our team can make it to New York City in the next six to eight hours?"

Robert frowns. "Well, we all could, if it was absolutely necessary. But I need some of them here to work on the virus. What's on your mind?"

CB scowls. "What's on my mind is that pretty soon I'm going to watch Toby die, and it's going to really piss me off. He says they have blood, hair, and skin samples of a lot of other 'useful assets' at their Corporate HQ. I plan to make sure no more are used after tonight."

Robert nods slowly. "I'm not sure that's tactically wise."

"Oh, I'm absolutely sure it's not," CB says. "But damned if I'm not going to do it anyway. That's why I want to pull out all the stops."

"Right…" Robert checks the time. "Give me an hour to track everyone down and work through logistics, and I'll tell you what your options are."

"All right," CB says. "Don't send Jenny."

"If Jenny decides to go," Robert replies, "I am not going to stop her."

CB slumps, mutters something under his breath, then smiles sardonically. "Yeah. Sorry. Don't tell her I said that. Moment of weakness, won't happen again."

"I'll contact you in an hour," Robert says. "I'll use the second line, just to make sure we're in the clear."

"Sounds good to me. Talk then."

The screen distorts, then goes dark.

Robert curses softly, then turns back to the computer monitor at his desk, displaying the latest research on the virus. He adds a few notes, scans it over, then closes the window. He leans back in his chair and closes his eyes, thinking furiously.

The news that *anyone* can carry the virus, metahuman or not, makes it significantly more dangerous. And it makes Haruspex Analytics, or whatever group is working through them, significantly more dangerous as well. The deaths of metahumans all over the planet is only their *secondary* objective. Their primary objective is to erase them from the gene pool entirely.

Robert pushes a button on his desk. "Jenny, are you still in the gym?"

A few seconds later he hears Jenny's voice over the desk intercom speaker. "Yeah, I'm here. What's up?"

"David Bernard was working on something in the meeting room. Can you get him, and both of you meet me in my office? I don't want to interrupt him, but we need his perspective on something."

"Did something just happen?" Jenny asks.

"Yes," Robert says. "Something definitely happened. I'll tell you about it when you get here."

"OK," Jenny says. "I'll see you in a few."

Robert turns in his chair, staring out the window at the ocean on the other side. He reviews all of the information he has onhand.

His desk beeps. He looks down—it's coming from the meeting room. He presses a button.

"Thorpe."

"Robert." There's an edge to Jenny's voice that immediately puts him on alert.

"What's wrong?"

"Well…" Jenny hesitates. "You said David would be here."

"That's what he told me," Robert says. "He asked me to reserve it for him. He's working on something."

"He's not working on it here," Jenny says. "The room is empty. Except for that thing he does."

Robert frowns. "What thing?"

"You know the black globe he creates that always floats on top of his hand? It's currently floating in the exact middle of the meeting room. The room is completely empty, except for that thing."

"OK, hold on a moment." Robert mutes the intercom. "Daniel, please report the location of David Bernard."

The computer responds immediately. "David Bernard is not currently on this vessel."

"What? How?"

"Unknown," the computer replies. "I have no record of him leaving the vessel. All craft save the one used by Curveball, Street Ronin, and Scrapper Jack are accounted for. There is, however, an unknown energy reading emanating from David Bernard's last known location."

"Right…" Robert stands, grabs a tablet computer off his desk, then hits the intercom button again. "Jenny, I'm on my way. Something's going on. Stay there and don't let anyone else in the room."

Part Six: City of Knives

Under normal circumstances, David wouldn't think that diving *toward* a near-infinite cosmic storm of unfathomable power was a good idea. But the dot of white fire now glows so fiercely that it hurts his eyes, and rapidly changing altitude is one of the fundamentals of avoiding artillery fire. Since the storm is already exerting force, trying to draw them down, he can dive faster than he can climb. So they dive, arcing away from the dot of white fire as they descend. The fire dims for a moment, as if surprised, then blazes even brighter than before. The roaring of the maelstrom swells around them, and David is convinced it is a sound of rage and fury.

Smaller dots of white fire appear along beneath them, and something that is neither lightning nor fire erupts from each point. David isn't flying in a straight line, however—he spent too much time flying as Sky Commando, is all too familiar with enemies trying to shoot him out of the air—and his weaving, twisting descent always places him in an empty space.

The maelstrom is powerful, but it is slow. It isn't used to dealing with something so small.

It takes an hour before the maelstrom stops trying to shoot him out of the sky. After that, the dots of white fire trail along after him, waiting for him to slow or stop. He does neither: he descends, and the storm grows ever larger, and its pull grows stronger. The roaring of the storm, dampened as it is by the golden sphere, is relentless and terrifying.

He has no sense of scale in this place. His only point of reference is the storm, which is much too large to measure by. They have descended to the point where he can no longer see the edge of it. He believes the distance between them is still vast; at the same time, it looks almost close enough to touch.

He's noticing more detail. From his original position the maelstrom looked like a purple cloud spouting fire—now it's apparent that the purple is a layer of clouds covering something else. He can see glimpses of it now: something churning with incredible, relentless energy, just hidden from view. Allard can tell him little about what it might be. Its kind do not willingly approach the storm.

Still, it notices something David has overlooked—an odd disturbance in the seething mass of clouds, at the far edge of his vision. The arcs of white fire that lance across the clouds stop, suddenly, when they reach the edge of it. Still descending, David changes course toward the disturbance. The dots of white fire change course to follow, undeterred.

Occasionally the clouds break apart, providing more glimpses of what lies beneath. Fire, if an ocean of flame were possible. As he reaches the disturbance, the clouds begin to thin, and finally he sees what it is: a massive whirlpool of fire, spinning furiously, sweeping the clouds into it where they are torn apart. The roaring is even louder here, and all David can think is *Abandon Hope, All Ye Who Enter Here*. If ever there was a gateway to hell itself, this is it.

An ocean of fire feeding a whirlpool of fire.

An ocean of... *living* fire? Allard claims the maelstrom is alive.

The maelstrom lives, Allard insists. *Whether the fire is maelstrom, or the maelstrom dwells beneath fire, I cannot say.*

"You don't talk the same," David says.

"No," he hears himself saying. "I do not... *masheud*."

As he crosses the lip (*the event horizon*, something that is not Allard whispers, and he forces the thought aside) he is overcome by a wave of vertigo. The sheer volume of fire pouring into the whirlpool's mouth, the violence with which it sweeps around and around as it spirals into the depths, the annihilation of every cloud that approaches the rim—all combine to overwhelm his senses. Allard's alarm spikes as it realizes David is losing all sense of direction, and the golden sphere wobbles, the surface rippling as David's concentration slips. If it drops, here, so close to the fire, they will surely die.

Again Allard notices what David overlooks. He feels his left hand extend, pointing out. His eye follows the gesture; as he focuses his vertigo falls away. There, high above the fire, roughly dead center of the whirlpool, is a cluster of indistinct shapes.

There, Allard urges. David, grateful for something to focus on, urges the sphere forward.

It is an island. It is a *series* of islands, tiny motes floating above an immense inferno, existing without explanation, apparently unaffected by the maelstrom in any way. As they approach the islands grow more distinct, and David sees the cities: buildings like knife blades rising out of the ground, jagged, unrelenting spires piercing the empty sky above. Straight avenues cut between jagged skyscrapers, ending at little, empty barren plots of land squeezed in between. Each island has one of these cities, each of varying size but similar in architecture and design. The islands are all connected by a spiderweb of bridges, and as he draws closer it becomes apparent that the islands aren't tiny at all. David might have no head for the size of things on a cosmic level, but he knows the scale of cities very well. The smallest city on the smallest island would dwarf New York. The larger cities are the size of small states.

And they are all, as far as he can tell, empty. The buildings exist. They were obviously created. The closer he gets the more obvious it appears that the buildings, roads, and bridges are in good repair. But he sees no *movement* anywhere.

He asks Allard, but the shadow knows nothing. These are not its people. They do not approach the storm.

A new sensation pushes at the border of his mind—a trickle of an entirely new kind of pressure. There is intent and awareness behind this pressure, and it is similar to some of what he felt when he first spoke his name aloud in this realm. At least one of the things that noticed him then has taken note of him a second time, and then in a thrill of alarm he feels the one awareness become two, the two become ten, and then, like a dam breaking, there are more minds than he can perceive, all slowly focusing on him.

The cities were never empty, David realizes. They were asleep. And now they are waking up.

Rise. Escape. The golden sphere shoots up, away from the storm, away from the cities of jagged blades. They are far enough across the whirlpool that none of the points of white fire can follow them, and it is suddenly more important to escape the minds that are focusing on his own, the same way a magnifying glass might settle on an ant on a sunny day. He pours his will into the speed of the globe, and the islands shrink beneath him. He moves faster than he thought was possible, and the islands are soon no more than specks beneath them.

He slows the globe, gasping for air. He didn't realize he'd been holding his breath.

What do we do now? David asks.

Up, Allard urges.

They continue *up*. The pulse of the storm lessens a bit more, and some of the fear dissipates. As they continue to rise, it becomes apparent that they are not alone: a huge, rubbery, manta-like creature soars silently past them. It is the length of a battleship, David thinks, though considerably wider, and on the back of this beast, he sees a smaller version of the cities they left behind. It reminds him of Robert Thorpe's mechanical island, only the buildings look like knives growing out of the island's back.

He feels no awareness coming from the island at this time. He moves the sphere higher, passing it quickly, not wishing to risk another inadvertent awakening.

He sees other creatures, from time to time. There is something like an anemone, little more than a floating ball of podlike appendages that flail uselessly until something wanders too close. Then the pods extend to razor-sharp tentacles, latching on to whatever it can. David sees one of them capture an uncolonized manta, burrowing deep into its flesh. He rushes past them, and is thankful that they disappear from view before the anemone can begin tearing the larger beast apart.

There are birdlike creatures as well—at least two species, as far as he can tell. One looks vaguely like a headless pterodactyl, all leathery hooked wings and long tails. The other looks more like the shadow of a bird than the bird itself. He only sees those out of the corner of his eye—great flocks of shadow birds that disappear when he turns to look at them directly.

Still they rise.

"I don't have a plan," David admits. "I don't know what I did to take us here. I don't know how to get us out."

A ripple of dread runs through him. It isn't his.

I may know a way.

"You don't sound happy about it."

It takes the shadow a moment to consider the word *happy*.

No. I am not.

"Can you explain it?"

Allard tries. Images flash through David's mind. Rigid, unchanging shapes that grow heavier the longer you look at them. Colors that burn. A mathematical equation that makes him want to scream. A memory of voices lifted in a song that devours the singers, the final note changing from a scream to a despairing sigh to utter silence in a matter of seconds.

"I don't understand," David admits.

Allard tries again. David sees a city—not the knife-edged cities of the floating islands, but one of regular geometric shapes, made entirely of dark glass, set in a methodical fashion against a backdrop of absolute darkness. Two rivers flow into the city from opposite directions, both running in perfectly straight lines, stretching on without apparent end. In the very center of the city is an obelisk that towers above everything else. A voice, or something like a voice, calls out from the rock.

"You want us to go there?"

No, that's not exactly right. Allard doesn't *want* to go there, but they must. The obelisk has the burning light that bends the worlds.

David tries to make sense of that and fails. "I still don't understand."

Trust, Allard murmurs. *This will require trust.*

David snorts. The shoe, it seems, is on the other foot.

"Very well," he says. *"I submit."*

There is startled silence, followed by brief laughter and grim amusement.

Good enough, Allard murmurs, and then the shadow takes control.

Part Seven: City of Glass

David doesn't like being a passenger in his own body, but he takes some comfort that he isn't a prisoner. He can, he realizes, retake control over his body and mind at any moment—it is *trust* and *active restraint* that is allowing Allard to take control.

Allard turns David's face away from the maelstrom, focusing on a patch of nondescript, empty space far in the distance. David can't see anything, but he can feel Allard's certainty that something is there.

The mix of golden light and dark shadow changes, the gold dimming as the shadow darkens, and he feels something shift around him as they move faster toward their destination. The pulse of the storm, though ever-present, lessens. In time it recedes to an angry murmur, an ever-persistent but not overpowering pull. David glances down—the storm is still spread out below them, still fills up most of his view, but it looks less like a raging storm and more like a slowly swirling cloud.

There, Allard murmurs, and David feels his head turn, his eyes focus ahead. Far above them he sees lightly discolored shapes emerging out of the darkness. Little pale gray dots, set in single file across the expanse.

Are they stars? No—at least, not stars as he would understand them. They're set too regularly, spaced too evenly from each other, to be natural. Now that he knows what to look for, he can see even more of the strange pale gray dots in the distance.

They continue on. The dots grow larger, now the size of a fingertip, and David notices a thin, spindly line extending from each, connecting them. The lines continue on, connecting each dot in turn, and as the lines grow sharper and more defined David realizes the dots *aren't* laid out in a straight line, they're *curved*. They arc across the empty space and curve down seeming to disappear behind the storm's horizon, like a…

"Is this a *ringworld*?"

David senses Allard's confusion, then feels the creature sifting through his memories, trying to find context. It considers the question.

Imprecise, Allard thinks. *But not wrong.*

David's eyes drift back to the distant pale-gray dot directly in front of them. "So what are these things? Islands, like we saw floating over the storm? Connected by roads?"

Not roads. Rivers. Great rivers between the empty spaces, connecting the Great Cities.

Rivers. Cities.

The pale gray dot grows larger, almost to the size of a half dollar. David can see more detail: the "dot" is actually a huge, flat disk, hanging in space, with a mass of smoke swirling and churning underneath. On top of that foundation he sees massive, looming architecture: regular geometric shapes, set in a methodical fashion, against a backdrop of absolute darkness.

"This is the place you were trying to tell me about," David says.

Yes.

"Each of the gray dots—each one is a city like this?"

Yes.

"And the connections between them are… rivers? Like you showed me in that vision."

Yes.

"All right." David looks at the smoke churning beneath the city platform, and frowns. Something doesn't look quite right. "Why is there all that smoke under the city? Is it an engine? Is that what keeps the cities in place?"

He feels Allard's tension rising.

No. Soon. You will see. Soon. Listen.

David listens. He can still hear the storm, now very far below them, a low, ever-present noise in the background. There is something else, though, very faint, just behind the roar of the storm.

"What is that?"

It rises, crests, and recedes, dipping back behind the roar, only to surge again. It sounds like voices. Strangely human-like voices, crying out in despair, each cycle a little louder than before. The sound rises and falls in time with the swirling of the smoke beneath the foundation, growing louder as the smoke expands, quieter as it recedes.

"What is—" David's question dies on his lips, unasked, because suddenly they are close enough to see the smoke in detail. In that moment, he understands that he is wrong. The smoke isn't smoke at all. It's a *swarm*, and the swarm is made of *people*.

Humanoid shapes, male and female both, struggle beneath the city foundation like ants in a collapsed colony. Their heads are empty, featureless, with only vague indentations where eyes and nose should be. The only distinctive features they have on their faces are mouths, which are always open and screaming. They turn blindly out into eternity, as if they can sense that freedom lies out there, but they are inevitably pulled back into the mass of bodies by others trying to claw to the outer edge.

"What is this?"

The movement is always down, away from the city. The farther up he looks, the less movement he sees, until finally the bodies aren't moving at all: eventually they twine together, arms and legs wrapped and bound and lashed to each other to form a chain of flesh that stretches across the city's foundation, stretches beneath the "rivers," stretches as far as he can see in two directions. People—not humans, perhaps, but people nonetheless—are bound together, holding up cities and the paths that connect them, stretching an almost infinite distance across nothing, potentially encircling the storm.

"What *is* this?" David's voice is hoarse. His cheeks are wet.

There is a trace of bitterness in Allard, and the emotions that run through it are fast and complicated and hard to separate. There is loss, homesickness, revulsion and fear, horror at what is happening and longing for a time when the knowledge didn't matter. It occurs to David that perhaps Allard can't answer the question, because it no longer understands, precisely, what it's seeing.

They are even closer now, and the wailing of suffering and despair grows as loud as the roaring of the maelstrom had been earlier. Allard changes direction, no longer flying directly toward the city but aiming to fly over it. The wailing is now so loud that it drives out any hint of the roar from the maelstrom below, and for a moment David is aware of every mind around him. He can feel their panic as bodies crush against them, their terror as they scrabble for every chance to reach the very outer layer, and their despair when they feel something loop around an ankle, or arm, and pull them deep into the pile, toward the city. There is resignation, then, and the will to fight flickers out and dies.

"Allard." David is panicking. There are too many voices in his head, too many, too distinct. "Allard!"

Close.

He is overcome with the urge to take back control and fly as far away from this place as he can. "Allard, I don't think…" Another wave of despair shoots through him. "I don't think I can do this."

Close.

And then they are past the net of flesh, and there is only stone and silence.

The pressure is gone. The wailing is gone. Even the faint sound of roaring from the maelstrom is gone. They are flying through a complete absence of sound, and for a moment all David can feel is an overpowering sense of relief. The relief turns to shame, prompting a brief murmur of irritation from Allard.

Perhaps Allard is right. There's no shame in being free of that feeling. He can't do anything for them—not now, not in their present circumstances—and forcing himself to feel that endless despair will do nothing but break him, in the end. He doesn't want to break. He wants to survive this.

He focuses on the stone that forms the foundation of the city. They are flying close to it now, and despite their speed he can take in an unusual amount of detail. What looks like a smooth, thin plate of rock from a distance is surprisingly uneven—it looks like the sides of the city's foundation melted, turning patches of it into glass. Rough stone is interspersed with smooth, irregular patches that rise up and twist into distended shapes, hills and bubbles and whorls, and even some extrusions that look like half-formed...

People?

And just as the truth of it begins to dawn, they shoot past the foundation and arc high over the city itself.

It is a city made entirely of glass. There is light everywhere. All the streets, all the buildings are lit by brightly shining globes of white, pushing back the darkness and reflecting off the glittering dark surfaces of the mirror-like buildings. The buildings themselves are geometrical shapes: half-globes, cubes, tetrahedrons suspended on long cylindrical columns. Four massive pyramids, each with thirteen sides, mark the four corners of the city. At its center, a massive obelisk rises above everything else.

They hang motionless over the city, the protective sphere around them intensifying, flaring up gold and shadow-purple as Allard gathers their strength for the next push. They float over one of the rivers that arches out across the expanse. Looking more closely, it is more accurately a canal: its shores are nothing more than broad stone walls holding it in. As the canal passes into the city it opens up into a lake, complete with docks and buildings along the artificial shore that might be warehouses. There are ships on the canal, each made of the same glass as the buildings, each lit by spheres of light.

And then they are moving, diving down into the city itself. David, surprised by the speed of their descent, feels a familiar thrill as they cross the city skyline, descend along one of the wide avenues, and head directly toward the obelisk at the city's center.

This city is not empty; there are creatures here. Many are humanoid, some looking like the faceless ones bound beneath the city, others looking entirely human. Many of them stand motionless, heads turned up, gaping at David/Allard as they race through the sky. There are other creatures as well, things that are *not* humanoid. They appear as dim shadows, barely distinct from the obsidian glass, standing tall above the crowds. They look vaguely like the shadows of jellyfish. Occasionally one thrusts a shadowy tendril into one of the humanoid creatures, who seizes up, screams, and falls to the ground, only to *sink into it,* never to be seen again.

The shadows, when they notice David/Allard, raise a shriek of anger— the first sound David has heard since they passed beyond the net of flesh. It is a terrible sound, many voices at once, some low, some high, all dripping with malevolence and rage.

David is overcome with fear. Allard is also afraid, David notes, but its fear is different. David fears the unknown. Allard knows what the shadows are, and that is why it fears.

The shadows leap into the sky, but David/Allard shoots past them, closing on the obelisk. The shadows gather in pursuit, wispy tendrils reaching out, but unable to pass through the globe of golden light and purple shadow. The globe trembles with each hit. Each time it trembles a little more. David wonders if it will hold.

It will hold, Allard says. *We are nearly there.*

The obelisk looms before them. Four main roads lead to its base, and four sets of massive double doors, all open, reveal a vast chamber within. Inside the chamber is a light so bright it is impossible to see anything distinct: there are dark silhouettes of robed figures, but David can see nothing else.

Allard's tension ratchets up another notch. It urges them on faster.

"Shouldn't we slow down?" David asks.

Allard doesn't answer. The shrieks of the shadow-things grow harsher, angrier.

"Allard!" David's calm breaks as some of the panic he has been trying to push back begins to break through. "We're going to have to slow—"

All at once they are surrounded by light. Harsh, smothering light that bears down on their globe with such relentless force that David hears it sputter and buckle under the pressure. All at once they come to a halt, there in the room of light, and David can feel searing *heat* leaking through the globe's walls.

Dream now dream now dream now dream now dream now dream now dream now dream now dream now dream now

Allard returns control of his mind and body as it continues to repeat the same command, over and over again.

Dream now dream now dream now dream now dream now dream now dream now dream now dream now dream now

David immediately thinks of his dojo, conjuring the flat stone floor, the dry plains, the warm sun beating down from a blue sky. He feels something tear, and suddenly the world around them disappears. Gone is the harsh, ever-burning light. Gone are the shadows, shrieking in impotent fury. Gone is the city of merciless glass. He stands on the cracked stone floor of an open dojo in the middle of an endless grassy plain. A warm wind blows, carrying with it the smell of dry soil. The sky is clear and blue, and the sun shines hot on his face and neck. He stands motionless for a moment, unsure whether what he's sensing is real.

It is real.

He feels something shift within him, then sees a dark silhouette remove itself from his body. It is different from the shadow-form it had taken when this first began. It is still shadow, but it is not an absence. It is fuller. More clearly defined.

"We're safe?" David asks.

The shadow dips its head. *Safe. We live. We are no longer there. We are here.*

David looks around his dream dojo. Then, in spite of everything, he starts to laugh.

"So you agree dreams aren't lies, then?"

Allard stares at him, then it too emits a rough kind of laugh. *You might perhaps have gone too far to make your point.*

David laughs harder. He lets himself laugh like that for a while. It is the prerogative of a man, recently escaped from Hell, to laugh at anything that strikes his fancy.

He stops when he realizes Allard is watching him, lost in its thoughts. David can't exactly tell what it's thinking, but he can feel it has come to a crossroads and can't decide which path to take.

"What now?" David asks.

Allard stirs. *I believe that is for you to decide.*

"Well," David says, "I know what *I'm* going to do. I suspect when I end this dream we'll wind up back in the meeting room where everything started. We're probably there right now, physically. So I'll stay, and I'll help Dr. Thorpe and the others as best I can. I... think that *the best I can* is significantly more than it was, before all this."

It is, Allard agrees. *I do not know how you managed to enter the True Realm, but to survive it you changed. You changed, and I changed with you. Neither one of us is entirely what we were.*

"You sound different," David says.

We were being destroyed by the Storm Beneath. We merged. You are part shadow, now. I am part… you.

"So what will you do now?"

I am part you, Allard says again, a bit impatiently. *I am bound to you. Your will bound me to you back on the ever-dreaming island, and while it changed in the True Realm, it did not break. If anything, it grew stronger.*

Now that Allard mentions it, David can *feel* it. There is a bond between them. There are *many* bonds between them, now, but the original one is still there. It's more of a leash than a bond, held by David, compelling Allard. And as David examines that leash, he can see that it cages the shadow completely. It can no longer attempt to vie for control of his body or mind. The thing David feared most—losing himself to the sentient fragment of Artigenian's power—is no longer a concern. The leash makes him safe.

He feels some regret when he wills the compulsion between them severed, but not much. He smiles when he feels the shadow's shock through the many other bonds that still exist.

You release your claim on me. It is almost a question, and the questions that lie behind the thought are too complicated to speak aloud.

David shakes his head. "That's not what happened. You named yourself, back there. You claimed a *soul*. I can't release a claim on you, because I can't *put* a claim on you. I mean, if it turns out you're still evil and you try to destroy my world, I'll certainly try to hunt you down and destroy you, but I can't keep you bound to me."

Why?

"Because," David says, "I will not build a city using you as my foundation."

The shadow does not reply. David steps forward, reaching out, and for a moment he sees his right hand shift—now flesh, now shadow, now flesh, now shadow again—before it rests on Allard's shoulder. A moment later Allard's hand falls on his shoulder in return. They stand there for a moment more, then Allard changes.

Allard's form shifts, shrinking and distorting, until it floats before him in the shape of a bird. One of the shadow-birds, David thinks, only sharper and more clearly defined. He lets his arm fall to his side as Allard soars into the air, streaking through the sky, then swoops back down to the dojo. It lands on David's shoulder, adjusting its weight as it settles into place.

I think I will travel with you awhile yet.

David smiles again. "Then I think we'd better wake up," he says, and opens his eyes.

Part Eight: Crossfire Safehouse

"It's starting."

Senator Morgan's voice cracks as he says it. His hand shakes as he sweeps a stray bit of hair out of his eyes. He is very pale, and sweating profusely. His eyes are wide, and terror shines out of them like beacon fires. But he's still hanging on, despite it all.

"I'm here." CB sits down on the couch next to the senator. "Right here."

"You might not want to be." Senator Morgan speaks more slowly than he usually does, concentrating on the words he wants to say. "I don't know how it works. You might get caught in it."

"Well, I'm here right now. We'll see what happens next." CB hates this. He's not good at *providing comfort,* and he knows it. This man is about to die horribly, and he's stuck sitting next to a guy who has hated him for decades. "You want a cigarette?"

The senator tries to laugh, but it comes out as a wheezing grunt. "I quit twenty years ago. I'm not going to let this be the reason I start again."

"Look, Toby—"

"Let's not do that," the senator says. "You all know now. You *know.* That's enough for me."

"Yeah," CB says. "All right."

The senator nods once. "I don't know exactly what's going to happen. I feel something cold. It's... paralyzing me. I can't move my legs. It hurts like hell. I thought paralysis wouldn't hurt. That doesn't seem fair."

He's starting to babble, but CB lets him talk. What else can he do? He looks at the hallway door. Street Ronin is down there, checking in with Robert.

"I regret nothing," the senator says, rage and defiance overflowing from every word. "I regret nothing. I regret—"

His face locks into a frozen mask of pain.

"Toby." CB stands, leaning over the man, peering into his eyes. "Toby, you still with us?"

The senator's breaths are coming in short, shallow bursts, the way you breathe when your ribs are broken.

"Toby!"

He's never felt so helpless. There's nothing he can do but watch the man die.

"Oh my God!" It's a woman's voice, directly behind him. CB whirls around and sees Jenny, dressed in her nondescript black body armor, staring at her uncle in shock.

"Jenny?" All CB can think is that Toby wouldn't want her to see this, but he can't bring himself to move. And then CB realizes that Jenny is supposed to be on the *Nautilus*. How did she get here?

Jenny stares in bewilderment at the man sitting in rigid agony on the couch. Then her expression hardens.

"David! He's here. Do what ya gotta do."

A man steps around the corner. For a moment, CB recognizes David Bernard as he takes in the room and moves forward. Then, for a moment, he doesn't recognize him at all, seeing instead a man whose skin shifts into shadow as much as he radiates a golden light that fills every corner.

CB takes an involuntary step back as the man (*just a man, he's sure it's a man*) stands before the senator.

"Is it too late?" Jenny's voice is steady. Detached. Professional.

"No." Dammit, it *is* Bernard. It's definitely his voice, though there's something strange about it. Something he can't place. "Not too late."

Bernard stretches out his hand, and the golden light gathers around his fingers, even as purple darkness seeps into the edges as if the light were bruised. He places his fingers on the senator's forehead and face. He presses down slightly, and the senator arches his back, face upturned as his mouth opens in a soundless, but very real, scream.

"Hey!" CB steps forward, his good arm outstretched. The world around him spins, then he's flying across the room, smashing face-first into a concrete wall. The air rushes out of his body, but he manages to keep on his feet. He staggers as he whirls around. Hands grab his arms and push him back.

"*No*, CB." His vision clears a little. Jenny stands in front of him, gripping him firmly. "No. I know it's weird, but David is here to *help*."

CB stares at Jenny's face until she comes into focus, then glances over at Bernard. His fingers are still pressed into the senator's face. The senator is still screaming soundlessly.

"It doesn't look like helping."

"David said it would hurt." Jenny's voice has lost a little of its detachment, and some of her worry and fear leaks through. "For a little while, until he can push it away."

"Push what away?"

"I don't know!" Jenny says. "I'm not the magic guy. He's the magic guy. *Trust your doctor.*"

Finally her words start to break through. "Right." CB looks at Bernard again, and forces himself to relax. "Right. OK. I'm good, Jenny. I get it."

She sighs in relief, letting go of him, then joining him against the wall. Street Ronin enters the room, looks at Bernard standing over the senator, and leans against the doorframe, watching quietly.

"Anyone else coming?" CB asks.

"The Feds," Street Ronin says. "Agent Hu came with those two. She's going to meet Agent Grant and coordinate some other assets. Red Shift, Vigilante, and Regiment are all working on something with Robert."

"That's too bad," CB says. "It'd be nice to have Regiment and Vigilante on hand when we try to assault an evil wizard's tower."

"Yeah," Street Ronin agrees. "Looks like we managed to snag our own wizard, though."

"It's been a really weird day," Jenny says.

"Yes," Bernard says. His voice has that strange edge to it again. "It certainly has."

The senator goes limp. CB tenses again until he sees the man's chest rise and fall in slow, deep breaths. Bernard adjusts the senator so that he's lying on the couch instead of sitting upright.

"There's a bed in the back," CB offers. The senator looks better—he's not in any obvious pain. Whatever Bernard did seems to be working.

Bernard shakes his head. "We can't move him much. Not at this point." He spreads his hands wide, and the tips of his fingers glow gold-purple again. He traces a circle around the senator's sleeping form. The lines hang in the air for a moment, then burn away as they fall to the floor.

"There," Bernard says. He relaxes, and the gold glow and shadows fade, making him look much more like himself again. "That will help for a time."

"For a time?" CB asks.

Bernard nods. "I can't save him. I can only keep the spell at bay. For a time. What I've bought you is time."

"Right," CB says. "OK. I can work with that. How much time?"

Bernard frowns. "A few hours? A day at most, but probably closer to a few hours."

"A few hours," CB repeats. "A few hours to do what?"

"This is an active ritual," Bernard says. "So they have to keep doing it until it works. If you want to save the senator, you'll need to... well, do what you were already going to do. Assault the evil wizard's tower."

CB stares at Senator Morgan, then at the others. He reaches into his flannel shirt's breast pocket and slowly pulls out a mashed-up pack of cigarettes. Only one left.

"Sounds good to me," he says. "But I'm gonna need to go shopping first."

Part One: A Comfortable Room

Artemis LaFleur sinks deeper into his overstuffed chair, lost in the sound of waves crashing against the beach. Sunlight streams through the thick-paned window, warming his face, and he closes his eyes as he momentarily loses himself in the comfort of it. The moment stretches into minutes, and the minutes stretch even farther on… until at last, almost regretfully, he opens his eyes.

It's a trap. He *knows* it's a trap, but the knowledge no longer carries the urgency it had in the beginning. Somewhere, in the farthest corners of his mind, he feels a vague stir of obligation, an obligation to *resist*—but he can't remember *why*.

He stares down at the book resting face-down in his lap. He remembers not being able to read it at first, just as he remembers not being able to look out the window. The book had been nothing but blank pages bound in leather, and the window… he frowns, trying to remember what he'd seen when he first looked out the window. Nothing, but a very specific *kind* of nothing…

The memory eludes him. He shrugs, staring out at the gulls playing in the surf. He can look out the window, now. He can read the books, now. He sighs, contentment and regret mixing together. He puzzles over that regret, recognizing it, unable to remember why it's there.

He should be doing something. Something other than this. Something important.

"It's taken hold. Interesting. I expected this to take longer."

A man sits in a chair on the other side of the window. A dark-haired man, with a face that pulls at old memories. His father's face, but the man is not his father.

"Given your focus and determination, I expected you to be more restless." The man smiles softly, staring at him with kind eyes. "I suppose it's harder to marshal such traits in a prison such as this."

"Yes…" Artemis sighs as he speaks. His gaze drifts back to the window.

"All the little things you want in life." The man with his father's face gestures to encompass the room and the window both. "In your lowest moments, when you are the least comfortable, the most irritated, feeling the greatest distress… these are the things you *long* for. A quiet chair, near a warm window, overlooking the ocean. Tea. A good book."

"Yes…" Artemis sighs again, and as his breath leaves him he feels a portion of his worry and despair leave as well. These are all the things he would rather be doing than... what did he call it? *Saving the world from itself.* And now, at last, he is doing them. Why was the other thing so important?

For a moment Artemis remembers being suspended in midair, watching a robed man with a soul of poisonous shadow screaming questions at him as he grows hungrier and thirstier each passing day. He shifts uneasily in his seat, trying to remember what it means. Who is that robed figure? Why was he hanging in the air? Why is the thing he remembers more clearly than anything else—more than the hunger, more than the thirst—an overwhelming resolve to *resist?* That commitment is the clearest part of the picture. He frowns as he tries, in vain, to find context.

"Some fight left, I see." The man with his father's face nods approvingly. "I'm glad to see it. I do regret this—it must be this way, you are far too dangerous to be restrained in a more traditional manner—but I am glad you resist to the end. It's what you *should* do. It is what is *right.* You will not win—it is, alas, only a matter of time until you succumb—but it is right that you refuse to accept it."

He stands, looking down, gently placing his hand on Artemis' shoulder.

"I promise you this," the man with his father's face says, "and in that most secret place where you are still fighting, I hope you find comfort in it. Some day, you will be released from this prison. Some day, it will be over and done... the die will be cast, and a new world will have risen from the ashes of the old. You will be free. You will find yourself again, and it will be in a world that you have dreamed of for a hundred years. Dreamed, but never achieved. I will do this for you. I will lay that world at your feet."

Artemis stares up at the man. His jaw tightens. "I..."

The words don't want to come. He forces them out.

"I... will... stop... you."

"No," the man says, voice gentle. "You won't."

Artemis' gaze returns to the window. He listens to the sound of surf crashing on the beach.

Part Two: Crossfire Safehouse

Red Shift stands in the garage of the Crossfire safehouse, staring through a portal at the conference room of the *Nautilus*. The portal is shaped like a Persian arch, its borders purple-back shadow mixed with radiant gold light—a combination difficult to stare at directly. Light warps around it, making the air at the edges ripple. The interior of the arch gives a clear view of the other side, and he can actually hear people moving around the conference room. That side of the portal is currently in the Atlantic Ocean, somewhere between Puerto Rico and Florida. He crossed from there to New York City in only four steps.

That's fast. Even for me.

He shrugs his right shoulder, trying to adjust his backpack without letting go of the overstuffed duffel bag in his right hand. The bulk is inconvenient, but he can't stop staring at the portal, through the portal... *around* the portal. He's worked with teleporters, and he's seen teleportation tech, but he's never seen anything quite like this.

"You actually walked through that thing?"

Curveball stands on a small platform set in front of the door that leads to the living area on the second floor. Stairs made of industrial concrete and steel pipe connect the platform with the garage. He isn't in great shape: his face is a mask of bruises, and one arm hangs limply by his side as the empty sleeve of a canvas shirt hangs over it. His eyes are sharp and clear, though. He looks at the portal warily.

"Sure did." Red Shift readjusts his grip on the duffel bag and walks to the raised platform. "Didn't melt or anything. That's a pretty useful trick the Doctor has."

Curveball blinks. "The *Doctor*? That's what he went with? He's gonna get his ass sued."

Red Shift laughs, then shakes his head. "He went with 'Doctor Enigma.' It'll take a while to figure out how to address him in the third person."

Curveball looks amused in spite of himself. "You could just call him *David*."

"*You* could," Red Shift says.

"You staying, or going back?" Curveball asks the question a little too casually for Red Shift to believe he doesn't care about the answer.

"Doctor Thorpe has plenty of biologists at his disposal," Red Shift says. "Most of them are better than me. I figure I'll be more useful attacking a… what did you call it?"

Curveball relaxes a little. "An evil wizard's tower."

Red Shift nods. "An evil wizard's tower." He hefts the duffel bag again. "Doctor Thorpe thought you might want a few force multipliers."

"Good." Curveball stands to one side, letting Red Shift through the door. "Thanks. It'd be nice if we could get Regiment and Vigilante in on this as well, but *hell yes* I'll take the guy who can break Mach 12."

Red Shift flashes an affable grin as he walks through the door.

* * *

Jenny Forrest stares down at the motionless form of her uncle and tries to figure out what, exactly, she should *feel*.

In some ways it would be easier if he were dead. If he were dead she could look past all the years—decades, probably—that he had been a self-important asshole who cared more about his career than his family. That's what you do with dead people, right? You overlook the bad, and focus on the good. So she could forget how terrible he was, and focus on how he died a hero, working with his grandfather to bring down a powerful conspiracy. But he's *not* dead—not yet. At the moment he's lying down on a ratty green couch, surrounded by a circle of that weird purple-gold energy David conjured out of thin air.

Looking down at the man, it's hard not to remember all the times she hated him—hated the way he used his grandfather's fame to further his own career, hated the way he tried to control everyone he met, hated that fake smile that everyone who wasn't part of the family thought looked exactly like Liberty's.

Still, looking down at him, seeing shadows of the pain and fear that were etched into his face just minutes before, it's hard to think of him as anything but a victim. But even *that* is wrong: if his statement is to be believed, he was working a long con with his grandfather. That means being a raging asshole was *part of the job*. That makes everything even *more* complicated. Has it all been an act? Does she know anything about her uncle at all?

"Jesus, Uncle Toby. Are you some kind of hero after all?"

"Looks like."

Jenny looks up to see CB standing in the doorway. Just behind him, Red Shift ducks into the weird room with the torture chair.

"I didn't realize I said that out loud," she admits.

CB smiles slightly. "Monologues are an occupational hazard."

Jenny tries to suppress a smile. "I thought only villains did that."

"They're just better at it, usually because they're standing off by themselves while their minions do all the dirty work. Heroes have to monologue while fighting, which makes effective wordplay challenging. On the other hand, we have *amazing* cardio."

She laughs in spite of herself, then frowns when she looks back down at her uncle. "Were you serious? About him being a hero?"

CB walks into the room, staring at the senator with a mixture of admiration and dislike. "Yeah."

"I always thought he was one of the bad guys," Jenny says. "Not exactly evil, but so wrong I never understood how he could be related to great-grandfather. His whole 'metahumans are unregistered weapons' spiel was pretty awful. But if he was acting all this time—"

"Pretty sure he wasn't lying about *that*," CB says. "Let's just call him complicated and leave it at that."

They stand in silence a while.

"How's your arm?" Jenny asks.

CB stretches it out in front of him, wincing slightly, then shakes it out, wincing a little more. "A little better. Red Shift brought an IV with some of Crossfire's weird regenerative concoction. I'll be fine after that."

"Red Shift?" Jenny asks, cautiously optimistic. "Is he…?"

"He is," CB says. "We get two-thirds of Crossfire for this. I'll take it."

The swinging door to the kitchen opens, and David Bernard steps through. He looks different, even since this morning: he's stronger, healthier, and no longer half-starved or on the verge of exhaustion. The hollowness in his eyes and cheeks has filled out to the point that he almost looks normal. That said, there's still something… off. Jenny can't put her finger on it, but the wholesome, all-American appearance is *flawed* somehow, as if it were covered in a nearly-transparent film smeared with a fine layer of ink.

"Lieutenant," CB says. He steps to the side to give David a better view of the senator. "Or, uh, *Doctor Enigma*, I guess."

David grins self-consciously. "Such a pompous name."

"And Sky Commando wasn't?" Jenny asks.

"It felt a little more earned…" David stares down at Senator Morgan, furrowing his brows in concentration.

Jenny feels a pang of worry. "What is it? Is he getting worse?"

David shakes his head. "Still holding steady. I'm trying to figure out how long we have until the thing I did stops working."

"Oh," Jenny says. "And?"

David frowns. "Three or four hours."

"That's what you said an hour ago," Jenny says.

"I know. But it looks like the people who cursed him didn't expect him to have any protection. They haven't tried to break through yet. They will. When they do, that's when the timer starts."

"In that case," CB says, "we need to get this show on the road." He turns to Jenny. "Red Shift brought something for you. He's in the armory."

Jenny blinks. "There's an armory in this dump?"

"It's a Crossfire safehouse," CB says. "There's *always* an armory."

* * *

The armory is cramped but well-organized, filled with lockers and weapons cases stuffed full of deadly things. Red Shift hunches over a workbench at the far end of the room, fiddling with a small, rugged-looking black box attached to a tactical harness.

He doesn't turn or look up when Jenny arrives, so she waits as patiently as she can, hoping he looks up soon. When he doesn't, she clears her throat.

"CB said you wanted to see me."

"Sorry," Red Shift says, still not looking up. "I did, I'm just a little distracted... your bag is the farthest on the right, in front of the lockers."

Jenny glances over the lockers—all closed—and looks down. Three backpacks sit on the floor, arranged in a row.

"My bag?" Jenny grabs the rightmost bag. It's bulky, but feels light.

"Gift from Doctor Thorpe," Red Shift says.

Jenny opens the top of the bag and peers inside. "Body armor?"

"The armor Street Ronin made for you out of Curveball's old gear was pretty basic. Doctor Thorpe has a complete fabrication facility on the *Nautilus*—along with every other type of scientific facility known to man, probably—so he worked up a replacement he felt would better integrate your new physical skills with your technical skills. I don't usually recommend using new gear before it's properly field tested, but Doctor Thorpe has a pretty good track record for this kind of stuff. He says you should watch the helmet demo before going out."

Jenny fishes through the backpack. "I don't see a helmet."

Red Shift straightens from the table, turns and stares at Jenny's bag. He snaps his fingers. "It's the hoop."

Jenny searches through the bag again and pulls out a heavy metal ring. It looks like a solid piece of metal, shaped into an oval. "This looks more like a headband."

"It gets better," Red Shift promises. "Lay it all out on the floor and I'll show you how to put it together."

"OK," Jenny says, and starts pulling out the contents of the bag, piece by piece.

There are a few rigid pieces—a small chestplate, two arm guards, and two shin plates—but most of the space is taken up by a bodysuit that looks like a coarse, thick blend of black and blue-gray wool. There is some semi-rigid tech embedded in the material, but it doesn't look like body armor at all.

"I think I'd rather wear what I have now," Jenny admits.

"It doesn't look impressive in this form," Red Shift agrees. "This is just for transport. Most of the really clever tech is in the chestpiece, but the rest of it—well, you'll see. OK, the chestpiece attaches to these sockets here..." He points out a series of disks that look like oversized snaps running down the length of the torso. "They snap in like magnets. Same for the arm and shin plates."

The plates line up and snap in just as Red Shift says, though Jenny isn't convinced they'll stay on during a fight. The last step is to attach the heavy metal circle to the neck. Once all the pieces are in place, a panel on the chestplate lights up, and a small square on the upper-right corner turns green.

"Put your thumb there," Red Shift says.

Jenny places her thumb over the green panel, which turns red, then yellow, then green again.

"It's keyed to you," Red Shift says. "Your DNA as well as your fingerprint. Next is to key it to your voice. Keep your thumb on the plate and say the word 'activate.'"

Jenny looks at the chestplate uncertainly, then shrugs. "Activate."

The entire chestplate lights up. Jenny jerks her hand back as the bodysuit inflates like a balloon, then gasps as it transforms before her eyes.

What appeared to be coarse wool flattens and smooths into something more rigid. In a few seconds the transformation is complete, and Jenny is staring down at what can only be described as a suit of armor.

The material is mostly blue-gray, with black running along the seams between the joints and outlining the chestpiece and arm and leg plates. The material isn't exactly solid: it looks like lots of tiny links, all woven together into a semi-flexible mesh.

"The mesh is kind of like chainmail," Red Shift explains, "only significantly stronger. It would be a little too cumbersome for most people— I'd find it very restrictive, myself—but with your enhanced strength you should hardly notice."

"It's not as intimidating as the all-black armor," Jenny says, running a finger along one of the arms, "but it looks stronger."

"A lot stronger," Red Shift says. "Small arms fire won't be a problem in that. It can technically resist light artillery, though the concussive force would probably still kill you."

"I'll keep that in mind," Jenny says dryly. Her gaze falls on the neck piece, where the thick metallic loop of the "helmet" fits seamlessly into the torso. "There's still no helmet."

"Put it up on its feet," Red Shift says. "It'll stand on its own when it's like this."

Jenny does so. She can tell it's heavier than it was—she's not entirely sure how that works, and decides the explanation would probably put her to sleep. As Red Shift predicted, it stands on its own.

"Now tell it to deploy the helmet."

"OK," Jenny says. "Deploy helmet."

Multiple paper-thin plates extend from the heavy metal loop set into the neck, assembling themselves into the form of a fully-enclosed helmet and visor. Despite having seen the helmet assembled with her own eyes, she can't detect any seams on its surface.

"Doctor Thorpe says he got the idea from watching a movie," Red Shift says.

"How do I get into it?" Jenny asks. "Do I have to deflate it first?"

Red Shift shakes his head. "It opens in the back."

Jenny starts tugging at her body armor. "Go back to working on your thing," she says. "I have a demo to watch."

Part Three: Haruspex Analytics, Jason Kline's Suite

Phyllis Tanner has many skills. Speed reading is one of them.

This is not a unique skill on Jason's team: reading through volumes of information as fast as possible is extremely useful in her line of work. Pretty much everyone has some degree of proficiency in it; the only one who never got the hang of it was Billy.

She closes her eyes for a moment, feeling and then suppressing the loss that comes when she thinks of him. She can't dwell on it now. She has to focus.

"Jason, I need your authorization to go further."

Jason Kline, head buried deep in a pile of printed reports, looks up distractedly. "Hm?"

"I hit another secure area," Phyllis says. "I need your authorization to continue."

Jason looks vaguely annoyed—not at her, specifically, but at the presence of yet another protected area.

"It's Russian dolls." Simon Yin rubs his eyes wearily, pushing his chair away from his desk, then stretches his entire body without bothering to get up.

"They're called *Marushka* dolls." Michelle Lawrence is barely visible from the depths of her over-sized hoodie. "And it's basically our fault."

"Whatever." Simon relaxes out of his stretch, letting his arms hang over the sides of his chair. "...I need more coffee."

Phyllis finds herself missing the situation room again. Jason's promotion brought with it an entire suite of offices. This means they each have offices of their own, something most people would consider a perk. But Jason's group works best as a group, so they've converted the reception area into a bullpen. It's essentially a smaller, more cramped version of the situation room, without catering.

The office suite is more private, and since Jason is now a member of the board they are directly linked into all the data they need. But the security breach they'd been brought in to investigate had occurred because board members had grown over-reliant on their staff, and one of the first remedies was to require board members to personally authorize access to information above a certain level of classification. Jason's team is auditing all the organization's security protocols... which means they constantly access information above a certain level of classification.

Jason stands, grumbling, and heads over to Phyllis' computer. He's about to place his thumb on the security panel when something on the screen catches his eye. He frowns, squinting, then his eyes go wide.

He pulls his thumb away from the panel.

"Jason?" Phyllis looks up at him, eyebrows raised.

"I… can't," he says. "I mean, I *could,* but I'm not supposed to. We're not supposed to access that data."

Phyllis looks back at her screen. "It doesn't look any different from anything else. How are we supposed to audit security protocols if we don't know what they are?"

"Yeah, I know, but…" Jason points to a string of symbols. "Anything with that on it is off-limits."

"What is it?"

Jason takes a deep breath. "Magic stuff," he says. "Mara has a different team dealing with that."

Phyllis looks at the locked file carefully. The title simply says "Incursion Protocols." The string of symbols beneath it was, she'd assumed, just encrypted information that would become readable once access was granted, but upon inspection, it's obvious they're not ASCII symbols… nor are they part of any of the extended Unicode typesets she's familiar with.

Magic stuff.

"OK," she says. "Off limits. I don't suppose you've read them?"

"No," Jason says.

Phyllis nods, careful to keep her expression neutral. She's worked with Jason for a long time, and he almost *never* lies to them. It happens so rarely that, while he's a pretty good liar in general, he's genuinely bad at lying to *them,* which is why she knows he just lied to her right now. She stares at him as he returns to his desk and sinks back into those reports. She's not the only one staring: Simon is also watching him, brow furrowed.

He knows Jason's lying, too.

She glances at Michelle, but whatever the young woman's reaction might be, it's hidden by her hoodie.

Phyllis thins her lips, then looks back at her screen. The Incursion Protocols sit there, staring back at her.

I bet I don't need his thumbprint, Phyllis thinks. She sets about proving herself right.

Part Four: Crossfire Safehouse

The safehouse is a small white building set right up against a public storage facility next to a run-down industrial park. It's so nondescript and boring that it's easy to overlook—the eye drifts naturally from the shiny storage units to the large concrete warehouses in the industrial park, skipping it over entirely.

Special Agent Lijuan Hu files that away for later as she stands in front of the heavy wood door with "MAIN OFFICE" stenciled on the front in cracked, fading letters. It's not the location of this building that matters— Crossfire will abandon it immediately after this op—but the psychology that went into choosing the location. They're allies at present, solid ones as far as Hu can tell... but she's pretty sure they'll wind up on opposite sides of something eventually.

That assumes, of course, that she still has a job when this is over. It's not guaranteed: what they've been doing strays pretty far outside the rules, and what they're *about* to do will probably get them thrown in jail if things go even a little bit south.

Maybe Crossfire will be hiring. She smiles in spite of herself.

The door *buzzes* and the lock releases, causing it to open just a crack. Hu slips inside, making sure to pull the door closed until she hears it *click* firmly in place.

The door opens into the garage. The portal to the Nautilus is gone, but in its place is Jenny Forrest—Zero—waiting for her.

The young woman isn't wearing the black tactical armor she had when they all portaled over. What she's wearing now looks much fancier, steel polymer with extra tech embedded in the chestplate. It looks quite a bit heavier than her old armor, but the difference doesn't appear to affect her any.

"New gear?" Hu asks.

Zero nods, grinning unabashedly. "A gift from Robert. Red Shift told me to tell you there's something for you as well."

"Oh?" Hu frowns. "That probably violates at least seven DOJ policies and guidelines, not to mention a few laws, but since we're about to attack the lair of an evil wizard I think I can deal with the fallout later. What's he got?"

Jenny shrugs. "Red Shift wouldn't say. You're supposed to meet him in the armory."

"Where is that?" Hu asks.

"Comm room, trapdoor leading down."

"OK," Hu says. "Thanks. Hey, Zero—what are you doing after we win?"

Zero looks at her blankly.

"You know," Hu says. "We fight the bad guys, we kick their asses, the virus is deep-sixed and the world goes on. What do you do next?"

"Uh…" Zero shrugs, her cheeks coloring slightly. "I guess I've just been super focused on this thing."

"Sure," Hu says. "Understandable. Well, look, you're Liberty's great-granddaughter and all that, so I'm pretty sure you'll have your pick of opportunities… but you should consider Division M."

Zero blinks. "Uh… you mean, like you and Agent Grant?"

"Like me, yes. Like Grant, hopefully not so much."

Zero laughs nervously, not sure how to reply.

"Just think it over," Hu says. "You'd make a hell of an agent."

Without waiting for an answer, Hu steps up to the raised platform and ducks through the door into the living area. When she reaches the comm room she runs into her second surprise.

"Travers!"

Pete Travers ducks his head by way of greeting, smiling that eternally polite smile. "Agent Hu."

"What are you doing here?"

Travers shrugs. "Helping. I'm not much good on the *Nautilus*, unfortunately. I can't help them find a cure. But I think it might be useful to have someone back here while you all tilt your windmill. Especially someone who is familiar with government response protocols."

Hu nods in agreement.

"Besides," Travers says, "David thinks someone should be on hand to keep an eye on Senator Morgan while you're out. We could hardly spare any of you."

"Grant could do it," Hu says.

"That's one less of him in the field," Travers points out.

"True." Hu spies the trap door at the far end of the room. "Well, I gotta go and see what Doctor Thorpe whipped up for me."

"You'll probably like it," Travers says.

"You know what it is?" Hu asks.

Travers shakes his head. "Not a clue. But I know him."

"Guess I'll find out," Hu says.

She climbs down the ladder to find Red Shift and Scrapper Jack standing over a large black duffel bag dangling from Jack's right hand. Jack looks like he's been through the wringer: his shirt is torn, the right leg of his jeans has been ripped off below the knee, and one of his boots is split down the back, while the other is missing a heel.

"Jesus, Jack," Hu says, "what happened? Get hit by a car?"

Jack looks up from his bag and flashes her a lopsided grin. "Funny you should ask..."

She files that away as something to follow up on later.

"Red Shift, Zero says you wanted to see me?"

"Sure did," Red Shift says amiably. "Just finishing up. Doctor Thorpe would like Jack to add a few things to his ensemble."

"It's to keep me from winding up naked every time something violent happens," Jack says.

Hu smirks. "I disapprove."

Jack laughs at that, then stares back down into the duffel bag. "Thing is, I'm not too keen on wearing spandex."

"It's not spandex," Red Shift says.

"You know what I mean. The closest I ever got to a costume was when I was still running with Artie, and most of that was just practical."

"This is practical too," Red Shift says. "You wear it under your clothes. If your clothes are destroyed, you're not flashing the world. And he thought you'd like the boots."

Jack rummages through the bag. "Yeah, OK, I do like the boots. What the hell, I'll give it a shot."

Jack hoists the duffel bag over his shoulder, then brushes past Hu to get to the ladder.

"Is that... engine oil?" Hu asks.

"I *literally* got hit by a car," Jack says. "Then I used it to hit *another* car."

Definitely following up on that later. Hu watches Jack climb up the ladder, then turns back to Red Shift.

The speedster points to a black duffel bag sitting in front of one of the armory lockers. "Doctor Thorpe would like to offer you an alternative to your 'bathing suit.'"

Hu stares at the bag for a second, then grins fiercely. "Hell yes!"

"That's refreshing," Red Shift says. "Usually people have questions first."

Hu scoops up the duffel and peers inside. "Oh, I have questions, but I'm pretty sure the smartest man in the world made me a fireproof outfit."

"Well," Red Shift says, "technically nothing is really fireproof—"

"Fire," Hu says absently. "Fire is fireproof." She pulls out a bundle from the bag and unwraps it.

"I kind of want to argue the point," Red Shift says, "but I'll defer to the expert."

Hu lets the duffel bag fall to the floor as she holds up the outfit. "Looks like a wetsuit."

Red Shift nods. "It's kind of the opposite, though. Doctor Thorpe says the suit isn't so much fireproof as it is 'fire-compatible.' It has a much higher heat tolerance than the asbestos atrocity you use now."

"How much tolerance?" Hu asks.

"Doctor Thorpe claims it will survive what you did when you blew up the tip of his island."

"Nice," Hu says. "Division M probably won't let me keep it, but I'll enjoy it while it lasts."

"They might, actually." Red Shift points down to the duffel bag. "In one of the side pockets he included the specs on the suit, so your people could study it and duplicate it themselves."

Hu looks back down at the duffel bag and picks it up. "Thanks. Good luck today."

"You too," Red Shift says. He turns back to a workbench sitting on the far wall, leaning over a small black box half-attached to a combat harness.

"What's that?" Hu asks.

"My present," Red Shift says. "It needs a little prep before I can use it."

He doesn't explain further, and Hu doesn't press him for more. She puts her new suit in the bag, slings the bag over her shoulder, and climbs up the ladder to look for a place to change.

Part Five: Haruspex Analytics

Mara Ioannou sits patiently outside the Chairman's office, both aware of and indifferent to the passage of time.

She meditates on a decision that will be made in the next few hours. She doesn't know who will make it, and she doesn't know what course of action will be chosen. She knows only that someone will be faced with a choice, and they will choose. She's been trying to understand the decision by hypothetically assigning it to different people and following the lines of consequence that branch out from it. It's an old gift; one of her oldest. It rarely provides a clear answer, but she almost always finds it useful.

The phone on the receptionist's desk buzzes, a harsh, low sound that hurts her ears. The nondescript man behind the desk picks up the phone, listens intently for a moment, then returns the receiver to its cradle.

"The Chairman will see you now." The nondescript man behind the desk doesn't bother looking up from his work. The wall next to the couch *clicks*, sinks inward, then slides to the right, revealing a warmly-lit room with dark, bare walls.

"Thank you." Mara stands, and all the creases in her white dress fall away. She walks into the Chairman's office, face serene. He stands next to his desk, waiting.

"Mara." He wears no shroud over his face—that has never been necessary between them—and his smile is genuine. "I'm surprised to see you at this hour. Not displeased, of course."

Mara's smile is just as genuine. She extends her hand and he takes it, bowing slightly, and kisses it once. It is a ceremony that pleases her. It's not a ceremony from the age in which she came into her power—it's far more modern than that—but it acknowledges the need to place walls between beings of power, and to regulate the ways in which those walls are willingly broken. A modern echo of a much older exchange. The Chairman is a young creature, but he understands such things.

"I would not have come," Mara says, "but I've been made aware of a problem that requires your immediate attention."

The Chairman nods, his expression growing grave. He half-turns, gesturing toward the glass-and-steel-framed desk—the only furniture of note in the room—and retreats to the large leather executive chair behind it. He sits as Mara chooses one of the two leather chairs set before it.

Both are just as comfortable as the Chairman's, Mara suspects. The only indication of a difference in status, in this room, are the positions of the chairs themselves. One behind the desk, two before.

He is not a man who revels in the trappings of his office, Mara thinks. Then, suppressing the brief desire to smile in wry awareness, adds *he is, of course, not entirely a man.*

It is a point they have discussed before, at length. A point the Chairman acknowledges as true, but dismisses as irrelevant; Mara is beginning to understand and appreciate his view of things.

"The artificers involved in the absolution of Senator Morgan have run into an unusual problem," Mara says.

The Chairman gazes at her from across the desk, one eyebrow rising in surprise. "They ought to have finished by now."

"They should have," she says. "I have examined every aspect of the ritual and judged all observances were followed correctly. Something... someone... appears to be blocking them."

The Chairman leans forward slightly. His eyes narrow. "Indeed."

Mara nods. "I was able to follow the trail of power, but I wasn't able to determine the physical location of its target. I ran into a barrier. I do not understand this barrier."

The Chairman eases back into his chair again, head tilted back, eyes closed. "Please continue."

"It is, at its base, power similar to our own," she says. "There are parts of it that *feel* the same. But it mingles with something..." Her voice trails off, and she *tsks* in annoyance. "I don't have words for it. It is a power, but I can't determine what it is. It suffuses the power I *know* with an energy I do *not*. Whatever it is, it's strong enough to prevent the ritual from reaching its target."

"I see." The Chairman's eyes are still closed. "Permanently?"

"No," Mara says. "The barrier does not renew itself. The ritual does. I instructed the artificers to continue with the absolution. The barrier will be overcome in a matter of hours."

"Good," the Chairman says. "The issue, then, is not that the ritual will fail. The issue is that someone outside this group has power to counter it, even for a time."

"Yes," Mara agrees. "But I caution you not to underestimate this. The power required to block absolution *at all* is immense. I might be able to do it, with the necessary preparation. It would require a temple dedicated to my cause, and the offering of much blood. There is no temple in this city other than our own, and there was no blood in the barrier I detected."

The Chairman opens his eyes, focusing on Mara. "But you did say there was a portion of the power you could not understand."

"If it used blood," Mara replies, "I would understand it."

The Chairman considers her words, then nods in agreement. "So. There is a new power."

"It seems there is. Something that incorporates the old powers, but also something that has evolved."

"Do you think this is one of the other elder powers, making a play?"

"Absolutely not." Mara speaks with absolute conviction. "The only powers that might have the flexibility to adapt to what I felt—and, more importantly, *didn't* feel—are the ones who stood before you and accepted our parley. They are as bound to the terms of our mutual pact as you are, and will be until their ties to the powers that came before can be severed completely. If there were ties to the powers that came before I'd feel them, just as I'd feel the power of blood."

"No ties at all?" the Chairman asks. "No signs of affiliation?"

"None."

"Hm." The Chairman stands, walks around his desk, and crosses the room, stopping before a lone picture set against an otherwise empty wall. It is the picture of his battlefield, Mara knows. He speaks of it from time to time. It is one of the great events that shaped him, even before he came to be. "You might have mentioned that sooner."

Mara thinks back on her words so far. "It is hard to describe a thing I don't understand," she admits. "It wasn't until you asked about 'signs of affiliation' that I realized I'd felt none."

"Yes, of course," the Chairman says. "I apologize, Mara, that was me being petty."

Mara smiles slightly, gets up from her chair, and stands to his right.

The Chairman laughs suddenly. A startling laugh—easy, delighted—it is reflected in his face, and in his eyes. He seems... *pleased.*

"It's finally happening," he says.

Mara looks at him questioningly, but says nothing.

"I had, of course, hoped that it would happen within our own group," he continues. "I had—and still have—high hopes for Nuzzo in particular. But it was inevitable that after I came to be, in apparent violation of all that we understand of our power, and the ties it has to the True Realm, that other deviations would appear."

He turns to her, eyes alight. "It means I am not a single *aberration*, in danger of being swallowed up and forgotten over time. I was the first, but more are coming. *Change is happening.*"

Mara feels herself smiling in return. She doesn't bother to hide it. They share the moment, and then when it passes they return to the matter at hand.

"Of course," the Chairman adds, "it is unfortunate that this change is manifested among our enemies. It complicates things greatly."

"Do you think it is one of the heroes?" Mara asks.

The Chairman shrugs. "One of them, or a newly acquired ally of theirs. Curveball and Scrapper Jack kidnapped the senator, with the aid of at least one other. And now someone has, at least for a time, prevented his death."

Mara nods thoughtfully. "It seems unusual that they'd deal with this power directly."

"Very," the Chairman agrees. "For the moment, let us assume there is a method they have devised that we don't understand. Perhaps one of their technologists has found a way to manipulate the power mechanically. We don't need to focus on it. I believe we will get a clearer picture soon."

"They will come here?" Mara asks skeptically. "That seems tactically unwise."

"Have you read the profiles Mr. Kline has assembled on that group?" Amusement runs deep within the Chairman's voice. "They all have histories of making 'tactically unwise' work."

Mara concedes the point. That is, after all, one of the reasons she wants to kill them.

"I think," she says, "that this may work to our advantage."

The Chairman looks doubtful. "I don't think they'll stop us, but I don't see a way to turn this into a win."

Mara smiles. "I think I do. Consider that we had to trespass in the City of Ravens because we had no true stronghold of our own... because we needed the power such a stronghold provides."

"We paid a heavy price for that trespass," the Chairman notes.

"We did," Mara agrees, "but it was necessary to pay it."

The Chairman nods.

"Consider also that right now the Board is considering how best to advance to the next stage of Project Recall. It has been presented with multiple scenarios. Some are more audacious than others."

The Chairman focuses his gaze on Mara, eyes sharp. "You wish to restore the First Temple."

"Yesterday if you had asked, I would have said no. Today…" Mara gestures. "If you are right… if these *heroes* are about to assault this building… well, even if we kill them all, this building and its people are lost to us. Anyone connected to this building will be sought out and questioned. We will have to *cut them loose* and ensure they reveal nothing."

The Chairman nods again, unwillingly, but he sees her point.

"There is another way, though." Mara says. "We don't cut our losses. We don't abandon our resources. We *build a pyre* and we *make an offering.*"

The Chairman says nothing. He turns his gaze back to the picture of the soldier's graveyard, brooding. Mara can hear her own heartbeat in her ears. The silence stretches on to painful lengths, but she forces herself to add nothing more. She's made her argument; it's his call.

He bows his head. "We will only be able to take a few with us. The rest of the Board will have to fend for themselves."

Mara exhales, pushing back the warm rush of victory to concentrate on the logistics of it all. "We signed what we signed."

"You did," the Chairman agrees. "So be it."

The question Mara had been pondering earlier—the decision that she knew would have to be made, but did not know who would be called upon to make it—suddenly grows still. *One more mystery revealed,* she thinks. She sees all of the potential futures branch out from that decision.

"There is peril in this," Mara says. "Peril for our enemies, perhaps, or peril for us. But overall I think this is right."

"We have never shied away from peril," the Chairman says. "So let us dance with it again." He looks around his office, and she's struck by the weariness and loss in his eyes. "I am proud of what we built here."

"I am, too," Mara says, "but it was never intended to exist beyond a certain point in time."

"True." The Chairman's mouth firms. "On to practical matters. There are some in the building now we will need to ensure get out. Doyle, of course. And Richter—he will continue to be invaluable. The inner circle, and I think we will add Mr. Kline to that number. We may still need someone with the insight he provides."

"His team?" Mara asks.

"Ah yes," the Chairman says. "His team…"

"They've been quite useful so far," she points out.

"An analyst," the Chairman says, "works from a distance. They make decisions and recommendations that other people must carry out. That other people, in the end, must *pay* for. Don't misunderstand me, I quite appreciate the necessity for that kind of separation, but Mr. Kline is transitioning *away* from that work. He is becoming a *leader*. But unlike you or I, who have been forced to bear the consequences of every decision we have made— who are going to be forced to bear the consequences of the decision we are making *right now*—he has been insulated as a result of his work."

"True," Mara says. "Is this to be a test, then?"

"It is," the Chairman says. "Make him aware of everything that will happen, and give him every opportunity to fail. If he takes up the mantle we offer, he must do so with the knowledge that those he loves will die."

"I agree," Mara says. "Kline is a potential asset, but he is useless to us if he us unwilling to commit… but *I* will tell him. If you tell him, his innate awe of you may override the very things we wish him to struggle against."

The Chairman sighs. "Agreed. We will deal with *that* unfortunate quality at a later date. While you deal with Mr. Kline, I will begin organizing our egress. Meet me back here in… let's say an hour?"

"An hour," Mara agrees. She turns to leave.

Part Six: Crossfire Safehouse

It's cold and the sky is overcast, blocking out the stars and turning the moon into a blurred, hazy blotch of light in the sky. So hazy, CB notes, that he can't even tell what phase it is. It was a detail he'd completely overlooked earlier, when he was focused on kidnapping a United States Senator. He suspects he'll be too busy to think about it later, when he assaults the fortress of an organization of evil wizards. He has time to think about it now, so he does.

He leans against the handrail of an old, rickety fire escape set outside the safehouse's second-floor bedroom window. He pulls out a wadded up pack of cigarettes—he forces himself to use his right arm, still tender but finally on the mend—and shakes the last two out. He lights one, takes a long drag, and watches the smoke as it rises into the cold night air.

Cold. Strange. He didn't think it had been that long, but it's hard to keep track of the passage of time when you're doing everything on the sly. All the time they spent in his bunker in Farraday City before assaulting the base under the warehouse. All the time they spent on Thorpe's floating island. Apparently it had been *months* rather than *weeks*. Not *many* months, but enough to have added up to... what? Four, five? Five months since Alex's murder. Not a lot of time, in the grand scheme of things... but long enough to skip summer in New York City.

Cold. And *dark*. Hazy moonlight aside, the only light comes from a few windows and two streetlights that aren't broken. One, at the end of the block, shines down on an intersection that leads to more populated parts of the city. One, about halfway down the street, is in the process of sputtering out.

The window behind him rattles. He turns just in time to see it open. Jenny sticks her head out and grins.

"Room for one more?"

CB waves her over. Jenny grunts as she awkwardly steps through the windowsill, then curses quietly as the fire escape shakes slightly from the added weight. He grins, glances over to her as she settles in on the rail beside him.

"What, no armor? I thought you'd never get out of that thing, once you put it on."

Jenny grins. "Well, I had to use the bathroom, and I'm not quite ready for the built-in catheters just yet."

CB stares at her. "You're... joking?"

Her grin widens. "Nope. I always wondered how the Gladiator armor handled it. Now I know and wish I didn't."

CB winces.

"I'm going to wait till we move out before I put it on again, and make sure I take care of business beforehand."

"Good plan," CB says.

"You OK?" Jenny sounds nervous as she asks the question.

CB shrugs, takes another drag, and waves his hand dismissively. "Arm still hurts. I'll be able to use it. I'm no Red Shift or Vigilante—well, nobody's like Vigilante when it comes to healing—but I do OK, and I'm used to working hurt."

"I guess everyone learns to do that, eventually," Jenny says.

"Comes with the job," CB agrees. "How are you?"

"I'm fine." She sounds defensive, and CB raises an eyebrow.

"Nervous," Jenny adds reluctantly. "I mean, we're going up against magic this time, right? And my uncle's life is on the line, and I *know* it's not exactly *fair*, but that makes this seem more important."

"I get it," CB says. "I don't even like the guy, and I think the stakes are higher, too."

"So why aren't we off storming the castle, then?" Jenny asks. "I've never really had an opportunity to be proud of my uncle before. Not in recent memory. I'd kind of like the opportunity to tell him I am to his face, at least once."

She does a real good job keeping her voice light, but he can tell it's an act. There's real anguish there, and worry, and he can't blame her for that.

"We're waiting for Agent Grant to get back," CB says. "He's telling his boss what's about to happen. And… Sky Commando, I guess? Hopefully they'll be able to keep the local LEOs from doing something stupid to make things worse."

"You mean going into the building to arrest us?" Jenny asks.

"Yeah," CB says. "Something like that. This is going to get pretty messy, it'd be good to have a few allies on the outside, doing what they can."

He takes a last pull from his cigarette, then flicks it out over the rail. He watches the burning tip spiral as it arcs through the air, landing on the pothole-ridden street, bouncing once on the asphalt, a second time against the curb, and finally coming to a halt right next to a sewer grate. It still burns, fading slowly.

CB shivers, overcome with the sudden feeling that they're being watched. Jenny's aware of it, too—he can feel her tense beside him.

"The end of the street," she whispers.

CB looks up. There, at the intersection where the working streetlight sits, are two silhouettes. One is short and thin, one tall and fat. Both appear to be wearing hats.

Bowler hats.

"What's with Laurel and Hardy?" Jenny asks, a dangerous edge in her voice.

"Good question," CB says. He puts his last cigarette to his lips, lighting it with deliberate casualness. "I haven't quite figured that out."

"Enemies?" Jenny asks.

"Eventually," CB says.

"You know who they are," Jenny says.

CB nods.

"Well?"

CB starts to answer, and feels the words catch in his throat. He frowns.

"Complicated," is all he can manage. "Uh, do me a favor. Tell Bernard. Tell him this falls into his range of expertise."

"Should I tell anyone else?" Jenny asks.

"Sure," CB says, "but make sure you tell him first."

Jenny frowns, but turns back to the window. It takes her much less time to get through than it did before.

"OK," CB mutters. "Let's see how much this is going to hurt."

He uses his sore arm as he vaults over the rail, stopping his fall as he dangles over the edge. It hurts like hell, but he can use it at full strength. That's good. He lets go, dropping two stories. He stands, dusting off his trenchcoat, and walks slowly towards the figures illuminated in the streetlight.

They don't move. They just stand there, waiting patiently as CB draws near. For his part, he refuses to run, even though the distance between them seems to increase the more he walks.

Eventually he is close enough to recognize them: the short, thin, sharp-faced man and his huge, expressionless companion. The large man appears utterly uninterested in his surroundings, as always. The smaller man, however, grins broadly as CB nears. His eyes—glittering, hawkish eyes—lock onto CB's every movement.

CB stops just beyond the reach of the streetlight. He pulls on his cigarette, making the cherry shine bright in the darkness. "You fellas are a long way from Georgia."

The smaller man's razor-sharp grin widens, and he doffs his hat, bowing low. "We are indeed, Oh Cat Who Observes Himself. We are strangers, wandering alone in this pale copy of paradise. But I find, to my *eternal* joy, that it seems we are alone no longer."

"Business?" CB pushes his hands deep into his trenchcoat pockets, trying to look unconcerned. "Pleasure?"

The small man, still bowing, looks up, spreading his arms wide in a theatrical fashion. "We take great pleasure in our business. It is our *calling*, after all. We spoke on that, as I recall, during our very first meeting."

"Right…" He pulls the empty, crumpled pack of cigarettes out of his pocket, tossing it carelessly into the street. "Control versus self-determination."

The small man's grin widens even further, contorting his face into a mass of jagged angles. He straightens, places his bowler hat on his head, then touches its brim with two fingers by way of salute. "Exactly the one! The struggle behind every struggle; the struggle that begins at life's first gasp, and ends only in its final ragged breath."

"The great struggle between good and evil," CB says, "interrupted by the great struggle between everyone wanting to do things their way, which is a way incompatible with everyone else wanting to do things their way."

The small man laughs, sharp and cutting, full of appreciation and devoid of any actual mirth. "You *gloss*, of course," he chides, wagging his finger, "but you still hit upon the truth of it. A battle not just for what should be, but how it will be achieved. *Politics* and *religion*. You will recall, we spoke on that as well."

"I remember," CB says. "The guys we're up against are a different… er… denomination, I guess. Right? They want what you want, in broad strokes at least, but they want to do things the *wrong way*. So you're against them."

The small man's jagged grin fades into an apologetic smile. "Normally, yes… but I'm afraid we're feeling rather more *ecumenical* today."

CB has just enough time to frown before something hits him *hard* and he flies into a cinderblock wall. Before he even has time to bounce off the wall the large man is there, his thick, meaty hand wrapped like a vise around CB's throat. The large man stares up at him—the first time, he thinks, that they've ever made eye contact—but there is no interest or reaction of any kind on his face. He looks *distracted*, if anything. As if he were merely going through the motions while thinking about something else.

CB grabs the large man's arm, trying to pull the hand away from his throat. It doesn't budge. It's like trying to move a statue.

"I would have been content to reserve your inevitable end for another time," the small man says. "It would have been more climactic, I think. But my partner is far older and wiser than I…"

He gestures to the large man, beaming with admiration.

"And he pointed out, quite correctly, that due to a sudden change in priorities, the reasons for our previous alliance were no longer valid."

CB kicks out at the larger man's stomach. His foot connects, sinks into soft flesh, but the larger man is unmoved.

"This celestial dance has, it appears, become more *complicated*." The small man adjusts his bowler hat ever so slightly, tilting it *just so*. "While you and I find your enemy mutually abhorrent—for different reasons—it appears he has introduced a new, rather remarkable tool that is… how to best say it? *Agnostic to process*."

CB tries to say something, but all he can do is choke. The pressure on his neck is immense. He can't breathe. The corners of his vision darken, and the world around him begins to spin. The large man keeps him pinned against the wall, face devoid of all feeling.

"A tool that *they* have offered to *us*. And it seems, oh Cat, that we want that tool more than we want a proper *denouement* with you."

With what little strength CB has left, he hooks one leg around the large man's arm and *pushes* with the other, the sole of his boot pressing against the large man's face with everything he can muster. Nothing—the man doesn't grunt, doesn't stagger back, doesn't so much as twitch. His strength, it seems, is limitless. CB's is fading fast.

"There were some logistical issues to work around, of course," the small man says, shrugging dismissively. "First, we needed to *find* you. You are not easy to locate, even in our own city, but my colleague found a way."

The small man gestures again to his partner, who makes no sign of hearing or acknowledging his words.

"I won't bore you with the details. They would mean little, though perhaps you would have been better served in life if you'd known what a *threshold* was."

He *tsks* to himself and shakes his head. "The point, oh Cat, is that we found you. Which leads directly to our second logistical challenge… *we had declared our neutrality.*"

CB tries to push again against the large man's face, but he can't keep his strength up. He needs to breathe. He can't breathe. *How do you fight when you just can't breathe?*

"Words," the small man says, adopting the tone of a professor lecturing his class, "carry power. They *mean things.* So if we agree, with our words, to be neutral in the affairs of our enemy, that is our constraint. We cannot move for or against them. We must maintain the *center.* Which might lead you to suspect that this action, here, might be a violation of those words, and you would be right—it would be, in most circumstances. But once again, my esteemed colleague proves he is far wiser than I."

In the blink of an eye the small man is by their side, peering up at CB's limply struggling form. "We *helped* you, you see. True, it didn't quite go as planned, but the intent was to aid you against a mutual enemy. But now the landscape has changed, and our previous assistance on your behalf has… unbalanced things, somewhat. Of course, our reasons were sound, *then.* No one would have questioned our right to do it, *then.* But *now*… well. Now we find the world has shifted around us, and we have, inadvertently, incurred some debt."

The razor-sharp grin returns to the small man's face.

"And we, oh Cat, take our debts *very seriously.*"

CB finally goes limp, his arms and legs dangling uselessly by his side. The darkness is almost complete. It's getting harder to hear, or think. *Where is Bernard? Jenny must have had enough time to contact him by now. There must have been enough time to—*

"Do not wait for your friends to save you," the small man says, voice almost gentle, almost kind. "They would, if they could. I am certain of that. Which is why we took *such great pains* to ensure that *they will not.*"

CB summons the last of his strength to try to spit on the small man. He fails, miserably, managing only to dribble saliva down his lip, onto the large man's wrist. The small man smiles knowingly, and says… something. CB can't understand his words. It's all garbled, as if he were speaking underwater. The world dims further, and now he can't even see the small man, just vague shapes, dark patterns on top of other dark patterns. He goes completely limp, and knows that, when he finally passes out, he will never wake up again.

With a final shudder, all struggles cease.

The world falls silent.

The large man continues to hold the motionless form of CB against the cinderblock wall, impassive, unrelenting. The small man looks on, nods once, then turns away, stepping into the light.

He hesitates before he takes his second step, then whirls, gazing down the length of the street, frowning.

"Is there—?" he begins to ask, but his words are cut off.

The world is surrounded by a great and mighty roar.

The world is surrounded a blinding light.

The world is surrounded by an impossible darkness.

Something rushes down the street, from the safehouse to the streetlight, a power that cracks asphalt and concrete in its wake. That *something* crashes into the large man, and CB, mostly blind though he is, has the satisfaction of seeing him widen his eyes in disbelief before it tears him away from his victim, throwing him into the small man, who barely has time to squawk before his partner knocks them both into the middle of the intersection. CB collapses to the ground and slumps over, clawing at his neck, trying to remember to breathe.

Moments later, David Bernard steps out of a crack in the world, surrounded by a nimbus of white light and purple-black flame. He places himself between CB and the two men.

"No." It is the only word David speaks. As he says it, the shadow of a predator bird settles on his left shoulder.

CB gags, lungs burning.

David takes a step closer to the men. The large one is sitting up, blinking slowly, a look of confusion on his face. The small one jumps to his feet, picks his bowler hat off the ground, and cocks his head at David, regarding him with interest.

"Another new thing," the small man muses.

David doesn't reply. He extends his arms, and the nimbus of light and dark fire spreads out from his hands, encircling the two men completely.

The large man gets to his feet, turning slowly as he takes in the ring of fire. Somewhere in the back of CB's oxygen-deprived mind he thinks it's the most he's ever seen the strange man move.

The small man appears not to notice the fire at all. He stares at David intently… curiously. Almost *eagerly*. Finally he grins, eyes sparkling, and doffs his hat.

"A good opening. A *fine* opening. Well played, oh yes! Well played!"

A look of uncertainty briefly crosses over David's face, but he sets his jaw.

"A trifle undisciplined," the small man continues, "though that is only to be expected, when one is so young. Indeed, you show far more control than I would expect."

The large man falls into place behind his partner, his expression once again distant and uninterested. The small man's expression grows somehow even more gleeful, his eyes wild with excitement.

"If this were to be a proper battle," the small man says, "I think you would find us more than a match. It would be a fine exchange, I believe, at least for a while... but you are so young. And we are so very, very old..."

He snaps his fingers, and when he does the flames of white and purple-black sputter out. David gasps as if struck.

"But." The small man raises a finger. "However. Our debt is for that one only." The finger points past David, centering on CB, whose gasping is starting to even out as his lungs remember how they work. "Engaging you would surely violate our terms, and we cannot have that. So, I say again. Well played!"

The small man applauds, beaming. He removes his hat, bows low once more, and the streetlight above them explodes. Somewhere between the sudden surge of light and the seconds it takes for their eyes to adjust to the new darkness, the small man and his companion are gone, leaving David and CB alone on the street.

David immediately turns and crouches in front of CB. "Are you all right?"

CB has stopped gagging and has graduated to long, raspy breaths. He nods, waving David away in order to get a little more room. David steps back.

"Took you... long enough." CB's voice sounds like dry paper being torn into strips.

"Sorry," David says. "Right after Jenny told me they were here, they did something... strange. With time, I think. I don't understand it."

CB nods again. He tries to struggle to his feet, and settles for getting to his knees.

"Who *are* they?" David asks.

"Bad guys," CB says.

"Yeah, OK." David looks abashed. "You shouldn't be talking right now, so I should shut up more."

CB shakes his head, clears his throat a few times, and his next attempt at speech is a little steadier. "It's a fair question. I just don't think I can tell you much."

David looks back over at the spot where the two had disappeared. "Right. Magic."

"Right," CB says. "Magic. I'll probably be able to tell you eventually. It'll just take a little time…"

"Well," David says, extending his hand, "we need to get you inside so you can rest."

"Nope." CB takes David's hand and gets to his feet, wobbling slightly. "We need to get this thing started. *Right now.*"

"Are you kidding me?" David shakes his head. "I don't think you're ready to—"

"I'll be ready," CB says. "A walk will do me good. But you know how you were saying they wouldn't be able to use your block to trace us, because they wouldn't really know what it was? Well, I'm pretty sure they know what *those* assholes were. And I'm guessing they just made a pretty big boom."

David frowns thoughtfully. "You're right about that."

"Then we need to go," CB says. "I want to bring the fight to them before they have a chance to figure out where we are. We've still got a senator back there, and there's no point trying to save him from black magic if they figure out where he is so they can just up and shoot him."

"Right," David says. "When you put it that way, the suicide frontal assault makes a lot more sense."

CB laughs, leaning on David as they make their way back to the safehouse. "Don't be so negative. I have a really good track record with bad ideas."

Part Seven: Haruspex Analytics, Jason Kline's Suite

Jason Kline stares at the text on his laptop screen and tries for the fourth time to actually *read* it. He fails, for the fourth time in a row, and sits back in his chair, sighing in frustration. He can feel Phyllis watching him, and he knows why. He lied to her, she knows he lied to her, and he doesn't know how to fix it.

He leans forward again, unwilling to look around the room, or risk accidentally making eye contact with the rest of his team. He doesn't work with idiots. They wouldn't be on his team if they weren't all brilliant. If Phyllis knows he lied, then the rest of them probably do as well. Things were already on thin ice after Billy died, with the team wondering but not quite willing to suspect that Jason knows more about that than he's let on, and this is just more strain.

He's got to find a way to make it right. He just can't find the words.

He almost laughs out loud at that. He literally *can't find the words*. He's not authorized to discuss the Incursion Protocols in any form with his team —he's requested to twice, and been denied both times—and he literally can't disobey. Any attempt to talk about them immediately renders him unable to speak. The only option he had earlier was to lie to Phyllis.

He wonders if it would be possible to lie *obviously*, in a pattern that Phyllis would detect. He could, perhaps, use one of the old cyphers they'd all worked on in the past. He opens a blank notepad and starts trying to work out if he can, in fact, communicate the information obscurely.

After a few minutes he closes the notepad and sighs again in frustration. There does appear to be a little more room to maneuver, but not enough. He can allude to things, but not speak of them directly.

Part of him finds the entire situation maddening. Part of him wonders if it would be possible to extend whatever built-in compulsion this part of the world uses to protect itself to other, more mundane uses.

A persistent, self-enforcing security system embedded in the information being transmitted… it's ingenious.

The office door opens. Everyone looks up as Mara Ioannou steps into the room, looking stylish and elegant in a white business suit and skirt that cuts off just below the knees. Her smile, genuine and warm, takes in the entire room before she fixes her eyes on Jason.

"Jason," she says, her voice friendly but businesslike, "we need to speak in private. Your office?"

Jason gets to his feet. "Uh, sure. Yes. This way please." He gestures to the open door at the far end of the room, and almost trips over himself as he follows her.

Jason's office is large by his standards—it has not just the traditional desk and three chairs, but a couch and two other tables. The tables are covered in boxes—the team has been using it to store everything they haven't unpacked yet—and the sofa has a blanket and a pillow, used by whichever team member needs a quick nap before resuming their work.

Mara looks around the room, amused. "Do you not like your office? Is it too small?"

Jason flushes as he fumbles with the light switch. "We all work better together, and the reception area is larger."

"Your team does have an interesting dynamic," Mara admits. She walks past him, smiles at the others who are staring at them openly at this point, then firmly shuts the door. "That has served you very well up to this point. Unfortunately, it may soon begin to work against you."

Jason frowns. "It will? Are we underperforming?"

"Not at all," Mara says. She moves to the couch, throws aside the blanket, and sits down in the middle, legs crossed. She gestures to Jason's desk and waits.

Jason, confused and concerned, moves two boxes off his desk, a third box off his chair, and sits.

"Your team is performing exceptionally well," Mara says. "That performance is what first attracted our notice. Mine, first, and then the Chairman's. And you lead them well. You understand them, and work with them, and bring out the best in each of them. It is one of the most effective analyst teams Haruspex has. And that is no small compliment."

"No, ma'am," Jason agrees.

Mara smiles. "I've asked you to call me Mara before. Now that we are peers, I must insist."

"Sorry... Mara," Jason says, and takes a steadying breath. "Old habits tend to resurface when I'm off balance. And you certainly meant to put me off balance just now."

"I did," Mara admits. "I'm pleased you noticed. And even more pleased that you drew it into the open in order to urge me to get to the point. You have a very unique skillset, Jason, that goes beyond traditional analysis work. You are certainly skilled in that area, but let's be frank. Most of the others on your team are better."

"Absolutely," Jason says. "Simon is leagues above me in infosec, and I can't hold a candle to Michelle when it comes to ciphers and codes. Phyllis is just all-around brilliant, and… well, when she and Billy—"

"But their gap," Mara says, interrupting before Jason can go too far down that road, "the area where *you* shine, has to do with *human interaction*. You read people, interpret their intent, and when you cannot determine intent, you position them and yourself in ways to create the best advantage for yourself when intent can be understood."

Privately Jason thinks that Phyllis is probably at least as good at reading people as he is, though she's not as good at using what she finds.

"Do you remember your first meeting in the board room?" Mara asks.

Jason nods. "It was excruciating, at first."

"Until you understood the trick," Mara says. "I watched you closely during that meeting. The room is designed to make people uncomfortable. You detected *how* relatively quickly, and as soon as you understood, it lost its power to influence you. These are qualities we want in our leaders."

"Thank you," Jason says.

"However, we are choosing *you* to lead," Mara continues. "Not your entire team. Only you. And that means you will be in possession of knowledge they will *not* have. It will separate you, whether you want it to or not. You are very likely already noticing this, to a certain extent."

"I… am," Jason admits. "Phyllis keeps asking about the Incursion Protocols."

"And you are unable to tell her anything," Mara says. "Even when you try. Which you very likely have, if you are anything like the man I believe you to be."

He feels it's best not to react to her comment.

Mara laughs. "It is not a mark against you, by any means. You want your team to know about the Incursion Protocols because they may affect them… and after what happened to Billy, you want to protect the rest of them that much more. It's admirable. That is why the Silence exists—because the knowledge it protects is terrible, and no single person can bear it."

Jason relaxes slightly.

"That said," Mara says, "the division *does* exist. It exists today. It will continue to exist, grow, and become harder to manage over time. And instead of trying to repair that division—which is what you will want to do—we need you to *accept* it."

He starts to protest, but Mara waves him off. "You are newly come to this world, so you are still viewing it through the lens of the world you know. In time, as you grow, as you learn more, that will change. You will eventually view this world through the lens of the new world you have been brought into. That will change the way you understand things, fundamentally. It will change the way you understand people… fundamentally. And your team will not be able to take this journey with you. If they could, we would already be taking the steps to bring them in. Only *you* were chosen. And there are consequences to that you must accept."

Jason looks away. He knows what she's trying to tell him. "This… isn't an easy thing."

"The worthwhile things never are," Mara says. "And it's about to get even harder."

He looks up at her questioningly. Her expression is grave.

"We expect this building to be attacked," Mara says. "At least some of the metahumans survived the attack on Thorpe's island. They have captured one of our assets and have, at least for the moment, managed to counter one of our attempts to silence him. A small group of us are evacuating. We will relocate to the location the Chairman has chosen to start the final phase of Project Recall."

"Evacuate?" Jason's eyes go wide.

"Yes," Mara says. "You have been chosen to be part of that group. *Only* you. Do you understand?"

He does. He understands only too well. He glances at the door, where his team sits on the other side. He nods silently.

"Good," Mara says. "We will meet in the Chairman's office in half an hour. Tell your team it's a last-minute business trip if you like. Say nothing else."

"I understand," Jason says, voice hoarse.

"Good," Mara says. She stands, smooths out her dress, then smiles. "The first steps into this world are terrifying, and they scar. But we've all had to take these steps. We understand the cost you will have to pay. You are not alone."

"Thanks," Jason says. Then, feeling the answer was inadequate, he adds, "Thank you. Very much."

"I'll see you soon," Mara says, then walks out of the room. She shuts the office door firmly behind her as she leaves.

Jason sits behind his desk, staring numbly at the clutter in the room. *The building is about to be attacked.* That means Phyllis, Michelle, and

Simon will get front-row seats when the Incursion Protocols are activated. He leans forward, elbows on his desk, and cradles his head in his hands.

They want me to sell out my team.

That isn't quite right.

*More. They want me to sell out my team **more**.*

He wouldn't be the first to abandon a good team in favor of a promising promotion—to become "a suit," as Billy would say. He didn't think he would ever become That Guy, but then again... he didn't think he would ever be given *this job*.

The things he has learned, even in this short time...

But he can't, can he? It's one thing to screw over your team by taking all the credit for yourself and leaving them to toil in obscurity. It's another to *leave them to die*, which is absolutely what he will be doing, if he does this.

Phyllis, Simon, Michelle... they don't deserve this.

Billy didn't deserve this. The Chairman actually said as much. That's the thing—the Chairman had told him, before it happened, that terrible sacrifices would be necessary. Jason hadn't thought much of it at the time. "Terrible sacrifice" is something you put on an analysis sheet in order to bring projected losses into perspective. But the Chairman, Mara... even Andrew Estovich, *especially* Estovich... they'd understood what terrible sacrifices were.

And he, it seemed, would understand as well. In time.

His go-bag sits in the bottom right drawer of his desk. It's a heavy leather briefcase, a bit larger than the standard executive model but not so large as to attract undue attention. He opens it, reviews the contents, and closes it with an authoritative *click* as it locks shut. He goes over to the executive washroom and splashes some water on his face, dries it carefully, then grabs the briefcase, opens the office door, and steps into the reception area.

Phyllis, Michelle, and Simon all look up.

"Ms. Ioannou—Mara—just told me I'm going on my first business trip as the newest board member for Haruspex Analytics," Jason says. "I don't know where I'm going, but I'm leaving in thirty minutes. I don't know when I'll be back. Phyllis, you're lead until I get back."

"You were in there some time, just for that," Phyllis says, unconvinced.

"Yeah." Jason sighs. "The rest of it was, uh, let's call it 'Executive Orientation.' They're concerned I'm not fully embracing my new role."

"Because you still work in the bullpen?" Simon asks.

"That's part of it," Jason says. "Look, uh, I know things have been awkward lately, and it's all on me. I haven't been in a situation where I'm *not allowed* to tell you things. Usually it's some other guy making the decision to withhold information from all of us. Now it's me being that guy. It sucks, and I want to find a way to make it right. I'll work on it when I get back from this thing. Whatever it is."

Nobody says anything at first. Then Michelle mumbles "'s cool," and Simon wishes him a safe trip. Phyllis just nods, and returns to her work.

"Right," Jason says. "Well. I can't imagine this lasts more than a few days. So... see you then."

He hurries out the door. It shuts behind him with a rattling thud.

"That little piece of shit," Phyllis says. "He just lied to me *again*."

Part Eight: New York City, Downtown

The graveyard shifts are always the worst.

Danny leans against the counter, rubs his eyes, and looks longingly at the cigarettes arranged on the rack behind him. Just a quick smoke out back, and he'll be able to make it through till sunrise. He glances balefully at the security camera, always watching, and suppresses a curse.

It knows. It always knows, and he can't afford to get written up again.

It's like they pay people to watch the cameras just to make sure I don't duck out the back. Jesus, imagine if your job was just to watch store cams all day.

He rubs his eyes again and considers getting another cup of coffee. His stomach gurgles in protest, and he sets the notion aside. He's not *that* desperate. Not yet.

The door jingles. Danny looks up to see a man with spiky, dark hair standing in the doorway, back turned to him. A worn trenchcoat, ripped in multiple places, hangs over his lanky frame.

"It'll just be a second," the man says, waving to someone outside. Then he turns, and Danny tries not to stare. Then he gives up, and just stares.

The man looks young, but *hard* young, like a guy who spends most of his time sleeping in a ditch. His face is mottled with black and purple bruising, and he limps slightly as he moves into the store, eyes locking onto the cigarette display.

The eyes shift to Danny, just for a second, taking in his expression.

"You should see the other guy." The man's voice is clear, at least— clear and steady, so probably not drunk or high. *Probably.*

"Yeah?" Danny keeps gaping. The bruising appears to go down the man's neck, but his t-shirt and trenchcoat cover everything else. He limps, though, very slightly, as he makes his way to the counter. "What does the other guy look like?"

"Not a scratch on him." The man delivers the line absolutely deadpan, with startling frankness. He turns slightly, examining the coffee machine. "Yeah, I got my ass kicked. Two packs of Reds. Hard packs. And a large coffee. And a QuickWin ticket."

The man stumps off to the coffee maker and reaches for a large styrofoam cup.

"Just one?" Danny suppresses a surge of longing as he grabs the cigarettes from the top shelf and puts them on the counter next to the cash register. "People usually buy at least five."

"Just one," the man says. He begins filling the cup with coffee. "This stuff smells terrible."

"It tastes worse," Danny says. "You'd do better just eating the cup."

The man laughs at that. He brings the cup back, now full of piping hot sludge, and sets it down next to the cigarettes. Danny suppresses a grimace as his stomach gurgles in response to the smell.

"Maybe you should just call it a morning," Danny suggests, staring at the coffee with distaste. "I can't think of anything worth staying up for if I had to drink that."

"No rest for the wicked," the man says, flashing a quick grin. "I gotta see a guy about a thing."

Danny snorts. He places a single QuickWin ticket on top of the cigarettes and starts ringing him up. "From the look of you, I figured you'd already done that."

"That... was a *different* thing."

Danny glances up at him quizzically. To his annoyance, he sees the man has already started rubbing off the silver ink from the QuickWin ticket with a quarter. He turns his attention back to the cash register and finishes ringing everything up. By the time he finishes, the man is holding up the ticket with a satisfied smirk.

"Take it out of this," he says.

Danny squints at the ticket. "Twenty-five bucks. Nice."

The man holds out the ticket.

"I'm not really supposed to do it that way," Danny says. He glances up at the security camera. "Screw it."

He takes the ticket and starts making change.

The man waits patiently as Danny counts everything out, shoves his cigarettes into a trenchcoat pocket, then toasts Danny with his coffee.

"Hope your morning gets better," Danny says.

The laugh that comes out of the strange bruised man is tinged with bitterness. "I doubt that very much."

With that, he toasts again, takes a sip of coffee, and gags.

"Maybe I *will* eat the cup," he mutters, then limps out of the store.

* * *

David Bernard stands outside with Special Agent Alan Grant, watching CB interact with the store clerk through the big storefront windows.

"He stopped for *cigarettes*?" Grant asks. He jams his fists into his trenchcoat—it's a much nicer one than CB's, black and made of heavier material.

"And coffee," David observes. He shivers slightly. It's not summer any more, and he's no longer on a tropical island. He's definitely not dressed for the season. Somewhere in the back of his head, Allard murmurs a spell that might work against the cold.

"And a *lottery ticket*," Grant adds. He's less annoyed, more amused at this point. "Jesus, it looks like he actually won something. What's his power again?"

"Beats me," David says. "He was a little before my time."

"Mine too, but we all had to read the PRODIGY case files. The best we have on him is 'makes weird shit happen.'"

The door jingles and CB stomps out. He hands the coffee over to Grant. "Hold this for a second."

Grant stares at the coffee, nonplussed. He sniffs at it, makes a terrible face, and holds it a little farther away from his body. "What'd you do, scrape the bottom of the pot for flavor?"

"The guy tried to convince me not to buy it," CB says. He pulls an unopened pack of cigarettes from his pocket and starts fumbling with the plastic wrapping. "Come on, let's get going."

He sets off on foot, not really paying attention to where he's going. David notes, however, that he is headed in the right direction.

"Why are we walking?" David asks. "We have faster ways of getting there."

"So they won't notice us," CB says.

Grant frowns. "I think we gotta assume if Haruspex is everything we think it is, it'll be child's play for them to link into all the surveillance cams the police have set up around the city."

"We should definitely assume that," CB says. The plastic wrapping falls to the pavement, gets picked up by the wind, and blows away. He pulls out a cigarette, sticks it in his mouth, and fishes around in a pocket for his lighter.

"So I don't think we can assume we'll evade notice," Grant continues. "Going on foot would make more sense in the middle of the day, but at night we kinda stick out."

CB stops walking for a second, pulls out his lighter, and lights up. He takes a draw on his cigarette. The cherry glows bright red. He closes his eyes, and for a moment David feels as if the world is whirling around him. A moment later, he feels it *stop* spinning, as if it were snapping into place.

"It'll be fine," CB says, and starts walking again.

Grant shoots David a look, shrugs, and hurries to catch up with CB, handing off the coffee and wiping his hand on his coat. David falls in behind them.

"So where's this other guy, Grant?" CB asks.

Grant points. "We're about two blocks that way."

We. David has only seen Grant do his multiples act a few times, and he gets prickly—well, more prickly than usual—when asked questions about it. He feels Allard stir uneasily as his gaze shifts between Grant and CB.

Two of them, Allard murmurs.

They're metahumans, David replies silently. *Just like everyone else.*

No, Allard replies. *They are not.*

David waits for Allard to explain, but it offers nothing more.

Well, at least you aren't screaming for me to murder them. It's progress.

Allard's laughter rolls through his mind, but it's nervous laughter.

"You still with us, Doc?"

David looks up to see CB and Grant staring at him, CB with caution, Grant with an expression of amused impatience.

"Sorry," David says. "Private conversation."

CB's gaze flickers to David's left shoulder—the place where, earlier in the evening, the large shadowy form of a predator bird was perched. David gives him a small, confirming nod.

"Well," CB says, "let's try talking *and* walking. I want to meet the new guy."

"There's a whole crew," Grant offers. "But at the moment it's just him and his sister."

"Sister?" CB asks.

"She's pretty awesome," Grant says enthusiastically. "She doesn't like me much."

"You're an acquired taste, Grant." CB smirks as he pulls on his cigarette again.

Grant laughs. "I get that a lot. People, they get intimidated by my overpowering charisma."

Two blocks down they find a bus stop sitting in front of an old playground. The bus stop bench is covered in graffiti. Standing in front of the bench are three figures, one white, two black. The white man is Alan Grant. The realization makes Allard stir uneasily for a moment, but the feeling subsides quickly as David takes in the other two.

The black man is very tall and very thin, dressed in a well-tailored suit with a white starched shirt, gray silk tie, and a black trenchcoat that looks almost exactly like the kind Grant favors. Long, thin dreadlocks are pulled back into a medium-length ponytail. Everything about the man radiates tension—he stands completely straight and still, his face a mask of rigidly enforced neutrality and control. The lamplight gleams against his dark skin, skin pulled so tight against his face that he looks almost cadaverous in the darkness.

The black woman is only slightly shorter than the man, making her at least an inch or two taller than David. Wearing black tactical pants, combat boots, and a white sports top, she looks much more like someone preparing to go into a fight. She also, David notes, sports a trenchcoat, but a decidedly more ragged one—closer to CB's than to Grant's.

"Gentlemen," Grant says—*their* Grant, not the one at the far end of the bench—"may I introduce to you Brother Judgment and Sister Sentinel. The leaders of the Bastions."

"Curtis," David says, nodding in greeting. "Lisa."

Brother Judgment's eyes widen, startled. Sister Sentinel breaks out into a grin.

"Holy *shit*," she says. "It's motherfucking *Sky Commando*, First Edition!"

Ignoring CB and Alan—both of them—she walks over to David and gives him a friendly tap on the shoulder. It hurts, as always, and he staggers back a step.

"You *know* them?" Grant asks, incredulous.

"Of course I know them," David says. "I was Sky Commando for four years."

He says it without bitterness, now. It seems only yesterday he thought that would be impossible.

"Might have been nice to know you had a pre-existing relationship with them," Grant says. "I could've saved all my charm for something else."

Brother Judgment's mouth presses into a thin, straight line.

"I didn't know you were gonna be on this," Sister Sentinel says. "The other Sky Commando, sure—she's all right, by the way, Curtis likes her but won't admit it—but not the original!"

David grins sheepishly. "Not the original any more. I, ah, go by *Doctor Enigma* now."

Lisa stares at him blankly, then breaks out into uproarious laughter.

"Why?"

"Because it's better than 'Doctor Weird, Warlock Supreme.'"

"Hey!" Alan Grant shakes his head in mock outrage. "Doctor Weird is a *fantastic* name, and some day you will regret not taking it."

"Does that mean you're going in with us?" Curtis turns to CB, frowning. "Look, I know I'm not calling the shots, but I *like* this guy, and I don't want to see him get killed. He was hot shit in his armor, but out of it he's just a normal. No offense David."

"None taken," David says.

"He's not normal any more," CB says. "He's the magic guy."

Both Curtis and Lisa study David more closely.

"He telling the truth?" Curtis asks.

David nods. "Long story. Magic island."

Curtis and Lisa exchange glances.

"Well," Lisa says, "you've already seen some weird shit, right?"

Curtis nods. "Yeah. He seems normal, though."

He turns to face CB, and sticks out his hand. "You're Curveball?"

CB juggles his coffee into his left hand, and shakes Curtis' hand. "That's me."

Curtis smiles slightly. "Read about you when I was a kid."

"Ouch," CB says.

Curtis snorts. "The Fed here filled us in, and I've got my team ready to go, but how exactly are *we* getting in to start the show? We kind of stick out."

"I figured we'd go in through the front," CB says. "Glad to have you on board." With that, he continues walking down the street.

Curtis stares after him, then turns to David. "He for real?"

David shrugs. "I haven't really seen him in action. Heard some interesting stories, though."

Curtis nods, and as if on cue they all start following CB. Lisa and Curtis fall into step beside David, Lisa to his right and Curtis to his left, making him feel uncharacteristically small.

David looks from Curtis, to Lisa, to Grant, then to CB. He sighs.

"Guess I need to start wearing trenchcoats."

Part Nine: Haruspex Analytics, The Labyrinth

The Labyrinth—the primary security hub at Haruspex Analytics—features the kind of cutting-edge surveillance tech that First World countries won't get for another ten to fifteen years. It also contains capabilities of a very different kind, a power that is unlikely to ever be used by any modern principality, and that combination requires the staff to be very deliberately chosen and trained for their task.

Ty Parks is one of the few members of the original team to survive the initial go-live date. He is not the man he was at the beginning, but enough of him remains to make him the de facto leader of the team that runs the Labyrinth today.

The Labyrinth, true to its name, resembles a maze—if Ms. Ioannou is to be believed, it uses the same floor plan as the first maze to carry the name. But while the first Labyrinth consisted of stone walls that led to a monster at its center, *this* Labyrinth consists of walls of high-definition video feeds. There is also a monster at its center, though the form and nature of that beast are significantly more abstract than the original.

Ty frowns at the video feed he is examining—the outer room of Board Member Kline's office suite, where his team is still working at their computers—finally dismissing the picture with a wave of his hand. Once upon a time, before the latest retrofit, he would have had to walk to the dedicated feed terminal and type in a command using a physical keyboard. Now, he simply waves his hand, and the electronic mesh inside his data glove returns the feed to the list.

The glove, and voice commands—that's all you need these days.

He gulps down half a cup of lukewarm coffee and turns to the young woman staring at him questioningly.

"Not yet," he says.

Ellen Murray is younger than the rest of the team, but she's resilient in a way most of the rest aren't. She's been in the Labyrinth for the better part of a year, and has displayed none of the obvious physical changes that usually manifest. There is only the slightest hint of darkening in her sclera, and the skin on the back of her left hand—where the data glove makes contact—is starting to mottle. "But she's trying to access the Incursion Protocols."

Ty nods. "And if she actually gets to them, we flag it and send it on up. But keep in mind, we were asked to monitor them because they were already doing that."

"I thought we were being asked to confirm it," Ellen says.

Ty shakes his head. "If they're asking us to *monitor*, they already know. If they ask us to *confirm*, it means they *suspect* but want proof, and if they ask us to *investigate* it means they have detected anomalous behavior but don't have context for it. *Monitor, confirm, investigate.* Those words are always chosen deliberately."

"Yes sir." Ellen accepts the information, even as she obviously chafes against it.

Ty favors her with a thin-lipped smile—he never shows his teeth any more. Too many people find it disturbing. "The board almost always moves slower than we think they should. They're almost always right."

Ellen says nothing. He knows what she's thinking: *almost always* means *sometimes not.* But she nods, accepting the instruction, and changes the subject.

"We got a hit on one of the flagged metahumans a few minutes ago."

Ty raises an eyebrow. "Which one?"

"Curveball. He walked into a convenience store. Bought some cigarettes and a cup of coffee. Looked like he'd been in a fight."

"Are we tracking him now?" Ty feels his pulse quicken. Curveball is one of the red flag targets—the Board wants to know *everything* about him.

"He's between cameras, but we're expecting him to show up again soon."

Ty nods, waves his data glove. "Track subject: Curveball."

The display shifts, showing a map of the last known location of Curveball, and the next seven possible locations where he can be picked up on camera.

Ty tsks in distaste. "Not a great part of the city for coverage."

Ellen nods. "City government hasn't finished rolling out the municipal video feeds. The poorer parts of the city aren't hooked in yet. We're supplementing with a few Internet security feeds, but adoption is low in that region."

"Well, we need to try to—"

Ty's order is cut short as all of the displays in the Labyrinth flicker, go black for a moment, then return.

Ty grimaces, briefly showing his teeth. He doesn't notice Ellen shudder as he turns in place, searching. "Abel! What was that?"

A stout, bearded man peeks out from around one of the corridors. "We're drawing too much power again. We either need to throttle back, or borrow from the city. Again."

Ty thinks it over. "Who did we black out last time?"

"Brooklyn."

"OK. Bronx this time. Throttle everything back until we have what we need."

"Give it about ten minutes," the bearded man says, then disappears around the corridor again.

Ty sighs, exasperated. Ellen shakes her head disapprovingly.

"They're going to notice, eventually," she says.

"They already have." Ty looks down at the empty styrofoam cup in his hand and sighs. "So far they're blaming it on increased internet usage and an aging power infrastructure. Ellen, our resources are about to be severely limited…"

As if on cue, the light dims in the Labyrinth, and half of the active video feeds abruptly wink out of existence.

"…but when it comes back up I want you to focus on re-locating Curveball. This is the first hit we've had on him in New York since the assault on the Forrest brownstone. The Board will want to know. In fact, since most of you will have a little down time, you should probably go ahead and send a preliminary report to the Board now, in case they have any specific instructions."

Ellen nods, shoulders slumping slightly as she realizes she just got suckered into doing paperwork. Ty twists his mouth into a tight-lipped smile.

"What will you be doing?" Ellen asks.

Ty jerks his head over to an elevated platform in an otherwise empty spot in the middle of the Labyrinth's center. "Eyes and ears."

Ellen shudders. She's never had to do that before.

"Paperwork's looking a little better now, isn't it?" Ty asks.

Ellen nods silently.

Ty chuckles. "Well, we've both got our jobs. Let's get started."

Ellen turns and disappears around one of the many video corridors leading into the center room. Ty steps up onto the platform, draws a symbol in the air with his data glove, and says, "Begin."

He feels a slight breeze as the two silver cables drop out of the ceiling.

As soon as the ends hit the platform they twitch, and as even more lengths of the cables spool down, the ends rise, snakelike and begin to coil around his body. One, two, three, four, five loops, and when at last the cables tighten, trapping him firmly in place, the ends have reached his temples.

He barely notices as they plunge through the sides of his head, force themselves through his skull, and touch his brain.

Immediately he feels the awareness enter him, and he swims in the sensation of seeing through two sets of eyes—his own, and the eyes of the building itself.

His body shudders involuntarily as his consciousness merges with the awareness that was imbued in the building's foundation when construction first started, then he feels himself go completely still. This is the point where so many of the others never came back, and Ty immediately focuses on his own will—not fighting against the other awareness, but refusing to cede what remains of his own identity.

Seconds pass, and they reach the balance they need. Ty opens his eyes—their eyes, for the moment—and speaks in a voice not wholly his own.

"We are the Eye of the Labyrinth."

He extends his right arm, now swarming with tiny, silvery-black cables that crawl in and out of his flesh with impunity. It doesn't hurt; he can't feel much of anything at the moment. Cables stream out, away from his arm, and embed themselves in one of the displays. A surge of warmth travels up his arm, through his chest, up his neck, and then he is floating in an ocean of images. Every feed in the building is streaming into his mind at the same time.

He can see the Chairman and some of the other members of the Board waiting in the uppermost chambers as helicopters on the roof are prepped for departure. He frowns, considering for a moment what it means: this is the core group—the Board within the Board. There are a few notable additions: Mr. Kline is there, as well as the metahumans Richter and Doyle.

They are leaving Haruspex Analytics, he realizes. *The next phase must be beginning.*

Ty is not technically a member of the Inner Circle—he doesn't make any of the decisions—but he knows all the secrets. It is unavoidable. He is the Eye.

He can see the artificers, hooded, faceless, maintaining their circle in the underlevel. A part of Ty's consciousness doesn't understand the words the robed figures are chanting. Another part understands them all too well, and this part stirs uneasily as he puts this together with the previous image.

They should have been finished by now, Ty thinks. *The senator should have been dead hours ago.*

The only reason to continue the ritual is if something has *prevented* that death. And if it is continuing, and the Inner Circle is leaving, that means they suspect an incursion.

Ty's mind recoils briefly at the thought of it, then he steels himself, forcing himself to accept what must be. He reaches out again, connects with the internal phone system, and makes a call.

In the first image, he sees the Chairman turn to look at an unobtrusive phone sitting next to an overstuffed chair. He picks it up.

"This is the Chairman." The voice radiates warmth and strength... and caution. Only a few people know this particular number, even among the Inner Circle.

"This is the Eye of the Labyrinth."

"Ty?" The Chairman sound surprised, but he glances up at the camera that feeds into the Labyrinth's systems. "I suppose I shouldn't be surprised. And I owe you an apology, now that I think of it. I should have called you an hour ago."

"Unnecessary." The various forms of social niceties that Ty would normally use when he was talking to their unquestioned leader fall away when he's in this form. *"I have surmised you are planning final egress from this citadel."*

"Correct," the Chairman says. "We are expecting a rather forceful incursion."

"Acknowledged. Ellen reported that Curveball was flagged in this city just before a power outage forced us to degrade operations until power is restored."

"It is very likely he will be involved," the Chairman says.

"Acknowledged. We will prioritize your egress, then the protection of the artificers until their task is complete, then the elimination of threat. What limits will you set?"

The Chairman falls silent for a moment, thinking. Then he speaks.

"Ensure that the first objective has been met. After that, take every opportunity to accomplish the third."

Ty feels a thrill run through him.

"Acknowledged."

Part Ten: Haruspex Analytics, Ground Floor Lobby

The Haruspex Analytics building isn't one of the tallest in the city, but it does look impressively *modern* when viewed from the street. Its design is similar to the Cayan Tower in Dubai, in that it drifts away from the traditional rectangular shape of most buildings by twisting it, making the edges of the building spiral around as it rises. It is further unique because the twisting shape of the Haruspex Analytics building is *not* a rectangle: it is a triskaidecagon.

The other way the building stands out from the rest of downtown is that it has *grounds*. It's not just shoved against the street—the front entrance is set behind a little park that has a long, straight path cutting through the center, leading to the double revolving doors that provide access to the building itself.

CB swirls his coffee—still hot in its styrofoam cup—and takes a short drag on his cigarette and sizes everything up. Agent Grant sidles up to his left, hands thrust into his trenchcoat pockets.

"Everyone's in position," he says. He keeps his voice low and his expression casual.

CB nods. "Then let's get this started."

Brother Judgment steps up to his right. "How are they not all over us, yet?" CB has never worked with Brother Judgment, or Sister Sentinel, or any of the other Bastions, but Crossfire seems to trust them almost implicitly. That in itself is remarkable.

CB shrugs. "There's even odds they haven't noticed us yet."

"Not likely." Brother Judgment jerks his head over to a traffic light a block down the street. "Most of those things have cameras. If these guys are as on their game as everyone says, they can tap into all the municipal stuff. They probably watched us coming."

"Yeah," Grant agrees. "That's what I'd do, if I was a bad guy."

"It's what you do *now*," Brother Judgment shoots back.

"We get a warrant first," Grant says. "I mean, usually." He smirks. "Unless we don't feel like it."

"Normally," CB says, ignoring the exchange, "that'd be a valid concern. I think we stepped around that problem this time. They'll notice us when we break down the front door. Not before then."

"How do you know?" Brother Judgment's tone isn't hostile, it's just *aggressively curious*. CB doesn't really blame him.

"I don't *know*," CB says. "I won't know till the eight ball's in the corner pocket... but the shot feels right. You're the telepath, right? Can you get a read on the building?"

The other man blinks. "The whole building? Nah."

"Too bad," CB says. "Then I guess we just go in and see what happens. Everybody put your game face on."

Brother Judgment and Sister Sentinel immediately put on sunglasses. Agent Grant relaxes into a cocky smirk. That leaves David Bernard, who looks... not quite there.

"Doc?"

"I'm here," David says. "I don't really have a game face yet, but I figure they're going to be too focused on trying to kill us to critique my stage presence."

"You think they're going for the kill?" Sister Sentinel does that thing where she makes a fist and cracks all her knuckles. CB has never been able to do it. It always looks cool.

"Oh yes," David says. "The sense I get from that building is... very similar to a place I visited recently. They're not gonna shoot you in the hand."

"Come on." CB starts walking toward the building, flicking the butt of his cigarette into the street with one hand as he holds his coffee with the other.

Grant looks down at the Styrofoam cup. "You gonna drink that?"

CB grins. "Nope."

They hit the park at a brisk walk.

"They got card readers at the doors." Despite wearing sunglasses at 4AM, Sister Sentinel can see quite well. "That means the doors are gonna be locked. May I?"

CB gestures grandly with his coffee. "Be my guest."

She steps out in front of the rest, not running, but quickening her step just enough to put a little space between her and the rest of the group. When she reaches one of the revolving doors, she doesn't stop—she steps inside, places her hands against the center shaft, and *pushes*. Steel shrieks against steel, something snaps, glass shatters, and then the entire door is shoved into the lobby, where it skids to a halt, spinning counterclockwise on its side.

Sister Sentinel steps through, beaming at the startled security guards on the other side. "Hi!" Her voice is bright and friendly. "Y'all are in big trouble!"

Part Eleven: Haruspex Analytics, Jason Kline's Suite

Phyllis, Michelle, and Simon say nothing for a moment. The only sound in the room is the *zwip* of the drawstrings to Michelle's hoodie as she pulls the left side out as far as it will go, then the right, then the left, then the right again. Finally Michelle pulls both, causing the hood to scrunch up over her face. Then she speaks.

"Why do you think he's lying?"

She looks and sounds very young, right now. Less sarcastic. A lot more vulnerable.

"I can read him," Phyllis says. "Usually when he lies like that it's because he's trying to protect us from something. Not today, though—today he's throwing us to the wolves."

"Jason wouldn't do that." It's more desperate rationalization than flat denial. "He's not like that."

"I would have agreed with you," Phyllis says. "Before... before Billy."

"He didn't know anything about that!" Michelle, deciding anger is the best fuel for denial, slams both hands down on her desk, one on each side of her laptop. Her mouse clatters to the floor.

"He did," Phyllis says. "He didn't know it would be Billy, but he knew what that woman was doing, and he knew what it meant. And now... I don't know, now, but whatever he's doing, it's not a business trip."

"He had his go-bag," Simon says.

Phyllis and Michelle turn to look at him. Simon is slumped in his chair, one hand tugging at strands of his spiky hair. His eyes have a faraway look.

"How do you know?" Michelle asks.

"I've seen it before," Simon says. "When I first joined the group he told me it was important to have one, and he showed me his. To give me an idea of what it should have in it."

"That doesn't mean anything!" Michelle throws her hands in the air in frustration. "He doesn't know anything about the business trip, so he takes his go bag. Just in case."

"That's *stupid*, Michelle." Simon's voice goes hard. "And you're *not* stupid, so *cut it out*."

"OK," Phyllis says, "let's take it easy. Michelle, I know you don't want to believe Jason would do this. I don't *want* to believe it either. That's why I'm so damned angry. But you don't take a go bag on a business trip. You take it when you're rabbiting. You know this."

"I wonder if he meant me to see it," Simon says thoughtfully. "Like, if management flat-out told him not to tell us anything, he wouldn't. But letting me see the go-bag, that's not telling us anything. Technically. It's letting me draw my own conclusions based on known behavior."

Michelle falls silent as she thinks it over.

"Something to think about," Phyllis agrees, "but right now I think we need to find out what the Incursion Protocols are."

Simon winces. "I can give it a shot, but given our timeframe I don't think I'll make much progress."

Phyllis waves her hand. "I'm already working on it. I know you outclass me with computers, but this isn't about cracking a security system."

Simon laughs and shakes his head. "If this isn't about cracking security, what it is it?"

"It's about *cracking Jason*," Phyllis says.

Simon stares at Phyllis blankly. Michelle barks out a laugh. "You're spearphishing your boss."

Phyllis smiles. Her laptop beeps. She glances at the screen and nods once, satisfied.

"I win the bet."

"You're in?" Simon leaps out of his chair excitedly. Coming around behind Phyllis to stare over her left shoulder at her laptop screen.

Michelle rolls her chair around to Phyllis' right, doing the same. "So what are they?"

"Give me a minute," Phyllis says, looking through the contents of the folder that opened on her desktop. It looks like there are a number of technical specifications and policy documents. She opens one of the policy documents and starts skimming through it.

Her eyes go wide.

"What is it?" Michelle licks her lips nervously. "Phyllis?"

Phyllis waves them both away. "Give me some room. I'll tell you what I know when I know it."

Simon and Michelle reluctantly return to their laptops. Simon tries not to fidget. Michelle plays with the drawstring on her hoodie.

Phyllis returns to her reading. She scans through the document, closes it, and opens another. Time passes. She closes that document, and opens a third—one of the technical specifications this time.

"My… God…" Her voice drops to a whisper.

"What?" Simon focuses on her, gaze intense. "What is it?"

Phyllis closes the document and rolls back from the laptop. "One of you bring up a schematic of the building. I don't care who, but do it fast."

"Phyllis," Michelle asks. Her eyes are huge beneath her hoodie. "What's going on?"

"We're in trouble, honey," Phyllis says. "I'll explain it when we have time. I don't think we have time right now."

At that, both Simon and Michelle spring into action, each working at their laptop furiously. Simon is the first to bring up a schematic. Phyllis looks it over briefly, then shakes her head.

"That's not real," she says. "It's too much of what you'd expect. I need to see the *real* building. But only look in the areas we're allowed to look in for now. Eventually they're going to notice what I did, and we don't want them to notice faster."

"I have something," Michelle says. "Look at this."

Phyllis gets out of her chair and leans over Michelle to look at her screen. The schematic is definitely the building, but there are parts of it that very much don't *fit*.

"This is what we need," Phyllis says. "OK. We're getting out of here. The three of us. Together. Problem is, we don't want them to *notice*. So we need to find an exit route that minimizes detection. Michelle, you see this floor?" She points. "It looks like the security system just isn't there."

Michelle's brow furrows. "Yeah. There's not a lot of anything there."

"If we can get there, I think we can take that stairwell down to the sub-basement."

"Right," Michelle says. "Then we can get to the stair leading to the delivery entrance."

"We just need to figure out how to get there without being noticed," Phyllis says.

"Show me," Simon says. Michelle spins her laptop around. Simon scrutinizes the screen.

"Give me a second."

Phyllis pulls her cell phone out of her jacket pocket and calls her husband.

Her husband sounds sleepy over the phone, which doesn't surprise her given the time. "Hey, you. What's up?"

"I'm gonna have to put in another long one," Phyllis says.

There's silence at the end of the line. When her husband speaks, he's a lot more alert. "Sorry to hear it."

"Me too," Phyllis says. "I'll call when I know more."

"All right. Don't work too hard."

He hangs up first. Phyllis nods in satisfaction. *They got Billy. They won't get him too.*

"OK, so I maybe have something," Simon says. "So the security system here is tied into this central—"

"The Labyrinth," Phyllis says. "Yeah, we all sat in on the same briefing."

"OK, OK." Simon shrugs. "Hopefully they're not *listening in* right now, or we're pretty dead. Anyway, they recently had an upgrade and it's been drawing more power than they can sustain. I think we can use that."

"How?"

"When they trip the power, they start drawing it from the city power grid," Simon says. "That's why there have been so many brownouts all over the city lately. But it takes about fifteen to twenty minutes, and during that time the system has holes in it. That's our window."

Simon starts describing all the locations where security will still be active, and he and Michelle plan a route that avoids most of them.

Phyllis nods in satisfaction. "Great work, you two. Now let's get *our* go-bags."

Part Twelve: Haruspex Analytics, Ground Floor Lobby

The lobby looks like a cross between a bank and a tomb.

The floor is polished marble tile, gleaming white beneath dimly lit fluorescent lights hanging from the ceiling. Standing in the gaping hole where the revolving door used to be, CB sees a row of faceless statues lining the wall to the left. The statues are vaguely Greek, stylistically. They all wear togas, and each has one arm raised in an authoritative manner, as if they were in the middle of teaching some great truth to the multitudes. Six statues in all, evenly spaced down the length of the long hall. At the far end are elevators, the stairwell, and a few other closed doors.

On the right is the lobby desk made of dark, polished wood, with a stone top that matches the marble floor. It's huge, stretching the entire length of the wall, and looks ridiculously oversized given that there are only three people behind it: two men, one middle-aged and balding, one younger with a full, dark beard, and an older woman with steel-gray hair pulled back into a tight braid. All three are dressed in guard uniforms—dark slacks, gray buttoned shirt, badges—and the men have drawn pistols. The woman with the steel-gray hair doesn't move at all, calmly taking in the scene.

Sister Sentinel stands in the middle of the long, empty room, next to the shattered remains of the revolving door still spinning slowly in place. The grin on her face is equal parts adrenaline and dare.

The woman with the steel-gray hair regards her impassively. "This is private property," she says. "You're trespassing."

"I'm gonna count to ten," Sister Sentinel says. "And if you haven't dropped your weapons by then, I'm gonna assume—"

The two men open fire. Both have excellent form, and they've obviously trained with their firearms. The shots all find their mark, bullet after bullet impacting somewhere on Sister Sentinel's body. For all their accuracy, the shots are ineffective: although she takes an initial step back when the first shot impacts, all the guns do is put tiny holes in her shirt and jeans. She looks down, annoyed, and then leaps through the air, closing the distance between them in seconds. She lands behind them, and before they can turn they're already disarmed. Holding a gun in each hand, she squeezes slightly. Both guns shatter.

Still not visibly reacting, the woman with steel-gray hair presses a button on the desk. An alarm sounds, something similar to the noise a fire alarm makes, but deeper.

She presses a second button. CB hears the hiss of hydraulics and springs forward, feeling the air move behind him as a massive, metallic *clang* rings through the air, shaking the ground. He half turns to see a thick armored wall where the gaping hole of the revolving door used to be. Moments later he hears a slight buzz thrumming behind the sound of the alarm.

The woman with steel-gray hair is shouting something into her sleeve as she backs away from Sister Sentinel. The men are also backing away, in the other direction, both fumbling at utility belts. The young man pulls out a taser; the older man pulls out a knife.

Sister Sentinel rolls her eyes. She's saying something, but CB can't make it out. The alarm is too loud. The young guard looks intimidated, but the older man and the woman with the steel-gray hair don't. They look... resigned.

CB frowns.

The older guard steps behind the younger, wraps his arm around the man's head and jerks it back, exposing his neck. Sister Sentinel starts in surprise, and the woman with the steel-gray hair takes the moment to press a third button on the front desk, causing the alarm to end and killing all the lights in the lobby. The sound of the deep klaxon is immediately replaced by the sounds of the young guard shouting in incoherent alarm, then changing to pleas of "No! *No!*" as he feels his head being forced back and his neck exposed.

CB draws deep on his cigarette, then throws the coffee.

Emergency lights switch on just as it leaves his hands. It's a perfect throw, tumbling end over end, the plastic lid firmly in place as tiny trails of coffee leak out the lid's spout. It crosses the width of the room just as the older guard steadies his knife on the side of the younger man's neck, ready to jerk the blade across exposed flesh. The styrofoam cup smashes against the side of the older guard's face, the plastic top facing the floor, and as the side compresses the lid slides off. Coffee that is still far too hot for drinking pours down onto the man's neck and shoulder; he screams. The knife tumbles from his hand as he stumbles away, clawing helplessly at his shirt and the beet-red flesh beneath it.

Sister Sentinel curses, grabs the younger guard, and shoves him behind her as she turns to keep herself between him and the others. The young guard stumbles, eyes wide. The woman with steel-gray hair draws her own knife.

CB starts running. Sister Sentinel angles herself to keep an eye on both guards—the woman and the burned man—and waits. CB is vaguely aware of a soft blur as Agent Grant blinks into the room, taking a moment to get his bearings.

The woman with the steel-gray hair jerks her head back, exposing her own neck.

"Stop her!" CB shouts. Sister Sentinel takes a step toward her, but hesitates, eyeing the burned guard. She'll leave the young guard unprotected if she moves in, and there's no guarantee the burns on the older guard will remain a distraction for much longer.

No, protecting the young idiot is the right call. But he's not going to get there in time; the woman's knife has already started to move.

With a quick jerking motion, the woman pulls the knife across her neck. The air blurs behind her and Agent Grant appears, grabs her wrist and twists sharply. The woman cries out in surprise and pain as her hand opens, knife clattering to the floor. A tiny droplet of red oozes from her neck, but nothing more.

Grant grunts as the woman twists in his grasp, then fades and disappears as her other hand slices across the air where he'd been a moment before. He reappears an instant later, inches away from her now-outstretched arm, and grabs it, heaving the startled woman over his shoulder and onto the marble floor with a thud.

"Jesus," Grant mutters. "They grow 'em *crazy* in here." He reaches down to take the woman's right arm, and as she struggles to get to her hands and knees he pulls it behind her back, slipping a pair of handcuffs over her wrist, then does the same with her left. She sags, then stops struggling, too woozy to act without the use of her arms.

"They were gonna kill me!"

The young guard keeps Sister Sentinel between him and his former compatriots, scrambling over the front desk and backing away, eyes wide with fright. He points in the direction of the other two, turning to CB, his voice rising in pitch and incredulity.

"Did you see that? He tried to slit my throat!"

"I saw," CB says. He turns to the guard and points at the heavy metal shell covering the door and windows. "Can you open that thing back up?"

"Two years!" The man's voice is getting hoarse now. "I worked with them for *two years*, and this is what happens. Jesus, they came to my wedding!"

"You got cuffs for this one, too?" Sister Sentinel points to the burned guard. "He's starting to calm down."

Agent Grant blurs for a moment, then a second Agent Grant appears over the burned guard, forcing him onto his stomach. "Good call," the first Grant says. He's staring down at a console set into the front desk, frowning.

The second Grant finishes handcuffing the burned guard, then turns to examine the metal shell enclosing the door.

"Brother Judgment can't get in," the second Grant says. "His telekinesis is pretty strong, but this doesn't want to bend. And the Doc can't portal in, either. Something's blocking it. I'm gonna guess there's an anti-teleportation field set up."

The young security guard is still wild-eyed, gaze darting around the room like a paranoid rabbit, but he's stopped babbling at this point. CB turns his gaze away from him for a moment to regard the heavy shell surrounding the building. "How'd you get in, then?"

Grant shrugs. "I work different."

"OK," CB says, "is the shell just this floor, or does it go all the way up?"

"All the way up," Grant says. "It's not the same, though. The ground floor looks like it was deployed from the second floor—dropped down like big metal blinds. The other floors look like they're just reinforcing windows and other weak points."

"Great," CB says. "What's the status of B Team?"

"Up, up, and away," Grant says.

"Outstanding. Maybe Sister Sentinel can do something about these plates—"

"Gas!" Sister Sentinel's warning is sharp and direct. Grant nods once, his image blurs, and a moment later he reappears, standing in front of both CB and Sister Sentinel, gas masks dangling from his hands.

CB takes one and slips it over his head. "You need one, too."

"I'm puttin' it on outside."

The masks are based on one of Robert's designs, both thinner and more rugged than the standard fare. CB slips his on quickly and it immediately seals itself over his face. A heads-up display on the goggles identifies the gas as a potent neurotoxin. It hasn't reached lethal levels, but it's rising steadily.

"We gotta get the guards out of here!" CB shouts. A tiny speaker set into the breather portion of his mask amplifies his voice, making it easy for everyone to hear.

"Get to the other side of the room!" Grant shouts. "We got incoming!"

Grant blurs again and reappears behind the front desk, much closer to the elevators. Sister Sentinel picks up the handcuffed guards, one under each arm, and hurries in that direction. CB curses, grabs the wild-eyed younger guard, and drags him along as he follows.

"Hey!" The young guard grabs at CB's arm, and tries to twist out of his grip. "Hey! Let go!"

"Shut up!" CB snarls. The guard lapses into surprised silence. "Come on, we gotta get out of the way." He half-pulls the man over the front desk, then hunkers down as he hears the dull rumble of a sonic boom grow louder and louder.

"Duck and cover!" Grant shouts.

"Dammit." CB drags the guard down to the floor and covers him with his own body.

Then the entire building shudders as a *boom* fills the air, shaking CB to his core. Stone and glass and metal fly overhead. The young guard screams in terror as chunks of the front desk immediately to CB's right and left are torn to shreds by flying debris.

A moment of silence follows. CB pokes his head up from behind the lone piece of front desk remaining in that section.

Red Shift stands just inside the building. Behind him, the entire wall is broken: the windows shattered, the metal turned to twisted bits of ruined steel and the concrete turned to flakes and dust. The outer shell buckles inward, and a small, smooth cylindrical hole, slightly larger than Red Shift himself, is punched through it. The edges of the hole glow white with heat.

CB climbs to his feet, brushing marble dust off his trenchcoat, then hauling the now-whimpering guard up after him. "How fast was that?"

"About Mach Nine," Red Shift says. "Too many obstacles to go full speed."

"Damn," Grant mutters.

CB checks the levels on his gas mask's HUD, then sizes up the hole Red Shift left in the shield. "Kinda wish the hole was bigger."

Red Shift shrugs. "Munroe effect. With any luck, it disrupted the—"

There is a low *hum*, sort of a mix between a buzzer and a chime, then a faint gold spark appears to Red Shift's right. He takes two steps to the left as the spark brightens, expanding into the shape of a Persian arch, its borders purple-black shadow mixed with radiant gold light. A moment later the interior of the arch shifts, and they're looking out into the pre-dawn sky.

"—anti-teleport field," Red Shift finishes.

Brother Judgment steps into the room. A gas mask has replaced his sunglasses. His eyebrows rise over the top of the mask.

"Damn," he says. He looks over at his sister. "What did you *do*?"

Part Thirteen: Manhattan Rooftop

Jenny Forrest shivers involuntarily as she waits on the rooftop with Street Ronin, Scrapper Jack, and Agent Hu. She's not cold—her new battlesuit is layered and heavy, and if it weren't for her enhanced physique she'd probably be pretty warm right now—but she's all nerves as she waits for the signal. Hu looks like she *ought* to be cold—the new, fire-friendly outfit Robert made her doesn't look like it has any insulation at all—but she appears completely at ease in the crisp weather.

It's because she's pretty much made of fire, I guess. That's so not fair.

They're about a block from the Haruspex Analytics building, on the roof of the Foster-McLaughlin Complex. It's a taller building—fifty-five stories to Haruspex's fifty—and gives them a clear, unobstructed view of the Haruspex Analytics roof. Street Ronin kneels on the lip of the low wall encircling the roof, staring through a sight attached to one of his many high-powered rifles. The image from his scope feeds directly into Jenny's visor as well as a small handheld screen, which Jack and Hu are sharing. The display shows two helicopters sitting on a helipad, with a few silhouettes scurrying around them.

"They're being prepped for takeoff," Street Ronin says. "We probably want to prevent that."

"Not yet," Jenny says.

Street Ronin sighs. "No," he agrees reluctantly. "Not yet."

"We'll move in if they start to take off," Agent Hu says. "Even if we're early. It's only two copters. That means they're evacuating the big guns."

"Probably Artie's evil twin," Jack adds. "If he's still here."

"Wait…" Jenny frowns, fighting back a sudden surge of panic. "Does that mean they know we're here?"

Jack shakes his head. "Just that they know we're coming. *Doctor Enigma* apparently made a lot of noise that the bad guys could definitely hear."

One of the sensors on Jenny's visor starts blinking red as Agent Grant appears out of nowhere and steps up to them. She takes a half step back, startled. Jack tightens one fist, then relaxes when he realizes who it is.

Street Ronin doesn't so much as twitch. "We almost there?" he asks.

"Yeah," Grant says. "We're going in now. Can you see the entrance with that thing?" He gestures toward the rifle scope.

"No," Street Ronin says. "We'll need your play by play."

"Well, first of all, Sister Sentinel is a *badass*."

Street Ronin nods in agreement. Jack snorts in amusement. Agent Hu just rolls her eyes.

"Um," Jenny says, "maybe you could be a little more specific?"

"She just pushed a revolving door out of the wall and shoved it into the middle of the lobby," Grant says. "Didn't even miss a step."

"Stronger than Vigilante," Street Ronin says. "Probably not up there with you and Regiment, Scrapper, but she's closer than most. Tough to boot."

"Yeah," Jack says. "I know who the Bastions are. I'm glad I'm retired."

Agent Hu stares up at him, then gestures toward the Haruspex Analytics building. "You're *terrible* at retirement."

Jack grins, his scar making the grin look lopsided and a little deranged. "I got a knack."

"*Shit.*" Agent Grant looks toward the Haruspex building, scowling. "They just activated some kind of impressively fucked up defenses. Big metal plates sliding all down the sides of the building."

"I got it on scope," Street Ronin says.

The scope feed updates in Jenny's helmet, and she's tempted to utter a curse of her own. A series of metallic plates, arranged like scales, cover nearly the entire surface of the building. The only gaps she sees are strips of the building where she assumes the metal plates emerged.

"There's an alarm, too," Grant says. "I can hear it from the outside."

"Who's *inside*?" Jack asks.

"Sister Sentinel and Curveball. Doc is trying to portal in, but it ain't working. He says there's interference. Scrapper, can you get through those things?"

Jack frowns. "Probably, but I bet it'd be easier to just rip 'em out of the wall. Even if they're made out of some kind of super-metal, the building looks like regular concrete and steel. Something would give somewhere."

"You don't sound like you like the idea," Jenny notes.

"Yeah," Jack says. "I don't. Tearing 'em off also means dropping 'em once they're free. They might hit someone."

"Easier to punch through the roof," Hu says. "Or burn through. We need to take out the helicopters anyway."

Street Ronin gets to his feet. "Agreed. Time for us to go. Roof is still our best shot."

"OK," Jack says. "You ready?"

"Hold on a moment." Street Ronin reaches down beside his rifle and slings a tightly-packed backpack over his shoulders. He checks his utility belt and gives his weapons a last once-over. "OK. Zero?"

"Ready," Jenny says, "though I don't think I'm gonna like the ride. No offense Jack."

"Heh." Jack grabs Jenny and Street Ronin, hoisting each up off the ground, one under each arm.

"Right behind you," Agent Hu says, then bursts into flame and shoots into the air.

Jack *leaps,* and Jenny suppresses the desire to shriek. This isn't like being carried into that shipping compound in Farraday City—then, it was almost impossible to tell where they were, what with the storm raging around them. Now she can see everything, and everything is *very, very far away.*

The buildings below them shrink, then as their arc changes from *up* to *down* they very quickly expand. The Haruspex roof comes into view, and grows larger far more quickly than is comfortable.

"Landing might be a little rough," Jack shouts, then they hit the ground.

Jack bends deep as he lands, absorbing as much of the shock as he can, but Jenny's head knocks up against the inside of her visor, causing her to see stars, and Street Ronin grunts in pain. Jack drops them on the rooftop, then springs away again, and Jenny can hear a high-pitched whining sound as something sizzles as it strikes concrete and steel.

They have point defenses up here.

"We gotta move!" she shouts, and scrambles to her feet. Her suit is undamaged, and the HUD shows that there are in fact four energy weapons placed at the corners of the building.

A column of white-hot flame streaks across the sky, slamming into one of the weapons, causing it to go up in a mini-inferno. Agent Hu streaks across the rooftop, drawing fire from the remaining three. Two hit her square in the back, but she doesn't seem to feel it. Street Ronin rolls to his feet, grunting in pain, and pulls out a silver disc. He punches down on one end; the other end flashes light, alternating red and yellow. He throws it like a baseball, then runs toward the still-burning weapon Hu destroyed.

It's a solid throw. The silver disc streaks toward one of the energy weapons, exploding just as it hits the base of the gun. The weapon pops up out of its base and falls over, scorched and smoking. Scrapper Jack leaps to the third, ignoring a hit to the chest as his fist comes square down on the weapon, punching through its shell. He draws his fist back out, pulling the weapon off its base in the process.

Which leaves only Jenny.

Lucky, lucky Jenny.

Gritting her teeth, she runs toward the fourth weapon, currently trained on Agent Hu. She speeds up, noting with satisfaction that while her armor is heavy, it doesn't seem particularly bulky: it fits well and doesn't slip.

She's about ten feet out when the weapon swivels toward her. Light flickers over the... *what do you call that? A muzzle? Energy weapons don't need those, do they? What do you call it then? Um, nevermind...*

She leans back into a slide, closing the rest of the distance nearly prone as the weapon fires over her head. She's there—now what?

I'm not as strong as Jack, but maybe I'm strong enough.

She rolls into a crouch, places her shoulder beneath the barrel, and stands, pushing with all her strength.

Fire lances up her back as she feels a sharp pinch in her spine. Metal groans, then something in the base of the gun snaps. The entire barrel jerks up sharply, then falls over to the side. The weapon is silenced.

That's when the rooftop lights up with gunfire.

People, Jenny remembers. *There were also people on the roof.*

She dives behind the ruined weapon as gunfire tears into the roof behind her. A second later she remembers the body armor is supposed to be able to resist small arms fire. She reddens slightly.

Well look, Robert is a genius but I'm not just going to take his word for it.

She rolls, grabs a broken bit of gun, and hurls it back toward the source of the gunfire. She hears a muffled cry of alarm, then footsteps in retreat as the metal bounces and clatters off into the night. Street Ronin pops up with his rifle and fires once, twice, three times. The rooftop is silent.

"Clear," Jack says, then walks over to the first helicopter. He starts ripping it apart with his bare hands, taking care not to fling parts of it off the building.

Agent Hu lands next to Jenny, eyeing the gun she destroyed. "Nice work. I thought you were gonna do something complicated, like hack the system in order to shut it down."

"That would take *way* too much time," Jenny says. She stretches. Her back pops. She feels a little better. "The direct approach seemed faster. Hurt like hell though."

Agent Grant blurs in beside them. "OK, things are bug-fuck crazy downstairs. The security guards just tried to knife each other, and now they're pumping neurotoxin into the ventilation."

"They tried to knife Sister Sentinel?" Jenny asks.

"No they tried to shoot her. They tried to knife *each other*. Like, one long cut across the neck. I don't get it. But that shell is definitely blocking teleporters, so we're resorting to drastic measures to punch through."

Jack stops ripping up the helicopter and turns to face Agent Grant. "How drastic, exactly?"

They hear a faint sonic boom in the distance.

"Right," Jack mutters. He goes back to dismantling the helicopters.

"Should we be worried about this?" Jenny asks, looking around for a handhold.

"Just stay away from the edge of the building," Street Ronin says. "It's probably just going to be a little—"

A loud *boom* fills the air, and the entire building shudders, causing Jenny to stumble.

"—shaky," Street Ronin finishes.

The building stops shaking almost immediately. Jenny looks around cautiously. "That's it?"

"I was expecting something more violent," Hu admits.

"Oh, it was plenty violent," Jack says. The first helicopter has been reduced to a pile of metal scrap. He heads toward the second. "It was just very *focused* violence."

Part Fourteen: Haruspex Analytics

The Chairman is on the phone again, speaking to the Eye of the Labyrinth.

"Your initial mode of egress is no longer available," the Labyrinth says. *"Metahumans have destroyed both helicopters. I am preparing a direct transfer to the remote site, but there are some limitations."*

The Chairman nods. "Go on."

"First is power. The power it will require for the teleporters to function will delay the full activation of tower defenses, and the delay will allow the attackers the time to progress further and inflict more damage before full reprisal is possible."

"I see," the Chairman says. He bows his head for a moment, eyes closed, as he thinks it through. "That may be unavoidable."

"Acknowledged and agreed. However, the greatest danger is that you and the other principals of Project Recall are still here. You are in danger because our defenses are not sufficient to stop the metahumans from reaching you. Our greatest asset, at present, is that they do not seem to know where you are."

The Chairman nods again. "We need to keep it that way."

"We cannot trigger the Incursion Protocols until you have left the building."

"Because of the power consumption?"

"Primarily. But also some in your group would be affected."

The Chairman glances at Jason Kline. The young man was doing a fairly good job appearing calm, but there are signs that isn't entirely the case.

"Very well. Do what you can, to the extent you can. Sacrifice what you must to ensure our exit."

There's silence on the other end of the line as the Labyrinth considers this.

"How necessary is it for the senator's ritual to succeed?"

The Chairman frowns. "I would prefer that it did. However, I believe I understand your gambit. It is acceptable."

"Thank you, Chairman. I will attempt to give the artificers enough time."

"Ty…" The Chairman hesitates for a moment, then pushes on. "I need to give you an extra objective. A very *important* objective. One that will be instrumental in allowing us to move to the next phase of Project Recall."

The silence at the other end of the phone is so complete that the Chairman actually checks to the display to make sure they didn't disconnect.

"Clarify, please."

"We require a pyre for an offering."

This time instead of silence, the Chairman hears one long, ragged breath.

"Understood. It will be done."

"Thank you, Ty," the Chairman says. "Your work has always been exemplary. I know you will continue to excel. Right to the very end."

"Acknowledged." There is a note of pride in the part of the voice that's still human. *"Good fortune."*

The line goes dead. The Chairman puts the phone back in its cradle and turns to the others.

"We have to get to the Thirteenth Floor," he says. "And we don't have a lot of time."

* * *

Outside the building, three figures—two handcuffed and propped up against a park bench, one standing on his own, shivering in the cold—are watching a glowing crack in the world.

The crack is shaped like a Persian arch, and one side of it is the grounds in front of the Haruspex Analytics building. On the other side is the lobby of Haruspex Analytics. It's a kind of teleportation, obviously, but it feels almost familiar to them… in a way that it shouldn't, given who created it.

"I can't believe you guys tried to kill me." The young man rubs his arms, feeling much colder than he should, even in the early morning air.

The older man sighs, then winces as he shifts his weight. The skin on his face is welting. "You are such a fucking *moron*," he says in a raspy voice.

"Hey." A man in a black suit and long, dark trenchcoat—one of the teleporters, it seems—half-turns toward them, looking annoyed. "Shut up. Cops will be here soon, then you talk all you want as far as I care."

The older man glowers at Mr. Trenchcoat. The other handcuffed figure, a woman with steel-gray hair, says nothing. Instead, Madeline simply *watches*. She watches, calm and remote, and waits.

The arch appears to have been created by a second man. This man, dressed in blue jeans and wearing a light tan jacket, is extending his hand toward the Persian arch and swaying slightly as if exerting effort. It's not a lot of effort, from what she can tell—he's not gritting his teeth, or sweating, or shaking from exertion—but it's something that's requiring most of his attention. That, from her perspective, is useful. Mr. Trenchcoat is more of a problem, since one of the things he's actively doing is keeping an eye on them. He's doing other things as well—relaying information to the man in the tan jacket, for one, and he seems to be coordinating the distribution of equipment to other teams, but that doesn't seem to distract him enough for them to do anything other than *talk*—and even that is getting harder to do, now.

It isn't until the second (third?) teleporter arrives with the other woman that he's finally distracted enough for her to make her move.

"Peter is right," she finally says, in a low voice. "You really *are* a moron."

"I called him a *fucking* moron," Peter says.

"Be quiet," Madeline says, and he obediently falls silent.

The young man stares at her, his expression a mix of defiance, anger, and betrayal.

"You weren't the one who was going to die, Justin," she explains. "You were the one who was going to *live*."

Justin goes very still. "Not like that," he whispers.

Madeline nods gravely. "Exactly like that. And you know why you will. Because one way or another, Haruspex will demand that you honor your employment contract, and this is the way you want to honor it."

Justin shakes his head violently. "Why would I want to honor it *that* way?"

"Because," Madeline says, "you love your wife and son so *very, very much*."

There is a moment of silence, then the younger man's shoulders shake as he suppresses giant, wracking sobs.

She lets him weep for a few seconds, then says, very gently, "We don't have a lot of *time*."

Justin takes a deep breath. He nods. He wipes his eyes with his sleeve. And then he looks around.

"Wait until those two go into the portal," he says finally. His voice is even, drained of emotion. "Then I'll need a distraction."

Madeline relaxes a bit. The kid is finally back in the game.

"I got this," Peter says. Then they wait.

Mr. Trenchcoat appears to be briefing the new man and woman about the gas, then his silhouette blurs slightly, and he's holding two more of those gas masks. He hands one over to each. They put them on and step through the glowing Persian arch, disappearing into the lobby.

Justin looks at Peter, his eyes clearly saying *now.*

"Because you *are* a stupid little shit!" Peter shouts. "If I'd known you were going to fold like you did, I would have cut your fucking throat *months* ago!"

Justin takes a step back, startled. Mr. Trenchcoat whirls on them, looking annoyed.

"What did I *say,* sunshine?" He blurs for a second, then holds up a roll of duct tape. He kneels next to Peter, waving it in his face. "Do I have to *gag* you? It's gonna be real fun trying to get it off your burned face. Might take half your face with you! Normally they'd have rules against me doing shit like that, but guess what, pal? I'm officially dead!"

Mr. Trenchcoat is focused completely on the older man, and the man in the tan jacket is torn between Mr. Trenchcoat and keeping that portal open. It's the perfect opportunity. The young man backs up slowly, angling not for the glowing archway, but for the man-sized hole cut out of the first floor blast shielding.

The hole is still glowing with heat at the edges, but Madeline approves of the choice. He doesn't need to make it inside undamaged. He just needs to make it inside undamaged enough to do his job.

"Right. Where exactly are you going, kid?"

Justin turns and gapes as he sees Mr. Trenchcoat staring at him. Madeline frowns as she looks between the Mr. Trenchcoat shouting at the older guard, and the Mr. Trenchcoat blocking the young man's way.

Metahumans are annoying.

"It's just..." Justin turns to point back at Peter and Madeline. "I don't want to stand next to them."

"Tough," Mr. Trenchcoat says. "Look, count your blessings. All he can do is shout at you, now."

"I wish that were true," Justin says. Then he maces Mr. Trenchcoat in the face.

They'd searched him, of course. They'd taken his knife, his taser, his sidearm, and his riot stick. But they hadn't searched him—any of them, really—as thoroughly as they *should* have. The mace was in a tube up Justin's jacket sleeve. Mr. Trenchcoat shouts in pain, disappears... then the one in front of Peter reappears next to Justin, grabs his arm, and *twists,* disarming him as expertly as he did Madeline earlier... complete with shoulder throw.

That was a tactical mistake. The throw placed the guard farther from the glowing arch, which was probably what Mr. Trenchcoat wanted, but it also put him nearer to the tear in the blast shield.

Mr. Trenchcoat pulls out another pair of handcuffs. "Christ Almighty, talk about *ungrateful*."

Justin rolls to his feet with surprising speed, racing towards the tear. Mr. Trenchcoat snarls, pulls down his gas mask over his face, and disappears.

The act of pulling on his mask cost precious time, but he still appears in front of the tear before the young guard reaches it.

At that moment, Madeline finally finishes burning through her handcuffs.

The acid splashes on her hand, causing her vision to blur from pain, but that's not important. She rolls away from Peter, who has almost cut through his own, and charges the man in the tan jacket. He turns, startled, and the portal wavers. Then a dark shape rises off his shoulder, something birdlike and fierce, and slams into her like a ton of bricks. She falls on her back, gasping, as the bird-thing rakes a claw across her face. She feels a deep cold seep into her. She fights the urge to pass out.

The man in the tan jacket turns to Peter. Peter grins wickedly, pulling his hands from behind his back. He holds a tiny revolver.

"Gun!" the man in the tan jacket shouts.

He reaches out his hand, a dark energy flickering over it…

…the bird-thing launches into the sky with a screech of rage, descending on Peter…

…and Mr. Trenchcoat blips into sight right next to him, kicking him in his gun hand so hard Madeline can hear the bones break.

She nods to Justin. Without hesitation, he bolts toward the still-glowing tear.

"*Crap.*" Mr. Trenchcoat blurs again, but Justin has already thrown himself through the gap, crying in pain as he brushes against still-glowing metal. The pocket knife in his right hand has already punctured his neck by the time he hits the floor.

Madeline sighs in relief as she feels the energy release. The kid did it.

Inside the Haurspex Analytics lobby, six vaguely Greek statues begin to move.

Part Fifteen: Haruspex Analytics, Ground Floor Lobby

Brother Judgment looks around the room. One wall is cracked where the metal shell buckled inward. Concrete and glass litter the marble floor. Dust hangs in the air, settling on their uniforms as fine white powder. He turns to face his sister.

Sister Sentinel shrugs. "I only did the door." She jerks her thumb toward Red Shift. "He did the rest."

"True," Red Shift admits. He scans the room slowly, lights on his visor changing colors as the built-in sensors take readings. "This toxin is pretty nasty stuff, by the way. We may need to seal off the breach to keep it from getting out."

"About that..." Agent Grant is peering down at the controls the guards used to activate the alarm. It's the part of the desk CB dove behind—defying all probability, it's still working. "*Doctor Enigma* says the only reason his portal works is because of that hole."

"I see." Red Shift glances at the portal, then at the hole he punched through the wall. "Well, it looks like the toxin disperses pretty quickly as soon as it gets outside. I guess we're OK for a bit. What's our status?"

Agent Grant doesn't immediately reply. His outline blurs for a moment, then he makes a satisfied noise in the back of his throat as he manages to open a menu of commands on the small security screen set into the desk.

"Blink and Derecho are outside. Zero's team found two helicopters on the roof. Looks like we interrupted a getaway."

"Good," Red Shift says. He nods down to the menu on the screen. "Can you get anything useful out of that?"

Grant shakes his head. "It's pretty locked down. You know, it's almost as if they don't trust us."

* * *

Hair stands up on the back of CB's neck as he stares at the portal standing in the middle of the floor. Looking through it he can see David, standing a bit farther down the sidewalk bisecting the park, head bowed, one hand raised.

Teleportation is weird, CB thinks, and shivers, trying not to think too much about how *this* particular kind of teleportation is being done. David is using *magic,* and even if his version is new and not quite like the kind CB is familiar with, it's still rooted in the same kind of power that murdered every single person in his old apartment building. There are echoes of that power... the way it feels, oily, hot and cold at the same time, a pulse of power muted through layers of filth. At the same time, there's something else mixed through it. Something grounded, firmly rooted in this world in a way that dilutes the sense of wrongness until it is merely *unpleasant* and *complicated*.

CB scowls under his gas mask as he fights down his desire to recoil from the arch. He saw Bernard save the senator's life, and he *definitely* saw Bernard save *his* life from the Bowler Hat Twins.

He can almost hear Alex lecturing him that good work and clean work aren't always the same thing.

Now is not the time for purity tests.

Agent Grant, not wearing a gas mask, appears on the other side of the portal. He steps up to David and murmurs something in a low voice. David cocks his head to one side, listening without breaking his concentration, and nods once. Grant steps away, out of view. CB looks over his shoulder to see Grant, *with* a gas mask, leaning over the security monitor, Red Shift standing to one side offering advice as they try to get through whatever software is locking them out.

Brother Judgment looks up, head cocked to one side. "The rest of my team is coming in."

"Knock, knock!" CB turns toward the cheerful greeting to see a short, athletic man with dark, shoulder-length hair step through the portal. He's about five feet, five inches tall, lean, and moves like an acrobat or a dancer. His face is obscured by one of Thorpe's gas masks, and he's dressed in tight-fitting but flexible body armor. He wears a shoulder holster—the fancy auto-locking kind that doesn't require a thumb break—and a web belt with a few closed but obviously full pouches. His only other weapon is a straight-handled baton strapped to his upper thigh.

"This is Blink," Brother Judgment says.

Blink sighs, steps away from the portal, and looks around the room. "Jesus." He has a slight accent—CB places it as "South American," but can't be any more specific than that. "What happened in here? Your sister is scary when she gets pissed."

"*It wasn't me.*" Sister Sentinel speaks through clenched teeth. "All I did was the *door*."

Blink chuckles softly, then the space around him warps for a second, as if light were bending around him. He appears a few feet away from his previous spot. "Good. It was only blocking me from the outside."

He disappears again, appearing at the far end of the room, taking a position where he can watch the elevator and the stairwell.

"And this," Brother Judgment continues, "is Derecho."

CB looks back to the portal. A tall, slim woman with long, straight black hair steps through. She's not wearing body armor: she dresses simply in faded blue jeans, a red tank top shirt, and combat boots. Her one concession to a uniform appears to be a web utility belt similar to the one Blink wears.

Derecho nods to the room, spreads her hands, and rises into the air, not stopping until she reaches the ceiling. A soft breeze fills the room, stirring the dust slightly, but nothing more. CB is impressed: they said she was a weather controller, but nobody bothered to mention how much *control* she had. Most weather controllers fly by conjuring winds to hold them aloft. Derecho barely stirs the air in the room, which means she's restricting the *violent* winds—the ones strong enough to actually lift her—so that they're only inches from her body.

"Wow," CB says. "Do you have that much control offensively, too?"

Derecho glances down. She doesn't say anything, but extends one hand. A tiny cloud forms over it. Light flashes, and he hears a tiny, almost cartoonish rumble of thunder echo through the room.

"*Wow*," CB says again.

"She doesn't like to talk much," Brother Judgment says. "But she knows her business."

"Looks like it," CB agrees. "Hey, you know, we probably should have warned you about this earlier, but these jokers have a fetish for weather controllers. They have ties to PRODIGY."

"Agent Grant mentioned it," Brother Judgment says. "Anything else we need to know?"

"Uh…" CB frowns. "Yeah, actually. According to what Senator Morgan said earlier, they're *terrified* of psychics. Telepaths especially."

Brother Judgment shrugs. "Good to know, but it's hard to think of them being *more* pissed off at us right now."

CB laughs. "Fair. Speaking of, is your telepathy working in here?"

Brother Judgment nods.

"You have Blink and Derecho on point, that's good, but I was wondering if you could sense if people were *behind* all the closed doors back there. They'll send someone eventually. Advance warning would be nice."

"Already on it," Brother Judgment says. "I'm not reading anything so far. But if they send in more meat robots like Darius I won't sense *anything*."

"… Meat robots?" CB asks.

"*Darius?*" Red Shift looks up from the security panel, zeroing in on Brother Judgment. "*Clive* Darius?"

"Uh…" Brother Judgment stares back at Red Shift. "Yes?"

Red Shift takes two steps toward the telepath, fists clenching with an uncharacteristic show of emotion. "What does Darius have to do with this?"

Brother Judgment eyes him warily. "He's the reason I got pulled into all this. Is there a problem here?"

"No," Red Shift says. "Not with you, at any rate. It's just that—"

"Crap!" Agent Grant looks up, gaze fixed on the portal. "Hold on a sec." His outline blurs and disappears. Everyone in the lobby stares at the portal in surprise as angry shouting comes through it. They hear Agent Grant raising his voice, then he shouts wordlessly in pain.

"Gun!"

It's David's voice. Red Shift blurs into motion, streaking toward the portal, but skids to a halt as it wobbles and almost collapses. A dark figure leaps through the hole in the blast shield, crying out in pain as it hits one of the still-glowing edges. It falls to the ground in a heap.

Red Shift is there in a fraction of a second. Just as CB realizes they're looking at one of the security guards—the young one—Red Shift turns him over. Something is sticking out of his neck; blood pools on the floor beneath him as he makes soft, wet, choking sounds.

CB rummages through his trenchcoat pockets, looking for something useful to stop the bleeding. "What the *hell*?"

Everything happens at the same time.

The young guard on the floor stiffens, baring his teeth, his arms jerking out to his sides as if he were making a snow angel. CB takes a cautious step back, only to be knocked to the ground by Red Shift as a large shadowy fist passes over the spot where he used to be. Sister Sentinel, Brother Judgment, and Blink all start shouting warnings at the same time, even as they race forward. The wind in the room rises.

CB blinks to clear his eyes, and then he sees it: the six statues lining the wall are all moving.

Red Shift is already on his feet. CB rolls to one side as the closest statue—very *uncomfortably* close—punches into the ground where he'd been prone moments before. The marble shatters, leaving a deep, fist-shaped hole.

"OK..." CB gets to his feet and backs up quickly. "We got six evil magic statues." He fishes through his pockets for a cigarette. "Weren't they *smaller* before?"

The young guard gurgles again. His body jerks once, then rises into the air, flying into the wall behind them. He hits it with enough force to crack the sheet rock, so hard that the impact sounds *wet*. But his eyes still move, taking in the scene. His hands clench, and the statues form a circle, standing back to back. His mouth stretches into a rictus grin.

Agent Grant blips into the room. "Those fucking guards just went batshi—" His voice trails off as he takes in the scene.

"Right. I'll get the Doc."

He disappears again.

"So," Blink says, trying to keep his voice light. "Anyone got any ideas? I kinda feel like maybe we shouldn't just be standing around."

What remains of the young guard laughs, trailing off into an unpleasant gurgle. He nods his head, and the six statues nod in sync with him, copying the motion perfectly.

CB sticks an unlit cigarette in his mouth and fumbles for his lighter. "Let's make some gravel." He charges.

"You did *not* just say something that *stupid*," Sister Sentinel growls, but she charges in after him.

CB drops into a slide, passing under the legs of one of the statues, lighting his cigarette as the statue tries and fails to stomp him into the floor. He leans right as a large stone fist flies past him, impacting solidly into Sister Sentinel. The force of the blow lifts her off the floor, but her only reaction is to grab the arm that hit her, place her feet against the statue's forearm, and *pull*. Stone cracks like thunder as the statue's forearm is torn away from the rest of the statue. She drops the arm, twists in midair to land on her feet, and steps into her swing as she strikes the statue, her arm sinking elbow-deep into stone. CB leaps to the side as the arm Sister Sentinel just removed rises into the air and flies into another statue. It shatters without causing apparent harm, and he hears Brother Judgment curse in frustration.

"Forget the statues!" Red Shift shouts, then disappears in a blur of red motion as he races straight toward the young guard's body, still half-embedded in the wall.

Instantly the statues shift their focus. Their arms rise, moving in a way that appears coordinated even though CB can't understand exactly what the pattern is. One of the arms shudders and Red Shift goes flying across the room, hitting the floor, bouncing multiple times before sliding to a halt. He's on his feet almost instantly, and all the statues turn to face him, twelve arms—no, only eleven, CB amends—continuing their strange shifting pattern. Red Shift hesitates a moment, then blurs out of sight again, this time causing a loud, rumbling *boom* to fill the room as he goes supersonic.

And again there is the sound of stone hitting flesh, and again Red Shift is swept to one side, this time crashing through the front wall and hitting the metal shield with an almost gong-like sound. And *again* Red Shift surges forward, and *again* he is swept aside by one of the statues' arms.

"How?" Sister Sentinel, thrown clear of the statue she was fighting when Red Shift first attacked, shakes her head in disbelief. "They aren't even moving that fast."

Red Shift goes in for the fourth time—this time not opting for a straight shot, but trying to weave around the statues to get at the remains of the guard—but even though he changes direction faster than CB can track, he still winds up being knocked across the room.

"They're not matching his speed," CB says. "They're predicting what he's going to do."

The realization shakes the rest of the group out of their reverie. As Red Shift picks himself off the floor yet again, one of the statues rises into the air, and with a grunt of effort from Brother Judgment, slams into the one next to it just as Sister Sentinel bears down on the one missing its arm. Her first strike knocks a large chunk of rock out of its midsection, the second cuts the statue in half. The wind in the room rises sharply, and the last three remaining statues wobble in place, momentarily unable to act as they're forced to fight to keep their balance. CB looks up to see Derecho, her attention now focused fully on the statues, holding out her arms, palms extended, toward the melee below her.

Agent Grant reappears next to CB in a blur. "Doc's coming." A moment later, Doctor Enigma—not wearing a gas mask, CB notes—runs through his portal, closing it behind him. He takes in the scene just as Red Shift, now opposed by three statues struggling to stay on their feet, streaks toward the embedded guard without any opposition.

Doctor Enigma's eyes go wide. "Stop!"

Red Shift's head turns slightly in response to the cry, but it's far too late to change anything. Once within reach of the guard, Red Shift's arms blur, and a moment later something the size of a basketball falls to the ground. It rolls to a stop just behind the statues. The security guard's head, mouth locked in a savage grin, stares sightlessly up at them. Almost immediately the remaining statues stop moving.

"Christ." Agent Grant takes an involuntary step back away from the severed head. "Jesus."

Red Shift slides down the length of the wall, landing on his feet. He stares at CB intently. "We have a problem?"

CB stares at the severed head, feeling a little sick, but he shakes his head. "Can't go halfway with magic."

"Red Shift." Doctor Enigma is standing next to CB, his body rigid, his voice crisp with command. "*Everyone.* Get away from the statues, now. This is *very important.*"

Alan Grant blurs, disappears, and reappears on the other side of the room. Sister Sentinel takes a few steps back, and Brother Judgment rises into the air until he's hovering next to Derecho.

Red Shift skirts around the rubble until he stops at Doctor Enigma's left. "What's wrong?" He cocks his head to one side, as if something new is occurring to him. "Trap?"

"Not exactly. More like a contingency plan." Doctor Enigma stretches out his arm, fingers spread. "I'm trying to stop it."

A blinding white light fills the room at the same time as a wave of force expands outward. CB feels himself lifted off the ground and hurled into the last piece of the security desk that's still standing. The air rushes out of his lungs as he rolls onto his hands and knees. For a few seconds all he can do is gasp for breath.

"Ow…" Doctor Enigma's voice comes from somewhere to his left. "That… didn't work."

"Guys…" Sister Sentinel's voice is as strong as ever. "Shake it off, OK? Something's happening."

CB forces himself to stand, blinking rapidly to try to get past the spots dancing in front of his eyes. David is still down. Red Shift is down but getting up. Agent Grant is at the far end of the room, next to Blink. Derecho and Brother Judgment are overhead, but Brother Judgment's trenchcoat is singed.

Sister Sentinel is standing where she had been moments ago. Her trenchcoat is torn in multiple places, but she looks otherwise untouched.

She points. CB follows the gesture.

The guard's head, mouth still twisted into that sickly, deranged grin, is *floating* seven feet off the ground. As CB watches, the rest of the body peels itself out from the indentation where it was stuck in the wall, then floats to place itself directly underneath the head. Stone cracks as the remains of the six statues break apart into tiny stone chips, the largest no bigger than one of CB's fingers. The stones rise into the air and begin to spin counter-clockwise, the corpse floating in the eye of a stone hurricane.

CB takes a step back. Red Shift, now back on his feet, takes a step back. Even Sister Sentinel takes a step back. And then, all at once, the stone hurricane collapses in on itself, covering the corpse, rock merging smoothly into rock, subtly changing texture and tone until it looks almost metallic. The surface of the rough humanoid shape ripples and smooths, gaining definition and refinement, becoming more distinctly human in shape though considerably larger. As the last of the rock merges into place, what remains is a single figure, a large humanoid shape about fifteen feet tall. A line of symbols in an unknown script trails down each arm and leg, and a single massive rune glows purple on its chest.

"Oh," CB says. "Crap."

Agent Grant blurs into view again, immediately to CB's left. "That looks familiar," he says. "Anyone else think that looks familiar?"

"Yes," Red Shift says. "Now that you mention it... I'm pretty sure this is going to be a harder fight."

Part Sixteen: Haruspex Analytics, Roof

Torn bits of helicopter are heaped into three neat piles at the center of the roof. The team gathers at the heavy security door leading to the stairwell. On a hunch, Jenny scrolls quickly through a number of different settings in her visor, chooses one, and waits as the display fades from the color palette of normal vision into the blues, yellows, and reds of heat signatures. The door is mostly varying shades of blue, with some yellows around the digital keypad that serves as an external lock.

"I don't think there's anyone on the other side," Jenny says. "Not reading any heat."

Street Ronin touches something on the side of his visor, then nods in agreement. He turns to Jack, who stands beside Agents Grant and Hu, waiting patiently.

Street Ronin gestures to the door. Jack flashes him a lopsided grin, steps forward, and with a single smooth kick the door buckles inward, tearing off its hinges and hitting then tipping over a guard rail. The sound of heavy metal tumbling down a flight of stairs follows.

Grant shakes his head. "Must be nice."

"Pretty nice," Jack agrees. "Come on." He steps through the now doorless frame and starts down the stairwell. Street Ronin follows, and Jenny steps in behind him as Grant and Hu take up the rear.

They descend a full flight of stairs and come out on a landing considerably larger than the one on the roof. The misshapen security door is here. Deep grooves cut into the floor from the stairs to the center of the landing, where the twisted rectangle sits, bending up like a misshapen toboggan. The stairs continue down, but Street Ronin places his hand on Jack's shoulder, and the large man steps onto the landing and moves over to the door leading out to the floor.

The door has another electronic lock, but it doesn't look nearly as sturdy as the one sitting in the middle of the landing floor. Street Ronin moves carefully to the left of the door and crouches. Jenny moves immediately to his left, crouching after him. Agent Grant hands Hu his pistol, then produces another. They position themselves farther back and to the right.

"Scrapper Jack goes in first," Street Ronin says. "Zero, you go in after. Agent Grant, Agent Hu... no offense, but I think it'd be better for you to hang back initially. Sidearms in a melee isn't a good mix."

"No shooting from the back," Grant says. "Got it."

"Zero, try to find a computer. We'll give you room to work."

"Got it." Jenny forces the tremor out of her voice. She wonders, yet again, if she'll ever get used to this.

Street Ronin raises his right hand, showing four fingers, and silently counts down.

four-three-two-one

Jack kicks. This time the door shatters, splintering into a shower of wood shards. Gunshots fill the hallway, and Jenny sees Jack's shirt ripple as multiple projectiles hit his chest. Jack nods once, then breaks into a run, disappearing from view.

Street Ronin stretches out on the floor, peering around the corner as he brings his rifle to bear. At the same time, Jenny launches past him, bolting through the door frame.

Her armored feet land on thick, red carpet—not the kind you get in regular office spaces, where the rank-and-file work. Jack barrels on, rushing past a set of doors as the gunfire somehow begins to sound more urgent. She can see three figures crouched about halfway down the hall, little bursts of light flashing from carbines. Jenny hears the crack of Street Ronin's rifle, and one of the figures falls over, gripping his leg.

Jenny focuses on the doors Jack just ran past. They're as good a place to start as any. She chooses the one on the right, shoving her shoulder into it with all her strength. She's not as strong as Jack, but the door rips free of its latch, swinging open so quickly that she nearly stumbles into the room.

She's momentarily surprised to find two armed men in the room, crouched by the door. They are nearly as surprised to find her.

The moment passes. The armed, black-clad men step back from the door, raising their carbines. Jenny lashes out, snagging the arm of one and pulling as she steps forward, placing him between herself and his partner. His weapon isn't fully raised and it discharges into the floor as he jerks forward. She twists his arm, and he cries out in pain as the carbine clatters to the floor. His partner takes a *second* step back, raising his weapon, fully intending to fire whether or not there's someone standing in his way.

Jenny pushes. The trapped man flies into his partner, both collapsing to the ground in a tangled heap. The second carbine fires wildly, leaving small holes in the ceiling and one of the walls—but not getting anywhere near Jenny.

She kicks the carbine out of his hand, hard, and it clatters uselessly across the floor. She looks down at the men, struggling to untangle themselves, wondering what to do next.

She knows what Street Ronin would do.

She doesn't know what *she* will do.

A gun fires immediately behind her. She whirls around to see Agent Grant standing in the doorway, firing across the hall into the now-opened door on the other side, where a third black-clad man carrying a carbine ducks behind the wall. Grant's outline blurs and he disappears. The room across the hall flashes as a gun fires, then she hears the wet thump of a body hitting the floor.

Grant steps into the doorway, giving her a thumbs up.

Jenny checks on the men on the floor. One has actually crawled to his knees, reaching for one of the carbines. Jenny drives her armored knee into the man's face, breaking his nose. He falls, head snapping back as his hands fly to his face. He hits the ground hard as blood spills through his fingers.

Jenny grabs the second man by his collar, dragging him upright only to shove him into the wall separating the office and the hall. It's not a load-bearing wall and it cracks where the man hits. He slides to the ground, unmoving.

Jenny scans the room quickly. It should be as good as any... she crosses quickly, stepping over the man still covering his face, and opens a faux wooden door at the far end.

Jenny activates her comm. "Found it. Down the hall, first door to the right."

"Copy." Street Ronin's voice is calm and measured. She hears careful, precise shots echoing down the hall. "I'll be there soon."

The desk is higher quality than the average office worker's, so Jenny figures it's probably a middle manager or a specialist's desk. On it sits an empty laptop cradle—the employee must have taken the laptop home.

That's OK; she doesn't actually need the computer.

Two ethernet cables extend from the back of the cradle, traveling down the length of the desk and disappearing into a floor plate. Jenny pries up the plate to reveal two ethernet sockets, one green and one red. She toggles the comm on again.

"Do you want fast or quiet? I can't do both."

"They already know we're here," Street Ronin says.

"Fast it is." Jenny removes the red ethernet cable, then pops open a panel on her armor's left arm. She pulls out the end of a ruggedized ethernet cable and plugs it directly into the red socket. Immediately her helmet's display shows its computer running through thousands of login scripts, trying to take advantage of one of the publicly known exploits before moving on to the creative stuff.

Seconds pass. A few more shots ring out, then everything falls silent. A moment later Street Ronin and Agent Grant appear. Street Ronin takes note of

Jenny, sitting on the floor with the ethernet cable running into her armor, and takes cover behind the mildly overpriced desk, his rifle trained on the door. Agent Grant stays in the outer room, occasionally peering up and down the hall.

"Where's Jack? Hu?"

"They got called to the lobby," Street Ronin says. "Apparently there's another giant magic robot."

"So it's you, me, and five copies of Agent Grant?"

"Not copies!" Grant protests from the other room.

"Two copies," Street Ronin says. "He's still being used as a relay until we punch through whatever's blocking our signal, so three of him are spoken for. Someone has noticed us, by the way. Travers is picking up a lot of crosstalk on the LEO bands."

"Not copies!" Grant insists.

"I hope this Agent Henry is as good as Travers thinks he is," Jenny says.

"He is," Grant says. "And the new Sky Commando is pretty on top of things."

"David thinks so," Jenny says. "He trained her."

She can *feel* the disapproval radiating through Street Ronin's visor. She sighs, exasperated.

"Fine. *Doctor Enigma* thinks so."

"The distinction is important," Street Ronin says.

"If you say so." Jenny doesn't bother rolling her eyes—it wouldn't do any good, since her face is covered. "Though I should point out that so far Crossfire is the only group I've met who seems to think that."

"Do you know if Doctor Enigma is going to want to keep his identity secret?"

"…No," Jenny admits. "How could I? He hasn't said."

"Then until he makes the explicit decision to reveal his identity to the world, maybe we should stick to calling him only by his code name. Especially while we're in a hostile environment."

Jenny tries to find a way around that point and fails. "I really hate how much that makes sense."

"At least you admit it," Street Ronin says, a hint of grim amusement in his voice. "How's it going?"

"Their security is *really good,*" Jenny says. "I've burned through all the script kiddie stuff and moved into 'be creative.' I wish CB was up here, I could use him to make it go faster."

Grant laughs nervously. "He's a little busy right now."

"Excuses…" Jenny mutters. She clenches her jaw, fighting back her impatience. They'll give her the time she needs, she just needs to make sure not to waste any of it.

She almost misses it because she assumes it won't be there to begin with. A very simple, basic flaw on an old network switch that doesn't look like it's been patched in years. Once she's past that, there are a lot more files to see. All she has to do is find an account with a poorly-chosen password… even in a company specializing in security, employees get lazy.

"I'm in!" she says. "I'm looking for something useful…"

It's not too long before she finds a schematic of the building. She goes through it quickly, looking for something obvious. She finds it.

"Found a building schematic. I think they need to get to one of the sublevels. Six floors down from the lobby."

"Good work," Street Ronin says. "Agent Grant, did you get that?"

"Yeah," Grant says. "Any chance I can see the map?"

Jenny looks around and spies a standalone inkjet printer set on a shelf next to the desk. "Hold on." She unplugs herself from the floor socket, then walks over to the printer, studying it quickly. She jerks a USB cable out of the side, then a USB connector extends from her left index finger. "This will only take a second."

The printer lights up, screeches once, then begins printing out pages. A minute later, she grabs the printout from the tray then walks into the other room, handing it to Grant.

Agent Grant scans the printout, quickly flipping pages. He stops at one and points. "Here?"

"That's the one," Jenny says.

"Right. Back in a sec." Agent Grant blurs for a moment, semi-fades from sight, only to reappear again, no longer gripping a printout in his hands.

"CB's a little distracted, but it looks like he's assembling a C team."

"Time for us to move, then," Street Ronin says. "Zero, are there any other interesting places on the map?"

"A few that don't look like places you'd find in an office building," Jenny says, "but they're unlabeled."

"Sounds like places to visit. Where is the closest?"

"Five floors down," Jenny says.

Street Ronin climbs to his feet, readjusting his grip on his rifle. "After you."

Part Seventeen: Haruspex Analytics, Also Not

Phyllis, Michelle, and Simon huddle around the door separating the stairwell from the rest of the floor. Everything is quiet—Phyllis resists the urge to tag *too quiet* to the end of that thought—and the few sounds they hear echo more loudly than they should.

The door itself is not your typical stairwell door: it's made of heavy, windowless, reinforced steel and sports a complex electronic lock surrounding the L-shaped handle. A thumbprint, shining bright blue in the dim light, is set into the grip.

"Has anyone ever been on this floor before?" Simon is whispering; in the silence it sounds like a shout. Michelle flinches, drawing away, and Phyllis has to force herself not to do the same. She shakes her head.

"I didn't even know it was here until I saw that floor plan," Phyllis says.

"I think we're stuck." Michelle's voice trembles as she forces it to be loud enough. "I don't think we're going to get that to open."

Simon nods in agreement. "Stuck." He's still whispering but his voice is tighter and sharper. He's trying to fight back panic.

"No." Phyllis keeps her voice firm and steady. "There's no going back now. Simon, how much time do we have until they turn the power back on?"

Simon stares at her dumbly, blinks, then forces himself to focus. He pulls out his phone and stares at the display. "Five minutes."

"Doesn't matter," Michelle says, pointing at the door. "It's still on. It obviously has an independent power supply."

"Obviously," Phyllis agrees. "But there aren't any eyes and ears. That means I don't have to be quiet about this."

Phyllis' go-bag is essentially an oversized purse. She catches all kinds of hell about that from her co-workers, but the whole point is that she can carry it in public and nobody thinks twice about it. Unlike her *actual* purse, her go-bag is very organized. She draws out a small square wrapped in cloth and unwraps it quickly.

Michelle and Simon exchange nervous glances.

"Is that what I think it is?" Simon asks.

"Probably," Phyllis says, holding it up.

Michelle shakes her head. "You carry a *shaped charge* in your purse?"

"I'm not going to carry it in the open," Phyllis says. "Besides, it's not primed." She studies the door for a moment, then places the charge an inch away from the opening edge. It bonds to the wall instantly. She pushes her thumb through the surface, and a moment later the entire charge lights up red and begins blinking rapidly.

"*Now* it's primed," Phyllis says. "We should probably head back up the stairs a bit."

The three of them move quickly up the stairs until the door disappears from view.

"I can't believe you—"

Simon doesn't get a chance to finish his sentence. A small but vigorous explosion *booms* beneath them; burning smoke rushes up the stairs past them.

Phyllis coughs, waving her hand in front of her face in a vain attempt to disperse the haze as she returns to the now-charred stairwell. The steel door still stands. The wall next to the door, however, has been blown to pieces, creating a gap large enough for any of them to step through sideways. She nods in satisfaction.

"Let's go," she says.

"Wait!" Simon doesn't bother to whisper at this point. "What if somebody heard that?"

"They'll think it's coming from the roof," Phyllis says. "Come on, we have to get to the other side."

With that she steps into the floor proper.

They stand in a long hallway, floor covered in a thick red carpet, walls gleaming white, drop tiles and florescent light panels set in the ceiling. The proportions of the hallway are *wrong*—the hallway is too wide, the walls are too tall, and they seem to curve in ever so slightly, putting all the angles off kilter. The smell of smoke fades rapidly as the whisper of unseen ventilation disperses the product of Phyllis' shaped charge. The other side of the steel door, also undamaged from the explosion, has a crash bar instead of an l-handle.

I guess they only want to keep people out? Or they have other ways of keeping people in... It's an unpleasant notion. Phyllis pushes it aside.

Michelle steps through the narrow gap in the wall and looks around. "How'd you know the wall would blow? If I were putting in a door like that I'd make sure the walls were reinforced steel, too."

"So would I," Phyllis says. "But the door was obviously added later. They had to work with what was already here, so they framed it with steel and relied on monitoring to tell them if somebody tried to pull a stunt like this. Only right now, monitoring has a lot of holes in it, and for the next four minutes or so, one of those holes is right here."

"Let's be gone before that hole gets filled in," Simon says.

"Agreed," Phyllis says. "Michelle?"

Michelle pulls out her smartphone, bringing up a map on her screen. She pinches at the image, expanding it, and scrolls around until she locates their position. She points.

"Left."

"Let's start moving," Phyllis urges, and they head down the hall at a brisk pace. "Clock is ticking…"

A full minute passes in silence, their feet making soft *fwit fwit fwit* noises as they brush over the unusually thick carpet. Phyllis can see their destination: another reinforced steel door with a crash bar.

Phyllis quickens her pace to a light jog. They have about three minutes until the cameras on this floor reconnect with the Labyrinth, and she doesn't want to be here when it happens.

"We're not getting any closer." Simon's voice is dead calm—a sure sign that he's just on the verge of breaking… not that she can blame him.

"Just chalk it up to *magic* and keep moving," Phyllis says. "If it gets too close to time, we'll duck into a side office and figure out a way to hide until the next brownout."

"*What* side office?" Michelle snarls. "There aren't any fucking *doors*."

That makes Phyllis stop in her tracks. She's so focused on the exit, she hasn't been paying attention to her surroundings, and Michelle is right. There *aren't* any doors. It's an impossibly long hallway with strange angles, and no doors at all.

"This… floor…" Simon's voice is still dead calm, but he's stumbling over his words. "It can't even fit in the building. And it's… just a hallway? Phyllis. We don't have enough time to figure this out."

"We gotta make the time, Simon, or we aren't getting out of this building alive." It's a risk, piling that on top of the emotional load he's already trying to carry, but compared to the strangeness of this floor it's a direct, relatable problem. She can see him focus on that, discarding everything else. He stares down the hall for a second, then turns to Michelle.

"The walls bend *in*, just a little. Do you see it?"

Michelle frowns and turns her head sideways, one eye disappearing underneath her hoodie as the other squints.

"Yeah. I think so." She runs one hand up and down the wall to her right. "I think it's an illusion. It feels straight when I touch it."

Simon nods, placing his hand against the wall, and starts walking toward the emergency exit. After ten paces he stops. "Door."

Phyllis squints. "I don't see anything."

"It's part of the illusion." Simon traces a door-shaped square along the wall, and for a moment the surface ripples like water. "The image is bending in, so it covers the door. I think that's what's happening."

"Mystery solved," Phyllis says. "Now I think we have just enough time to—"

Down the hall they hear the very distinct *ding* of an elevator, followed by the sound of a door sliding open. Simon's eyes widen in shock.

"Shit." Michelle places her hand against the wall, tracing over part of the region where Simon claimed to find a door. Her hand closes on something and she pushes. A crack appears in the wall, opening to reveal a space beyond. Michelle shoulders Simon, who stumbles into the room, then slips in behind him. "Come on!"

Phyllis follows, immediately closing the door behind her and placing her ear against it.

"Phyllis…" Michelle's voice catches slightly.

"Shhh. They're coming this way." Phyllis closes her eyes, trying to focus only on sound.

Multiple footsteps, all muffled by the carpet, but there are enough to register as a crowd. Phyllis hears voices as well, growing louder and more distinct as they draw near.

"…think you should let me take care of this," one of the voices is saying. It's a rough, older voice, obviously a native of the city.

"Absolutely not." Phyllis tenses at the all-too-recognizable voice of the Chairman. "You have had two opportunities to deal with your animus toward that one already, and you failed both times."

"Not because of *him*." The rough voice turns sulky and defensive.

"Irrelevant, and I will hear no more of it. We are moving to the next phase *now*. You are needed for that. There is little time for anything else."

"…Yes sir." The rough-voiced man chokes out the words reluctantly, voice laced with bitterness.

"Why are we here?" That's a German accent. Richter? If so, that means the rough-voiced man is probably Plague. Phyllis grips the doorframe as a wave of what she hopes is psycho-somatic nausea washes over her.

"We need an alternate point of exit," the Chairman says. "A room has been prepared for us. I regret this experience will be... unpleasant. It should not, however, be fatal."

"Fatal?" A calm voice, with just an edge of concern. Phyllis recognizes it instantly, and her lip curls in disgust.

"It will be *fine*, Jason." *That* is Mara Ioannou. "It will be unpleasant, nothing more. That said..." She hesitates. "What of our guest?"

"Our guest..." Phyllis hears footsteps growing closer, and suddenly the Chairman's voice comes from the other side of the door. "Thank you, Mara. In all the excitement I had forgotten."

Phyllis takes a sudden step back, breath catching in her chest as the door handle begins to turn.

"We cannot take him with us," Mara warns.

The door handle stops turning.

If he opens this door it's all over.

"We cannot *leave* him, Mara."

"We don't have a place prepared." Mara's voice is gentle, but firm. "We can't *contain* him. Besides, he isn't *necessary*."

"I take your meaning," the Chairman says, "but I quite disagree. Still, there may be a third option..."

Phyllis feels a sudden wave of cold emanating from the other side of the door—a cold so unrelenting it's all she can do from gasping at the sudden change. The hairs on the back of her neck stand on end as cold radiates from the door in one, two, three pulsating waves, then the cold is gone.

"Ah!" Mara says. "You've cut him off."

"Yes," the Chairman says, "on this end. Whatever may happen to the rest of this place, he will be wholly unaffected by it—and will be unreachable by all, until I restore what I severed. We'll retrieve him when we have what we need on hand to contain him. It's not what I would prefer... but he should be quite secure until we're ready."

Seconds pass, then something *clicks* on the other side of the hall, and the footsteps move off carpet, onto stone. The door *clicks* a second time as it swings shut. The hallway is silent once again.

Phyllis lets out the breath she didn't realize she was holding, and allows herself to relax a little.

"We're going to miss our window," she says. "But at least they didn't come in here."

"Phyllis." Michelle's voice is low and soft, as if she were trying to soothe a wild animal. "Turn around."

That brief moment of relaxation fades as Phyllis opens her eyes, turns, and takes in the room for the first time.

It is, to all appearances, a small Victorian parlor. Bookcases line two of the walls; a small fireplace, fire cracking merrily in the hearth, sits just to the left of the door. The final wall is taken up with a large, thick-paned window, curtains open, revealing the scene of a small cliff overlooking a long, sandy beach. The sound of surf crashing against the shore, and gulls crying in the distance, mix together with the crackling fire to create a calm, soothing environment. Two chairs, one set on each side of the window, are divided by a small table supporting an elaborate tea set. Neither of the chairs quite fit with the rest of the Victorian décor, but they look comfortable.

Sitting in the chair furthest from the fireplace is an older man, perhaps in his mid-sixties, refined and elegant, with thinning, snow-white hair. He stares out the window, his expression a mixture of contentment and hopelessness. He doesn't appear to have noticed them.

Simon glances at Michelle and Phyllis, looking for direction. Michelle pulls at the drawstrings of her hoodie, disappearing behind the hood as it closes over her face. Phyllis stares at the old man, thinking furiously. Finally she speaks.

"LaFleur?"

The man's gaze moves from the window to her, focusing for a moment into something impossibly sharp and calculating, then soften as his gaze starts to drift back.

"Overmind."

The eyes sharpen again, soften again, but this time they stay on her.

"Who…" The man's voice is dry and cracked, the voice of a man lost in the desert, dying of thirst. "Who are you?"

Phyllis glances at her companions. Simon is gaping at her in bewilderment. Michelle is still turtled in her hoodie. Her resolve firms.

"My name is Phyllis Tanner," she says. "And these are my friends. We're leaving. We thought you might like to leave with us."

LaFleur—she's positive that's who he is—furrows his brow, as though the concept were foreign to him. "Leave?"

"That's right," Phyllis says. "Leave. I think your friends are here. I think you might want to help them."

At the word *friend*, LaFleur's gaze focuses even further. "Jack. Jack is my friend."

"OK," Phyllis says. "Jack. Good. Let's go look for him. Let's go find your friend."

LaFleur nods slowly. He blinks, once, and his gaze drifts away from her again—but this time, it's as if he's taking in his surroundings for the first time in a very long while.

"How?" The question is so plaintive, so utterly lost, it almost sounds as if it was asked by a child.

Phyllis takes a deep breath. "Well," she says, "I think we start by getting you out of that chair." She extends her hand. "Come on. Let me help you up."

His gaze focuses on her hand, sharpening again. Slowly he extends his own hand to grasp hers. The grip is faint at first, his hand feeble, but as it closes on hers, strength returns.

"Yes," he says, a spark of life returning to his voice. "I think... I think I would very much appreciate your help."

Phyllis nods, pulling up. LaFleur rises to his feet, brushing against the table slightly as he rises. The tea set rattles, tea spilling out of a cup set carelessly on the table's edge.

LaFleur sways slightly, and Phyllis steps forward, allowing him to grab her shoulder for support. He's shorter than she is, Phyllis realizes, and for a moment he looks so frail she's afraid he'll collapse into her arms. The moment passes, his balance returns, and all fragility falls away. He lets go of her shoulder, squeezes her hand once, and then lets go, standing on his own.

"Thank you," he says. His back straightens, and while he's still shorter than Phyllis he suddenly seems like the tallest person in the room. "Thank you *very* much."

Part Eighteen: Haruspex Analytics, Ground Floor Lobby

The massive stone fist misses CB by inches. The floor shatters, stone chips flying into the air like shrapnel, forcing CB to twist even further to avoid the debris.

He stares at the fist, gaze traveling the length of the golem's arm, taking in the intricate blue-glowing runes cut deep into the stone. Three of the runes at the wrist have gone dark. Each time a rune goes dark, the golem repairs itself.

There are a *lot* of runes on that arm. And the other arm. And both legs.

"This is getting old..." He tries to keep his voice casual as he rolls to his feet, noting the golem shifting its weight as it prepares to advance.

"He's not ready yet." Agent Grant's voice *is* casual—of course, he's on the other side of the hall, kneeling in front of David Bernard, watching him closely. David sits cross-legged on the floor, eyes closed, muttering something beneath his breath. "His eyes aren't open yet."

CB grimaces. David said he wouldn't be able to speak while preparing, so that was the signal they were looking for. "Well, great." He takes a deep breath, yells, and charges directly at the golem.

He wouldn't have minded a little more backup, but this needs to be done right... and if everyone is in the middle of a grand melee when it starts, it won't be. So he has to do it the hard way.

I hate the hard way...

He feels the world shift around him as possibilities begin to fall into place. If he steps *here*, then turns *there*, twists at *just the right angle*, at *just the right time*...

The golem's fist swings uselessly over his head as CB slides between its legs. He's on his feet before the golem has a chance to turn, and then in two steps and a jump he's on the thing's back, one arm wrapped around its neck.

He hears laughing. Thin, ragged laughter, muffled through layers of stone, rises out of the golem's torso. The security guard—or, more accurately, the guard's *corpse*—is in there, somewhere, and he finds this *amusing*.

The golem stops turning and straightens to its full height. It's *growing*, and is now so tall that CB can touch the ceiling if he really wants to. He inches to the side as one of the golem's hands tries to grab him. Stone fingers brush his trenchcoat, but close on nothing.

The golem turns sharply, trying to shake CB off. It backs into the wall where it had once been six Greek statues. CB lets go just before the golem strikes, ducking into a roll as he hits the floor. He's on his feet again as the golem pulls itself out of the wall. He takes a ragged breath, preparing for its next move…

"Eyes open!" Grant shouts.

CB steps back.

A stiff wind rises, followed by blinding white light as lightning arcs across the room, enveloping the golem in a halo of blue and white fire. Its torso smokes, the stone turning glassy and smooth where the lightning hits. It staggers, but doesn't fall.

A loud *booooom* splits the air as a red blur streaks across the room, smashing into the golem at Mach 2. The impact would tear any normal statue to pieces—in this case the golem staggers again, arms flailing for balance, and finally topples over onto its back. Red Shift rolls nimbly off to the right as Sister Sentinel, shouting at the top of her lungs, lifts the torn revolving door and brings the entire weight of it down on the golem's right leg.

The leg shatters, bits of stone and stone dust flying everywhere. She doesn't take a moment to appreciate her work: instead, she hefts the door up again and brings it down on the golem's *left* leg. This time, it's the *door* that breaks, unable to handle the second blow, but it takes a chunk of leg with it. Sister Sentinel drops the remains of the door, clenches her fists, and starts pounding away at the crater in the left leg. One, two, three blows, and the leg splits at the upper thigh.

The golem is not idle, however—it props itself up with its left arm while its right fist descends, at great speed, toward the small of Sister Sentinel's back. CB starts to shout a warning, but the fist stops abruptly, inches from the woman as she kicks the lower portion of the left leg away from the body. CB glances at Brother Judgment. He stands rigid, left arm extended, hand trembling. He can't see the man's expression, his face covered by the gas mask as it is, but he can see sweat on his forehead.

"Sis." Brother Judgment's voice is shaking too. Restraining the fist is taking a lot of effort.

Sister Sentinel looks up and starts in surprise as she sees the fist. Then she wraps her arms around the wrist and steps aside. "Got it!"

Brother Judgment relaxes. The Golem starts to raise its arm again, trying to pull her off the floor, but she flips over the arm, places both feet against its side, and pushes, twisting with her waist. Stone *snaps* and *cracks* as the forearm breaks off, causing the remaining stump to flail uselessly.

Red Shift descends on the other arm, fists blurring, generating a continuous string of sonic booms as he leaves small holes in the golem's sole means of support. Just as Sister Sentinel tears off the right arm, the left collapses on itself, and once again the golem is prone.

"Now!" Sister Sentinel shouts, as she and Red Shift race down the length of the lobby to the far end, where the others are waiting. CB backs away, still facing the creature, just in case he needs to distract it again.

The air above the golem's torso ripples and blurs, and then Agent Grant and Blink appear, both crouching on its chest, each holding what looks to be a miniature claymore mine. They both set their munitions on the golem's torso—Blink's near the waist, Grant's near the neck—and then the air ripples again, and both are gone.

"Come on, Chief!" Grant calls. CB turns to see that he and Blink are both holding detonators in their hands.

CB runs toward them.

"Now!" Grant shouts, and he and Blink both close their hands in the same way. The room fills with yet another loud *BOOOOOM*, and CB turns to see the golem—or what's left of it—lying in absolute ruin, its limbs destroyed, its torso blown apart. He can see bits of white mixed among the rubble, and realizes with a shudder that he is staring at pieces of bone.

The room is silent a moment, other than the sound of heavy breathing through gas masks, and then blue light shines from the destroyed golem, bright enough to fill half the room.

"It's starting!" Red Shift calls out, and CB can see the dust and rock and yes, the bits of bone start to move. The torso comes together in a rough outline, and in a matter of seconds the pieces of rock fuse together as the golem begins to reform.

Still, it isn't happening instantly. This one is going to take a little time. That was the point—to break it down enough that repairing itself would take *time*.

David Bernard runs forward, passing CB with his arms extended, purple-white energy swirling around them like miniature alien storms. He stops in front of the reforming golem, thrusts his hands forward, and the energy pours out of his hands into the reforming torso. The golem twitches, then goes still, seams in the torso reappearing and widening. More blue light flares, and the rocks begin to fuse together again. Bernard sets his jaw, narrows his eyes, and the purple-white light grows brighter, causing the rocks to start falling apart again.

And then the blue light flares. Again.

Jesus, it's still going, even with our own wizard.

"Help him!" CB gestures to the reforming rocks. "Break apart the big pieces. Make it work harder to do less!"

Red Shift is there in a blur, arms almost invisible as he starts punching holes into the golem at supersonic speeds. Sister Sentinel is only a few steps behind him, pounding at its torso with such force that she breaks off a quarter of it even as more blue light flashes and other bits reform. Some of the stone skittering across the floor toward the golem slides *away* from it as Brother Judgment passes his left hand across the floor in a sweeping motion. Even Agent Grant joins in, having acquired a sledgehammer from somewhere. The black-suited man starts pounding away at the arm Sister Sentinel tore off the golem, sending stone chips flying.

CB looks up at Derecho, floating just below the ceiling, overlooking the scene. She notices, and shakes her head slightly. She can't use her lightning with everyone right on top of the target.

Derecho can't get a shot, and Blink and I are pretty useless right now. Outstanding.

The blue light flares again, brighter this time. Once again, the torso starts repairing itself, and once again the rubble in the room is dragged toward it.

"How many times is it gonna do that?" Brother Judgment asks. He sounds tired. CB doesn't really understand how telekinesis works, but he knows that interacting with magic makes everything more difficult.

"Depends on our wizard," CB says.

"Hmm." Brother Judgment's voice is wry behind his mask. "Not sure I'm ready for a world where that's a thing."

CB snorts. "You and me both…"

He takes a moment to assess their progress and shakes his head. "Grant! We need more firepower. Can you spare Jack and Hu?"

Grant brings his sledgehammer down on a corner of the separated arm. A chunk of stone breaks off and almost immediately moves back into place, filling in the hole as if nothing happened. He swears and swings at the same spot. "On it."

They redouble their efforts, but it soon becomes clear they're only managing to just barely keep the golem's ability to heal in check. That's fine in theory—letting the golem burn itself out trying to rebuild itself is a workable tactic.

Unfortunately, everyone is getting tired.

Light pours through the Red-Shift-shaped hole in the outer wall, and Agent Hu, already transformed into living flame, flies through. She gives the room a once-over and focuses on the golem.

"Clear out!" Hu positions herself directly over the golem. Red Shift and Sister Sentinel back away. Agent Grant teleports to the other side of the room.

The blue light flares again. Immediately the torso begins to close up, and the right arm slides across the floor, placing itself into the stump. Then *Hu* flares, and a stream of white-hot fire erupts from her hands, burrowing into the golem's chest. An enormous wave of heat washes over the room; CB feels his eyebrows singe. At almost the same time, Derecho—who finally has a clear shot—summons lightning striking nearly the same location.

The torso *shatters*. It reminds CB of seeing a pane of glass being dropped to the floor. He vaguely remembers reading that extreme heat can make stone brittle, and wonders exactly how much heat Hu is generating.

Blue light flares up again, but it's different this time. It flickers erratically, like a fluorescent light just before it goes out. When the last trace of blue flickers away, David Bernard sinks to his knees, shoulders slumping, and exhaling heavily.

"It's done." The man sounds impossibly weary. "It almost didn't work."

Hu rises slightly into the air, surveying the damage. She looks over to Derecho and nods once. Derecho nods in return.

At that moment, Scrapper Jack leaps through the hole in the wall. He hasn't bothered to put on a mask, which doesn't surprise CB at all. The guy is almost as impervious to gas as Vigilante.

Jack takes in the room and frowns. "I thought there was another magic robot."

"Too slow," Hu says, sounding smug. "I took care of it."

Jack looks vaguely annoyed, then glances up. "We left Zero and Street Ronin alone."

"Hey," Grant says. "I'm still there. It's fine. Zero just found a building schematic. She says our objective is probably six floors down. She's printing out a floor plan. Speak of the devil..."

Grant blurs and disappears for an instant, then reappears right in front of CB, holding a printout of a floor plan in his hands. CB takes it, studying it closely.

"Right." CB looks toward the far end of the hall. "Everyone take a minute."

Brother Judgment's head jerks up, and he swivels to look at the stairwell. "Don't take a minute. Something's coming."

"What is it now?" Bernard climbs to his feet, swaying slightly.

"It's…" Brother Judgment hesitates, uncertain. "They're not meat robots. But they're not… quite… human, either."

CB stares at the stairwell at the end of the lobby, then at the group, still recovering from the golem. "How many?"

Brother Judgment shakes his head and shrugs. "I stopped counting at fifteen? A *lot* more than fifteen."

Part Nineteen: Haruspex Analytics, Upper Floors

The deeper they go, the darker it gets.

Deeper? Jenny frowns as something gnaws at her. *Deeper* isn't quite right, but she doesn't really know why.

She scolds herself for letting her mind wander. Semantics can wait—right now, she needs to focus. The deeper they go, the darker it gets.

The stairwell echoes with their footsteps as they reach the next landing. Street Ronin crouches, his rifle trained on the closed door—rugged metal with a thin rectangular window traveling up the top half—separating them from the rest of the floor. Agent Grant stays in the stairwell, watching for anyone coming up or down the stairs.

Jenny keeps below the window's line of sight, creeping up to the door's right. A subvocalized murmur activates one of her helmet's fancier sensors, and it quickly scans the hallway beyond.

Nothing. She shakes her head. Street Ronin nods in reply, gestures to Agent Grant, and they proceed down the stairs to the next landing.

The deeper they go, the darker it gets.

It's not right—it can't be right. Whatever they're doing, they're not going *deeper*. She grinds her teeth in frustration as she tries to force the thought back. What does it matter? Sure, they're thirty floors above ground but they're still going *down*, and without any windows they might as well be underground. "Deeper" works as well as anything. Why is she so stuck on it?

It's the *darker* part that should be bothering her. The fluorescent lights in the stairway are still on, still glowing white—but they might as well be a child's nightlight for all they actually light the space around them. She squints as she looks down the stairs, noting they are almost at the landing that marked the halfway point between floors. Two floors up, she remembers being able to see the halfway point clearly from the top of the stairs. Not any more—she's halfway there before she can see the shape of it.

It's even darker past the landing (*the deeper they go*) and Jenny activates a low-light display on her helmet. She turns it off again in irritation—the image is washed out, as if the light were at normal levels.

The stairwell echoes with their footsteps as they reach the next landing. Street Ronin crouches on the landing tile, his rifle trained on the closed door—rugged metal with a thin rectangular window traveling up the top half—separating them from the rest of the floor. Agent Grant stays in the stairwell, watching for anyone coming up or down the stairs.

Jenny crouches, keeping below the window's line of sight, and creeping up to the door's right. A subvocalized murmur activates one of her helmet's fancier sensors, and it quickly scans the hallway beyond.

Nothing. She shakes her head. Street Ronin nods in reply, gestures to Agent Grant, and they proceed down the stairs to the next landing.

The deeper they go, the darker it gets.

Her dissatisfaction with the notion of *deeper* surges up again, and her irritation nearly turns to anger at herself for being distracted by word choices. She's usually only like this when it comes to her job, when imprecise language creates misunderstanding.

Well, I guess this is my job now too, isn't it?

She thinks about that for a second. Yes it is—at least for the moment—and she needs to focus on doing it. They've reached the midpoint again, and Jenny is gripping the railing loosely with one hand in case she misses a step.

How did it get this dark? And if it's this dark, why are the lights still shining?

The stairwell echoes with their footsteps as they reach the next landing. Street Ronin crouches on the landing tile, his rifle trained on the closed door— rugged metal with a thin rectangular window traveling up the top half— separating them from the rest of the floor. Agent Grant stays in the stairwell, watching for anyone coming up or down the stairs.

Jenny crouches, keeping below the window's line of sight, and creeping up to the door's right. A subvocalized murmur activates one of her helmet's fancier sensors, and it quickly scans the hallway beyond.

Nothing. She shakes her head. Street Ronin nods in reply, gestures to Agent Grant, and they proceed down the stairs to the next landing.

The deeper they go, the darker it gets.

She considers the possibility that if this is her job, and she's *treating* it like her job, then it might be appropriate to consider why she's reacting so strongly to the word "deeper." She's reacting, she realizes, the same way she would if she were reading an explanation from an engineer who'd made an assumption that was fundamentally *wrong* and had based an entire design around it.

Street Ronin stumbles on the stairs ahead of her, just for a moment. She can barely see his hand tighten on the rail for support. Her own hand grips the rail. She can't really feel it through the gloves of her own suit. Just a vague pressure. It's so dark they can only see a few feet in front of them.

This is wrong. But how?

The stairwell echoes with their footsteps as they reach the next landing. Street Ronin crouches on the landing tile, his rifle trained on the closed door— rugged metal with a thin rectangular window traveling up the top half— separating them from the rest of the floor. Agent Grant stays in the stairwell, watching for anyone coming up or down the stairs.

Jenny crouches, keeping below the window's line of sight, and creeping up to the door's right. A subvocalized murmur activates one of her helmet's fancier sensors, and it quickly scans the hallway beyond.

Nothing. She shakes her head. Street Ronin nods in reply, gesturing to Agent Grant.

The deeper they go…

"Stop."

Jenny blinks in surprise as she realizes the command came out of her mouth. And it *is* a command: crisp, clear, brimming with authority. Street Ronin and Agent Grant both stop, turning to face her. Neither speak. Both wait.

"Something's wrong," Jenny says. "Give me a second."

Deeper. That's what I'm stuck on. I'm stuck on the word "deeper," and I can't find any rational reason why.

Either she's become a completely different person in the last twenty-four hours—it's possible, she concedes, given all the crazy things that have happened—or some part of her brain that is treating this as her job has reached a conclusion about the word "deeper," but hasn't figured out how to tell the rest of her yet. Option B makes more sense to her, so she quickly reviews every remembered irritation surrounding the word.

Deeper isn't quite right

Whatever they're doing, they're not going deeper

not… going… deeper…

Imprecise language creates misunderstanding.

The problem, Jenny realizes, is that she's assuming she's being picky about word usage when she's actually objecting to the declaration of motion. It's not that "going deeper" doesn't accurately describe descending a staircase from the top of a building in Manhattan, it's that *the phrase assumes they're moving to begin with.*

And they're not. They're not moving at all.

The darkness surrounding them disappears. Jenny blinks involuntarily as the near total darkness is replaced with cold fluorescent light, only to realize her eyes don't hurt.

She stands in a stairwell landing, facing a rugged metal door with a thin rectangular window traveling up the top half. Street Ronin stands to her left, hands at his side, his rifle lying on the floor at his feet. Agent Grant stands to her right, eyes glazed, expression remote.

"Hey." This time, Jenny's voice doesn't sound crisp, or clear, or full of any kind of authority of any kind. It's cracked, and hoarse, barely above a whisper. Her tongue feels thick and swollen. "You guys OK?"

They don't respond. She can't see Street Ronin's features under his visor, but Grant doesn't react to her voice at all. He simply stares into space, blinking occasionally.

"Hey!" Her voice cracks as she tries to speak louder. "Ronin! Grant! Snap out of it!"

Still no reply. Whatever weird place they were in a few seconds ago, Jenny is the only one who managed to get out. And, she realizes with alarm, that may only be temporary: the room is steadily growing dark.

Oh crap oh crap oh crap oh crap oh crap

Jenny grabs Street Ronin and Agent Grant, each by an arm, and does her best Scrapper Jack impression by kicking the metal door with all her strength. It doesn't shatter, but the frame does, and with a *pop* and *screech* of tearing metal the door flies down the floor's main hall until it topples over about a third of the way in.

Jenny heaves, throwing both men forward. She's certainly strong enough, but they aren't cooperating, and dead weight is awkward to control. Agent Grant slams into Street Ronin just before they pass through the door, causing the armored man to clip the door frame with his shoulder. Jenny winces as his shoulder takes out a chunk of sheet rock before he crumples into the carpet just on the other side. Grant goes a little farther, hitting an office door then collapsing into a heap about five steps past Street Ronin.

The deeper they go, the darker it gets.

Jenny can barely see. The stairwell echoes with their footsteps as they reach the next landing. Street Ronin crouches on the landing tile, his rifle trained on the closed door—rugged metal with a thin rectangular window traveling up the top half—separating them from the rest of the floor. Agent Grant stays in the stairwell, watching for anyone coming up or down the stairs.

No. That's not right. She kicked down the door. She threw Street Ronin and Agent Grant through the door. They *aren't there any more*, so why is she—

Jenny crouches, keeping below the window's line of sight, and creeping up to the door's right. A subvocalized murmur activates one of her helmet's fancier sensors, and it quickly scans the hallway beyond.

Nothing. She shakes her head. Street Ronin nods in reply, gesturing to Agent Grant.

The deeper they

Someone shoves her, hard, and then she's flying through the broken doorway, sprawling on the floor next to Street Ronin. The air in front of her shimmers and Agent Grant appears, bent over, wheezing and coughing.

"What... the... *fuck*?" Grant gasps for air, coughs, then looks through the doorway into the stairwell, horror and revulsion stamped into his face. "What the fuck was that?"

Jenny starts to retch, realizes what a bad idea that would be in her helmet, and forces back her gag reflex. She gets onto her hands and knees, noting with surprise that she hurts all over. Grant's abilities are weird and useful and impressive, but super strength isn't one of them. She's pretty sure he isn't responsible for this.

"Uhhhh..." She takes a deep, steadying breath. Some of the pain recedes. "Evil magic spell, I think."

"Right." Grant stands, then quickly props himself up against a wall to keep himself from falling again. "Well. It sucks."

Jenny climbs to her feet, crouching, hands on her knees. "Well, hopefully that's the—"

All of the lights in the hall go out, engulfing it in darkness. Then the hall is flooded with red as emergency lighting activates. A rasping, high-pitched shriek comes from the far end of the hallway, followed by others.

"Nice job," Grant says. "You were going to say 'hopefully that's the worst of it,' weren't you?"

"No!" Jenny protests. "I was going to say 'hopefully that's the *last* of it.' I wasn't tempting the Gods of Escalation, I swear!"

"How is that better? You dodge the Gods of Escalation by calling on the Gods Of Yet Another Goddamn Thing?"

As if on cue, the shadows at the end of the hall come to life and try to kill them.

Part Twenty: Haruspex Analytics, Ground Floor Lobby

A single rasping shriek, high pitched and rising ever higher as it goes on, emerges from somewhere behind the stairwell door. Almost immediately it is joined by dozens of other voices, similar in pitch and frenetic despair. The phrase *Chorus of the Damned* runs through CB's head. "How long?"

Brother Judgment stands in the middle of the broken lobby, concentrating. "A few minutes? They're a few floors down." Another scream, much fainter, and farther away, causes him to look up. "And many, many floors above."

David Bernard stands, swaying slightly, then straightens. "You said they weren't quite human." He sounds tired. CB wonders what kind of toll all this is taking on him.

"That was then," Brother Judgment says, voice dry. "I've gotten to know them a little better. It's complicated, and I won't be sleeping for a week."

David nods. "I definitely get that part. Still, if you could give me something I might be able to narrow it down."

Brother Judgment thinks it over. "An ocean of murder poured into human skin?"

David frowns. "That's not as narrow as you'd think."

"It's... evocative," CB says.

"They're here to *kill us*," Brother Judgment says. "That's pretty much it. It's their purpose, their calling. I want to say 'divine calling,' but that's not quite right, but it's a purpose that fills them so completely there's no room for anything else. They won't stop, won't surrender, and won't accept ours. And they're... *happy about it*."

"Come on," Grant says. "That is *not* the tortured screaming of a happy man. Except for this one place in the Village—"

"Shut up, Grant." Hu is floating near the ceiling, still engulfed in flame, but she's dialed back the heat quite a bit. "The point is we're not going to be able to deescalate this. Are we?"

Brother Judgment shakes his head. "No way that I can see."

"Then we don't," Red Shift says. "Lethal force."

Nobody says anything.

"It's pretty clear-cut," Red Shift continues. "These are not *innocents*. They've been performing medical tests on *human beings*, and discarding their *corpses* when they get what they want. We just saw one of them *willingly slit his own throat and turn into a monster*."

"Come on, man." Blink shakes his head, looking at Red Shift in disbelief. "You can't think *everyone* in this building is in that deep. I mean, a whole building in the middle of the city? There's gotta be some people who just took a job. Cleaning staff. Temps. Interns. That kind of thing. These people could be mind controlled."

"I don't think so." David Bernard shakes his head sadly. "Not the way Brother Judgment describes their thoughts."

Another scream, much louder this time. They can hear the faint echo of many feet stomping up stairs.

"The kind of power they're tapped into isn't natural to this universe. It can't exist on its own. It needs either victims or collaborators. The victims it kills, for power and sustenance. The collaborators... it changes them. It scoops bits of them away, filling up the empty spaces with something that makes nihilism look kind. Assuming Brother Judgment's description is correct—which I do—then these people have had so much of themselves scooped away there's nothing left to recover. They're genuinely monsters, now."

CB exhales, his gas mask fogging a little. "I am so tired of this shit."

He pulls off his gas mask, letting it fall from the fingers of his left hand just as he places the cigarette in his mouth with his right. Everyone in the room looks on in surprise, some going so far as to shout a warning, or a more generic but equally appropriate *"what the fuck are you doing?"* but he ignores them. He doesn't inhale until the lighter makes fire: when he finally does, the cherry burns bright red and the entire world clicks into place around him. After that he breathes in deep through his nose. The air smells metallic, but that's it.

"You can take your masks off, now," he says. "I made it go away."

Everyone just stares at him. Then Red Shift touches something on his visor, and the mouthpiece opens and retracts. "How did you do that?"

"I'm *pushing*," CB says. "Because that's where we are right now."

Red Shift grimaces. Jack looks startled. The others have no idea what he's talking about.

"Look," CB says, "our objective is six floors down. Whatever these things may have been an hour ago, *right now* they are monsters dead set on murdering us. I am dead set on getting six floors down in order to stop the Junior Senator of New York—a guy I *really don't like*, for the record—from getting murdered by an evil magic spell. We're running out of time and I am all out of fucks to give."

Another series of screams cuts through the air, very close this time.

"Here's what we're going to do. These jokers are gonna pour through that stairwell door like water and we're gonna pound the ever-loving shit out of 'em. Hold back only so far as not to bring the building down on us. A minute into the fight, some of us head downstairs. Me, Agent Grant, Blink, Doctor Enigma, Brother Judgment. The rest of you are going to keep these assholes busy. Follow when you finish."

Sister Sentinel frowns. "I get the basic plan—we draw fire while you slip away—but how are you handling the slipping away part? If they're coming in through the stairwell door, it's not going to be easy to go through the stairwell door."

"We're not using the stairwell door," CB says. "They've turned off the elevators, but it's still a straight drop down."

Blink raises an eyebrow, then turns and jogs to the elevator. "You know, if I get down there first, I can pop back and grab the rest of you one by one. Save a lot of time."

"It'd be safer if we go as a group," CB says.

"No time!" The floor is shaking now. They're getting close. "Look, me and Grant will go. Pretty sure we can infiltrate to a safe place and bring the rest of you in easier and faster than the group can."

"I like it," Grant says. "Don't get me wrong, it's a terrible plan, but it's got *moxie*. Let's do it." He turns to follow Blink.

"Don't die, Grant!" Hu shouts.

"Don't blow up the building!" Grant shouts back. "The city gets touchy about that stuff."

They duck into the elevator and disappear from view. Seconds later, the stairwell door flies out of its frame, and a wave of living shadow streams into the room.

Part Twenty One: The Swarm

The stairwell door bursts outward as shadow pours out from behind it like currents of angry, blackened steam. The shadow is *cold*, and CB is suddenly overcome with despair, filled with the urge to do nothing but *wallow* in it.

He recognizes the attack for what it is and shakes it off. The others do as well, fighting back the deadly malaise by leaning into their more defiant traits. Hu's flames flare up, annihilating the shadows around her. Sister Sentinel shouts wordlessly, equal parts defiance and taunt. Red Shift does a lap around the room, shaking off the tendrils of darkness that can't keep up with his speed, and when he returns to his original position he's vibrating in place, that weird force field he projects when he moves keeping the darkness at bay. David mutters some kind of spell, causing a brief flare of purple-white light to surround him like a halo, Brother Judgment contemptuously brushes imaginary dust off his shoulder... and Jack just shifts his stance, ever so slightly.

The only person who doesn't seem to react is Derecho. CB worries the mist may have affected her, but then a stiff breeze kicks up and the mist is blown into an empty corner of the room.

The creatures come.

They are human-shaped, men and women, dressed mostly in business casual khakis and button-ups, plastic badges swinging wildly from lanyards hung about their necks as they rush the room. But above the neck it changes: the creatures have no heads. Where a head should be is a roaring font of darkness, bursting forth like purple-black flame.

And each creature is screaming that strange, rasping shriek.

The world swirls around him, and CB steps smoothly to one side as the first wave rush past, going straight for Scrapper Jack and Sister Sentinel. They never reach their targets: a *boom* fills the air as a red blur cuts across their advance. They appear to *explode* into clouds of black mist; something wet sprays across CB's face. He wipes his face with one arm while he reaches into a trenchcoat pocket with another, pulling out a long length of weighted chain.

A roar erupts from the ceiling as Agent Hu sends a stream of liquid flame directly into the stairwell door, prompting howls of anguish from the creatures trying to force their way into the room. Almost immediately the fire stops—she's trying not to burn the place down—but even the short burst has done impressive work. Shadow creatures are burning, staggering blindly into the room where they are struck by rapid bursts of lightning from Derecho. The few who manage to get through are lifted into the air by invisible force as Brother Judgment slams them into the wall so hard they crack the stone.

But Hu *is* trying to keep the building from burning down, so the stream of fire isn't constant. When the stairwell door isn't on fire, more creatures barrel through. And more. And more.

And more.

CB crouches, lashes out with the chain, and pulls. The end wraps around a leg and a creature falls to the rubble-strewn floor, bringing down two others with it. Not bothering to stop, CB launches himself at a fourth, kicking hard at its neck. He feels bone break beneath his heel, then the chain—still wrapped around the first creature's leg—tightens. He pulls on it sharply, causing him to twist in midair and land in a crouch as the fourth creature falls backward, still. He pulls on the chain again, and it releases its grip on the leg, arcing into what would have been another creature's head.

Only it doesn't have a head. CB curses as the chain passes through the shadowy mass of flame, apparently doing nothing at all.

The creature turns toward him, only to be knocked down by a second. CB glances at Jack, who grabs one by its tennis shirt and throws it into two more. Sister Sentinel stands just to Jack's right, laying into three at once, her face a mask of grim determination. Two more creatures rise into the air and smash into the far wall, leaving two more cracked indentations.

Then David casts a spell: the air *hums* with energy, and a purple-gold wave washes over the room. Half of the creatures in the room fall on the spot, but all of the ones still standing abandon what they were doing and immediately turn on him, charging with murderous abandon. David's eyes widen in surprise, then he kneels, crosses his arms across his chest, and is suddenly surrounded by a purple-white sphere. The first creature strikes the sphere, bounces off, then springs back to its feet to charge again. That's when more liquid flame rains from the ceiling, making a circle of fire around David, and lightning falls around the flame, jumping from creature to creature, leaving blackened spots at their feet.

They fall, but the stairwell is unwatched, and more creatures are pouring through.

CB's attention is diverted, momentarily, by the sudden appearance of Blink. He teleports next to the hole Red Shift punched through the outer wall—a good choice, since it's out of the general melee and gives him a chance to take in the situation. He sees David lower his force field, notices him swaying on his feet, and in an instant he's right next to him, placing his hands on the weary man's shoulders, and saying something CB can't hear. They both disappear in a flash of light.

CB twists to avoid the outstretched hands of a shadow-creature. He flicks his chain out, and the end wraps around a wrist. He leans back, pulling sharply, and the creature stumbles into the one next to it. He jerks again, releasing the chain, and drops low to kick at a third's legs. Three down, and the ones behind it are forced to route around, giving him time to put distance between them. Then the light around him flashes, and Blink is placing his hands on CB's shoulders.

"Here we go!"

The entire world tips violently to his right, as if someone were throwing him across the room, but before he hits anything he is suddenly falling, landing awkwardly on his hands and knees as he strikes a concrete floor. He grunts in pain.

"Sorry," Blink says, then disappears in a flash.

He hears the sound of someone quietly retching beside him.

"I gotta admit, it's a neat trick." Agent Grant's voice comes from somewhere above him, not too far away. "But it doesn't look like it's a smooth ride for passengers."

"The first time…" David Bernard's voice is very raw, and he coughs and spits before trying again. "The first time I ever did this I had a massive concussion. I assumed that was the reason I threw up."

He laughs ruefully. "Apparently not."

Part Twenty Two: Manhattan, Alpha Checkpoint MCV

Alishia Webb sits alone in the back of a Mobile Command Vehicle, watching all the feeds coming in from the relay points set up around the target. She wishes yet again that she were in the Sky Commando armor, airborne, directing the action from there… but it's not quite time for that. The big suit is currently tethered to the MCV, acting as a power source to most of the equipment until the generators show up. Which, according to latest reports, should be soon.

All the streets around the Haruspex Analytics building are closed now, and they've set up five checkpoints with the oh-so-creative names of *Alpha, Bravo, Charlie, Delta,* and *Echo.* It's still very early morning, so it hasn't disrupted morning traffic—yet—but it will. And even now, outside of business hours, it's generating a steady stream of angry complaints from City Hall. Webb looks at the blinking message light on the screen in front of her and scowls. She's only taking calls from certain people at the moment, and the Junior Attaché to the City Department of Transportation isn't one of them.

Not *again,* at least. The first time was more than enough.

A second notice on her visor is more welcome—the surveillance drones are finally in place, and they have full coverage around the building. She opens the feed, flipping from view to view, trying to get a feel for what's going on.

The alloy shell encasing the building is clearly visible in the predawn light, as is the man-shaped hole punched through a section near the lobby. The two handcuffed security guards stowed in the little park in front of the building have been carted away, and the arresting officers have retreated back behind the dubious safety of the barricade. There are signs of a fight on the roof of the building—the remains of at least one helicopter along with what she's sure is point defense artillery.

A third notice appears in her visor, from one of the priority channels beeps: the one dedicated to the Metahuman Division. She activates it immediately.

"Captain Banks."

"Sky Commando." Captain Paul Banks has been head of the MTHD for at least as long as there's been a Sky Commando program. In the beginning, from what she understood, he saw Sky Commando as a competitor for funding and political clout. That changed over time, as the two groups learned what each could and couldn't do, and now they were pretty reliable allies. "I received the official briefing on my way to the scene. Is there... anything else I should know?"

"Yes." Webb tries to put as much emphasis as she can into that single word. "Face to face?"

"Oh." Captain Banks sounds startled, then lapses into a soft, thoughtful *hmmmm*. He's not a stupid man—he knows that if she's requesting a face-to-face meeting that there's something irregular going on. "Where are you?"

"Alpha Checkpoint MCV," Webb says. "I can come to you."

"Not necessary," Captain Banks says. "I'm not far. I'll be there in five minutes." The line goes dead, and so she waits.

It's an odd situation to be in. She's only a sergeant, and hasn't even been one for very long, but in this specific situation Banks reports to her, and will until the 10-A5 is resolved and the stand-down order is sent.

Which, under most circumstances, only she can send.

Someone raps sharply on the MCV door, three times, then it swings open and Captain Banks steps into the vehicle. He's an older man, in his early-to-mid-fifties, and has managed to remain fairly trim despite spending much of his time behind a desk. The head of the MTHD doesn't usually go into the field. At least, not in one of the suits.

Webb half-rises as he steps up into the space, ducking his head to avoid hitting the low ceiling. He smiles sardonically at her show of deference as he waves her back into her seat—he's just as aware of the awkward clash of rank and authority as she is, probably even more so—then turns to close the door behind him. He glances over the perimeter monitors and drone feeds, just as she did, then slides unceremoniously into the swivel chair beside hers. He looks at her expectantly.

She gestures to the monitors, each showing the Haruspex Analytics building from a different angle. "We have a potential repeat of the TriHealth fiasco, only exponentially worse."

Captain Banks raises his eyebrows. TriHealth had turned out to be pretty bad. They'd learned that one of their best and brightest officers had been dirty, and that someone had stolen and copied the MTHD's Metahuman Response Suits.

"I'm working with Division M on this," Webb says. "And they are working with civilian groups that are probably going to make this entire thing a nightmare when it really hits the press. But I felt you needed to be brought in on this, and the Division M lead agrees."

"Agent Henry, right?" Captain Banks wasn't the kind of guy to ignore the other players in the city. Webb nods.

"Right…" Banks stares at the building thoughtfully. "What do I need to know?"

"First," Webb says, "I'm going to play you a statement that was apparently made by Senator Tobias Morgan."

Captain Banks' eyebrows rise even higher. "He's been found?"

"Not… exactly," Webb says. "Watch the statement first."

She presses a button on the console in front of her. One of the monitors switches from the feed of the drone to the one queued up in the Sky Commando suit. A picture of Senator Tobias Morgan, sitting on a ratty couch in some hellhole apartment somewhere, comes into focus. The timestamp on the image claims it was recorded only a few hours ago.

"The government is full of cabals," the image of the senator says. *"It's unavoidable, in the long term."*

Webb doesn't bother watching the tape. She's already seen it. She watches the captain, trying to get a read on how he's taking it. She notes the flicker of uncertainty in his eyes when the senator says *magic*. That's the part that's going to trip everyone up, she thinks, but that uncertainty is quickly replaced with horror.

"That's right," the senator's image says. *"Remember when I said the first virus—the one that didn't kill people—was discarded because it didn't last long enough? The virus stays in your blood. Given enough time, it does more than that—it alters your DNA. It becomes a virus that is transmitted through your DNA. You are given tiny little building blocks that embed a kill switch into any human with the metahuman gene. And then—"*

"My God," Banks whispers.

"And then," the image continues, *"after all the male metahumans are dead, the rest of the world will go back to their lives. And that involves* **having children.** *"*

"It's not about killing the metahumans we have now," someone off-camera says. *"That's just collateral damage. They're making sure there are* **never** *any metahumans again.* **Ever.** *"*

The feed ends. The drone footage returns.

Captain Banks turns to Webb, no longer trying to mask the emotions on his face. Alarm, shock, fear… horror. All there. Not as much doubt as Webb had feared.

"Is this true?" the captain asks. "Is that really the senator? Are we sure he hasn't been coerced?"

"Division M has people working with the group who made the footage," Webb says. "I know the people, and trust them. The group as a whole is... politically complicated. It involves the use of... extralegal assets."

Banks' mouth thins. "Do I want to know?"

"You *need* to know, if you're in," Webb says. "I can't have your people shooting at the ones on our side. The stakes are too high."

The captain, face sour, nods reluctantly. "I see your point. What's the worst of the group?"

"Agent Grant," Webb says promptly. "But in the way *you* mean it, it's a tossup between Crossfire and Overmind."

She watches sympathetically as the all-too-familiar look of panic blooms, noting the tension rising in Captain Banks' posture, and raises her hand just as he opens his mouth, cutting him off just before he's committed to shouting.

"It's *bad*, Captain. Bad in a way that, historically, cuts across old boundaries. You've worked city-wide threats before, and you've worked with criminals to put those threats down. This is the same situation. The people in that building are much worse than anyone in that group could hope to be, on their worst day. We're talking *genetic plague*, Captain."

The captain shuts his mouth. His tension has receded, or at least is masked so that it only displays as an unhappy frown. He stares at the images of the Haruspex Analytics building thoughtfully.

"I understand. I don't... like it, much, but..." He glances at Webb. "You haven't been Sky Commando very long. I knew Bernard much better. I wish we'd had more time to work together before we got forced into a spot like this."

"So do I," Webb says.

"And then there's the question of why you even bothered to bring me in," Banks says. "You're Sky Commando. You're in charge here, no matter what I personally think about it. You don't *need* to brief me on this. Why do it?"

"I disagree," Webb says. "These guys are connected to TriHealth, which means they have access to MTHD tech. I'm going to need to put your people between them and the rest of the city. I won't do that with you in the dark."

"How do you know I'm not working with them?" Banks counters. "That statement the senator just made makes it hard to trust anyone, assuming he's right." He shakes his head. "Which I am, I think. Damn it all."

"I'm pretty sure you're on the level," Webb says. "If I weren't, we wouldn't be doing this. But we're going to be completely sure of it in a few seconds."

As if on cue, someone knocks on the MCV door. It opens before either of them has a chance to react, and a tall, slim black man dressed in a three-piece black suit and wearing sunglasses steps up and in, letting the door shut behind him.

"Hello Captain Banks," the man says. "My name is Special Agent Phillip Henry. Before this goes any further I'm going to need to ask you two questions."

Part Twenty Three: Haruspex Analytics, Upper Floors

Everything is cold.

Wood bursts into splinters as Jenny's shoulder clips the doorframe, the force of the blow sending her spinning out into the stairwell as the creature follows, shrieking in triumph. She isn't hurt, not physically—her new armor soaks up everything she isn't able to dodge or block—but her right hand is still numb from her last attempt to punch one of those creatures in what she'd thought was a face.

She takes a knee, letting the floor halt her spin and reorient her perception, then rolls to the side as the shadow zombie reaches out. It overextends, stumbles, and Jenny takes the opportunity to grab its legs and lift it over the railing. The shriek rises in alarm, then stops as it strikes the rail on one of the lower stairs. She hears it strike a few more as it tumbles, then nothing.

She flexes her right hand. Still numb. Not even needles. She glances at the corner of her visor that shows her physical condition. As far as her suit's diagnostic computer can tell, her hand appears normal.

Gunfire erupts from the hallway—steady, controlled bursts from Street Ronin's rifle, mixed with the quick, staccato shots from Agent Grant's pistols—causing the shrieking to rise in volume and pitch. Jenny flexes her hand one more time, just to reassure herself that it still works, and pushes her worry aside to focus on more immediate problems.

She subvocalizes the command to activate the comm channel. It registers two active listeners—Street Ronin and Agent Grant. The plan had been to have the entire group on the same channel throughout the operation, but something is blocking them... which is why every group has Agent Grant.

"Where are these things coming from?" Jenny keeps herself as low as she can as she runs back into the hall. Street Ronin crouches inside an office doorway. Agent Grant is farther down, where the hall opens up into a cube farm. Another pack of creatures emerge from the stairwell at the far end of the building.

Street Ronin switches to single fire, taking time to aim before pulling the trigger.

"I'm gonna go with 'Human Resources,'" Grant says. As soon as Street Ronin stops firing, Grant's image blurs, reappears down the hall *behind* the latest group, and fires twice. Two creatures drop, and the group's charge falters: some try to turn to face the new threat, others crash into the ones trying to turn. He grins, waves once, then disappears as Street Ronin detaches a metal sphere from his belt and rolls it down the hall. It speeds on its way, straight into the confused mass of shadow creatures.

Street Ronin's hand clenches into a fist. The sphere explodes in a ball of bright, hot light. The high-pitched shrieking of the creatures rises even higher.

Street Ronin is very proud of those little bombs. He claims they burn themselves out so hot and so fast that there's practically no chance of starting accidental fires, and so far his claim is holding out. All that's left in the hall is scorched carpet, walls, and the charred remains of bodies.

Jenny's glad she can't smell anything through her helmet. The look on Grant's face tells her everything she needs to know.

"I think we've got some time," Grant says. "There's an army of these things in the lobby. We have the heavy hitters set up down there as a diversion."

A loud *boom* echoes from far below them, causing the floor to shake.

"That's probably them. Pretty sure that's who they're gonna focus on for a while."

Street Ronin nods, swaying a little as he gets to his feet. It's easy to forget that he's the "normal" one—scary good with his weapons, but he doesn't have the kind of enhanced endurance Jenny does.

"You OK?" she asks.

Street Ronin nods again. "Sorry about the one that got past me. Thanks for taking it on."

Jenny flexes her numb, cold hand again. "That's what I was there for."

"What happened to it?" Street Ronin glances down the hall to the stairwell.

"I threw it down the stairs," Jenny says. "It stopped shrieking, so I assume it's dead."

She tries not to notice how casually she says that. For a second she remembers a security guard, eyes wide with terror at the sight of his own gun pointed at his face. She pushes the image back, anger rising. *Not now!*

Street Ronin turns to Agent Grant. "Where are you right now?"

"I'm with Curveball, Blink, Brother Judgment, and Doctor Enigma," Grant says. "We're a few floors below the lobby. We went down the elevator shaft." He very quickly fills them in on the plan—distraction in the lobby as a smaller team goes after the objective. Street Ronin nods in agreement. "So what do we do? Zero?"

Jenny manages to push the lingering traces of bad memory aside. "I vote keep going down. Though maybe faster than we have been. I don't want them to figure out they can come up *both* stairwells."

Agent Grant grimaces. "Yeah. Let's hope they don't get smart."

"Zero." Street Ronin stares at Jenny's hand. She realizes she's been flexing it unconsciously the entire time. "What's wrong with your hand?"

Jenny raises it, wiggling her fingers. "Not sure. I... when the thing broke past you, reflex took over and I tried to punch it in the face. Only, you know, no face. As soon as my hand passed through that... shadow fire, or whatever it is, it went cold and numb. I can still move it, but I can barely feel it."

"Take off your glove. Let's get a look."

Jenny hesitates, then releases the latches that attach the suit's right gauntlet.

"Holy shit," Grant says.

Dark patches of deep purple run along the front and back of her hand. Tiny dark purple threads extend from the patches. She can't tell if that means the patches are growing or receding.

"Well," Jenny says. "*Fuck.*"

Street Ronin takes her by the wrist, moving her hand slightly to catch the light better. "That doesn't look good."

Jenny snorts. "There's that Crossfire gift for understatement. The good news is, it doesn't hurt."

Street Ronin shakes his head slowly. "I'm not sure that's good news."

"Well... yeah, OK, now that you point it out, it seems like a bad sign." Jenny tries to keep her voice light. "But there's not a lot we can do about it right now. I can still use it, it doesn't hurt, and we're kind of in the middle of something. So we keep going."

As carefully as she can she reattaches her gauntlet to her armor.

Street Ronin nods in agreement. It's not like they have many options. "I'll go first," he says. "Zero, you follow, Agent Grant, bring up the rear. I don't like the thought of those things swarming over us from above."

They resume their descent. Three flights down they see the broken body of the creature Jenny threw over the rail, its "head" still a burning shadow. They gingerly step around the corpse. Jenny's hand throbs as she passes by.

For a time, they hear nothing but the echo of their footsteps, and the occasional rumble from the fight below. The rumbling is severe enough that it makes the rail tremble in return.

"What are they doing down there?" Jenny glances over her shoulder at Agent Grant, who shrugs helplessly.

"They're the distraction," he says. "They're being distracting."

"You can't check?"

"No," Grant says. "I'm almost back up to five, but it'd be stupid to try that in this kind of situation. Last thing we need right now is for me to get confused about where I am and fire my gun in the wrong location."

Jenny smiles slightly. "You're weird, Grant."

"So I've heard."

"Seriously. Most people with your talent would talk about how many copies they make. You talk about how many places you can be."

"That's because *I don't make copies.* I don't understand why what I do is so much harder to grasp than someone who creates photocopies of themselves out of thin air."

"What's our status?" Street Ronin interrupts their bickering with a wholly appropriate question. For some reason, that aggravates Jenny immensely.

"Our little strike team is exploring the level at the bottom of the elevator shaft," Grant says. "Not much to report so far. I'm not at the diversion, so I can't report on that, but that's also the group I'm least worried about. You're here with me, so no point in reporting on that. It's getting interesting outside. Sky Commando's on the scene. I think she's meeting with Agent Henry. I'm trying to keep my distance for now, on account of me being officially dead and all. No one has approached the bunker. The senator..." His voice trails off. Jenny can feel him staring at her. "He's not in good shape. Whatever Doctor Enigma did is wearing off, and it's starting to hurt."

Jenny grips the rail a little tighter, but says nothing.

Conversation drops off until they reach the next level, then Jenny stops in her tracks.

"Do you hear that?"

The other two stop. Agent Grant frowns and shakes his head. Street Ronin cocks his head to one side, then stiffens. He hoists his rifle. "Fighting."

"That's our decoy group," Agent Grant says. "Partying it up in the lobby."

Street Ronin shakes his head. "This is only a floor or so down."

As if on cue, the faint sound of shrieking wafts up from below. Jenny flexes her hand. Still nothing.

Agent Grant sighs, then checks his pistols. "I was getting used to not fighting these things."

"What I want to know," Street Ronin says, "is who exactly is fighting these things? Unless some other vigilante has broken through that alloy shell, it's a pretty short list."

Jenny's eyes widen in shock. "You don't think..."

All three break into a run, descending the stairs at unsafe speeds.

Part Twenty Four: Haruspex Analytics, Below

The robed figures stand silently, one to each side of a rusted metal door set flush against a concrete wall. Their robes might have been mistaken for oversized hoodies if the context were different, just as they might have been mistaken for bouncers if they were standing outside a nightclub. But the sound that filters through the heavy door isn't the low bass of electronic music. The sound might charitably be described as *chanting*, but it's not precisely musical. Most people would find the sounds physically painful, literally so: they contain sounds and cadences that living things instinctively don't want to hear. The chanting has been growing louder over the past hour, growing more urgent, more eager, and while it hasn't yet reached its peak there is a taut energy in each new sound that suggests it's getting close.

The robed figures, guardians of the door, ever silent and watchful, appear unmoved by those sounds.

pat pat pat pat pat

Running feet splash through shallow pools of water condensed on the concrete floor: someone not yet in view is closing, quickly. The guardians exchange glances, then the one on the left moves forward, placing itself between the footsteps and its partner, which slips a large hand beneath its stone-gray robes to draw out a simple, oversized key. The first guardian drops into a crouch, fists clenched at its side, waiting. The second guardian cups the key in its right hand and whispers something in a language that echoes the chanting beyond the door. The key begins to glow faintly in the dim light.

thwack, thwack, bkak SNAP

Too far off to properly see, something bounces off one wall, then the other, then blurs over their heads to rebound against the heavy metal door with a loud *clang* before a baseball smacks into the second guardian's outstretched hand, bounces off, ricochets once last time off the floor, then buries itself into the back of the first guardian's knee. The second guardian cries out in pain—a high-pitched, thready sound—as the key flies out of its grasp and skitters across the floor, disappearing into the shadows. The first guardian, stung but not hurt, spins around, fists raised to strike.

The second guardian, still preoccupied by the sudden mixture of numbness and pain shooting through its right hand, looks past the first just in time to see the air ripple and a scruffy-looking man wearing a brown trenchcoat appear out of thin air, cigarette dangling from snarling lips, right hand clutching a long steel chain.

The second guardian opens its mouth, perhaps to cry out a warning, perhaps to snarl defiance. It never gets the chance.

The man in the trenchcoat snarls, his face twisting in rage. The first guardian halts its spin, half-turning back to the sound just as the steel chain wraps around its neck. The man in the trenchcoat rushes past and lets his weight and momentum pull the first guardian into the second. The second staggers back, struggling to get out of the way. The man in the trenchcoat, rapidly reaching the end of the hall, doesn't slow his pace: he jumps, twists in midair, and launches himself off the metal door toward the second guardian. It hesitates, unsure how to react. Seconds later the first guardian crashes into it from one side as the man in the trenchcoat spins and kicks it sharply in the temple from the other. It hisses in pain as it collapses. Two more swift kicks to the temple, and the lights finally go out.

* * *

CB unwraps the chain from around the hooded thing's neck, trying to avoid actually touching the strange, semi-scaled skin as he does. The others finally appear from behind David's spell, fanning out in a semicircle around the two inert figures and the metal door.

"Key to the door slid off that way." CB points briefly, then returns to his work.

"Pretty fast, CB." Blink goes over to the wall, then squats down, peering at the floor. "Sure you ain't a speedster?"

"It wasn't *that* fast," Agent Grant says. "Pretty impressive for an old man, though. You're pushing fifty now, right?"

"Passed that one a while back," CB says. The last of the chain works free of the robed creature's neck, and he begins to rewind it around his knuckles. "Blink, you find that key?"

Blink reaches down to grab something off the floor, then quickly draws back his hand. "It's hot."

"I think they were trying to destroy it," CB says.

"I got it." Brother Judgment extends his hand, and a small object rises off the floor and floats over to the door.

Blink picks up a second item from the floor. "Found your baseball, CB." He stares at it for a second, eyes widening. "It's signed by Mike Cuellar?"

CB laughs. "Yeah."

"How the hell did you get that? He was a little before your time."

"Pretty sure I stole it." CB looks up to see everyone staring at him blankly. "What? I used to be a villain. I think I made the Liberty Ten Most

Wanted in '85."

"Yeah, but weren't you some kind of political terrorist?" Grant chimes in. "Stealing a baseball seems kind of random."

"It's really not that complicated." CB stretches out his hand, and Blink tosses the ball back to him. "I called myself *Curveball*. It was signed by *Mike Cuellar*." The ball goes back into his trenchcoat pocket, leaving not so much as a bulge.

"We need to hurry." David's voice is strained. "They're almost ready."

The key, hovering in front of the metal door, slides smoothly into a keyhole just above the door handle. It turns clockwise. The door clicks softly.

"I don't suppose you know what's on the other side?" CB asks.

"Just an informed guess. The ritual will have a focus, someone leading the chant. And it'll require a release at the end, so expect the ritual leader to try to, uh..."

"Kill himself?" CB asks. "Like that kid upstairs?"

David grimaces. "Just identify the leader and take him down. After that the whole spell falls apart."

"Right," CB says. "Well, let's go get their leader."

Brother Judgment flicks a finger, and the door swings open wide. CB takes a long pull on his cigarette, then dashes through.

* * *

CB's first thought is that he's stepped onto a football field in Hell.

He's standing at one end of a vast, rectangular space, illuminated by a thick, dull red light that radiates from strange, twisting rock formations snaking through the walls. The walls are high, rising at least thirty feet, and looking down its length he thinks it really *is* the size of a football field. The metal door behind him is the only entrance or exit that he can see.

The chanting draws his gaze to the... fifty-yard line, if he's going to continue the comparison. There, bathed in that eerie red light, thirteen black stone columns rise twenty feet into the air, encircling a marble-white stone dais with more of that strange red rock growing out of it. Robed figures, all chanting, encircle the dais. Standing in its center is another robed figure, face obscured but turned up, arms raised. In its right hand it grips a long, curved knife. There is power in that knife. CB doesn't know what kind of power it is, but it's so strong it makes his teeth hurt.

Fifty yards.

He takes another pull on his cigarette and begins to run as hard as he can toward what he can only assume is a circle of evil wizards. Evil, chanting wizards.

Something blurs into view about fifteen yards from the stone pillars. It's Blink, looking around in confusion as he appears in a location he obviously didn't choose. A moment later Grant appears beside him, causing both to jump in alarm at the other's proximity.

The evil wizards, it seems, have a way to counter teleportation.

The two men recover quickly, running straight toward the pillars and the wizards and the cultist in the center with the knife. As if on cue, four robed figures step back from the circle, turn, and raise their arms high.

The chanting continues.

Blink goes right, Grant left. A surge of darkness streaks from a robed figure's hand, lancing across the space toward Grant who immediately fades out and reappears fifteen yards from the stone pillars. He swears in frustration, running toward the pillars again just as Blink, evading a similar assault, appears fifteen yards out from the stone pillars.

OK, fine, nobody thought the teleportation angle was going to work in the first place. Just keep running.

He hears running footsteps to his right. Looking over his shoulder he sees David Bernard managing to keep pace with him, at least for the moment. Even though he looks it, David isn't really recovered from his time on the island—that kind of thing takes a long time to fully bounce back from, so he's performing on sheer stubbornness and willpower. Not the smartest play, CB thinks, though he can't think of a better one at the moment. He turns his attention back to the evil wizards, which is when he realizes that only two of the four figures who stepped out of the circle actually did anything.

The chanting continues.

The third figure clenches both fists and pulls them down to its side, as if breaking an invisible stick. A fissure appears in the concrete, starting at one of the pillars and streaking toward CB as chunks of the floor tumble away into an apparently endless chasm of darkness. Without missing a beat CB leaps just as the ever-widening crack reaches him. He *just barely* manages to reach one side, then drops into a roll to force a little more space between himself and a very long way down.

The fourth figure clenches both fists and brings them together over its head. Smoky darkness gathers around it, then expands to fill the room, black strands of smoke hanging in blood red air. As soon as the darkness falls CB finds he can barely move—the smoke presses against him, resisting every effort to move forward. He stumbles in slow motion, immediately adjusting his balance to keep from falling, but finds to his consternation that "immediately" takes seconds to accomplish.

The chanting continues.

Something shifts behind him. He hears Bernard's voice, muffled in the strange mist but not slurred or slowed, and then a blazing purple-white light cuts through the darkness and burns the smoke away. CB can move again, and he resumes his charge. The fourth robed figure staggers back as if the light struck him a physical blow. Eight more robed figures step out of the circle and turn to face them.

Blink and Grant reach the pillars again, and again they break in opposite directions. A surge of darkness begins to gather in the first robed figure's hand, but a loud *crack* booms through the room and the robed figure crumples to the ground. Grant dives behind one of the columns for cover as he fires again, hitting a second figure in the leg.

Eight more robed figures step out of the circle, turning to face them. Minus the first one Grant shot, CB estimates they're facing at least twenty robed figures, with only four or five left performing the ritual.

They must be pretty close to finishing if they think they can spare all that firepower, CB thinks. He grits his teeth and tries to push his legs harder.

The robed figures all raise their hands in unison, and smoky darkness floods the room once more, immobilizing them. David's voice rises sharply in return, and the air above them ripples as purple-gold disks burst into reality roughly ten feet above each figure. The creatures cry out in alarm, then the black mist in the room recedes, gathering into globes around each disk. The disks try to expand, the globes try to shrink. The struggle appears to reach a stalemate, neither able to make any progress against the other, and CB can move again.

He stumbles as all the effort he expended trying to fight the mist suddenly comes up against nothing, then recovers into a flat run, closing the gap between him and the figure still standing in the center, gripping its knife.

Closing, but not fast enough. He sees the robed figure's fist tighten around the dagger's hilt.

"Now!"

Another robed figure just to the right of center—one of the few continuing the chant—squawks in surprise as it shoots into the air, slamming into the thirty-foot ceiling where it stays, pinned by an invisible force. Something falls from its hands, clattering to the stone floor below: a slender blade, not as ornate as the one held by the center figure, but obviously sharp. As the pinned figure screeches in rage and protest, the chanting around them falters... and CB feels the power around them dissolve.

They broke the spell.

The robed figure in the center shifts his grip on the knife, assuming a fighting stance. CB lashes out with his chain, wrapping it around the figure's wrist and pulling sharply. The knife clatters to the ground and CB kicks hard at the robed figure's knee. He hears bones break as his opponent falls, screaming.

He twists, avoiding a jab from a third cultist, and punches it in the neck. It falls to its knees, gagging, as Blink appears behind another, placing his hands on the cultist's shoulders. They both disappear. Blink reappears an instant later—alone—and CB hears a shriek of terror followed by a loud *thump* as a robed figure falls from the ceiling to the concrete floor.

Agent Grant fires his pistol again. Another cultist falls.

The smoky-black barrier between the outer ring of cultists and the disks of gold-black light disappears, and the disks all *thumm* in unison as they race downward, transforming into pillars of light that engulf the cultists beneath them. The room fills with a different kind of power, and then everything is still. The light fades. The outer ring of cultists have turned to stone.

David sinks to his knees, shaking from the effort.

CB looks around him. The cultist he just hit is on the floor, gagging for breath. The one with the busted kneecap is also on the floor, twitching and trying hard not to scream. His knife lies by his side, and CB kicks it away. It scoots across the floor, bounces off the leg of one of the room's new stone statues, and comes to a stop just outside the ring of pillars.

"I think we did it," Blink says, both pleased and surprised.

"Yeah." CB looks up at the cultist pinned to the ceiling. "Even though they tried to pull a fast one."

Brother Judgment floats down to stand next to CB. He's been airborne the entire fight—not exactly a hiding place, but the others had put on enough of a show to keep the cultists from looking up. "Almost didn't find him in time. They've had a little training. But I did..."

Brother Judgment looks up at the cultist on the ceiling, actively pinned there by the force of his mind. "Guess that's why they don't like telepaths."

Part Twenty Five: Haruspex Analytics, Also Not

Artemis' form blurs, then silvers as he assumes his battleform—a humanoid shape consisting entirely of an alloy that, aside from his instantiation, exists only in theory. He turns to the side, sweeping his right arm across the hall. Humanoid monstrosities scream in fear and rage as his arm, currently a razor-sharp blade almost the length of his body, cuts them in half. Their screams end abruptly, though the monstrosities taking their places shriek all the louder for it.

One of the people behind him gasps in shock. He thinks it's the young woman, the one in the hooded sweatshirt, but he doesn't have time to check. He turns again, his other arm sweeping across the width of the hall, and a second line of creatures is cut in half. It is not an elegant strike, but he has no time for finesse.

He sweeps his arm across the hall. Bodies fall. He spins, letting the force of his turn carry his other arm around. Bodies fall. He faces forward, crouching slightly, shortening his forearm blades as he prepares for closer work.

There's no end to them that he can see. A seething mass of headless, faceless, shrieking creatures, intent on tearing them limb from limb, and he is the only line of defense between the oncoming horde and the three who rescued him from his prison. He's not confident of their chances: He's tired, and sluggish, and still shaking off pieces of the odd, comfortable haze that was worming its way into his soul as he sat in that damned room. Even now, knowing what it was, he yearns to return to it.

He sweeps with both arms. Bodies fall to the ground in two pieces. He ignores the smell filling the hall, and concentrates on the still-living monsters still bearing down on them.

Twist. Cut. Turn. Slice.

His head swims. His arms feel heavy. He's not sure why he still gets tired in this form: at the moment he literally doesn't have cells. But despite the complete lack of a biological structure, he still feels an ache in muscles he currently doesn't have, and burning in lungs that are not there.

Twist. Cut. Slice. Spin. Stab.

He grunts in pain as one of his arms-turned-blades passes through the intensely cold purple-black fire erupting out of a creature's neck. He notes with alarm that the initial, sharp stab of cold fades into a general cold numbness... and that the numbness is slowly spreading.

The shape of the blade wavers a moment. His mind conjures an image of a comfortable chair by a window with an ocean view. He can almost hear the crackle of a warm, inviting fire in a fireplace as the cold metallic color of the blade softens into something close to flesh.

And then there is shrieking, many hands grasping at his arm, a mob of shadowed fire surrounding him, trying to knock him over or tear him apart. The blade reforms and he spins once, knocking bodies away and cutting them to ribbons in the same motion. The struggle begins anew.

He can hear the three people behind him talking in low, even voices. He can't hear what they're saying, but he notes the lack of panic in the back and forth: they're discussing their options, making use of the time Artemis has given them to determine their next steps. That impresses him, even as he's sure they're deciding there's not much they can do beyond trying to make for the stairwell that isn't blocked by an army of monsters.

It would be better if they did. I can be more effective if I'm not protecting them.

But he *is* protecting them, at least for the moment, and whatever the tactical advantages might be, he doesn't want them wandering off. If it weren't for them, he'd still be sitting in that chair believing he was looking out the window, staring at the ocean...

The fog in his mind grows a little thicker. He can almost smell leather-bound books.

He pushes the thought away and cuts savagely at the crowd in front of him. He overextends as he attacks, momentarily putting his balance at risk. He's in no real danger—so far the only thing that hurt him was accidentally touching the strange fire that takes the place of their heads—but it requires more energy to pull back. He sucks in a breath and tries to convince himself his arms don't feel heavier.

"It's Overmind!"

The voice—electronically distorted, but almost familiar—comes from *behind* the creatures. The ones closest to Artemis don't react, but even as he cuts more of them down he can see the ranks at the very back burst open: a figure covered in blue-gray armor grabs one of the creatures and throws it into a group of others. They all collapse in a heap, howling in rage.

"LaFleur!" The voice is coming from that armor, which is *absolutely* Thorpe's work, though he's positive it isn't Thorpe wearing it. He watches the armored figure duck low and perform a nearly flawless spinning kick that knocks two of the creatures to the floor. He recognizes the style immediately: it's very close to how Liberty used to fight, which would make the armored figure Jenny Forrest, or "Zero." She'd been wearing a makeshift armor before; apparently Thorpe decided an upgrade was in order.

He takes advantage of the new confusion to cut out a little more space between himself and his foes. The attention of the shrieking mob is divided now, roughly half on him, half on Zero. That's better news for him than it is for Zero—while he's certain Thorpe put actual *armor* in that armor, it doesn't look like it can withstand half a crowd of supernatural monstrosities.

"Down!"

Another, more familiar voice shouts out a single command, and Zero drops to the floor. Artemis turns, gesturing sharply, and his three liberators immediately drop to the floor without comment. A rapid succession of ear-splitting *booms* echoes down the hall, and Artemis feels bullets impact across his lower back. Creatures scream, and fall, and scream again. Street Ronin, he assumes: someone who clearly knows Artemis won't be hurt by small arms fire in this form.

Interspersed between the rapid discharge of Street Ronin's rifle is another firearm: a semiautomatic pistol, firing a steady, rapid stream of shots... steady, but the sound travels up and down the hall in a pattern that doesn't track with linear movement.

Teleporter. Agent Grant, most likely.

He turns to view the room. It is indeed Agent Grant. He and Street Ronin are coordinating their attacks surprisingly well. As soon as Street Ronin stops firing, Grant teleports into the midst of the creatures, shoots, relocates, and shoots again. This disrupts their initial surge toward Street Ronin, at which point Grant teleports back behind him and begins firing again. Zero stays close to one wall, avoiding the spray. Before Artemis has time to gather his strength and rejoin the fight, it's over.

The last creature falls, the last shriek ends in a rasping, choking cry. All that is left is silence.

"Overmind..." Zero takes a step forward, her foot landing in something wet that *squelches* audibly as it lands. She stops, looks down, and shudders. "You all right?" Her voice is tight, almost strangled. It looks like her gaze is fixed on the blades extending from his arms.

He allows the blades to shift back into hands, but maintains his battleform. "I appear to have injured my hand in the fighting."

"How?" Zero steps forward in alarm, her own right hand clenching and unclenching repeatedly. "Was it from that shadowy fire? That's not good—"

"*Stop!*"

Street Ronin stands twenty feet down the hallway, rifle trained on Phyllis Tanner and her two companions. For their part, the trio stands completely and utterly motionless. None of them look afraid, but they're all paying their undivided attention to his rifle.

"Who are you, and what are you doing?"

Zero turns to face Street Ronin, helmeted head cocked to one side in curiosity, then her gaze drifts to the three new faces. Agent Grant, despite not covering his face at all, is even more unreadable—he has that bland, noncommittal "cop face" that isn't quite anything.

It's interesting to see the government agent read the room and agree with the terrorist's tactical assessment. Artemis wonders if the tactical assessment is wrong. It's a trick question—the assessment *is* wrong, but there's no way for them to get the right answer with the information they have.

Besides, he didn't immediately open fire. He's making allowances for being wrong.

He considers jumping to their defense, but holds back.

"Phyllis Tanner." Phyllis doesn't take her eyes off the gun. "My colleagues are Simon and Michelle. We worked here."

"Past tense?" Street Ronin sounds skeptical.

"That's right," Phyllis says. "But not too far past. When we found out what they were planning to do to us, we tried to escape. Only made it this far. I think there's something about this floor—or maybe just this hall—that kept us from turning into..." Her eyes drop to the floor, her gaze resting on one of the creatures' bodies. "...them."

"How'd you find out what they were going to do?" Street Ronin asks.

"We broke through their network security," Phyllis says. "Those things are part of something called the 'Incursion Protocols.' We decided we didn't want to be part of that."

Street Ronin appears to relax a little, but he doesn't lower his rifle.

"We would like to defect," Phyllis continues. "I don't know if we have any specific information that will be useful to you, at this point, but whatever we have is yours."

Street Ronin stares at them for a long time. Nobody speaks. Finally, Artemis breaks the silence.

"They are responsible for freeing me from my prison. We had planned to seek the rest of you out together. We were interrupted by this 'Incursion

Protocol.'"

"I think it checks out," Zero says. Street Ronin nods but doesn't otherwise react.

"Seriously, I think we can—"

"Hold on a moment." Agent Grant raises one hand, waving away the rest of Zero's words. "We just breached the ritual site."

"Really? What's it like?" Zero asks.

"Really annoying. They're doing something—it's hard to describe—but everything's bent and turned sideways. Can't really get a tactical picture. Magic is creepy and sick, just in case you were wondering."

"No kidding," Zero says. "What *can* you notice?"

"Shit. Uh... well, this better work. The senator isn't doing too hot. I think they're about to break through whatever it is Doctor Enigma did."

"What?" Genuine alarm from Zero. "What's happening?"

"He's thrashing around, like in a nightmare. Except it... uh... looks like it hurts. Sorry."

Artemis frowns. "What senator? Who's Doctor Enigma?"

"Not now," Grant says. His brow is furrowed, his voice frustrated. "I'm trying to get to the center, to get a clear shot at the leader, but something keeps—*Jesus*, the room keeps tilting sideways every time I flip..."

And then his eyes widen in surprise, and a slow grin spreads across his face. "Holy *shit*. I think we did it!"

Zero sucks in a breath. Street Ronin has actually half-lowered his gun at this point.

"Yeah. Yeah! Curveball and Brother Judgment worked out some kind of play in advance. The cultists were trying to hide the identity of the ritual leader, but apparently it's hard to do that when you're going up against a fucking telepath. Brother Judgment just really ruined their day."

"What about my—" Zero stops herself. "What about the senator?"

"It's like throwing a switch." Grant smiles at Zero. It's a genuine smile, not a trace of mockery in it. "He's, uh, unconscious, but he's definitely not in pain. Breathing normally. Pulse steady. I don't think I've ever actually seen an unconscious man look *relieved* before."

Zero sighs, relaxing slightly. Street Ronin nods approvingly and lowers his rifle. Phyllis Tanner stares at Agent Grant, brow furrowed, calculating. Artemis wonders how much intelligence she has on everyone. Does she know of Grant as a teleporter only, or is she aware of his other, more obscure gift?

She notices one of Phyllis' eyebrows lift slightly. Whatever she didn't know, she just figured it out.

"Wait." Phyllis takes a step forward, then stops when Street Ronin immediately raises his rifle in reply. "Look, not trusting us is a smart play, but it's a bad one right now. If you're right, and you just disrupted some kind of ritual of theirs, that means they're about to escalate *everything*."

"Oh..." The asian man exchanges glances with the woman in the hoodie. "Oh... *that*."

"That what?" Agent Grant looks from the asian man to the woman in the hoodie, then back. "Simon and Michelle, right? What's going on, Simon and Michelle?"

"The Incursion Protocols," Phyllis says.

Agent Grant looks at the bodies on the floor. "Looks like they're not much of an issue just now."

Phyllis shakes her head. "There were more than one."

The entire building begins to shake.

Part Twenty Six: Haruspex Analytics, The Labyrinth

All the monitors in the Labyrinth are dark now; Ty Parks no longer needs them. As the Eye of the Labyrinth, he sees every part of the building simultaneously... and much of the outside grounds as well. He sees the police setting up a perimeter around the building. He sees the press, finally clued in to strange happenings in the predawn morning, trying to find ways to sneak past. He sees civilians, fewer than there would be if it were midday but still present, standing farther back, smartphones at the ready.

And, of course, he sees the *heroes* in the building itself.

There are three groups: the largest in the lobby, the next in the sublevels, and the third in the hallway, meeting up with the Chairman's prisoner and three traitors who have thus far managed to escape their fate. In each instance, the building's defenses have proven insufficient for the task at hand.

It is, perhaps, to be expected. They took advantage of the brownout—they may even have been responsible for it, in some way—and most are rated in the upper tiers of power based on internal threat assessments. On top of that, they have, of all things, an artificer of their own. One of considerable power, judging by his ability to mask their presence just before the assault on the ritual chamber.

It appears the senator will survive to see the sunrise. The thought angers him.

He pushes the anger aside. He will need it soon, but not now; he has to focus on the task at hand. The building has been breached. The Chairman and his people are safe, the mission continues, but this place—this sanctuary, where so many of their victories were won—is compromised beyond recovery. There is only one role left for it to play.

It must become the pyre.

He takes a deep, steadying breath. This won't be like before. This time he will merge with it completely—they will become each other, each losing themselves in order to become something wholly different—and it's going to hurt.

The monitors in the Labyrinth flicker on, bathing the room in cold blue light, then flicker out, plunging it back into darkness. Ty hears the soft rustle of cables descending from the ceiling, and the pain begins as they burrow deep. Each connection is pure agony, burrowing into flesh and soul alike. The pain will end soon enough.

The awareness stirs, restless. He feels it every time he links with the system, but compared to what's coming that link is shallow and fleeting. The connection is deepening now, sharpening and resolving into substance. The awareness can sense him as well, and while Ty hesitates to attribute any kind of human emotion to it, he can't help but think of it as *eager*.

He hears a final exhalation of breath to his right—the last of the volunteers has died. Ellen, probably—she was the strongest of the ones who stayed behind. Pride and regret swell, then fade as a new wave of pain washes over him. Something cold and immense slithers into his mind. It regards his own conscious with a mixture of curiosity and distaste as it realizes that this soup of meat and chemicals is the only interface it has with the outside world—the only conduit that will provide it the access it needs.

His mouth opens to scream. He cannot.

The awareness begins to integrate, grudgingly preserving what remains of Ty's sense of self, stitching it into its own. It is at that moment, when the last of the walls between Ty and the intellect fall and he is exposed directly to the full depth and breadth of its thought, that the last of Ty's sanity is utterly destroyed. What remains is rational madness, clinical, self-reflective lunacy.

I am the Labyrinth.

How many times had he said that simple phrase, so utterly ignorant of what it truly meant? He had been a shadow of the Labyrinth because the true Labyrinth had no way of reaching into the physical world. Now it does, through him. He is—no, *they are* the Labyrinth.

He is no longer simply a man in a body; that is now a single facet of something much larger and more complex. The Labyrinth is no longer the thirteenth floor of the Haruspex Analytics building; the Haruspex Analytics building is no longer a building. The Labyrinth is a mind, the building is its body…

…and the body begins to move.

Part Twenty Seven: Metamorphosis

It begins with a tremor, then a sound.

The tremor is brief, noticed only by the very few people on the grounds within the police perimeter and those still in the building itself. It's strong enough to shake the ground and rattle windows, but it doesn't carry beyond the police barricades and goes mostly unnoticed. The sound, on the other hand, is hard to overlook: low and rumbling, like the very beginnings of a fog horn just before it opens up, then rising slightly as the sound expands into a baritone *thummm* that feels like it fills every bit of empty space. Shortly after the sound, the tremors return.

A wind rises, racing through the corridors of downtown New York, strong enough to blow hats off heads, and cause the ends of jackets and scarves to flap. As the wind rises, so does the sound, the *thummm* growing louder, and behind it a second sound. An echo of a sound, really, the kind of thing a person thinks they hear until they focus on it, and then it disappears. The second sound, the sound that is only barely there, is the sound of inhuman voices chanting.

And then the wind dies off. The tremors stop. The sound stops, abruptly, and for a moment the city is unnaturally silent.

Silence, interrupted by bursts of static and garbled messages sent over police radios. Sirens in the distance, sounding in short, urgent bursts. Car horns honking, even farther off.

And again, it begins with a sound: the echo of metal tearing away from metal.

The massive shell surrounding the Haruspex Analytics building—the armored covering that only recently appeared—starts to peel away from the building like flakes of dried skin. It starts at the very top of the building, thirteen plates from thirteen sides all toppling back and away. As the topmost pieces of the shell break free, the next pieces begin to tear away in turn, and so it goes as each floor sheds the armor surrounding it.

The building is fifty stories tall. The last pieces to fall away—the ones attached to the first ten stories of the building—all land within the area the police have cordoned off. That leaves five hundred and twenty pieces of ultra-dense metal, deadly petals falling from a steel and concrete flower, that catch the air and fall beyond the emptied area and into the rest of the city.

The oversized shrapnel sails through the air until it hits steel or stone, then each piece slices through either with almost artistic grace. The effect they have on buildings varies, depending on the angle of impact: some hit lengthwise, doing little more than shaking the building and shattering its windows, but the ones that strike the buildings edge first have enough force to pierce the walls. Some stop, wedged in the building, slowly wobbling in place until they works themselves out, often taking a piece of the building with them as they finally fall away. Others pierce the building completely, tumbling and crashing into other buildings or into the street below. One building a block and a half away from the perimeter has an entire corner sheared off, clipped by a passing flake. The corner falls fifteen stories into the street below, sounding like a bomb as it hits.

The ones that don't hit the buildings straight on are potentially worse. They glance off, ricocheting from one to another until finally they hit the street. They tumble, the edges tearing up asphalt, ripping into cars and trucks, cutting through traffic lights, cutting through power lines… cutting through people.

This assault doesn't go uncontested: Flashes of yellow, red, orange, and green light up the sky; sounds of crackling energy and the *booom* of hypersonic flight cut through the air, and some of the flakes swerve, slow, miss their targets. One wobbles to a halt just before it pierces through a skyrise apartment building, gently lowered to the ground encased in a shimmering multicolored field, settling to rest at the feet of a masked woman in a red-and-gold uniform. A few flakes are knocked out of the sky by flying figures that smash them to the ground. More costumed figures work the streets, keeping men and women out of the way of the flakes as they fall, pulling people from cars, evacuating them from buildings. New York City is not without its heroes. But for each flake of metal they manage to keep under control, there are at least three beyond their reach.

When the last of the armored shell flakes away the sound starts up again. The *thummm*, the chanting—clearer now, a discernible subtext within the sound—and with it more, stronger tremors, strong enough to make windows rattle.

Thunder crashes. A dark line shoots out of one of the mid-level floors, streaking across the sky, burrowing into the ground with such force that showers of dirt erupt from the impact. It is a series of cables, braided together into a cord thicker than a man's shoulders, running from the ground to the building, drawing itself taut. Another crash of thunder, and a second cord shoots out of the building, end burying itself beside the first. Again and again, thirteen times in all—one for each side—and by the end of it thirteen cables run from the ground to the building, all drawn taut, making the building look like a deranged maypole in the pre-dawn light.

The baritone *thummm* grows louder, the vibrations in the ground grow stronger, and the building... *shifts*, leaning to one side as if buffeted by wind. The cables on the far side strain, but hold, and the ground shudders.

The building begins to tilt in the other direction. It cracks and groans, swaying left and right, until finally the first twenty floors of the building split into two columns. Streams of broken concrete, steel and glass fall to the ground as the fissure in the building widens, and then one half *shifts forward*, as if it were an unwieldy leg. Half the cables tighten, pulling the building forward, and the *other* column takes its first step. The last bits of loose concrete and steel fall away, and suddenly the lower half of the building can move freely. What were legs in appearance are now legs for all practical purposes.

The cables release from the ground and whip into the air, flailing wildly. Some of them swing out in a wide arc, smashing into nearby buildings and nearly cutting one in half. Others hang in the air, more like tentacles than cables, moving of their own accord, coiling and uncoiling as needed. The building moves, stepping out over the green park that surrounded it and squarely into the now-abandoned street.

Light flickers along its sides, an ugly purple light that gathers and resolves into strange symbols.

One symbol per floor. One symbol per side. Six hundred and fifty runes, all identical to the ones embedded in a certain golem CB and his companions had fought earlier that evening.

The Haruspex Golem towers over the rest of the city, and the rain of destruction begins in earnest.

Part Twenty Eight: Haruspex Analytics, Below

It starts with a tremor, then a sound, then all of the cultists bursting into flame.

In the immediate aftermath of the fight Agent Grant brings everyone up to speed on Jenny's group. Then the building starts to shake: the tremor is brief, but strong enough for CB and his group to stop what they're doing and focus completely on the cracks forming through the stone floor. When the sound starts, it's alarming enough that CB is about to suggest that they take the wounded and get David to make one of those convenient portals to hurry through when suddenly they are surrounded by fire, heat, and light. The strange red stones in the room and infused in the walls are engulfed in flame, followed shortly by every cultist in the room. Even the ones who turned to stone burst into blue-white flame. It's an unnatural burn—it takes no more than a second, as all the cultists' bodies and red stone are consumed like flash paper—and then all that is left are piles of ash scattered across the broken floor.

CB looks at the others. Blink is on the other side of the room, an instinctive reaction to suddenly being surrounded by fire. Brother Judgment is airborne, for pretty much the same reason, wisps of smoke rising from the hem of his trenchcoat. David appears untouched, though he's swaying as if trying to catch his balance, and that strange shadow-bird of his hangs in the air, motionless.

The only one who appears physically hurt is Agent Grant. He grimaces, thrusting his right hand between his left arm and his side. CB can smell charred flesh.

"Grant?"

"Just a sec." Grant speaks through clenched teeth, forcing back a gag. "I was trying to triage one of those assholes. Fuck, this *hurts*..." His outline blurs for a second, then he sighs in relief. The smell of charred flesh disappears, and as he drops his hand to his side CB can see no trace of burns at all. "Now what the *hell* is going on?"

The trembling starts again, stronger this time.

"Curveball." Brother Judgment floats down beside him and points to the door. "Exit's gone."

Correction: Brother Judgment points to where the door *used to be*. There is no longer any trace of it, just a solid, stone wall that is cracking the longer the building shakes.

"What the hell?" CB races over to where there ought to be a door. "Doc, is this some kind of illusion?"

David frowns at the blank spot on the wall. "No. Give me a second, and I'll summon a portal. Where do you want to go?"

"Good question," CB says. "Grant, tell Travers to reach out to Sky Commando. Looks like we need to group up."

* * *

"Shit!"

Alishia Webb banks sharply, the Sky Commando suit responding far more nimbly than its size would suggest, as one of the building's cables flies past her in a blur. The end strikes the side of a nearby building, knocking out a human-sized chunk of concrete and causing spider fractures to form around the impact.

"Status!" She's yelling, an unnecessary but altogether reasonable reaction given all the adrenaline pumping through her right now. She'd assumed all those metal plates being scattered across Manhattan was the worst-case scenario. She was so very, very wrong.

The building's right leg *(the building's right leg??? How the hell is that a thing?)* stands on the street, its left on the edge of the small park. The building is too large to fit entirely on the street; it can't go any farther without pushing through other buildings first.

This is clearly what it intends to do.

"We've expanded the perimeter." Captain Banks sounds a little calmer than Alishia—on the other hand, he's not dodging sky tentacles. "Sky Commando, we're lucky, I suppose, that this is happening now. Not as many people here. But there are still people…"

"Understood. I'll get you more support." She switches channels, activating the band reserved for civilian metahumans who assist law enforcement. "This is Sky Commando, calling all Licensed Metahuman Assets. You unlicensed ones, too—I know you're listening in. We need any metahumans with abilities or resources that can assist in evacuation to report to Captain Paul Banks as soon as possible. I'm sending his location now. We need you to focus on getting people *out* instead of engaging with the…"

Her voice trails off as she tries to find a word that accurately describes the walking building without actually calling it a walking building. She can't find one.

"Kaiju?" Whoever is making the suggestion doesn't bother identifying himself.

"You know what, at some point someone is going to post this entire conversation on the Internet and there will be a subreddit devoted to how wrong that is, but I can't think of anything better right now. If you are tasked with evacuating civilians, *do not engage the kaiju*. The point is to get the civilians *out of the way*. Air Force is en route, I don't want civilians caught in the middle when they show up."

Another channel lights up—one of the reserved ones. Alishia gains a little altitude to bring herself above the writing cables, then activates the reserved channel. "Sky Commando."

"Hello, Sky Commando." The voice is pleasant, professionally friendly, and exceptionally calm. "This is Pete Travers."

"Travers!" Alishia feels herself tense. "Agent Henry told me to expect your call. What's the status of your people?"

"It's complicated," Travers says. "Most of them are in the building at the moment, but we're about to extract them somewhat rapidly. Can you give them a safe place to exit? Keeping in mind that we would prefer they not be shot at, or arrested..."

"Since none of them are a fifty-story-tall walking building I think that's not going to be a problem," Alishia says. "Get them to the Alpha MCV— sending location now. Agent Henry and the rest of his team are already there."

"That's convenient," Travers says. "Location received. I'll contact again once everyone is out."

"*Hurry*," Alishia says. "The Air Force is on its way."

Part Twenty Nine: Downtown Manhattan

According to Alishia's instrumentation, the Air Force won't be on the scene for another twelve minutes. This poses something of a problem.

The Haruspex Analytics building is too wide to travel down city streets, so it is trapped in a relatively small space—the area where the building originally stood, and the small park placed in front of it. It can't move beyond this spot because the buildings surrounding it are too tall. This is a good thing: Alishia has been directing the police to evacuate the area for hours, and at the moment it is the least populated part of the city. Unfortunately, the building is not content to stay put, and it has reacted to the presence of other buildings blocking its way by attempting to tear one of them to bits.

Thirteen cables/tentacles bore into the side of the Foster-McLaughlin Center, punching through the concrete and glass with negligible resistance. Stone cracks, and the cables burst through the sides, causing sheets of rock and glass to fall to the street below. The ease with which the cables can cut into and tear away pieces of building is chilling, and as each piece of wall or roof slides to the ground Alishia feels as if a fist is slowly closing around her heart.

The good news is that for all that it can easily rip off chunks of building, it hasn't yet destroyed enough of the building to let it pass by. For the moment, it's still hemmed in.

Alishia means to take advantage of that.

"Sky Commando to Operations. Have our new arrivals arrived at the Alpha MCV Site?"

"Affirmative." Captain Banks doesn't sound thrilled by the admission. "I, uh… I knew who was coming, but it's not quite the same as seeing them arrive."

"Just one of those days," Alishia says. "Do they have earpieces yet?"

There's a moment's silence. "Yes," Banks says. "LMA Band."

Alishia switches over. "This is Sky Commando. All Licensed Metahuman Assets and police monitoring this channel: understand that as of this moment any metahuman not actively engaged in criminal activity has a twenty-four-hour amnesty, regardless of criminal status, so long as they assist with the current crisis. There are *no exceptions* to this rule."

She takes a moment to let that sink in, then continues. "Now: Scrapper Jack, are you receiving?"

"Here." The voice is deep, rough, and just a little cautious.

"You're probably the strongest person here, and the most durable. So I'm going to have to rely on your judgment for this next part. We currently have the... er... *kaiju*..."

"It's a golem," Scrapper Jack says.

"Well thank God for that. We have the *golem* hemmed in but it's trying *very hard* to break out. The Air Force will be here in eleven minutes, and we need to make sure it doesn't leave before then. This is currently the most evacuated part of the city—if it gets out, casualties go way up."

She tries not to think about the devastation those fucking bits of metal shell already brought down on rest of the city, and focuses on making sure nothing else goes FUBAR.

There's a brief silence on the other end, then Scrapper Jack says, "I'm pretty strong, but I don't think I can fight a skyscraper."

"I want you to assemble a team to keep it occupied. I'm putting you in charge of that task."

Another short silence. "Understood." She can hear him start shouting orders before his connection ends.

Over the Operations channel Captain Banks says, "I hope you know what you're doing."

She switches over to Ops, making sure the meta channel is muted. "I do. Whatever his career has been, Scrapper Jack has always been about minimizing casualties."

"I get it," Banks says. "But there's going to be fallout after. You know... the *stupid* kind."

Right. Politics.

"The guy who wore this suit last almost got killed doing the job," Alishia says. "Least I can do is risk getting fired."

"About that," Banks says. "I've taken the initiative to give one of our 'new arrivals' access to our Ops channel. He has some intel you might find useful, and... well. You'll see."

A moment later an unexpectedly familiar voice comes over the line. "Heya, Webb."

Alishia blinks. *"David?"*

David Bernard, the-guy-who-wore-this-suit-last, laughs ruefully. "I'm going by *Doctor Enigma* now."

It takes a moment for Alishia to match the name with the descriptions

Agent Grant had provided before everything went down. *"The magic guy?"*

"What?" David sounds a little defensive. "Things happened. There was a magic island. Anyway, you need to know something about this golem."

"Magic island?" Despite her best efforts Alishia can't keep the incredulity out of her voice.

Before David can respond, things start happening on the LMA Band.

"This is Scrapper Jack." The low, rough voice doesn't wait for any acknowledgment before continuing. "Red Shift will open the show by trying to plow through the left... leg, is that what we're going with? Leg. After that, I want me, Sister Sentinel, and any other metahumans with strength, mobility, and *durability* converging on the source of the cables. Tentacles. Whatever. We're trying to rip 'em out of their sockets. We won't succeed, but that's the best to keep it occupied. We'll go up the east side as Derecho summons as much wind as she can from the west to try to push the thing back. Any metas with energy attacks should provide artillery support, but *do not close*. When the Air Force gets here we need to get as far away as we can, as fast as we can. Doc, give us about a minute, and if we don't have its attention, do something flashy. These guys seem to really hate you a lot."

"Understood."

If Alishia was doubting it was really him before, the doubt is gone now. She remembers that tone. It was the way he sounded just before he placed himself between Rampage and a bus full of civilians. Weary, unhappy, but all in.

"Red Shift," Scrapper Jack continues, "I'm gonna let you start the—"

Something red catches the corner of her vision. It starts a few blocks up Murray Street, but by the time she turns her head to look, the Haruspex Analytics golem *staggering* as something tears through the leg on the street. The sonic booms, more than she can count, follow shortly behind.

Five figures—Scrapper Jack, Sister Sentinel and three others Alishia recognizes as street-level strongmen—leap into the fray, coming from the east and almost immediately disappearing behind the golem. Seconds later, an incredibly strong wind tears down Murray Street and slams into the west side with such force that she can almost feel the impact from her spot in the air. Rain and lightning follow soon after.

Alishia looks to her left and sees Derecho, hanging in midair, one slender arm outstretched toward the contained but savage storm currently battering the golem. Derecho inclines her head in a brief nod.

Alishia tries not to gape in amazement. That woman has serious control. According to Sky Commando's instrumentation, she's directing winds at speeds of fifty miles per hour, and she's not letting a bit of that weather exist beyond the width of the street—no rain, no wind, no lightning, nothing.

Because the weather is so focused, it only hits the right half of the golem. Because Red Shift has torn through a "foot," it isn't stable. It sways, and for a moment Alishia thinks it might actually fall over. Before she can decide if that would be good or bad, one of the cables lashes out and burrows into a relatively undamaged building next to the Foster-McLaughlin Center for stability. More sonic booms, and more pieces of "foot" go skittering across the street as a crack at the base of the "shin" widens slightly.

Alishia flies around the golem, eyeing the other twelve cables cautiously until she sees the five figures scaling the side of the building. Scrapper Jack is almost at the twenty-fifth floor, the apparent source of the cables, and Sister Sentinel is not far behind. Their climbing methods are direct and effective—they simply punch through the concrete wall to create handholds and pull themselves up with little effort and a lot of speed. The other three trail behind, using the same tactic but requiring a little more effort.

Scrapper Jack gets there first. He moves to the closest cable, kicks through a piece of the wall to lock himself into position, and reaches up to the base of the cable. It's wider at the base—the width of three men, shoulder to shoulder, but it's braided. He doesn't try to grab the entire cable, he just grabs one of the braids and pulls.

The golem's response is immediate: two cables abandon their attempts to tear through the Foster-McLaughlin Center and lash out at Scrapper Jack. He ignores them. Alishia wonders if he intends to try to take the hit, but it becomes clear that the golem doesn't precisely know where he is. One cable aims a little too high, one a little too low. Both leave huge gashes in the wall.

He's too small, Alishia realizes. *It knows he's at the base of the cable, but it can't pinpoint his location. It's like trying to scratch at a flea in the dark.*

She's not sure Scrapper Jack would appreciate being compared to a flea.

She hears more booms in the distance: Red Shift is starting another run. A third cable snakes around, getting ready to strike at Jack, but by this time Sister Sentinel has grabbed a cable of her own and is also starting to pull. All of the free cables snake around the building, lashing out towards where both might be. Most of them miss.

Most, but not all. One of the cables strikes Scrapper Jack in the arm, and the force of the blow causes him to lose his grip, slamming him into and then through a wall. The cable retracts, and the others shift their focus to Sister Sentinel. She adjusts her position, putting the base of her cable between herself and the ones closing in.

Time for artillery.

Alishia flies closer to the golem, readying a volley of anti-vehicle missles stored in the armor's right shoulder. They're nothing like the payload the jets will bring, but she figures it will at least get the thing's attention. She focuses them all on the base of one of the cables attacking Sister Sentinel and lets them fly. Eight miniature missiles streak across the sky, six finding their target, two going wide. Fire and thunder light up the sky, and then Alishia has to bank hard to avoid three cables shooting out toward her.

Apparently she's easier to see.

She activates the LMA Band. "The cables have a much longer range than previously displayed."

"They hurt, too…" Scrapper Jack's voice is shaky. "Try not to get hit dead-on. I'm gonna bruise."

"Yeah…" Sister Sentinel grunts as the sound of something heavy smashes in the background. "I got grazed by one. I'm bleeding a little."

"How bad?" Alishia recognizes Brother Judgment's voice.

"It's *not* bad. It's a *scratch*. A *real* scratch, not an I'm-too-tough-to-admit-when-I'm-hurt scratch."

Another boom, as Red Shift tears down the street again. Alishia checks her instrumentation. "We gotta keep it busy another three minutes." She corkscrews in the air, weaving through multiple cables as they all try to knock her out of the sky, thankful that Sam finally fixed that damn wobble.

"Sky Commando, MTHD teams are ready to assist." Captain Banks' voice breaks in over the feed. "How can you use us?"

"I can't yet," Alishia says. "They'd make a great distraction but they'd never be able to clear in time when the Air Force shows up. Right now focus on expanding our perimeter. If the golem breaks through that building we're going to want all the extra space we can get."

"Copy." She can almost feel the unhappiness and frustration coming out of the captain's voice. She can't blame him, but there's nothing to be done. She's not going to order them to charge, only have to them blown apart when the Air Force starts dropping bunker busters, or whatever they're armed with.

Two other cables shoot toward Sister Sentinel, both missing and burrowing into the wall next to her. That gives Alishia an idea.

"The golem tears itself up pretty bad every time it tries to attack one of you. Any chance we can use that our advantage? Get it to attack itself, do some of our work for us?"

"No." Sister Sentinel almost gasps the word. Alishia sees her hanging from a cable, legs windmilling as she tries to catch a corner of the wall with her foot. She eventually pulls herself up onto the cable, straddling it for support. "We've run into this before. Look at where they just attacked me."

Alishia looks over and chokes down a curse as she sees the holes the cables made *filling themselves in.*

She hears another boom, and even as she sees Red Shift tearing through the foot she can tell that it's already managed to repair much of the damage he's caused.

"It *regenerates?*" Alishia doesn't even try to hide her consternation. It's the most ridiculous thing she can think of, a self-healing monster skyscraper that can walk and attack people with cables.

"It's the runes." This is David's voice. "You see those symbols covering every inch of the golem's outer surface? Any time it needs to repair itself it burns one of those symbols. You'll have to force it to burn through *all* of them before the damage starts to stick."

Alishia forces herself to fly back, get distance from the fight so she can take everything in. There are more of those things than she can count. She can see a few blank spots on the wall, places where it looks like the building has already used a few for self-repairs, but... they're not going to be able to bring it down this way.

But maybe they won't have to. Her HUD beeps furiously, and as she takes in the new information scrolling by her display she sees they've successfully run out the clock.

"That's it! Everyone on the building, get off the building. Derecho, drop the storm. Red Shift, stay away...

"The Air Force has arrived."

Part Thirty: Air Support

The five figures on the twenty-fifth floor don't go down the way they came up: they just jump as far as they can manage. For all of them that turns out to be pretty far. The three local strongmen manage to get almost all the way to the building's original location before they hit the ground, and in two more jumps they're back at the Alpha MCV Site. Scrapper Jack and Sister Sentinel make it to the Alpha MCV with a single leap each. Red Shift was a few blocks up when Alishia sent out the call, so he just stays where he is, waiting. Derecho's storm ends in seconds, fading from gale to drizzle to nothing. And just like that, the Haruspex Analytics golem stands alone, nothing between it and the rest of the city except for a building that has already been torn to shreds...

...and five of the Air Force's most advanced interceptors.

New York City doesn't have an Air Force base—the closest is seventy miles out and is actually part of the Air National Guard. Still, it became apparent that a city with abnormally concentrated levels of metahuman activity would benefit from access to air support, so the FBMA, DoD, and Air Force made sure that along with the Sky Commando program there was also access to more traditional airborne offense. No one has ever needed to activate it until today.

The jets are working a little outside expected parameters at the moment: the assumption was they'd be called in if there was an attack from the harbor, or if metahuman forces were coming in from the air. No one, it seems, had ever planned for a scenario where a skyscraper would somehow come to life and start attacking the rest of the city. As it happens, this unplanned scenario actually works to their advantage: the skyscraper, while not the largest in the city, is still a large, slow-moving target. This means they can attack it without getting close.

They come in high and from the east, giving them a comparatively open target. Alishia hears the chatter from the pilots as they confirm radar and computer targeting have locked on. They're eight miles out when they fire the first volley of attacks, and there's a delay of a few seconds between when the missiles are fired and when they strike the golem.

The force of the explosions combined with the sonic booms of the missiles themselves almost knocks Alishia out of the air. The entire west side of the building opens up, briefly revealing shifting, slithering blocks of cable and steel that look like grotesque parodies of internal organs. The loud *thummmm* that was ever-present at the beginning returns in force, almost like a prolonged cry of pain. The golem sways around its center like a bowling pin not quite ready to fall.

The pilots scatter and reform, preparing for another run. Smoke and pulverized concrete dust hang in the air, but Alishia can see glimpses of the building within. Two of the thirteen sides—the two facing most fully west—are completely gone. Strips of cable lie on the street, ripped away from the building by the force of the blast, still twitching through some unseen power, but not able to strike or coordinate in any effective manner. The golem groans, tilts, then steadies itself. Slowly it begins to turn, allowing fresh walls to face toward the new threat even as the damaged walls start to seal off and repair.

More chatter as the pilots prepare for the second volley. Target acquired, target locked, and again she sees the explosion before she hears the missiles streaking past. Again the air is filled with flame and dust, again the westmost sides of the building open up. As Alishia takes in the damage the jets are inflicting on the building she begins to hope that even if the jets *can't* ultimately take it completely out of the game, maybe they can force it to burn through enough of those weird little symbols that they'll still have a chance of finishing the job on their own.

That, unfortunately, is when the golem begins returning fire.

A loud *snap!* reverberates through the air as a cable, fully extended, launches a piece of debris the size of a small car at the fighter planes. There's a burst of panicked radio chatter, then Alishia hears the *boom* of a distant explosion. Her HUD confirms it—one of the planes is down.

The golem scoops up rubble strewn around it—some from the building it's been tearing to bits, some from its own injuries—and throws it across the city. The method the cables use is strange and eerily accurate—they coil back, like a snake wound around itself, and then unspool straight toward the target, releasing the debris only when the cable has reached its full length.

All of the cables have debris now, all roughly the same size and shape as the first. The jets prepare for another attack, but just before they fire thirteen chunks of concrete hurtle across the city, and two more jets go down. The remaining two open fire, and again the side of the building explodes in fire and dust, just... not as much fire. Not as much dust. It's not enough to completely tear it open, and Alishia can see symbols on the golem pulse and fade as the wall begins to knit itself closed.

Then thirteen more chunks of debris hurtle across the sky, and one more jet bursts into flame, breaks apart, and falls to earth.

One jet remains.

It banks sharply, dropping altitude quickly as it rolls to make a more difficult target. The tactic works as the next volley of rocks aims too high, missing it entirely. However, the jet is too low to get a clean shot at the building, and Alishia realizes it will have climb higher, exposing itself, if it wants to take the shot. When Alishia hears the command for the jet to break off and abort, she's not surprised. In a matter of seconds, the scenario changed from devastating attack to devastating loss.

They're on their own again.

Alishia takes a quick scan of their surroundings. Unfortunately, the attack did more than simply damage the Haruspex Analytics building—it also turned what was left of the Foster-McLaughlin Complex to rubble, removing the only thing keeping the giant golem from venturing into the rest of the city.

Alishia activates the LMA Band. "It's on the move. It's no longer penned in and we no longer have air support. We need to stop it in its tracks, now!"

A red blur and a sonic boom announce that Red Shift is back in the game, and once again the "foot" splits open as he moves through it. This time, however, the golem has access to projectiles, and Alishia winces as the concrete smashes through cars and buildings, and burrows deep into the road.

None of them hit the speedster. Mach 12 is hard to track.

Derecho whips up her gale again, and the golem, which was just beginning to move forward, shudders and falters. Each time it seems to force its way forward, the strength of the wind increases and it falters once more.

Unfortunately, the level of concentration Derecho is using renders her motionless, in midair, one arm extended. A perfect target for thirteen thrown rocks.

Alishia races through the air, calling for Derecho to drop to the ground *now*, dammit. Derecho's head swivels toward her, eyes widening as she sees the armored form of Sky Commando racing her way.

This is probably going to hurt her, Alishia realizes. But it probably won't hurt as much as getting hit by anything the building *throws* at her.

The Sky Commando sensors show all thirteen cables coiling back, preparing to strike. Alishia only has seconds to act; she uses them as efficiently as possible. She deploys a stuckey, hitting the woman full on and instantly encasing her in a hardened lumpy sphere. Not slowing down, Alishia rams her shoulder into the sphere, pushing it out of the way as the first rock hurtles by, missing it by inches. Alishia grasps the stuckey, digging into it with metal fingers as she pushes *down* with all the strength her flight system can muster, narrowly avoiding two more rocks thrown in short succession.

Gripping the stuckey tightly, Alishia swoops behind an eight-story building as two more chunks of concrete whistle past, bursting into a twelve-story building on the other side of the street and shattering the top three floors. She sets it down on the sidewalk and sprays it with the release compound. Almost immediately the stuckey dissolves and falls away.

Derecho, disoriented, begins to shiver and cough.

"Are you all right?" Alishia peers at her in concern. Being cocooned in stuckey isn't fatal, but it's not pleasant either, and can trigger latent claustrophobia.

Derecho shivers again, draws a deep breath, and nods. "Thanks." Her voice is soft, barely above a whisper. "I didn't see them coming."

She flinches at the sound of two more impacts, farther up the street.

"Work your way back to the Alpha MCV if you can," Alishia says, "but stay on the ground as much as possible. If you can set up that gale while keeping out of sight, do it, but don't make yourself a target."

Derecho nods again. Alishia takes a few steps back, turns, and launches back into the air.

She flips on the metahuman channel. "Derecho is OK." She risks gaining altitude in order to get a picture of the battlefield. The golem is now officially out of containment: it has moved past the remains of the Foster-McLaughlin Complex and has hit a patch of two- and three-story buildings. Alishia doesn't expect them to slow it down.

It is, however, taking the opportunity to cause as much damage as it can as it slowly ambles along, its cables lashing out at anything it can hit.

The metahuman channel is still open. "I need options," Alishia says. "Sister Sentinel, you said you ran into this before. How'd you handle it?"

"We—" Sister Sentinel hesitates. "Well, we…" She trails off.

"I killed the man controlling it," Red Shift says, voice calm.

"Not exactly." David again. "The man was already dead. Sky Commando, there are different ways these golems can be made, but the most powerful require a human to willingly die in the act of its creation. When that happens, the body becomes a conduit between the physical world and the realm that makes these things go. So… destroy the body, destroy the link."

Alishia stares at the behemoth on track to destroy every part of the city it touches. "Same with this one? Destroy the body, destroy the link?"

"I'm positive of it," David says. "The problem is, the body is somewhere in there, and I don't know how to find it."

"I know how to find it," a new voice says.

Alicia frowns as she tries to place it. "Who is this? How will you find it?"

"This is Curveball," the voice replies. "And in order to find it, I need someone to get me a fresh pack of cigarettes."

Part Thirty One: Ingress

The Alpha Mobile Command Vehicle site is an odd mishmash of uniformed police, armored police, and CB's team. CB's team is currently divided into "people who can reasonably do something to fight a giant walking animated skyscraper" and "people who will reasonably be turned into a carbon smear if they try to do something to fight a giant walking animated skyscraper." The people in the first category are currently out there trying to keep the building from moving farther into the city...

Jenny shakes her head as she takes that in. *Trying to keep the building from moving farther into the city. That is actually a thing we are trying to do today.*

That consists of Jack, Red Shift, Sister Sentinel, and Derecho, plus a few other New York heroes who showed up to help. They're young, and CB has never heard of them, and compared to a guy like Jack they're not really in the same league—but none of that really matters at the moment. They *are* helping, and CB's the last guy to discount something like that.

The rest of his team isn't really suited to taking on "the Kaiju," as the other metas on the scene have been calling it. Well, Agent Hu is, but CB needs her for something else, so she's at the Alpha site standing next to her partner and another man—a black man in the same kind of suits they wear, only this time with sunglasses—and fuming.

Jenny is fuming as well, though after seeing what those armor plates did to the city outside the evacuation area she's more interested in being part of the evacuation and recovery efforts, figuring that's where her talents would be more useful. Street Ronin stands silently, keeping apart from the cops but obviously monitoring more than just the LMA Band they were all given access to. Brother Judgment and Blink are standing together, Brother Judgment's gaze fixed on the building, while Blink occasionally shoots CB a questioning look. Each time CB shakes his head no.

Not yet. Getting there, but not yet.

That leaves LaFleur, David, and the turncoats. The supervillain known as Overmind is standing watch over his rescuers: a middle-aged black woman, a young asian man and a hoodie with legs. They look desperately unhappy to be where they are, though also a bit relieved at the same time.

David Bernard is trying to explain to the new Sky Commando how the end game has to play out. It's not a pretty ending, but to her credit Sky Commando isn't dismissing it out of hand. She's asking questions, trying to poke holes in the plan, and trying to find other options—something she *ought* to be doing—but she's not actively opposing it. She wants to know that when the blame for everything falls on her shoulders, she's willing to take what comes because there was nothing else to do.

A uniformed officer comes up to CB, expression unreadable. CB faces him, tensing slightly, wondering what this is about.

"Captain said I should give you this." The officer reaches out, an unopened pack of cigarettes in his hand.

CB takes them. "Thanks," he says.

"This is gonna help?" The cop is an older guy, thick dark curly hair mixed with streaks of gray, thick mustache and sideburns making him look more like a fixture from a 70s cop show than an actual police officer.

CB looks down at the cigarettes. They're exactly the kind he smokes. He expertly tears the plastic around the top and pushes back the cardboard, revealing full rows of unlit cancer.

"Yeah," he says. "It's kind of a trigger for what I do. It'll help a lot."

The cop shakes his head. "My wife won't believe it. But I'm gonna tell her anyway..."

CB smirks, reaches into his trenchcoat pocket, and pulls out his lighter.

Jenny sidles up to him, watching him go through the process of lighting up. She's helmeted, so he can't see the expression on her face, but he's pretty sure he knows what that expression is.

He pulls and the cherry brightens then fades as he exhales, watching the smoke curl. The world, ever spinning, suddenly clicks into place.

Time to push. He's *been* pushing, almost constantly, ever since they breached the lobby, and it's giving him a headache... but it's time to push *more*. Time to go all in.

Push. Push. Push.

His brow furrows as he concentrates, and the world starts spinning the way it always does—but it's *not* the way it always does. It's different this time. This time, he's *controlling* the spin, just a little, making it wobble this way and that, letting him see more angles and possibilities. It reminds him of the early days, when all he could see were angles and ricochets, lining up shot after shot to determine which was the best.

"I found him!" Brother Judgment points up to near the top. "I know Ms. Tanner said the guy originally worked on the thirteenth floor, but apparently he moved. He's about a quarter of the way down from the top."

With that announcement the world shifts a little. Possibilities change.

CB nods. "Good enough place to start." He activates his comm link to the metahuman channel. "Let's group up. Agent Grant, Zero, Overmind—you're with me. Jack, you and the rest keep doing what you're doing. Brother Judgment, we need you to stay here so you can link us without getting killed. Blink, you're shuttle service, and Agent Hu… you OK with this?"

"I'm ready when you need me," Hu says, looking grim.

Brother Judgment grits his teeth, but nods in agreement. "Hate staying behind. Makes sense though."

"What is going on?" Sky Commando sounds very much aware that things are happening whether she approves them or not, and is not happy about it at all.

CB walks over to David, tapping him on the shoulder. "You have one of those headsets that goes over the special channel, right?"

David nods.

CB holds out his hand. "Let me borrow it for a sec."

"Curveball?" Sky Commando's voice grows a little sharper over the line. "What is going on?"

David removes the headset and hands it over, CB slips it on and opens the Ops channel. "Sky Commando. Let's talk over here instead."

There's a second's delay as Sky Commando switches channels. "How did you get on this line?"

"I borrowed Doctor Enigma's headset. I figure you probably don't want to have this conversation in front of everyone. I'm kind of bad for discipline when that happens."

"Fine," Sky Commando says. "What exactly is going on?"

"Nothing," CB says, trying to sound innocent. "I don't have a reputation for pulling these kinds of stunts at all, and you won't find a single cop on the force who will swear uncontrollably when you mention my name."

There's a brief silence on the line, then Sky Commando says, voice tight with anger, "There are a lot of people putting themselves on the line right now, and you better not be playing games with any of them."

Fair reaction. He tries to keep the snark out of his voice this time. "No games, Sky Commando. We have a way to take out the golem. Look, I know you're at the top of the chain here, but we know how to take this thing out and if you tell us to stand down we absolutely won't."

He sees David wince visibly at that. CB shrugs. There isn't any time.

There's another brief silence over the line. The noise in the city grows louder as the building finds new parts of New York to destroy.

The LMA Band opens again. "This is Sky Commando. Curveball is leading a team into the building to neutralize the threat. Our task is to keep it occupied to keep it from going farther into the city. Render all aid to Scrapper Jack and... Doctor Enigma. Captain Banks, I want MTHD forces to close and engage with heavy weapons. We're *not* going to bring it down, but we *can* keep it occupied. We need to do that for as long as possible."

CB opens the Ops channel again. "There will be a point when Brother Judgment will tell everyone to pull back. That will be just before the target gets neutralized. We... don't know what will happen to the building at that point."

Sky Commando switches back to Ops. "What's the worst-case scenario?"

CB thinks it over. "Timber?"

"Shit."

She switches back over to the metahuman channel. "When I give the order to pull back, I want everyone to take that seriously. Put as much distance between yourself and the target as you can. Don't stop until I tell you to stop. Try for two football fields if you can."

She switches back to the Ops channel. She sounds angry, but controlled. "If Brother Judgment will be your coordinator, I think you better give him that headset."

"Right," CB says. "Curveball out."

He walks over to Brother Judgment and hands him the headset. "It gives you direct access to management."

Brother Judgment smirks, takes the headset, and puts it on. "We doing this now?"

CB nods. "Link us up."

He feels a brief sensation of vertigo, then his mind is filled with thousands of thoughts that he knows aren't his own. There's a brief moment of panic, as his brain grapples with how to reconcile all these conflicting thoughts and preserve his own sense of self, but he fights it back and waits patiently for Brother Judgment to finish.

It's strange, waiting for someone else to reach into his brain and deliberately control parts of it, but it's not his first time dealing with a telepath. It's still uncomfortable: he can feel Brother Judgment at work, almost as if he were reaching in and flipping switches on and off to filter out some thoughts and let others in. When he's finished, the unending babble is gone. All that remains is an ever-present awareness of every other linked mind—an awareness that includes the exact location of every mind at every moment—and the understanding that if he "speaks," they will "hear."

"Testing, one-two, one-two..." He's only thinking, forming words in his mind, but he perceives it as speech. "This thing on?"

"Loud and clear." Jack sounds like he's standing right next to him, though he's actually halfway up the building trying to rip out one of its cables.

"This is weird," Jenny mutters. "Uh... sorry, I didn't mean to say that out loud. Or *think* it out loud, I guess, OK no offense Brother Judgment I know this is really useful but I really, really don't like this at all."

Brother Judgment chuckles. "Yeah, that's a common reaction. And I get it."

"Let's get to the important part," CB says. "Blink, can you use this to port to any one of us?"

"Sure," Blink says, sounding unconcerned. "We do it all the time. I sort of lose the connection for a second when I'm porting, but it comes right back."

"All right, then let's get this started. Doctor Enigma, start the show."

It's interesting watching David at that moment, seeing his outward stoicism and contrasting it with the immense sigh that comes through the link. He notices CB, gives him a thumbs up, then rises into the air.

The golem doesn't react at first. David is small, he's not attacking, and it is currently under assault from Red Shift, the strength metas, and a small army of heavily armed and armored police. It isn't until David surrounds himself with that sphere of purple-gold light that the golem responds, but when it does it abandons everything else it's doing and focuses *entirely* on David.

Thirteen tentacles launch themselves at the floating man. All are repelled by his shield, though CB can clearly feel the impact of each strike as if it were *his* shield instead of David's. David grunts from the effort of resisting, but the shields hold.

"Think it noticed me," he says.

"Think you're right," CB agrees. "Jack, we need a door."

"On it." Jack abandons the cable he was wrestling with and begins climbing higher up the building. "Just tell me when to stop."

"Keep going," Brother Judgment says.

Jack climbs using the same method as before, punching holes in the wall and making his own ladder.

"Right there," Brother Judgment says. "Target is actually probably a little higher, but if you get much closer I think he'll notice."

"He?" CB asks.

"Feels like a dude to me," Brother Judgment says. "Sort of. There's something else there, too. *Not* human. Anyway, Scrapper, right there."

"Got it," Jack says. He reaches in through the hole he made with his free hand and casually starts tearing out chunks of concrete. CB notices he aims the chunks carefully, avoiding any spots on the ground with people. His aim is pretty good; each chunk lands harmlessly, usually among the broken remains of the Foster-McLaughlin Center.

Jack pulls himself up, disappearing from sight. CB can still feel his presence, and has a vague impression of the space he's in. It was, at one time, an office, but the shape of the room is broken up by many, many other shapes.

"I'm in," Jack says.

"On my way," LaFleur replies. His battleform gleams as the sky brightens, the morning sun rising but unable to filter through the buildings that are still standing. He disappears, and CB feels his mind shift locations, appearing next to Jack.

Agent Grant says nothing, and while he doesn't appear to move at all, suddenly CB is aware of him in two places simultaneously... and when he concentrates he can dimly perceive him in a *third* location, much farther away. He immediately draws his own mind back from that, instinctively recognizing that if he tried to focus on it too closely the world would stop making sense.

"I'm here," Grant says. "And Jesus, this place has really gone downhill. The reorg has not gone well."

"That leaves me, Zero, and Street Ronin," CB says. "Blink?"

Blink ports over to Jenny, placing a hand on her armored shoulder. "You might want to open your faceplate," he says. "Not everyone takes this well."

"What—?" Jenny starts to ask, then she disappears. CB feels a mild rush of panic and discomfort when she joins the others. A surge of concentration pushes it back.

"Oh," she finishes, voice weak. "Yeah, neat trick. I hate it almost as much as the brain link."

Blink laughs, reappears next to Street Ronin, and moments later he's gone as well. Finally Bink appears next to CB, grabs his arm, and this time it's CB's turn to try to avoid puking.

A moment later, Blink disappears, returning to the ground, waiting for the next part.

"Well," Agent Grant says, "here we all are. Anyone need to send a fax? I think I see one in the corner."

Part Thirty Two: Haruspex Analytics Golem

One half of the room looks normal, the other half looks insane.

The part of the room closest to the door is in almost pristine condition: there are two cubicles set face to face, and a stand in the far corner that does in truth have one of those fax/copier combinations resting on it. Nothing looks out of place, except for the lack of any kind of window and the gaping hole Jack tore in the side. The building stopped having windows shortly after the first air force attack, and even the gaping hole is being repaired before their eyes.

The rest of the room isn't so much a "room" as it's an ever-shifting series of shapes passing through, traveling from one part of the building to another. It reminds CB of conveyor belts, or maybe trains pulling very strange cars behind them.

"What now?" Jenny stares at the large conveyor contraption, then turns to the rest of the group. "I'd suggest just following that, to see where it goes, but for some reason I half expect it to start passing through a series of hammers and anvils and cleavers."

"You want us to start the distraction now?" Jack asks.

CB nods. "Might as well."

"OK then." Agent Grant turns to Jack and LaFleur. "You two are pretty much immune to munitions, right? I don't have to worry about friendly fire?"

"I'll be fine," Jack says.

"As will I." Even LaFleur's voice sounds metallic in that form. "Depending on what part of the Crossfire munitions stash you're stealing from."

"Hey, it's not stealing," Agent Grant protests, gesturing to Street Ronin. "He's the one who showed me where it was."

"As long as you're there," Street Ronin says, giving his equipment a once-over, "I could use an ammo refresh."

"Sure," Agent Grant says. His outline blurs as he hands over a cloth pouch. "Two more left."

Street Ronin nods his thanks, hooking the pouch onto his utility belt. "I don't think there's anything there that'll hurt you, Overmind. Which means, Agent Grant, you should feel free to be as distracting as you can possibly manage."

Agent Grant actually grins at that. "You have no idea how many forms I'd have to sign at work to do what I'm about to do right now."

CB pulls on his cigarette. The world is right there, waiting. He pushes, watching the way it starts to tumble. He moves to the outer wall, Jenny and Street Ronin following. "Make some noise, gentlemen."

Jack grins, then charges through the conveyor belt, pushing deeper into the building's center.

Jack Barrow is, as far as CB knows, one of the world's strongest metahumans. His only rival in that department is Regiment, which means that the amount of damage Jack can do, if he really sets his mind to it, is hard to quantify. This is mitigated somewhat by the fact that this building is held together by magic, which is why Jack couldn't just tear off each of those cables he wrestled with earlier.

Still, attacking from the *inside* is different. Even magical extra-dimensional beings from a different reality tend to focus more on defending against enemies from the *outside* trying to force their way in—things are different once the enemy find themselves already *inside*. Jack tears off a cube of concrete from one of the "conveyor belts" and throws it into a column, shattering both. Almost immediately the building responds, dropping swarms of cables from the ceiling, all reaching out to grasp Jack, but even as they wrap themselves around his limbs, he tears them off their moorings.

LaFleur enters the fray, metal form disappearing and reappearing to Jack's right, bladed arms sweeping, cutting through concrete and cable alike. Even more cables drop from the ceiling, seeking to tangle LaFleur as well, but any time he's unable to cut through enough of them to remain free he simply teleports to one side and continues his fight.

"My turn!" Agent Grant shouts gleefully, as he rolls two cylinders along the floor, each coming to a rest near LaFleur and Jack. They flash red twice, then explode, causing cable and bits of concrete to go flying. Neither LaFleur nor Jack appear to be affected by the blast in the least, though Jack's outer clothing is in tatters.

"Bad news, Hu," Grant says. "Looks like Dr. Thorpe gave Scrapper Jack some kind of invulnerable bodysuit."

Even though she's not with the group, her sigh is clearly audible through Brother Judgment's mental link.

CB takes a moment to tune in on the events outside. The building is still focusing most of its energy on Bernard, who is still managing to keep his shield up. Red Shift has stopped punching through it, taking some time to recover spent calories instead. Thorpe gave him a new device that more efficiently replenishes his energy when he runs, but when he pushes for too long his body still burns faster than it gets. He's been pushing through the whole fight. Derecho is back in action, having found a place that gives her a good view of the building while keeping mostly out of sight, but she has to be more selective about what she does now that there are more forces on the ground.

In short: they're holding their ground. There's still time to pull this off.

CB turns to Jenny and Street Ronin. "OK. We split up. Shout out when you find the brain."

Jenny and Street Ronin nod. CB takes another drag of his cigarette, watches the last of it burn away, and flicks it into the corner. "Let's do this."

* * *

Other than sparring with her great-grandfather, Jenny has never done any formal training in much of anything. She exercised regularly and learned to fight hand-to-hand from one of the greatest melee combatants of all time. As impressive as that might be, looking at the constantly moving shapes she has to navigate through she kind of wishes she'd taken some parkour classes when she'd had the opportunity.

Due to all the disruption Jack, LaFleur, and Grant are causing—Grant has now appeared with a freaking *flamethrower* on his back and is cheerfully demonstrating that the inside of this monstrosity is not up to fire code standards—she's starting to see gaps between the moving rock and writhing cables that are wide enough to pass through. The problem is that she has no idea if they actually *go* anywhere. She sees Street Ronin choose one at random, grab some cables that are busy attacking Jack, and swing himself up and through, disappearing from sight. CB takes his time, choosing to light another cigarette first, then simply walks past the fight, disappearing behind a curtain of cables as if he was going into the back room of a tattoo parlor.

Jenny absently flexes her right hand, trying not to notice that she doesn't have any feeling in it beyond *pressure, not pressure,* and *numbing cold.* The cold is now creeping up her forearm, though the numbness and the cold isn't nearly as severe.

She tries not to notice. The hand still works, and that will have to be enough.

Jenny follows Street Ronin's lead, grabbing a mesh of cables and climbing onto what looks like a catwalk stretching across the fight below. It's not really a catwalk; it's another conveyor, though she can't tell what exactly it's conveying because there's nothing traveling across it. She crouches, letting the conveyor pull her along its path, ready to leap aside if there really are any random anvils or hammers or chopping sawblades appearing out of the ceiling.

There are no anvils, no hammers, no chopping sawblades. It seems the building is focusing its attention on the three madmen who are trying to wreck it from the inside out. She glances down at the melee as she passes overhead—Jack is nearly sinking through the floor as he creates an ever-widening and deepening crater as he punches, kicks, and smashes everything in sight. LaFleur isn't damaging infrastructure, but anything sent his way is sliced to pieces. His blades must be incredibly sharp to do that to stone. And Agent Grant cuts the most bizarre figure of the bunch: at first glance he appears to be choosing targets at random, letting loose with the flamethrower at anything moving, but any time something tries to hit him he always winds up teleporting to one of the spots he cleared away just moments before, giving him a moment before the building heals itself where he can select a new area to burn clean.

She returns her attention to where she's going and tries to keep her movements as limited as possible. The catwalk/conveyor continues on for a minute, moving so slowly she's tempted to start crawling on her own to make up lost time. But then she notices that the "catwalk" turns sharply downward, and if she stays on it she'll wind up being dumped down what might be a very deep hole.

Down is the wrong direction. Brother Judgment placed them below the target. She needs to go up. She starts scanning above her for anything that might give her a way up. It's then that she finally recognizes where she is: a brief flash of a metal door and some torn carpet through a mass of stone and cable and she realizes she's near the stairwell.

She waits as long as she can, then rolls off the catwalk, slipping through a tangled mesh of cable as she falls. For a horrifying instant she's convinced the cable will immediately constrict around her, but it actually slithers away as it feels her brush past. She lands on her feet, in a crouch, and makes her way forward.

This part of the building has fewer conveyor systems, but it is positively teeming with cables. Most of them appear to be Ethernet cables, which she finds interesting. The external cables look more industrial, like the kind you'd use to pull elevators around, but the internal cables look almost exclusively like the heavy-duty Ethernet cables you'd find on a data center floor. They drop from the ceiling, writhing like snakes, but they never drop farther than halfway to the floor. And they're all moving, some traveling farther down the floor's main hallway, others traveling back the other way.

Jenny crouches low, practically crawling down the hall to keep as much distance between herself and the cables as she can. She doesn't know what will happen if she touches one—they seemed to regard her as something to be avoided or routed around when she fell through them—but she doesn't want to risk being wrong. She crawls down the hall until she reaches the metal door, then pushes against the crash bar. The door opens into the stairwell; once she crawls through she lets it close shut behind her.

There are no cables here. There's not really anything: other than the lack of light it appears exactly the same as it did when they were descending it earlier. She activates the nightvision function in her helmet and begins jogging up the stairs at a brisk pace, keeping an eye out for anything out of place.

"Hey." Calling out through her mind still feels weird, but she's starting to get used to it. "If you can reach the stairwell, it doesn't look like it's used for anything."

Through their link, she can sense the position of both Street Ronin and CB. Street Ronin is actually pretty close to her position—he's in one of the offices just a little way down the main hall, if she remembers the layout correctly. CB is a level above them, on the other side of the building. She has no idea how he got there.

"I thought I recognized this room," Street Ronin mutters. "OK, heading your way."

"I'm gonna... stay here," CB says. "I don't think I can go back the way I came. But the cables aren't moving around like claymation snakes any more, so that's something."

"What are they doing?" Jenny asks.

"They're... just being cables. Like, have you ever sliced open a telephone cable?"

"Sure," Jenny says. "But Dad doesn't know, so don't tell him. He thinks it was 'hooligans.'"

"Well, it's like that. They're all flowing the same direction. I'm gonna see where it leads."

The fire door opens, and Street Ronin crawls into the stairwell. When the door closes behind him he stands, stretches, and sighs in relief. He nods to Jenny.

"Why isn't there anything in the stairwell?" he asks.

Jenny shrugs. "I really have no idea. Honestly, it looks like the building has been shifting its insides around for repairs and things like that. I don't know why it would *need* a stairwell. If I were in control of a big skyscraper monster that could shift its insides around, I wouldn't keep it."

"Part of the spell..." David Bernard's voice sounds a little shaky, and *very* tired. The cables haven't managed to get through his shield yet, but he's had to decrease its size to conserve energy. "Most golems are human shaped—or animal shaped. Shaped like a thing intended to move. So it's easy to get it to move, because it has a consistent form. This building was *never* intended to move. I don't even know what gave them the idea to do this. But in order for it to work, there has to be some kind of constant that runs through the entire length of the structure. Stairwells and elevator shafts are pretty obvious choices for that."

"That makes as much sense as I guess anything about magic ever will," Street Ronin says. "What I want to know is, why isn't it guarded?"

There's a brief silence. Jenny can almost *feel* David shrug.

"Hubris?" David suggests. "That's all I got."

"I'll take hubris," Jenny says.

"Maybe." Street Ronin doesn't look convinced. She suspects a healthy amount of paranoia is useful in his position.

"Let's climb up," Jenny says. "It's either hubris, which means we get easy access to the bad guy, or it's a deathtrap and we'll wind up starting another distraction so Curveball can save the day."

That provokes a sharp bark of laughter from Curveball. Street Ronin stares at her for a moment, then shrugs. "Nothing better to do right now..."

They trudge up the stairs single file, Jenny first, Street Ronin trailing behind. At the next landing Jenny stops dead in her tracks, staring at the door in mute astonishment.

Street Ronin steps up beside her. "What...?"

"Yeah."

Cable twists around the doorframe, starting from the floor and traveling around the length of it, forming an arch of its own.

"Sorta feels like there might be something interesting behind that door," Jenny says.

Street Ronin doesn't reply, but he gives his rifle a quick once-over.

Jenny turns the handle. The door clicks and easily swings open.

Whatever this is, it's not the kind of room you find in an office building.

A brightly polished marble floor stretches before them, gleaming in the soft light of lanterns hanging from a high ceiling. Rows of glass display cases are organized along the walls of the room, with more set up in a grid across the floor. A simple white card is set on each display.

"Be careful," Street Ronin says. "This could be a—"

Jenny steps into the room.

"...nevermind," Street Ronin finishes. He doesn't follow.

The marble echoes softly as Jenny walks to the closest glass table. It's not very wide—about the width of a small drafting table—but the only thing in it is a small clump of what Jenny finally realizes is hair. Thick, blonde hair. She looks at the card. It's someone's name—she doesn't recognize it.

"Anyone know someone named Marvin Ellis?"

"There's a governor named Marvin Ellis," Agent Grant says. "Nebraska, I think? Or maybe Kansas. One of the ones in the middle."

As Jenny takes in the names of some of the other displays, her throat starts to tighten. "Hey… uh… remember when my uncle said these guys were keeping samples of powerful people so they could threaten to kill them with magic? I think we just found their stash."

She doesn't recognize the name on every card, but every name she does recognize is a congressman, or a senator, or a governor, general, or someone highly placed in the bureaucracy.

"Jesus," she says. "Is that the Attorney General of New York?"

Street Ronin is now in the room, moving quickly from display to display, taking note of each name.

He's probably recording them, Jenny thinks. *Wish I'd thought of that.*

"What's it doing here?" Street Ronin asks. "It wasn't here on the way down. We would have noticed this."

"It wasn't here before," Jenny says. "The building probably moved it here when it… you know… changed. After we escaped."

There's a blur of an outline, then Agent Grant is standing next to them. Jenny has to block out the sensation of Agent Grant's presence. He was already in three places; four is just too weird.

Agent Grant looks around. "I think this was probably close to the place where they were casting that spell. If we'd had a chance to nose around a little we probably would have found it."

"What should we do now?" Jenny asks.

"I still have the flamethrower," Agent Grant suggests.

Jenny thinks it over. It might not make a difference at this point, but this does represent a hold Haruspex has over people. It's not the kind of thing that should just be left hanging around.

She looks at Street Ronin. "You get pictures of everything?"

Street Ronin nods.

"OK." She takes a deep breath. "Curveball, looks like we're about to create a third distraction."

Part Thirty Three: Haruspex Analytics Golem, The Labyrinth

CB follows the trail of cable down a long, doorless hallway. Faint red light surrounds him—it's not much, but it's strong enough to allow him to follow the cables.

He forces himself to keep walking, to keep alert. He takes another drag on his cigarette—his third so far—and lets the feel of the world spinning around him continue unimpeded. Right now there's nothing to do but follow the trail and see where it leads. He notes the hallway always turns right, and is doing so with with ever-increasing frequency. It's a spiral: he started from the outside and it's leading him ever closer to the center. When he sees a much brighter red, flickering light emanating from the turn up ahead, he suspects he might finally have arrived.

CB keeps close to the wall as he approaches. The air is filled with the sound of clicking. At first he thinks it might be some kind of bug, but he quickly realizes the sound is too regular to be natural. This is *mechanical* clicking, like a series of relays opening and closing in complex patterns.

The clicking is interrupted briefly when a massive explosion booms below him, carrying enough force to shake the floor. It comes from the general location where he senses Jenny and Street Ronin—that must be Jenny's "distraction." As if in response, the clicking grows louder, faster, almost frantic.

Somewhere below him, someone is firing an automatic rifle in short, controlled bursts. That would be Street Ronin. The short bursts turn into longer, more sustained bursts—Street Ronin becoming *concerned*.

"They were not happy about that!" Jenny shouts through the link. "*Very* unhappy cables!"

Pressing close to the wall, CB peers around the corner.

The room reminds him of one of the server rooms Robert had at the old Guardians base, just before he moved everything in. It's a big rectangle, a raised floor with panels covering the entire floor. Some panels are open, and each open panel radiates that red blinking light. Ethernet cable is everywhere: falling from the ceiling, creeping out of the panels, coming out of the walls… and all of it converges on something at the very center of the room.

There, suspended from the ceiling, is a… man? Woman? A human, or something human-shaped. It's difficult to tell, precisely, because cables appear to burrow into every inch of it. Each cable blinks red at the point where it touches flesh; each time it blinks, it makes a clicking sound. That's where the sound comes from. Right now it's blinking and clicking like crazy.

CB has to take a moment to remember not to talk out loud.

"Found the target."

"You sure?" Brother Judgment asks.

CB takes in all the cables—every cable in the room—as they snake across the floor and inevitably wind up somehow attached to the figure dangling in the center.

"Pretty sure." He scans the room slowly, judging distances. "I'm going to need to get closer. Blink, start with the extractions. Do Street Ronin and Zero first—I think they made some uncomfortable friendships in the last few."

"We did!" Jenny confirms. "I think we would like to leave now!"

"On it." Blink's presence disappears from his mind for an instant, appears somewhere below, then disappears with Jenny and reappears at the Alpha site. The automatic fire is replaced with the deep boom of a shotgun, followed by two small explosions.

Very cautiously, CB takes a step into the room. Nothing happens.

He senses Blink move again, this time extracting Street Ronin. The sound of gunfire and explosions stops.

CB takes another step forward. Nothing happens.

"Now?" Blink asks.

CB gauges his distance from the figure. "Not yet. I need to get closer. Everybody clear the building. Brother Judgment, tell Sky Commando to call the retreat. I'll yell when I'm ready."

In a matter of seconds LaFleur and Agent Grant disappear from the building and reappear at the Alpha site. Jack takes a little more time, but doesn't seem to be any more inconvenienced: he knocks a new hole in the side of the building and jumps. Curveball can sense Sister Sentinel, still fighting on the building's exterior, doing the same. And then he senses Red Shift moving, for the first time in a while. It takes CB a second to figure it out, but he finally realizes the man is using his speed to help the ground forces get out of range.

My turn, then.

CB takes a long pull on his cigarette, notes the world spinning around him, and very deliberately tells it to *stop*.

"Hey!" he shouts. He winks.

Somewhere in the distance, there is a very faint *pop*.

The air *buzzes* as a swarm of cables streak toward him. CB dives to one side, hitting the floor hard as they pass overhead. He keeps rolling as they twist in midair, thudding into the floor where he lay only moments before. He pushes himself off the ground, and jumps *just in time* as two more cables lash out beneath him. He twists in midair, trying to dodge a third, but he finds only partial success—the cable misses his chest, but tears through his trenchcoat and slices across his shoulder, knocking him aside just as four more try to rip through his back but miss. They all tangle together into a writhing mass as he scrambles off the floor, hissing from the pain as he forces his shoulder to work.

His trenchcoat is wet with blood. He tries to ignore it.

He catches movement from the corner of his eye and drops into a forward roll as more cables stroke form both sides. He feels something tear through the meat of his lower leg and curses, but again the cables tangle together, tying themselves in knots as they all attempt to follow.

He gets to his feet, shouting from the pain and trying to ignore all that bleeding. The cables switch tactics, whipping around the figure in the middle of the room at speeds that would certainly slice CB to ribbons if he tried to get too close. He stops a few feet away and decides he's close enough.

He smiles as the world, frozen in place, waits.

"Now!"

Instantly Blink and Hu are there. Hu takes an involuntary step back from the whirling cables of death.

CB puts a hand on her shoulder. "Ready?"

She blinks, focuses, and nods.

He moves his hand to Blink's shoulder. An instant later they're both at the Alpha site.

He looks up just in time to watch the entire top of the building get blown to bits.

Part Thirty Four: Aftermath

Jenny knew it would happen fast, but she wasn't quite prepared for *how* fast.

One second Blink and Hu are at the Alpha site, waiting. Another second they're gone, and a second after that Blink and CB are at the Alpha site, waiting. Then the world shakes from a truly massive explosion, and a second later Blink disappears, then reappears five feet in the air, holding the limp form of Agent Hu. They both fall hard, Blink managing to hit first to cushion Hu's body. He grunts, and spends a little time wheezing as Brother Judgment and Agent Grant lift Agent Hu off him. Brother Judgment kneels to check on his teammate as Grant throws one of Hu's arms around his shoulder to walk her over to a medic. David sinks to earth and sheds his shield, almost collapsing on the spot.

Then the sand begins to fall.

The amount of overpressure Hu can generate is impressive enough—it did take a chunk off the tip of Thorpe's island, after all—but there was more going on in that explosion than just her. Previously unnoticed sensors on Jenny's visor report traces of unidentified energy that she quickly re-categorizes as "magic." Whatever it was Hu blew up apparently decided to blow up a bunch of other things, and the end result was that the parts of the building that exploded were almost entirely pulverized. No large chunks of stone fall to earth, just fine powder and sand. It is, Jenny thinks, in some ways the *cleanest* explosion she's ever seen.

And the rest of the building does... nothing. It does *not* topple over, or even sway in a stiff breeze. It was, apparently, standing in a perfect state of balance when Hu blew off its "head," and it continues to stand, unmoving, as sand falls from the sky.

They did it. They won.

She realizes she can no longer feel the rest of the team in her head. She panics for a second before realizing that Brother Judgment ended the link. They didn't need it anymore. She looks over to see him sitting on a low brick wall, head between his knees, with Sister Sentinel crouched beside him, making sure he's OK.

Jenny looks for CB, and sees *him* leaning against a police van, talking to one of the police officers—an older guy with a weird 70s vibe. They both laugh at something the older guy says, and CB offers him a cigarette. Jenny rolls her eyes.

She methodically goes through the rest of their group. Derecho is standing with Brother Judgment and Sister Sentinel, but Blink is nowhere to be found. Agent Grant is standing next to Hu, who's being loaded into an ambulance. Near him is a tall black man in sunglasses wearing the exact same suit as his. They're talking in low voices. Jenny could enhance the audio on her helmet if she wanted, but she doesn't bother.

Scrapper Jack, LaFleur, and the three Haruspex employees who rescued him are nowhere to be found. That doesn't surprise her. Equally unsurprising is the disappearance of Street Ronin and Red Shift. What *does* surprise her is the reappearance of Blink, carrying the semiconscious form of Senator Tobias Alexander Morgan, blinking blearily as he tries to make sense of his surroundings. Blink yells for a medic, and as soon as everyone figures out who he's carrying the service is *excellent*.

That leaves David. She walks over to him as he tries to climb to his feet. She starts to offer her right hand, hesitates, then switches to her left. He takes it, but she notices his gaze lingering on her right hand as he stands. She flexes it, wondering if she can still feel pressure, or if she just *thinks* she can because she knows she *should*.

"Thanks, Zero." He sounds exhausted. He sways a moment as he gets to his feet, then steadies. "Are you okay?"

"I'll be fine," she says. She flexes her right hand again.

The sound of jets roars through the air, and moments later Sky Commando lands a short distance from the two of them. It's an impressive piece of machinery up close. Jenny notices David's eyes linger over it with just a hint of longing as it opens up and the pilot steps out. She's covered head to toe in some kind of battle armor, but it's obvious David knows her.

She walks over to them, regarding the Haruspex building as she nears. "Doctor... Enigma, is it?" There's the definite hint of a smile in her voice.

David nods. "I wasn't a huge fan at first, but it's growing on me."

Sky Commando shakes her head. "I just saw you fly."

"You've seen me fly before."

"I saw you fly *without jet engines*," Sky Commando clarifies. "And you tanked a *skyscraper*."

David grins. "This is New York City. That was *barely* a skyscraper."

Sky Commando laughs, then pulls a very surprised David into a quick, tight hug. "You set a really hard example to follow, jackass."

David's grin fades as he looks around. "Oh, I don't know about that. I *never* had to deal with something like this. Today Sky Commando managed to contain a monster that would have utterly destroyed Manhattan. At *least*

Manhattan. Probably more. I think you did pretty good."

He pauses.

"The Mayor's gonna try to get you fired, obviously."

"Obviously." Sky Commando's voice is dry.

"But he'll fail. Hey, have you met Zero?"

"No…" Sky Commando turns to face Jenny. "Zero, is it? Odd name."

"I was short on time," Jenny says. "And it turns out I'm terrible at names."

Sky Commando laughs. "There are entire social media sites devoted to voting on the best names for new heroes. Just hang out there for a while and read the comments."

"Never read the comments," Jenny says automatically. "Also, the top choice for every new hero is always 'Hero McHeroface.'"

Sky Commando laughs even harder. "I think I like you. Look, I have to go coordinate something before someone ropes me into getting shouted at for a few hours. Take care." She turns back to David. "I mean it."

David grins—a cocky grin that Jenny hasn't really seen on him much—and half-salutes.

She walks over to one of the uniformed officers and starts giving orders.

"She's pretty cool," Jenny says.

"Yeah," David says.

Jenny looks over the wreckage. "So what now? Do we help clean up?"

David frowns, considering. "No," he says finally. "Normally, yes, that's what you'd do, but part of our group only has a twenty-four-hour pass before someone with more enthusiasm than sense starts trying to arrest them. And because the rest of us were actively coordinating with one of the world's most infamous supervillains, that would make us 'persons of interest.' And oh yeah, there's still the matter of that metahuman virus."

"Shit." Jenny feels herself deflate a little. "I hadn't really thought about it, but when you put it that way, we didn't really win, did we?"

David shrugs. "I don't know about that. We were trying to save the senator's life. We did. That was our objective, we met it. They tried to retaliate by leveling the city. They failed. We didn't win the war, but we won this battle."

Jenny looks around again. "So what now?"

David starts looking through the crowd. "Now we round everyone up and go back to the *Nautilus*. Then we probably sleep for a few days. Then we try to figure out what to do next. We've still got a lot of work to do, and we can't do it from here."

Jenny looks up at the sky. It's morning now. Even though the sun can't get through the Manhattan skyline, the sky is bright and blue and cheerful. David is right: this wasn't a loss. As brutal a fight as it was, it was an act of desperation from an enemy that had run away. They've done what they've come to do: saved her uncle's life. And along the way they recovered LaFleur, acquired three new assets, and destroyed the leverage these assholes had over a bunch of very powerful people.

And, just as important, that wasn't the end of it. There was still more to do. She finds herself making a fist again—not because she's worrying about the numbness in that hand, but because making a fist feels like the right thing to do when there's still something left to fight.

"Right. I'll tell the others. Time to get back to work."

"Time to get back to work," David agrees.

So they did.

WRITER'S NOTES

Curveball Year Three started in 2015, and is only just now wrapping up, in 2022. That is seven years for twelve issues, which is... not a great metric. It gets better if you take out Issue 36: Issue 35 was published at the end of 2018, bringing it down to *three* years. Still not spectacular, but a lot better than seven.

Yeah, Issue 36 was a real pain to write.

Year Three was supposed to be the end of the story. When I started writing Year Three my intent was that the final battle at the end of the year would be The Final Battle Of The Entire Story – but it became clear, the further into it I wrote, that there were too many loose ends. By the time I started on Issue 35, I'd decided that the end of Year Three wasn't actually the end of the story, it was just *setting up* the end of the story. When I started Issue 36 I figured it was simple enough. I just needed to move all the characters to the points they needed to be where I could start the final arc...

...and it took me four years to finish.

Issue 36 was a monstrosity that took four years to get through. I spent a lot of it gripped by writer's block, writing words but never quite able to move the story forward, deleting words and re-writing words, staring at words trying to remember why I'd written them, staring at blank pages and wondering why I couldn't write the thing that was sitting in my head. I tried to get to the point I knew I could write, but couldn't start writing until I knew how the story had arrived to that point, and then when I arrived to that point I decided I'd done it wrong and started over. The deeper in to the issue I wrote, the harder it was for me to see how they would get to the end.

Oh, and there was a pandemic. That was a little distracting.

I did get through it, though! One of the greatest days of 2021 was when I realized I was going to finish the story *before* I turned fifty. The thought that I might turn fifty and still be struggling to finish a superhero story I'd started when I was 46 both terrified and depressed me. When I managed to beat that particularly nasty expectation I was giddy for almost an entire weekend.

Issues 25-36 – Year Three – is the longest part of the story so far. One hundred sixty five thousand words is more than I've written for *anything*. I look back on it the way I look back on pretty much everything I've written so far: I see parts that I like, and I see parts that I'd like to set on fire and throw into the ocean. Nothing to be done about it, at this point, other than to move forward and try to make different mistakes next time.

We're not done yet. One more arc to go...

C. B. Wright (http://www.curveball.xyz)

ABOUT THE AUTHOR

Writer, former musician, occasional cartoonist, and noted authority on his own opinions, C. B. Wright's weakness for tilting at windmills has influenced every facet of his adult life. He enjoys reading and writing fiction. He also enjoys writing about himself in the third person. He refuses to comment on whether writing about himself in the third person also qualifies as fiction. He currently lives in Alabama with his wife, daughter, dog, and his overpoweringly large ego.

ABOUT CURVEBALL

Curveball is an ongoing story published monthly as web fiction, then through retailers in eBook and paperback formats.

http://www.curveball.xyz

ALSO BY AUTHOR

Curveball Year One: Death of a Hero (eBook, Trade Paperback)

Curveball Year Two: That Which Does Not Dream (eBook, Trade Paperback)

Pay Me, Bug! (eBook, Trade Paperback)